THE HEART STONE

MÓRDHA STONE CHRONICLES, BOOK 6

KIM ALLRED

STORM COAST PUBLISHING, LLC

THE HEART STONE
Mórdha Stone Chronicles, Book 6
KIM ALLRED

Published by Storm Coast Publishing, LLC

OTHER BOOKS BY KIM ALLRED

The MÓRDHA STONE CHRONICLES series:

A Stone in Time - Book 1

Keeper of Stones - Book 2

Torc of Stone - Book 3

A Stone Forgotten - Book 4

A Druid Stone - Book 5

The MASQUERADE CLUB series:

The Lion & the Gazelle - Book 1

The Wolf & the Butterfly - Book 2

The Huntress & the Hawk - Novella

With special thanks to the Rain Dogs - Beth Schmitz, Jeff Gossett &
Lisa Gossett

Time is a companion that goes with us on a journey. It reminds us to cherish each moment because it will never come again. What we leave behind is not as important as how we have lived.

Jean-Luc Picard
    Captain of the starship USS Enterprise

1

England - 1804

Beads of sweat trickled down AJ Moore's temple. The light breeze that stirred the leaves shielding her location did nothing to dry the perspiration. It wasn't a particularly warm day, but the tension from perching in the tree strained her muscles. She'd been staring at the stone building for the last twenty minutes. She was growing impatient but forced her limbs, which were beginning to go numb, to remain still.

Other than the slight rustling of leaves, nothing else stirred. Even the birds seemed to wait in quiet anticipation. The peacefulness was so complete, the twang of the bow startled her, but she tracked the arrow as it flew toward its target, hitting the first guard in the chest. The second guard turned when his partner fell. He bent down, which was his dumb luck as the second arrow—that AJ was sure had been aimed at his chest—struck him in the head, piercing his skull.

AJ nocked her arrow, moving her bow from left to right, searching for the other guards. A man approached from the left side of the building, stopping in front of the door when he noticed the other two guards down. He scanned the clearing, musket drawn and ready to fire. Without hesitation, she aimed at the man's chest and loosed the arrow. She knew when the arrow left the bow that she'd lifted her head too soon. Instead of hitting the guard's chest, the arrow pierced his left arm and, fortuitously for her, pinned him to the wooden door. An instant later, a second arrow hit him in the chest, finishing the job.

"Sorry," AJ muttered.

"That's all right, love," Beckworth whispered. "You set up the target for me." He'd been sitting in the crook of a second branch, just off AJ's left shoulder.

She shifted position and gritted her teeth at the painful tingling of nerves in her right leg. Ignoring her discomfort, she nocked another arrow. Fitz had surveyed the area earlier and confirmed six guards, assuming no other men had arrived before their team moved into place.

"Besides." Beckworth rested against the trunk of the tree. "It's good to know you haven't quite worked up the urge to kill anyone."

She glanced at him before turning back to sight her arrow. "Not yet."

He snorted at her clear reference to him. "I know you've been tempted." Then his tone turned serious. "But once you take a life, the world is never quite the same. Make sure the first one you take is worth the price."

She blinked, suddenly quite attuned to her hesitance in striking a killing blow. Hadn't Finn once mentioned something like that, or maybe it had been Ethan. A slight movement in the trees to the right of the building made her twist to take a closer look. Her arrow flew when she saw the tip of a musket point toward a copse of trees where Ethan and Lando hid. A man fell from the tree, an arrow in his shoulder. When he tried to roll away, Jamie appeared out of nowhere and slit the man's throat.

At the same time, Lando moved out of the trees behind another guard who had emerged from the left side of the building, his musket moving from side to side as he searched for the enemy. The guard barely turned before Lando grabbed him and stabbed him through the neck with his dagger.

AJ stared at the man as he dropped to the ground. She might not be able to deliver the death strike herself, but the fact the rest of her team could with such dispassion didn't faze her.

Not anymore.

One more guard was out there somewhere.

A light gurgle came from their right before Fitz stood, the unfortunate guard at his feet. A spray of blood soaked the front of his leather tunic, and more blood dripped from his broadsword. The weapon was a surprising choice for someone of shorter stature, but Fitz's muscle-bound chest and arms handled it efficiently.

They waited another five minutes before AJ nodded to Beckworth. He whistled a dove call before they both scrambled down the tree. The team covered the thirty yards to the door in seconds. Jamie and Fitz took a position to the left of the door while the remaining four lined up on the right side.

On a silent count of three, Jamie reached for the door and yanked it open.

2

Baywood, Oregon - Current Day - About one week earlier

Wind chimes rattled as a cold wind blew in, chased by dark, threatening clouds. Rain would soon lash out. AJ drew the heavy blanket closer, relishing the numbness in her cheeks and hands.

"You should make her come in." Her mother's anguished, hushed voice filtered out through the open window, adding to AJ's heavy heart. Helen hated to see her children suffer. What mother didn't?

"She'll come in when she's ready." Adam's reassuring voice would do little to ease their mother's worry.

"I've made coffee." Stella's voice boomed from the kitchen, almost making AJ smile.

Almost.

"She's been like this for a week," Helen crooned. Then footsteps faded away.

When AJ heard nothing more but the crash of the tempestuous waves and the frenzied cries of the seagulls, she closed her eyes. A single tear traveled a lonely path down her cheek, and she let the wind dry it.

Some days, time had no meaning when she did nothing but watch the sea and clouds continue their march toward shore. She considered going into the house but didn't have the energy or desire to rise. Her limbs weighed her down, heavy as stones.

The French doors opened, and someone stepped outside. "I'll give you fifteen more minutes, then I'll carry you in whether you're ready or not." Ethan Hugh's tone brooked no argument. When AJ didn't respond, the door closed.

"How's Maire?" Stella sounded close, probably staring out the window at AJ. If AJ knew her friend, Stella would want to shake her. That made AJ almost smile again.

The group had either been silent while AJ lost herself in the coming storm, or they had returned from wherever they'd gone because the conversation picked up.

"She's almost as unresponsive as AJ." Ethan sounded tired, unable to do anything to help the women who suffered from Finn's disappearance. "When she's not going through her translations for the hundredth time or locked in a room with AJ talking about who knows what, she sleeps on the new couch I bought. She won't sleep anywhere else. She stares out to sea, just like AJ."

"It's been a week," Adam said.

AJ tuned them out. She couldn't listen anymore. She knew exactly how long it had been—down to the minute. A week here meant almost three months in the eighteenth century. No one understood the shift in time. She snorted. No one really understood how the druid stones worked at all. The incantations used with the stones to create the fog that took people through time had been guesswork from the start. Only Maire, Finn's sister, with the help of Sebastian, a French monk, was able to translate the druid's writing in *The Book of Stones*. The book explained how the stones had been created on an eclipse-darkened night, centuries ago, during a freak lightning storm. Talk about a perfect storm. The book also explained how the druids had created the silver torc to keep the six stones together, amplifying the power of each stone. The problem was that the book had been written in ancient Celtic, and there were very few people who could piece the language together. To make it more difficult, the druids had written in a secret code, hiding the individual words of the translations throughout the text.

Maire had deciphered the original incantations and modified them, making the time travel more reliable—to a point. They couldn't select a specific time or place to go, nor were they certain where they'd arrive when they traveled back in time. Though they had traveled enough times to have a decent guess.

Only five days had passed when AJ returned with Ethan and Maire, though she had spent almost two months in the eighteenth century. Where Finn had been left behind, with no one knowing what happened to him. Her heart clenched as the wind whipped, banging a bird feeder against a post. The early storm, unusual for the dog days of summer, matched her raging anger and deep, unfathomable ache of loss.

Someone had betrayed them. That was the only explanation. Ethan assumed it had been Beckworth, but that made no sense to AJ. Beckworth had fabricated situations in the past, and his earlier actions while working for the Duke of Dunsmore hadn't made him any friends. AJ was convinced Beckworth acted out of survival mode. But had he? His hatred for Reginald, his half-brother and full heir to the duke, was real. She was positive about that. And everyone despised Dugan, originally the duke's right-hand thug and now Reginald's man-at-arms.

She considered their last evening at Waverly Manor in England. Their team had sneaked into Reginald's masquerade ball to steal a second book that spoke of the stones. The druid's book, referred to as *The Mórdha Stone Grimoire*, had been written by a druid who had traveled through time. The team believed the man to be the druid chieftain who had written a journal of his time jump experience and continued experiments to repeat his time travel. This book, also written in ancient Celtic, was thought by some to be the ravings of a crazed man.

At some point during the party, Dugan's men had cornered the team. AJ, Ethan, and Maire had escaped through the fog, returning to present day. They had no idea if anyone else made it out. Maire wouldn't have if Finn hadn't changed the plan at the last minute, forcing Maire to take the book and run for the carriage. Had Finn suspected Beckworth? And why hadn't Finn used the individual stone he'd carried to return to the present? If he'd lost it or someone had taken it, Finn would have found his way to France to get another stone from Sebastian. He should have been able to accomplish the trip to France in the three months that elapsed in the earlier century. But he hadn't. No matter how she looked at it, there were only two possibilities.

He was either dead or captured.

She ran her fingers over the Celtic etchings of her wedding band that was still bound to the necklace and Heart Stone. When she closed her eyes, she could hear his voice on the wind, see his lopsided grin, a longing in his emerald-green eyes, and a lilt on his tongue.

"I'll always come for you, sweet lass."

One week. It seemed like months.

The vibration of her phone jarred her from her contemplation. She opened her blanket to peer down at the glow from the phone resting on her lap.

It was a short text.

"It's time."

AJ blew out a long breath. Finally.

She pushed herself out of the Adirondack chair, hugging the

blanket close, the edges dragging on the ground behind her as she entered the house. The group stared at her, probably waiting for her to say something, but she ignored them as she passed the dining table. She marched up the stairs and dropped the blanket on the floor of her bedroom. After changing to a warmer sweater and getting her tangled hair in order, she ran down the stairs, grabbed her purse, and was shutting the front door when she heard Stella's voice call out, "Where are you going?"

She was in her car, screeching out of the parking lot of the inn by the time the front door opened. Through the rearview mirror, she caught a glimpse of everyone standing on the porch before she made the first turn up the tree-lined drive.

———

Ethan cursed under his breath as AJ sped away. He should follow her, having a fairly good idea where she was going. When he turned to ask Stella's opinion, she'd already gone back inside. Only Adam remained on the porch.

"Come in, Ethan. We need to talk." Adam patted his shoulder then waited at the open door.

"I need some time, Adam." Ethan dropped into one of the porch chairs and stared at the empty drive.

Adam shuffled his feet, but after a long sigh, returned inside.

Ethan pulled his jacket closer, thankful the house blocked the wind. He shook his head and stared at the stand of trees across the parking lot. He'd anticipated this moment since their last jump and Finn hadn't followed. He'd known for sure when Finn hadn't arrived the next morning. Would they ever be safe from the stones and those blasted books? Maire and AJ thought he didn't want to go back. That he would just leave Finn for whatever fate had decided.

They should know him better than that, but when he

considered his mood this last week, he understood how his actions appeared. No matter how he broke it down, Maire would have to go with them, and he had no idea how to keep her safe. He couldn't follow her everywhere she went for the unforeseeable future. It would grate on her and their relationship.

He huddled deeper into his jacket, the cold wind seeping into his bones. Everything had been so simple living with the earl, though it was a lonely life. He'd never thought he'd find a woman he'd want to share his future with. Had never looked for one. The first time he stepped through the fog, he never expected to return home. Now home was anywhere Maire was. And being Finn's sister, Maire would never rest until they found Finn. And he would never let AJ go back alone.

There had only been one option, and he would have to wrestle with his own fears. She might chafe at his actions, but once they stepped through the fog, Maire would have a permanent bodyguard. And if it strains what they had together—so be it. Her safety was more important than his happiness.

He stared at the drive for another hour before the chill drove him back inside. When he trudged back to the kitchen, Stella stood in front of the coffee pot, bouncing with impatience as she waited for the final drips to finish. She glanced at him, her brows drawn, her expression unsure. When he nodded, the worry lines disappeared, and she returned her vigilance to the coffeemaker.

Helen, who looked pale and withdrawn, struggled to smile. She looked nothing like the sparkling person she'd been at her birthday party, which, in this timeline, had been only a week ago. Stella refilled the mugs before sitting next to Helen, patting the older woman's hand. Helen immediately grasped the proffered hand and studied Ethan as if she was waiting for the worst possible news.

Adam stood in front of the bay window but returned to his chair when he noticed Ethan had returned.

"Why do I feel you've been planning something behind my back?" Ethan asked as he lifted his cup and tasted the fresh brew. He gazed at the three of them over the top of his mug as they huddled around the table.

"Because you're a smart man." Stella's other hand fidgeted, and she kept glancing at the paper napkins on the table.

Ethan forced back a grin. She was dying to release Helen's grip and return to making her little birds.

"It's not that we've gone behind your back, per se," Adam started.

Ethan waved him off. "It's because I've been too stubborn to listen, is that it?" When no one suggested otherwise, he blew out a sigh. "It's not that I don't want to do something about Finn. I just wanted to give him time to find his own way back."

"So that you wouldn't have to go get him?" Adam asked.

Ethan sat back, shocked at the truth of what they thought of him. "There's never been a question of whether or not Maire and I would return."

Adam and Stella exchanged glances.

"That's not the impression we got from your brooding." Stella hunched forward, her intent gaze trying to read some underlying meaning in his response.

"Maire and I don't belong here." He brushed his hair back, unwilling to voice his true fear. He wasn't superstitious, but he couldn't help believing if he shared his concern for Maire out loud, something horrible was doomed to happen. "I didn't want AJ going back." He shrugged. "I'd hoped Finn would have found a way home on his own. Since he hasn't..."

No one questioned what he was thinking. They'd all known, though no one would say it out loud.

"AJ is stronger than she looks." Helen's calm voice surprised him, but apparently not the other two, who simply nodded in agreement. Helen's cool brown gaze held a steel edge he hadn't expected nor seen until now. "I know something of loss. As much as it still crushes me to remember the day the state trooper came to my door to tell me about Joseph. As horrible as his death was, I had a body to bury. He was there for me to say goodbye." A tear slipped down her face. "It was the hardest thing I'd ever done, burying my husband. But something I had to live through." She glanced at Adam. "For my family."

She released Stella's hand and leaned toward Ethan. "All AJ has been left with is a mystery. Is Finn alive and, for some reason, unable to find his way home? Or is he dead? As much as I don't want her to leave, knowing she may never return..." She paused when her voice hitched, and she blinked away the tears. "His loss will haunt her. She'll eventually return to her life, but she'll forever be watching the sea, wondering if her husband will return."

As much as he wanted to argue, he knew Helen was right. Had always known as each day turned to the next and the fog never appeared.

"She'll end up like that old geezer who built the McDowell house. Staring out to sea, quietly going mad." Stella seemed calmer, her hands now free to fold her origami figures.

"Just like the old fool that lived here at the inn, closed off in the upper rooms, still watching for Japanese Zeros long after the war had ended," Adam added. "Only instead of the Zeros, she'll be watching for the strange fog like we've been doing all week."

"Sometimes I think love isn't worth the pain." Ethan hadn't meant to say the words out loud, but he couldn't stop the fear that clamped a cold hand over his heart and squeezed until he could barely breathe. He knew they had to go back, knew Maire and he didn't belong in this time. But Maire's knowledge made her vulnerable.

"Of course, it is," Helen barked, waking Ethan out of his stupor. "It's everything—pain, happiness, irritation, bliss, anger, and passion. You can't have just one side of love. It simply doesn't work that way."

Ethan gave her a sad smile. "I know. I think I've felt every one of those emotions since I've known Maire." He moved his coffee cup out of the way and placed his elbows on the table. He hesitated, then decided to tell them the whole story. It was something he should have shared with them as soon as they'd returned, but their focus had been on AJ and Maire. "We haven't told you everything about that evening, other than we had to flee without Finn." He picked up his cup again, more to have something to do with his hands than needing any more coffee. "We'd been surrounded. Dugan's men had been waiting for us."

"Someone betrayed you?" Adam appeared startled.

Ethan nodded. "It's the only explanation."

"Beckworth?"

Ethan shrugged. "Unknown, but likely. We had a tight team. Everyone had worked together before. The only team members we didn't know well were the people Beckworth brought in."

"Could it have been someone from that other man...what was his name? Hensley?" Stella laid down the origami, her focus solely on this new information.

"I don't see how." Ethan ran a hand through his hair, then sat back. This particular topic had been just as frustrating as wondering what had happened to Finn. "Hensley's men didn't arrive until the day before the ball. They were told the basics, but none of the details."

"You had mentioned earlier that Dugan's men knew where to find the coach. Is it possible someone spotted it being driven someplace it shouldn't have gone and just suspected something was up?" Adam asked.

Ethan studied Adam. He kept forgetting Adam was a lawyer

with a logical mind that would have come in handy when they'd planned their assault on Waverly. "I supposed anything is possible. But the guards were all over the manor, searching rooms." He stopped, remembering something Maire had told him when she first found Ethan and AJ running from the manor.

"Tell us," Stella said, obviously recognizing he'd remembered something.

"It was when Maire ran into us and told us the coach had been compromised. I'd asked where everyone else was. She said Finn had changed plans. He decided it would be better if they split up. He worried about someone catching them with both the book and the stone he carried. So he told Maire to leave the manor a different way and meet us at the carriage. If that was impossible, she was to find Eleanor and hide until it was safe to leave."

"And what does that tell us?" Adam asked.

"If Beckworth was the one who betrayed us, why would he be okay with Maire leaving when both she and the book were within his grasp?"

"My thoughts exactly," AJ said as she marched to the table and sat down several paper bags infused with tantalizing aromas.

For a moment, everyone appeared startled. They had been so engrossed in Ethan's story, no one heard the car arrive, the front door, or the rustling bags.

"That's why you raced out of here like ghosts were chasing you. Dinner?" Stella chided.

"Not the only reason. I had a few other things to pick up."

They all stood and stared as Maire lumbered into the room, dragging two duffels. After dropping them, she moved into Ethan's open arms and kissed his cheek. "We weren't sure Ethan would play along with all his brooding. So we thought it best to wait until we had everything we needed."

AJ pulled paper containers from the bags. "Let's eat. Then we'll share what Maire and I have been up to."

Ethan could only stare at AJ. Her stoic resolve was gone. She moved with purpose, and appeared more vibrant and fierce than she had before the masquerade ball. He knew that look. She was prepared for battle.

3

Ethan picked through the two duffels. "What's all this?"

"Weapons. I thought that would be obvious." AJ shrugged with an apologetic smile at Ethan's raised brows. She hadn't meant to be flippant, and she forced her shoulders to relax. Another few hours were all she needed. She placed two maps and a single sheet of note paper on the table.

Maire worked behind Ethan, restoring the duffels to order after he'd rifled through them.

"We have to assume Eleanor, and possibly Bart, have been compromised." She paused. "Worst case, they're dead."

She glanced first at her mother and then at Stella. Discussing time travel like it was an everyday occurrence was one thing, talking about dead bodies and brandishing weapons was quite another. Yet neither woman batted an eye, though her mom did look a little queasy. Time was of the essence. The clock continued to tick away in her head, its icy hands abrasive on her frayed nerves. She would have jumped back immediately, but Ethan was adamant about giving Finn more time. It was Maire who forced her hand.

Maire had insisted they give her time to translate the rest of the grimoire, loosely known as the druid's book. AJ gave Ethan and Adam copies of the stolen letters that spoke of Langdon, a high-placed earl who worked with William Pitt in the war effort against France. Langdon had been lifelong friends to Sir Ratliff.

Long ago, during the Reign of Terror in France, shortly after the French Revolution, Sebastian and the Prior of the monastery had been worried about the theft of ancient artifacts from churches. To protect the torc, which held the six druid stones, and *The Book of Stones*, the two men had split the book into three parts. They scattered the torc, the three sections of book, and five of the druid stones deep within the underground rooms and secret passages of the monastery. The only exception had been the Heart Stone, the largest of the six stones, and the one they'd thought controlled the other stones. The monks felt the stone might be too powerful by itself, so the Prior sent it to an old friend in England, Sir Ratliff, to protect. That single act would eventually form the chain of women, referred to as the Keepers of the Stone. Through the generations, these women passed down the Heart Stone to their daughters and granddaughters, protecting and disguising it until it was mistakenly sold to AJ earlier that year. Her singular purchase launched AJ into the crazy world of time travel, a mad duke, and the arms of the dashing, if irritating, Captain Finn Murphy—the love of her life.

Just another day in the neighborhood.

Though the duke had been killed, his son, Reginald, who turned out to be Beckworth's half-brother, returned to England with one of the smaller druid stones. He'd also found the grimoire and had begun practicing druid magic, or so he thought. His goal had been to learn the secrets of time travel. To that end, he'd somehow discovered Ratliff had that century's Heart Stone. Ratliff ended up dead, no doubt by Reginald's hands, but the Heart Stone was still safe with Ratliff's daughter, Elizabeth. The letters found in Reginald's office spoke of Langdon, a family friend of Ratliff and the bearer of the surname of the first Keeper of the Stone. The letters included his daily routines and travel plans. AJ, and most of the team, assumed Langdon was being targeted. What Reginald hoped to gain was simple, he had his sights on the Heart Stone. The question was, why did he believe Langdon knew anything about it? AJ had overheard Adam and Ethan discuss the letters, but neither man had come up with a definitive guess.

Helen leaned over the maps. "What are these maps?"

"This must be Waverly." Stella laid down a half-formed origami figure and tapped one of the maps. Her head was pressed near Helen's as they both studied it. Then Stella pointed to a spot lower on the map. "This is the town?" She glanced up at AJ, who just nodded.

Adam pulled the map away from Stella and positioned both maps in the middle of the table, forcing everyone to lean over so they could all look together.

"Corsham," Maire confirmed. "It's about five miles southeast of Waverly."

AJ stared at her mother and Stella. These two women were her rock. If she'd asked them to go back to help find Finn, they would. They'd get themselves killed, but just the knowledge they'd do anything to help family was enough. She pulled up a chair next to Maire. "Using the Heart Stone incantation to go back will probably land us in France again." She glanced at Maire, who gave her a firm nod. "We think we should use Ethan's stone and incantation. That should take us directly to England. The question is, will it take us back to Hereford where Ethan last used his incantation, or will it take us back to Waverly Manor where he last jumped with the stone?"

All eyes turned to Maire. She shrugged. "This isn't science. There are still many things we don't know about the stones. The only thing I believe is that his stone should return us to England. That is how the stones worked when Finn first took AJ back. He arrived where he first jumped—the cottage in Ireland."

"But you modified the incantations," Ethan interjected.

"True. But I don't think they specifically modified how the stones interacted—starting point to return point. I think it just made the jumps more accurate, less scattered in time if you will." She shrugged again. "It's all speculation, of course."

"Of course," Ethan muttered.

"So why do you think Ethan's stone would take you back to Waverly? You used the Heart Stone's incantation to bring you back home." Adam stood to pace, hands in his pockets. He only made it as far as the bay window, where he stopped to stare out to sea.

"Wouldn't landing at Waverly be a problem?" Stella asked. "That's kind of like landing in the heart of the Death Star."

"That could definitely be a problem," Ethan agreed.

"It's not like anyone would be expecting us." AJ understood Ethan's concerns. He'd be overly cautious whenever Maire was involved, which also meant he'd catch any gaps in the plan they hadn't thought of. "We were a fair distance from the manor, deep in the woods. If we expect the same three-month time gap for the week we've been back, which the last two jumps have confirmed, then it will be spring. The leaves will be out, which will provide more cover."

"Except for the strange fog." Adam rocked back and forth in full lawyer mode. "I would think they'd remember that."

AJ ran her hands over her face before pushing her hair back. She knew they needed to walk through the problems—there were plenty of them. She'd been on slow burn ever since Maire had convinced her to wait until the grimoire had been translated. Her anxiety had been hidden under the numbness of Finn's fate. Until now.

"Look. I know there are problems with either stone and incantation we use. Worst case, even using Ethan's stone, we could end up back at the monastery. Then we'd have to wait for one of the smuggler ships, preferably the *Daphne Marie*." She stopped and caught her breath. "Assuming Jamie made it out of Waverly." She cleared her throat. "But I don't want to wait weeks or months to get back to England. We have to take the best chance to get to England the fastest way possible, and that leaves Ethan's stone. If we end up in Hereford, we'll be at the earl's estate and can make plans with the earl and Thomas." She paused. "Assuming Thomas survived."

The thought that none of the team had made it out alive quieted the group.

"So, let's find the safest plan in case you arrive at Waverly." Adam returned to the table and leaned over the maps. He took a quick look at the map of Waverly and Corsham, then pushed it aside to focus on the second map, which represented a closer look at the grounds of Waverly and the inside of the manor. "Where were you when you jumped?"

"Here." Maire pointed.

Adam absently checked his pockets as he noted the spot where Maire had laid her finger. "Okay. And that's all forested?"

"For the most part." Ethan ran his finger across the backside of the estate. "The tree line runs along here. There are other trees in the garden and small alcoves, all places we might be able to hide."

Adam glanced around the table, then checked his pockets again. "I need a pen."

Stella jumped up and pulled paper, several pens, and a pencil from a side drawer. She tossed them on the table, then refilled cups. "You arrive on foot, and what, hike to someplace safe?"

"Depends on what we find." Ethan ran his finger along an imaginary line. "We might be able to skirt the trees to the west of the estate."

Adam grabbed the pencil and drew a line from their possible reentry point along the line Ethan had shown. "Where's the stable?"

"It was here." He pointed to a spot northwest of the manor.

"Will they have fixed it by now?" AJ asked.

Ethan nodded. "They'll need someplace to keep the horses. The base of the building was stone. With the foundation still in place, it wouldn't take them long to rebuild."

"Dugan has more than enough men to have it rebuilt quickly. But he'll still have guards on constant patrol." Maire's tone held an edge. It came out whenever she spoke of Dugan.

AJ held the same anger toward the despicable man. Dugan would be a problem. AJ almost sneered, wondering who would put a sword through that man. "Beckworth mentioned that Dugan liked to change the patrols. Different times and rotation of men."

"How far to another manor or farm?" Stella asked.

AJ stared at Ethan and Maire. The only places she remembered were Eleanor and Bart's farmhouses. There were other neighbors, but she'd never paid attention.

"They're scattered but get closer toward town," Maire responded.

"We could walk the five miles." AJ pointed toward the back of the estate. "There's a road on the far side of the manor. We rode in from that direction when Beckworth led us to the building where Maire was being held. We traveled from the west. I assume the road continued toward town."

"Agreed. This close to Corsham, most roads would point

toward the town or connect to another road that heads that way." Ethan glanced at Maire then AJ. "But you don't want to go directly to town."

She sighed. It would be so tempting to check the building where Maire had been held. If only to check for guards. She noticed Maire's tight lips. Though Maire had been eating better since their arrival, the dark circles under her eyes proved how little sleep she'd been getting, her entire focus spent translating the grimoire.

AJ's reluctance to push Maire had frayed her own patience. What she wanted to do was take a couple of AK-47s back with them and just blow everyone away until she found Finn. Every morning she had to talk herself down. She knew it was her own frustration and idleness, but the thought helped get her through each day.

She couldn't help but smile at her last thought before refocusing on her plan. Ethan had to agree to it. "We need to play it safe. We can't afford to let Dugan or Reginald know we're back. If there are too many of Dugan's men about, we get the hell out of there. But if for some reason the guard is light, we should make an attempt to check out the building where they kept Maire." She hated to beg but, if she had to, she'd grovel on her knees for Finn. "We only need to see if it's guarded to know if someone's being held there." She held Ethan's gaze.

He nodded before returning to the map. His reluctant agreement should have calmed her, but it didn't. Did he think they were on a fool's mission to rescue a dead man? A painful stab slammed into her chest, and she pushed out the breath she'd been holding.

Ethan shrugged, as if reading AJ's concern. "We'd just have to come back to check. If it's not far, and we have the opportunity, we should take it. Then we go to town and get horses."

"How far away is Hereford?" Stella asked.

"I remember someone mentioning it was a two-day ride." Adam stared at the map where Hereford and Bristol had been written in.

"A hard two days," Ethan confirmed.

"Hensley is less than a day away." AJ pointed to a spot just east of Bristol. "After we get horses, or maybe a horse and cart, that's where we go."

4

AJ wiped tears from her eyes. She couldn't remember how long it had been since she'd laughed so hard. A tinge of guilt swept over her, but she tucked it away. Once their plan had been thoroughly discussed, the group turned to the savory aromas seeping from the paper takeout containers. The maps and grimoire were moved aside, temporarily forgotten while Adam and Stella shared tales of family misadventures. One or two, to Ethan's dismay, included him.

She had forgotten how well Adam could weave a tale. His animated stories reminded AJ of their father, and she had no doubt he'd mastered his skill through bedtime stories with his children. Adam shared his first meetings with Finn and how terrified he'd been of the man, but he added his own brand of humor that made Maire laugh so hard she blew tea out of her nose. That made everyone laugh harder. And while the laughter might have been dampened by her imminent departure, AJ knew the stories were cathartic for all of them.

After dinner, with the kitchen cleaned and another pot of coffee emptied by the team, the seriousness of the next hour reclaimed them.

"Why don't you wait until the early morning, like four? You won't have to wait too long for daybreak," Helen suggested as AJ dressed in pants she'd found at a thrift shop that were passable for the early eighteen hundreds.

AJ had also found a shirt, but it had been too pristine. She'd doused it with coffee, wine, and anything else she thought would leave hard-to-get-out stains. Then she ripped it and cut a hole in the fabric before practicing her sewing skills to repair it. After washing the shirt and approving of its well-worn appearance, AJ repeated her efforts on the pants. Once she was happy, she added the extended secret pockets she'd designed before, making a few enhancements.

She'd scrounged for the most comfortable shoes that would be passable without too many questions. If they could make their way back to Eleanor's, she'd have more clothing, but she couldn't depend on that. Even with the anticipated loss of three months, Dugan was sure to have a guard or two watching the old farmhouse.

"We hope to arrive at night. If we don't, we'll have to find a place to hide. Moving around the estate will be easier in the dark and give us more time to attempt the stables. If we end up having to walk to Corsham, it would also be safer at night."

AJ finished tying her shoes and faced her mother. Her expression was one AJ had hoped to never see again, split between loss and stoicism. The two women moved silently, drawn instinctively to want to protect the other, and their long embrace tempered the two years they'd spent such little time together. They both still grieved the loss of a father and a husband. Joseph Moore's departure had created a gulf between the two, and both had to find a way to heal in their own way. Now AJ was leaving with no guarantee of her return.

A knock at the door broke them apart.

"I'm sorry to interrupt." Stella remained in the doorway. "Ethan's getting anxious."

AJ wiped her eyes and snorted. "Do you remember the first time we met him? He'd always seemed a little broody, but he smiled more."

"That was before he fell in love." Stella laughed.

AJ retrieved her dagger from the dresser and stuffed it in the secret pocket of her pants. Then she picked up a single sheet of paper and turned to face the women.

"I made a list."

Stella and Helen glanced at each other and drew closer as AJ approached, handing the page to her mom. Helen grabbed the paper and leaned toward Stella so they could read it together.

They both stared at AJ, but Helen spoke first. "I don't understand. These look like tourist sites or old estates in England and northern France. And there's some town in Ireland?"

AJ nodded.

Stella looked over Helen's shoulder. "What are these symbols?" She pointed to the bottom of the page.

"They're Celtic. It spells Mórdha, which, if I never told you, was the root word for Moore."

"They're a message," Stella whispered.

"For what?" Helen asked, then she drew silent. "Places where you might leave a message if you don't return."

AJ nodded, tears filling her eyes. "I want you to know that we were okay but, for whatever reason, couldn't return home."

———

E than stood at the end of the dock, his legs wide as if braced for waves on the deck of a ship, his arms folded across his chest. The wind had picked up after dinner, but down in the small bay, only a minor breeze ruffled his hair. He'd changed into the breeches, waistcoat, and jacket he'd worn to the ball. The footsteps and chatter reached his ears long before the group arrived at the dock.

He didn't turn, but kept staring out to sea, playing out possible scenarios of what they might find when they arrived. Reginald and Dugan might have suspected the three of them had escaped the masquerade ball by traveling through time. If the thought had occurred to them, Reginald and Dugan wouldn't know when they might return. Three months was a long time to maintain a shift of guards in the woods, but Dugan had proved to be unconventional in his tactics.

There was only one decision—arrive prepared for battle. It might be overkill, but they had to survive the first five minutes of disorientation. The fog was unrelenting in its treatment of a traveler. After all his trips, the jumps never got easier. He rested his hand on the hilt of his sword. He'd asked Maire to carry a primed pistol. It was dangerous, especially through the fog, but she was an expert with the flintlock, and she'd instantly agreed with his request. He laughed at the memory, and his chest filled with overwhelming warmth. He was pretty sure she'd arrived at the same decision before he ever asked.

The women had bantered about the best way to arm AJ. The bow had been Maire's first thought, but if anyone waited for them, it would be close-quarter fighting. AJ was good with the bow but not practiced enough for quick release. While AJ and Maire had been busy with their plans, believing Ethan had been wallowing in his own thoughts, he'd been busy preparing for their return. AJ's weapon of choice was her dagger, and she always kept it close. Over time, she'd improved her throwing techniques. Ethan had traveled up and down the coast, buying several smaller daggers appropriate for throwing. There were several things he loved about this century, the espresso machine being top of his list. He also enjoyed movies, and they'd given him inspiration. He devised a strap for AJ to wear over her shoulder and across her chest, where she could store the new daggers for easy reach. She would keep her main dagger in her pocket as a last resort.

When he turned to the group, his instinct and readiness for battle surged, along with his heart when he spotted Maire and AJ. Even with the heavy duffel, Maire held her head high, a look of determination making her face glow. AJ's expression was grim, her shoulder harness strapped tightly over her chest with bits of silver seeping from the holstered daggers. If anyone had run into the two women as they appeared now, Ethan was sure the person would cross the street. Stories of the Valkyries came to mind, along with the Wagner music AJ had played for him during an earlier jump. He only hoped the slain bodies they retrieved would be Dugan's men.

Helen, Adam, and Stella chattered nonstop. He expected tears, and maybe they would still come, but the three staying behind appeared as full of purpose as the rest of them. In some way, their wait would be harder.

He couldn't take his eyes from Maire. She dressed in her scullery maid clothes, minus Eleanor's artful makeup. She was stunning. Her wheat-colored hair was tied back in a tight bun, which only emphasized her high cheekbones. She'd gained additional weight in the last week, filling in the shadows, her cheeks rosy from the chill in the air.

When AJ stepped away from the group toward the middle of the dock, Maire hefted her duffel and joined her. Ethan left his lone spot and walked past the women to shake Adam's hand.

"If all goes well, this should be the last time we meet." Ethan studied Adam's face. He'd changed since they'd first met. Though Adam had always been a good father, he had finally taken on the role of patriarch for the Moore family. Not to run the family, but to have everyone's back when needed. The distance Helen, Adam, and AJ had placed between themselves after the death of Joseph had disappeared. Their secrets had been laid bare, leaving a new understanding of who they each were. They were stronger for it.

He hugged Stella. "I think I'll miss you most of all."

"I knew it." Her grip was tight. While still holding her close, he pulled Helen in with his other arm and gave her a light hug. He bent his head, placed a kiss on both of their foreheads, and whispered, "I promise. Whatever it takes. I'll send AJ back home to you."

5

———

Corsham, England - 1804

AJ pulled her hat down as she inched her way into the mercantile behind an older woman who moved in time with the swing of her scarred cane. Thump, then slide, as the cane dragged across the uneven wooden floor. Each thump made AJ cringe. She thought the old woman would be a good person to follow. Most people had merely glanced and nodded at her when she ambled up the sidewalk. She'd expected the same simple acknowledgment at the mercantile, but it seemed several other women had been waiting for her.

Just her luck to have followed the town gossip. With each continued thump, AJ was sure someone would notice her. After gaining several feet into the store, she stepped behind a stack of crates to stare at a bin of root vegetables, waiting for someone to call after her. No one did. The old woman was surrounded, everyone talking at once. The store owner, Mr. Covington, trailed after the group, probably hoping to glean new information to share with his customers throughout the day.

Her visits to the apothecary and the inn told her nothing. After edging around the smithy without anyone noticing her, she'd worked up the courage to try the mercantile. Ethan worried she'd be recognized, considering her visits months earlier asking about Maire. Maire had applied a layer of dirt to AJ's face, making her appear more boyish, and advised her to round her shoulders and hunch. As if AJ didn't have enough to think about, now she had to focus on how to walk.

Their trip back to England had been quick and exactly as they'd planned. When the fog had come, blinding white light and horrendous nausea notwithstanding, Maire's incantation with Ethan's stone had placed them almost to the spot of where they'd last left Waverly. Once they'd been able to stand without puking, Maire had wiped her mouth and gloated.

"See? Right where I said we'd be."

Ethan and AJ glanced at each other with a slight grin.

If anyone waited for them, they could've easily taken the three of them while they emptied their stomachs. Ethan turned in a circle, one hand brandishing his sword, the other out in a gesture for the women to stay back. Maire had pulled out her pistol. When no one approached, he sheathed the sword. "If anyone was here, they've run like frightened rabbits."

"I'm pretty sure I'd do the same thing standing in the dark while three people magically appeared out of some mysterious fog." AJ ran a hand over her shoulder harness and the array of daggers, enjoying the extra armament and comfortable fit. She had to admit—she felt like a ninja.

"If someone was here, they've run to signal the alarm. We should get moving." Maire pocketed her pistol and turned for the stables.

"Wait." Ethan reached for her arm, but she grabbed his instead.

"We agreed to try for the stables. If someone was sounding

an alarm, I think we'd still hear his screaming." Maire sprinted away.

AJ shrugged at Ethan's questioning glance before racing after Maire.

With his slight curse, mumbled loud enough for AJ to hear, Ethan brought up the rear. Maire darted from tree to tree when they reached the more open landscape of the estate. Breathing hard, AJ bumped next to Maire behind a small outbuilding. They had reached the western edge of the estate with both the manor house and, as Ethan had speculated, the rebuilt stables in view. They had arrived in darkness, as they'd hoped, but had no indication to the exact time.

"I don't see any light in the manor, so it must be past midnight but not early enough for the kitchen staff." Ethan edged in front of Maire.

"And the moon is nothing more than a sliver low on the horizon. Seems we've caught a bit of luck." Maire began to move out, but Ethan stayed her arm.

"Me this time. Let me take care of anyone that might be in the stables." And without waiting for an argument, he ran for the building.

When Maire rolled her eyes, AJ chuckled.

"You have to let him do something," she chided.

"There was a time I wouldn't question his constant need to do everything. I don't know if it was all those months being locked away or your influence. But it has become rather annoying waiting for a man to do what I can do for myself."

"Yeah. I'm afraid that feeling will never go away."

"How did you work through that with my brother? He's as protective as Ethan."

AJ smirked. "I'm still working on that. It helps to not always be storming into danger or running for our lives."

"Point taken." Maire nodded.

Thirty minutes later, the back of the stable opened, and the shadow of a man led three saddled horses into the open. The women didn't hesitate and, after a quick scan of the area, broke into a jog toward Ethan. AJ closed the stable doors as Maire mounted a horse. Ethan waited for AJ to mount before swinging onto the third horse.

Ethan forced them to maintain a slow pace as they walked the horses down the tree-lined drive away from Waverly.

When they were far enough away, AJ asked, "Was there anyone in the stables?"

He shook his head. "No. I'm beginning to wonder if there are any guards here at all. There were only six horses."

"Maybe it wasn't a good idea to take them."

"Maybe. But if we're discovered, I'd rather rely on a horse than nimble feet."

The women hadn't argued. After leaving Waverly, AJ had been tempted to check Eleanor's farmhouse but decided it was too risky to investigate without daylight.

Dawn was on the horizon by the time they reached the edges of Corsham. They positioned themselves behind the old brick building where Beckworth had waited for her the previous times she'd entered the town. AJ waited until the sounds from town grew, suggesting it would be easier to enter unnoticed. Leaving her shoulder harness and horse behind, she practiced her hunched walk as she entered town. She kept her head down and stuck close to the buildings, hoping to eavesdrop where she could.

A high-pitched laugh woke her from her musings, and she stepped closer to the group of women. If there was something interesting happening in town, this was where she would hear it. Then she noticed Covington's heated gaze as he followed her movements. He'd been the one who'd given her the cryptic message months before to stay away from town. At the time, AJ assumed he was trying to protect Eleanor. Had something changed since then? Did something happen to that dear woman, all because of them?

She would never get close enough to the women to hear anything of value with Covington watching her. After selecting a few items, she screwed up her courage and placed them on the counter. She kept her head down as Covington totaled the sum. She slid a few coins Ethan had given her across the counter, grabbed her packaged purchase, and remembered to hunch her shoulders on her way out. She felt the man's eyes on her back until she cleared the door.

Holding her package close, she decided to return to Ethan and Maire. They could eat and regroup. She made it past the first alley and had planned on turning down the second one when a gruff hand wrapped around her waist, lifting her a few inches off the ground, while a hand covered her mouth. They were around the corner of a building and down the alley before she realized what was happening and began to struggle.

She kicked her legs and planted a solid hit to a knee. They went down. A man's voice yelped a curse in her ear as they hit the hard ground. Unfortunately, she landed first, and it knocked the wind out of her. She pushed up, only needing enough space to reach a throwing dagger, but he was too heavy.

The man grunted when she elbowed him in the ribs. Her hand reached the dagger, but she froze at the man's mumbled words.

"God's blood, woman. Please don't stab me again."

"Beckworth?" AJ twisted so she could get a better look as her captor's grip loosened.

They untangled themselves, and she dragged herself away, turning to sit, one hand still in her pocket.

Beckworth leaned against the building, or at least what she could recognize of him. He had a short beard, unruly and unkempt. His hair had grown long and was thick with dirt. He'd lost some weight from a previously slim frame, but when she caught his gaze, his cornflower-blue eyes sparkled with amusement.

"It took you bloody good time to return."

AJ stared. Her mouth was probably open in shock, and she wiped it, just to check. "What are you doing here?"

"Besides waiting for you?" He stood, brushed himself off, pulled at the sleeves of his filthy overcoat, then reached down to grab her hand and help her up. He gave her a once-over. "Newer clothes." He reached out and tapped at one of the holes she sewed up. "I assume you made these holes. Nice to see you've learned a thing or two from Eleanor."

"Is she all right?" AJ braced herself for the worst, and she had dozens of more questions, but she had to know this one thing.

When he nodded, she almost felt dizzy with relief.

"I sent her to London for a few weeks, but she returned and has been staying with a friend. She couldn't abide London, even when I set her up in a nice townhouse. She can return home, but I wanted to wait another week. To be sure."

Elated to hear Eleanor was safe and partly relieved to know Beckworth had seen to her safety, she asked the next question everyone would want to know. She shoved her hands into her pockets and stared at her feet. When she gained enough courage, she glanced up.

Beckworth arched a brow and waited. When it seemed she wasn't going to ask, he sighed. "I suppose you want to know if I'm the one who betrayed you."

She blinked. Then she returned to studying her shoes, embarrassed by having to ask. He had been Ethan and Maire's first guess, but the more everyone thought about it, it hadn't made sense. But with Beckworth, one never knew.

"I'm sorry I have to ask." Her tone seemed to confirm her words because Beckworth held out a hand, the first time he'd ever done that.

She stared at it for only a moment before grasping it and meeting his gaze. Her breath stuck in her throat and, if he didn't answer soon, she'd pass out from lack of oxygen.

"I swear to you, it wasn't me. It was Dodger."

AJ stumbled back a step, now grateful she'd taken his hand because he pulled her close and grabbed her shoulder to steady her.

"Dodger?" She pulled her hands away, crossing her arms across her chest, feeling a cold breeze.

"Yes. I'll explain everything, but we should find a safer place. It's not quite as dangerous since Reginald left Waverly a few days ago, but he'll be back soon. His men usually scour the town before he arrives."

"How did you even know I was here?"

"I've had the townspeople watching for you. We began to wonder if you'd return, but then I remembered the time difference. How long has it been for you?"

"A week."

He nodded, his gaze on a distant point before he refocused on her. "Someone thought they saw you at the inn earlier. I could have followed all the sightings, but figured you'd go to the mercantile before leaving town. You're not alone, are you?"

"No. Ethan and Maire are with me."

He nodded again. "Thought they might have vanished with you."

"They're at the old building."

He glanced down and retrieved the package of food, somewhat squashed from the two of them landing on it. He brushed it off and handed it to her. "Then let's be off."

She grabbed his arm again. "Finn?"

He wouldn't look at her. When she tugged at his arm again, he placed a hand over hers.

She'd turned stone cold, now sorry she'd asked.

He lifted her chin. His face didn't hold the pity she'd been expecting. His gaze was earnest. "Now, don't go thinking the worst. I believe he's still alive."

———

E than paced along the narrow trail that ran the length of the old crumbling building. The path continued on both ends of the building, the one to the south heading into the trees, the other leading toward town. The building wasn't the most isolated of places, but if Beckworth had used it before, it was probably safe. But who knew what was safe when it involved Beckworth?

AJ didn't believe Beckworth had betrayed them, but he wasn't convinced. Yet, Maire had been right. Based on her version of Beckworth's actions the night of the ball, it made no sense to let her leave with the druid book if he was the one who turned on them. Ethan had to get word to the earl and Hensley. If anyone else had made it out of the fray, they might discover the truth.

"Come sit with me," Maire called from under a young elm tree.

"Is my pacing bothering you?"

She smiled, her soft green eyes crinkling at the corners. "It's a beautiful spring day, and we're alone. Let's enjoy each other's company before the state of affairs crushes us."

He laughed and joined her. He wrapped an arm around her and kissed her temple. "There's the doom and gloom of the Irish I've come to expect."

She punched his side. "It's not without merit, our history notwithstanding. But we don't know what happened the night of the ball. How many we lost. What's happened since."

"I know you're worried about Finn. We'll know soon." He lifted her chin and plucked a strand of hair that had caught on the edge of her lips.

He kissed her. He'd meant for a light kiss. Reassurance that confirmed he'd be there for her, regardless of what they discovered. He hadn't expected the heat of her return kiss, the touch of her tongue on his lips seeking more.

He shifted as he brought her close, the kiss deepening as he responded to Maire's urgent need. He let her take the lead. She ran her hands up his chest then over his shoulders before her fingers moved through his hair. He couldn't stop the rumble of a growl as he pressed her close. He kept one hand around her waist as the other ran over the finely shaped bum underneath her dress.

He squeezed it, heard her own mumble of desire, and casually wondered how much time they had before AJ's return.

"Good to see you're keeping watch so no one sneaks up on you."

The two sprang apart as if they'd been doused in icy water.

Beckworth broke out in a hearty laugh, his expression full of amusement. He winked at Maire.

AJ's blush deepened, and she dropped her gaze, digging her toe in the dirt. Her grin widened when she finally glanced up. "I found Beckworth."

7

———

Two agonizing weeks followed the reunion with Beckworth. The group reestablished Eleanor's farmhouse as base camp. Before they could move forward with planning, Maire and Ethan had to hear Beckworth's version of events the evening of the ball. Everything he recalled from the search for the druid's book in Reginald's bedroom matched Maire's story, including Finn's changing the plan and forcing Maire to take the book and run.

"Finn and I went back out the secret passage, but when we arrived at the bottom of the stairs, Dugan's men were waiting for us. One of them thanked Dodger for his aid, and Thorn..." Beckworth turned away, walking to the hearth to pull the kettle from the fire. He poured a small amount in his cup, grimaced, then pushed the kettle back over the flame. He tugged on his sleeves. "Thorn was obviously upset. He didn't understand. None of us did. But then Dodger mentioned Peele, and he blamed me." Beckworth shrugged. "I suppose he was right."

"And that made it all right to turn on all of us?" AJ had tried to control her bitter tone. Now, Finn was paying for Dodger's betrayal. Maire laid a hand on her arm, but it didn't help.

"We never considered what his brother's death might have done to him," Ethan said. "And Thorn must not have seen it either."

"Probably lost in his own sorrow." Maire squeezed AJ's arm before sitting back. "I didn't know Thorn well, and he hid most of his emotions behind his cavalier attitude. Much of that is just hiding from one's own grief."

"Thorn and I had a history, misunderstood as it was. But he'd put that aside for the common good. Dodger wasn't able to." Beckworth's simple analysis seemed cold, but AJ knew better. Beckworth was still recovering from his own reaction to the events of the ball. For three months, he'd been isolated with only his own version of events to relive.

"Anyway," Beckworth continued, "Thorn turned on Dodger. The fight didn't take long. Thorn was always the better swordsman." He turned his gaze to Ethan. "I think that was what Dodger wanted all along."

Ethan held his gaze, then nodded in understanding.

"One of Dugan's men engaged Thorn, and while they battled, another guard stuck a blade through Thorn's back." Beckworth growled with pent-up anger. "Filthy dogs. Just like Dugan." When he looked up, a fire burned deep in his gaze. "I grabbed Finn, and we ran back up the stairs. Going back through Reginald's room was too dangerous. There was another passage I hadn't told anyone about." He slammed a fist in his hand. "We could have both made it, but Finn didn't think we'd have enough time." He bent his head, barely able to glance at AJ. "I tried to get him to go first, but he gave me back the stone I'd given him. Said he couldn't let the stone be taken, and he mumbled something about having a way to stay alive. He pushed me through and slammed the door behind him."

He turned pleading eyes to AJ, and, for the first time, he

seemed lost, as if he still couldn't understand Finn's decision. She wasn't sure she understood Finn's reasoning either, but she understood her husband. It was his mission, and he felt responsible for the team.

She turned to monitor Maire's reaction. Ethan held Maire's hand, and he pulled her close. They stayed that way for a minute before Maire stood. She stepped to Beckworth and placed a hand on his shoulder before she walked out of the farmhouse. Ethan didn't follow.

———

Ethan sent dispatches to the earl and Hensley, providing limited information in the posts should the letters be intercepted. Beckworth, feeling more confident that help was on its way, sent for Eleanor. She was happy to see everyone alive but seemed more excited to be home. When Beckworth hugged her, she advised him in no uncertain terms that she would never leave her home again, regardless of what trouble he stirred up. Once her sentiment had been shared, she cooked and baked the rest of the evening.

While they waited for responses from Ethan's missives, the hunt for Finn began. During the months Beckworth had been on his own, he'd watched the building where Maire had been held. Spring growth was the only change around the empty prison. Dugan wouldn't be foolish enough to use the same building again. Beckworth expanded his search to other vacant buildings in the vicinity, but nothing appeared to hold a prized prisoner.

No one spoke about what that could mean. After a week of searching in new areas and backtracking everywhere Beckworth had previously looked, a paralyzing fear took root. An unease that AJ was unable to shake. She'd suffered the same despair the first day after they'd returned to Baywood without Finn.

She'd been sitting on the back deck of the inn, entranced by the sea as she reexamined their steps at the ball, wondering where they'd gone wrong. Ethan had been irritated with Beckworth, and as much history as everyone had with the man, Beckworth appeared to be the only one who could have betrayed them.

AJ's instinct told her it wasn't him. If Beckworth had thrown his chips in with his half-brother, he would have been no better off than he'd been with the duke. Would he be satisfied living under the rule of Reginald and Dugan? She knew Beckworth would rather chew off his right arm.

"How long are you going to sit out here?" Stella dropped into the matching Adirondack after placing a bottle of wine and two glasses on the small table between them. She placed a small stack of napkins in her lap.

"Until dinner."

"And then?"

AJ gave her friend a sidelong glance. "Probably come back out."

Stella poured the wine and handed a glass to AJ. "These late summer evenings have been getting chilly. I found a down sleeping bag at that pawnshop next to city hall. It completely unzips. I think it will keep you warm enough, but you'll need a cover if it rains."

AJ blinked away the tears. She assumed Stella would cajole her back inside as her mother had tried. When Helen's attempts to persuade AJ didn't work, she made Adam move the sofa near the bay window so AJ could watch the ocean from the comforts of a warm house. But AJ didn't want the warmth. She craved the cold—anything to keep her numb.

She reached out and grabbed Stella's hand, giving it a light squeeze, honestly touched by her friend's support. "Thank you."

"Let it work for you."

"The wine doesn't seem to have the same impact anymore."

"Not the wine."

She glanced at Stella, who had stopped folding the napkin and was studying her. AJ suspected Stella was gauging her emotional state. "What are you talking about?"

"That week you were gone. The first time, when Adam and I had no idea where you went. For the first few days, I let fear grab hold. I let it run me. It wasn't until I accepted what happened and used that unfounded doubt to fuel me that everything changed. Don't let the fear paralyze you. Mold it into something useful—anger, inspiration, determination." She placed the napkin on the table and leaned back, turning her focus to the sea until she mirrored AJ's repose. "Kick it in the ass, AJ. You know that whatever happened—it's not over."

The scene became a daily ritual. She stared out to sea, wineglass in hand. Stella hovered next to her, making her birds. The woman must have folded hundreds of them, the two rarely speaking. But when they did, Stella never mentioned giving up.

On the second day, Stella had prepared her own agenda. "Have you thought what to do next?" Four origami swans sat on the deck railing. The light breeze had toppled a couple of the earlier versions over the edge.

AJ shrugged. At that point, she wasn't sure what Stella expected her to do.

"I got the impression from Ethan that Maire has her nose buried in that book you brought back."

"The druid's grimoire."

Stella shuddered. "Just the name gives me the creeps—grimoire." After a moment of silence, Stella pushed on. "I just find it curious."

AJ arched a brow and shifted her position to get a better look at her friend. It was at that moment she realized Stella had changed. The revelation made her consider everyone around her. Her family had changed, and not only in becoming closer. Each of them had developed an inner courage, a deeper tenacity than they had before. Stella no longer glossed over a difficult situation with jokes. She still used humor to calm a situation, but she wasn't trying to convince AJ to do the sane thing.

"What do you find curious?" AJ found her interest piqued.

"I don't know what Maire is expecting to find in the book. Maybe she'll discover something that will suggest your next move, but either way..." Stella bent her head, refocusing on her origami before she huffed out an exaggerated breath. She dropped the bird to stare at AJ, her brows pinched together in what AJ knew to be confusion. "Shouldn't you be training or something?"

AJ couldn't have been more shocked had her mother asked the question. "What do you mean?"

"I'm no expert on weapons or kung fu, but it seems you're just sitting here getting rusty."

AJ barked out a laugh at the unexpected mentoring. "Kung fu?"

"You know what I mean. I know Ethan says just give it time, but let's face it. We all know you're going back if Finn doesn't show up soon. Shouldn't you be, you know, practicing, staying sharp."

In fact, AJ had already begun her practice sessions when Stella and her mom hadn't been hovering. Now that she was back in England, each time the fear began to eat away at her when their search for Finn came up empty, she remembered what Stella had told her. She spent every waking moment when they weren't searching practicing with her bow and daggers.

Earlier that morning, after retracing their steps on the

eastern edge of Waverly, the group had returned to Eleanor's just as disheartened as when they'd left. Beckworth stayed for only a few minutes before he left for town. Eleanor said the innkeeper had wanted to speak to him.

Refusing to get her hopes up, AJ grabbed her set of daggers and spent thirty minutes practicing more advanced exercises. She ran for short bursts, turning and taking only an instant to aim before throwing. At first, her aim was sloppy, but halfway through, she began hitting her target. Soon after, she lost her accuracy and distance. Both arms ached, and she struggled to even lift them, but she continued. She had to build her stamina.

She threw her last dagger, which hit the tree dead on. Unfortunately, she'd been aiming at the tree next to it. She dropped to the ground, picked up a stick, and threw it. She watched it sail end over end before silently landing twenty feet away.

"You become lazy with the dagger and change to sticks?"

She spun around so fast as she tried to stand that she tripped and fell to a knee.

Lando.

She'd barely stood when he reached her and dragged her into his arms. He squeezed the stuffing out of her. She let the tears flow as she grabbed on and refused to let go. "I thought you might be dead."

He laughed. "Not yet, little one."

When he stepped back and let her down, he frowned. "Are these tears for me?"

She could only shrug, not wanting to reveal they were for all of them.

"As you can see, I'm in one piece." He drummed a fist on his bulky chest and turned to study the dagger buried in the tree. "You had good aim and distance for the first ten minutes. We need to build on that." He waited for her to collect her things before putting an arm around her shoulders. "Come. We have plans to make to find our Finn."

She lowered her head, unable to speak with the tears following.

"Don't give up." He jabbed a finger in his chest. "I'd know if Captain Murphy no longer resided in this world. He's out there, little one. We'll find him."

8

———

When AJ and Lando returned to the farmhouse, she spotted Jamie and Fitz sitting on the front porch, boots on the railing, their heads back, eyes closed. Another sliver of muscles relaxed along her back, her relief at seeing her friends alive temporarily muffling her fear for Finn.

Lando bent close, "We'd just docked in Bristol when we received the news you'd returned. Hensley had a man waiting for us. Jamie left the ship's care to the bosun and we rode straight here."

"Did you come from the monastery?"

"No. We wanted to be close. We'd just finished running cargo to Dublin and north. Jamie and Fitz, well, we all wanted to be out searching, but Hensley advised us to be patient."

"Hensley's been searching?"

He redirected his gaze to the other side of the clearing where Beckworth must have arrived not long ago. He was removing his horse's saddle. "He's been receiving letters from Beckworth."

AJ paused. She'd assumed everyone thought Beckworth was the traitor. "They were working together?"

He shook his head then led her to a bench under a poplar

tree. "We would have all been lost that night had the fog not come. We were outnumbered. Dugan had men surrounding the manor. When the fog came, it scared Dugan's men. They didn't know what the strange mist was, only that it wasn't normal." He chuckled. "Dugan's men knew the false viscount was playing with black magic. The fog made it all real for them."

Ethan had told AJ the fog might save them. Lando's confirmation made her feel better about their decision to leave. It didn't change the fact she should have returned sooner.

"By the time we made it back to Eleanor's, we'd lost three men that we knew of. We left for Hensley's once we confirmed we must have been betrayed. When Thorn and Dodger didn't return, we assumed we lost them as well." He turned away from her, but he wasn't finished. His shoulders tensed and then relaxed. "I thought Finn had left with you. I would never have left had I known."

AJ placed a hand on his upper arm. "And then you'd be dead or wherever Finn is." When he turned back, the torment buried deep within his gaze broke her heart. "This wasn't your fault. Now tell me the rest."

He nodded and put an arm around her. "Beckworth sent a message explaining Finn's capture, Dodger's betrayal, and the loss of Thorn. Hensley didn't believe his story, but Beckworth continued sending letters, at first every week, then every two. He never again explained what happened or asked for anyone to believe him. He simply informed Hensley where he'd searched for Finn and what he knew of the viscount's short trips around Bath and Hagersham. When the notes kept coming, Hensley began to believe him. Yet, he wasn't truly convinced until he received Ethan's letter."

"What have you heard from the earl?"

"Thomas is on his way with ten men. The earl will send more

when they return from other assignments, but it could be a few weeks. We'll have to work with what we have."

"And that should be more than enough based on my latest intelligence." Beckworth tugged at his sleeves before leaning against a neighboring tree and folding his arms across his chest.

AJ sat up, hope blossoming at the wry grin on Beckworth's face. "You found him?"

"I think so. Never thought to look within neighboring estates, but a new rumor is spreading about Reginald's interest in acquiring more land. He's set his sights on the baronet's oldest daughter." He visibly shuddered. "From what I understand, they met at his masquerade ball before we burned down his stables. The old baronet has one foot in the grave and has no sons."

"And how do you know this man has Finn?" Lando sounded doubtful.

"I don't think the baronet has Finn. The property line between the two estates has always been a bit blurry with the lake and all. But there is an old hunting lodge near the lake in complete disrepair. About a quarter-mile from that is another outbuilding. From what my estate manager told me when I first surveyed the property, the baronet used the building to hold vagabonds and gypsies that trespassed on his land."

"You think Reginald put Finn in this building without the baronet knowing about it?" AJ dared not hope because it sounded like a long shot.

"As I said. The baronet is beyond old, and his entire estate has been deteriorating for years. I doubt he knows half of what goes on under his nose."

"And you haven't checked before now?" Lando asked.

Beckworth shrugged. "I went by there during my first perimeter sweep when I knew Reginald had left the estate. The buildings were empty. With Reginald in residence, it's too dangerous to return alone."

If Reginald was in residence, then Dugan and his men would be back. Why was Beckworth mentioning the building now? When she glanced at him, his eyes gleamed.

"What aren't you telling us? You must have brought this up for a reason." A spurt of anger rose, and AJ tried to temper it but failed.

Beckworth maintained his nonchalance yet his gaze gleamed. "You may think I'm untrustworthy." He shrugged. "You're probably right."

Lando grunted, but AJ caught something in Beckworth's expression, and for the barest moment, felt sorry for him. He'd done a lot for them these last few months, but he never received a thank you, just more distrust. But if he'd found Finn, that could make all the difference.

"Get to the point, please." AJ allowed her burst of temper to keep a rein on her growing optimism. Beckworth wouldn't lead her on. He knew how important this was to her, and somewhere, in his own personal code, he felt he owed Finn.

"If the building is on the baronet's estate, then why would Dugan's men be guarding an old rundown building in the middle of a forest?"

9

The team left the horses on the perimeter of the baronet's property and moved in by foot. They split into teams of two. Lando and Beckworth took a wide approach, skirting the building and coming in from behind it. Jamie and Fitz broke to the right while AJ and Ethan flanked on the left.

AJ followed Ethan, bow at her side, her shoulder harness full of throwing daggers in addition to the dagger hidden in her pocket. Her body thrummed with electricity as they approached, their footsteps measured, avoiding anything that might make a noise. The silence was deafening, and the closer they got, the louder AJ's heart pounded until she heard nothing else. Three weeks since she'd seen Finn. The last was when he'd been running for his horse after their swift kiss. She had been sitting in the carriage dressed in the finest gown she'd ever worn. He'd been dressed like a midnight pirate. His smile had been forced when he'd give her a last glance. Did some inner instinct tell him they'd missed something important?

She had that same feeling now as they approached the stone building on the baronet's estate, fifty yards from the Waverly property line. Everything seemed too quiet. Not even the birds liked this place.

Ethan stopped behind a row of laurel bushes. She didn't like his expression when he turned to watch her approach. Not one bit. His frown and wrinkled forehead made her heart sink. Something was wrong.

She knelt next to him and peered through the shrubs. "Where are the guards?"

"I don't know." Ethan barely spit out the words.

The stone building sat in the middle of a small clearing, surrounded by dense thickets of brush and trees. One overgrown path, barely wide enough for a cart, was the only way in. Brush rustled on the far side of the building, which AJ assumed must be Lando and Beckworth. Jamie and Fitz should be on her right. If they were there, and she was positive they were, they gave no indication.

Someone whistled. Not a quick whistle that might signal an alarm. They hadn't made plans for a whistle, only a bird call. This whistling held a melody, the sound of someone walking through the woods without a care.

When Beckworth appeared, boldly strolling up the old trail, Ethan cursed.

All the strength went out of AJ, and she grabbed the nearest strong branch for support. The electricity that had coursed through her moments ago drained away, leaving a heaviness in her chest. A feeling so crushing, she could barely take a breath.

Ethan grabbed her elbow, forcing her up and through a thin spot in the laurel as he led her into the clearing. The other men followed as they moved out of the trees to huddle where Beckworth had stopped several yards from the front of the building.

The men glared at Beckworth, who shrugged. "The man I spoke with was beyond reproach. His word has always been good in the past."

"Yet the building seems woefully light on guards," Ethan growled.

"I doubt Dugan would leave the building unguarded if anyone was in there." Jamie spat into the dirt, his expression as grim as the others.

"Maybe the guards are inside," Fitz offered, but his tone told them he knew different.

The team glanced at each other. AJ didn't need to see it. She already knew. Dugan would never have left Finn unguarded.

"Maybe they got what they wanted from him then left him to rot." Beckworth winced at AJ's glare. "Sorry. Just a turn of phrase."

"Let's find out." AJ sprinted for the door, leaving the rest to catch up.

AJ gripped her bow in her left hand, her quiver over one shoulder, and a throwing dagger clutched in her right as she raced lightly to the door that had begun to rot on the edges. She slung the bow over her shoulder before reaching for the door. Lando pushed her aside as the other men surrounded her. Ethan tugged her elbow to force her away from the entrance and against the building. Beckworth, Jamie, and Fitz lined up on the other side of the door.

On a short count, Lando yanked the door open and jumped back.

AJ prayed for the sound of a musket or pistol, anything to give her back an ounce of hope. The only sound was the return of a lone chickadee, calling for its mate.

Lando went in first, a pistol in his hand, followed by Jamie, Fitz, then Beckworth. Ethan nodded for her to go next as he covered them from the abandoned clearing.

The inside of the building was simple. An open space with a wooden table and four chairs and one single cell, enclosed on three sides by the stone walls of the building. The fourth wall of the cell was iron bars, the door swung partway open. She could clearly see what her heart refused to believe.

The cell was empty.

Finn, if he had ever been there, was long gone.

The last of AJ's spirit drained away as she sank to the floor.

Jamie crouched next to her, Ethan on the other side as if they protected some injured fawn. She wished they would all go away. Her vision blurred, and she blinked several times to no avail. All the pent-up emotion since walking through the fog broke like a storm wave against a stone wall. The tears fell and she hung her head, curling into herself until Jamie and Ethan left her.

She didn't know how long she'd sat there. She'd cried herself out, upset that she'd shown weakness in front of the men like some little girl. Heaving a deep, shaky breath, AJ stood and glanced around. She walked into the cell and slowly turned, taking in every inch of the cell. A filthy pad lay in the corner farthest from the door. An empty bucket near the door. Nothing more.

With hesitant steps, she approached the pad. Dried blood spatters marred the ordinary brown stain of age and dirt. A small flame of hope sparked. If Finn had been here, there wasn't nearly enough blood to have killed anyone. It didn't mean much, but she held on to that slim string of hope. Her lifeline.

She turned and left the building.

———

 hen AJ emerged from the building, she raised an arm to shield her eyes from the sudden brightness. The men had found a place under two trees where they'd sprawled on the early spring grass. They paid no attention to her, and no one spoke as they ate the simple lunch Eleanor had made. The men seemed lost in their own thoughts, or maybe they just didn't know what to expect from an emotional female. She pushed that aside, realizing, not for the first time, that these men were just as disappointed in not finding Finn.

Ethan patted a seat next to him, and she dropped down, ignoring the bread, cheese, and meat pie he'd saved for her. She took a sip from the skin he passed her, wiped her chin, and grinned. She'd been expecting water but was grateful for the wine. She needed the sharp edges of the day to be softened, so she savored a longer drink.

"If Finn had been in the building, how long do you think he's been gone?" Jamie asked.

Ethan shrugged. "Hard to tell by what blood was there, but I'd say a week, no more than two."

Lando and Beckworth both nodded their agreement. The silence returned.

AJ closed her eyes, surprised to hear more birds and the light rustle of leaves. When she opened them, the beauty of the woods was intoxicating, warring with the deep pit she found herself in. Beckworth had been right as usual. She'd waited too long. Arriving a single day earlier could have made all the difference. They might have found him while he was still here.

She wrapped her arms around her waist, hugging herself against the torrent of emotions raging to be set free. If she didn't push them down and lock them away, she'd start screaming and never stop.

"Has he been here all this time and they just moved him? Do

you think they might be moving him every few weeks?" Jamie had become relentless with his questions, seemingly unable to process what went wrong.

After a lengthy pause, Beckworth tugged at his sleeves and scratched his beard that he hadn't yet shaved. "I have a thought."

When everyone stared at him, he lifted his chin. "I know, I know. You can't wait to hear the brilliant idea."

When the stares morphed into glares, he sighed.

"Fine. To the point then. I've had two men following Reginald's weekly midnight excursions. Just to keep an eye on him. He switches locations every few weeks. No one knows why. I assumed he was either afraid of being caught or it was some druid thing." He shook his head as if to say who knew what those crazy kids were up to. "Anyway, what if they're keeping Finn close to the gatherings?"

Ethan sat up. "They move him when they move their gathering spot."

"When was his last move?" Lando asked.

"Six days ago." Beckworth stood and brushed off his breeches. "We have a general idea of where he went, but it's not an area I'm as familiar with."

The team scrambled, stowing any leftovers. Their previously defeated emotions evaporated, leaving them with new purpose. While they might still carry doubts, smiles and camaraderie resurfaced, leaving no one unaffected by their new direction. Beckworth was on to something.

AJ picked up the bow, quiver, and dagger she'd dropped by her horse. She hung the bow and quiver on the saddle and slid the dagger into her shoulder harness. A tiny voice told her she was refusing to accept reality, but a more vibrant one tamped down the negative thoughts and shoved them into the background. For the first time since arriving, this felt right.

10

Once they returned to Eleanor's, Ethan took Jamie and Fitz to meet with Beckworth's man in Atworth, some six miles south of Waverly. Lando and Beckworth remained behind to guard the women.

No one had seen much of Dugan's men, but that didn't mean they weren't out there. No one could predict what Dugan might do. Had he concluded the team had been dismantled and no longer presented a threat? AJ hoped so. She'd like to see the surprised fury on his face when he returned to where they held Finn to find him gone.

As the day stretched into several, AJ kept to a daily routine that included long walks in the woods. They never said anything and were never seen, but either Lando or Beckworth always followed even though AJ left the cottage well-armed. On the third day, as dusk approached, AJ stopped at a small creek. She removed her shoes and dipped her toes in the frigid water. She absorbed the icy chill that crept from her feet to her knees. The numbness growing in her legs reminded her of Baywood and her days on the back deck staring at nothing. She'd asked Maire for a sleeping aid the previous night. When they found Finn, she wanted to be on top of her game.

She stretched back on the soft grass and stared up at the trees, breathing deeply to relax aching muscles from her earlier training session. A warm breeze stirred the leaves, and birds jumped from branch to branch in response. Any other time, the setting would provide all the solace she needed. But not today.

"Come out and talk to me. I need a distraction."

A few seconds later, the soft pad of feet grew closer. She had become familiar with the movements of the team during multiple searches, so she wasn't surprised when Beckworth plopped down next to her.

"Your feet are blue." He fell back so he laid an arm's distance from her, his own gaze staring into the canvas of branches.

"I've lost feeling in them." AJ continued to stare, a peacefulness finally falling over her.

"It's not your fault," Beckworth stated. "You did right to wait and prepare. I'm just sorry I wasn't able to do more."

A clenching of her gut momentarily dispelled her calm. She'd come to the same conclusion the day before. The entire afternoon was spent analyzing her decisions the week they'd been back in Baywood. Second-guessing previous actions did little good. She'd already berated herself days ago for not returning quicker. Now, Beckworth came to the same realization —they had to be prepared for the long game.

She reached out and patted his arm, wanting to give him a small bone. "If you'd gone straight to Hensley, someone would have shot you before asking a single question, believing you to be the traitor. Then where would we be?"

"You give Hensley too little credit. I don't know much about the man, but what little I do know, it's easy to see why Finn trusts him. He's a master of his game."

AJ smiled. "And what game is that?"

"Spymaster."

She turned her head, but Beckworth continued to gaze at the trees. "I hadn't thought of him that way before, but it makes sense. He does seem to always know what's going on in London. And I know the smuggling jobs he sends Jamie on, much like he had with Finn, are mostly a ruse for gathering information."

"I have a good feeling about today." Beckworth folded his hands over his chest, looking like someone posing for their effigy.

She snorted. "I find myself agreeing with you more and more each day."

Beckworth chortled in return. "Now that's a delightful sign that you've come to your senses. I can be a very bright sod."

"And for once, I finally agree with you, little man." Lando stepped next to them.

AJ sat up so quickly she splashed water over Beckworth. Neither of them had heard Lando's approach. She tried to get up, but her feet were numb, and Beckworth grabbed her as she fell. They both stared up at Lando as AJ massaged her feet to get the blood circulating.

His huge grin made AJ's hopes skyrocket, and she forced shoes over her still-wet feet.

"They've found Finn."

———

E than shared what they'd discovered in Atworth as they ate dinner. The group had broken into two teams, but after a thorough search of the lands around the town, they'd come up empty. When they met at an inn to review the areas they'd searched, Fitz left to perform his own style of reconnaissance. He spent the evening at a run-down pub at the edge of town. An old man, deep in his cups, had spoken of an old oak forest, farther east than they'd been searching.

The next morning, the men searched the new area, eventually coming upon the smaller village of Shaw. Dozens of Dugan's men milled about, staying close to the Waverly coach parked at the only inn. Reginald was in town. Clearly outnumbered, they retreated to continue their search for the old oak forest.

The old forest turned out to be three oak trees, one almost dead, but the remaining two stood proud in the waning afternoon light. A quarter of a mile away, Ethan and one of Beckworth's men found what they'd been seeking. Two dozen men guarded a stone building.

They waited for dark while the guards settled down to eat and prepare for sleep. Fitz went in alone under the assumption the evening patrol would be light. His small stature and stealth would make him difficult to spot. And if he was found, he could easily pass himself off as a drunkard. He'd returned quickly. Dugan had posted too many men for Fitz to get close.

"If they'd only posted three or four for the evening, I could have gotten a better look. But they had double that." Fitz finished off his mug of ale and poured another.

Beckworth eyed the group around the table. "It's a good sign the building is so heavily guarded."

"I would have preferred a dozen less men. We'll need reinforcements." Jamie had moved his plate out of the way and was scratching out a letter.

"It could take days before they arrive. We'll need someone to monitor the location in case they move him." Ethan squeezed Maire's hand when she began to squirm. A quick glance at AJ confirmed she was ready to march to Shaw on her own. For all they knew, Dugan held some other prisoner. And if it was Finn, what condition would he be in after all this time?

Beckworth shook his head. "We leave before daybreak and greet the guards at sunup."

When the men looked at him as if he was crazy, the women leaned forward, eager for action. Beckworth lifted his hand to halt Jamie's response. "According to my old butler, Barrington, Reginald is due back before morning. He tends to stay close to his gathering spot for a day or two, but after their midnight meeting, he returns home. Servants are roused earlier than normal for his arrival."

"We're still outnumbered." Jamie finished his letter and sealed it. Ethan suspected Jamie's letter mentioned Beckworth more than Reginald or Dugan. Hensley would want confirmation from Jamie whether he believed Beckworth's story about the fate of Thorn and Dodger.

Beckworth shook his head. "Most of those men are there for Reginald, not for whoever is in the building. I guarantee there will only be a small detail left behind."

On the news that Reginald would be leaving for Waverly, Ethan found himself agreeing with Beckworth. But Jamie growled as he stood, tucking the letter in his jacket. He opened a cupboard and pulled out a bottle of Irish whiskey he'd brought from Bristol. Eleanor placed small port glasses around the table, and Jamie poured a splash in everyone's glass.

The group raised the whiskey in a toast. Jamie, Fitz, and Maire shouted, "Sláinte," and they all drank. It was decided. A team would leave before dawn.

AJ collapsed on a mat near the hearth. She didn't want to sleep in the guest room, preferring to be close to the men. As light snoring enveloped her, she couldn't sleep. She wanted to leave now. But the men were in agreement. They wanted to ensure the majority of Dugan's men were gone before they arrived.

The waiting and disappointment had put her on edge. If she didn't think they'd tie her up for going loony, she'd go back to the creek for a midnight bath. She could use the numbing water to stop the frenzied thoughts that refused to be banished. Would they find someone else in the building? Finn might be long dead. She squeezed her eyes shut, forcing that image away. She had to stay positive for just a few more hours.

After tossing for what seemed like hours, she decided she might be a bit touched after all because she heard a voice as clear as if he'd been lying beside her.

"I'll never leave you, lass."

Silent tears erupted, and she let them flow as she watched the embers grow cold.

The next thing she knew, a boot nudged her shoulder.

"Get up, woman. We have your man to rescue."

She grunted as she rolled over and opened one eye. Beckworth smiled down at her, her shoulder harness in his hands.

Dugan's men were more alert than the team had anticipated. Fitz and Beckworth had scouted when they first arrived and found that Dugan had already left. Best guess was the remaining guards had been awake for at least an hour. The only good news was the confirmation there were only six men to deal with. Even odds with the six of them. No one knew how many might be inside.

One step at a time, AJ thought. Restless nerves prickled against her skin, and she focused on her breathing. She had to remain steady. Scratching her ear with the tip of her bow, she considered their hiding spot. Between their well-covered perches in the trees and the dense copse circling the front of the building, their small band would be difficult to find.

The skirmish ended as quickly as it began. Most of the men were taken down by arrows. Jamie finished off one guard when her arrow had stuck but hadn't killed. The only one of their own dressed in blood was Fitz. If AJ didn't know better, she'd bet he'd done it on purpose. His short stature appeared more formidable covered in drying crimson.

They lined up next to the door as they'd done at the baronet's building. On the silent count of three, Jamie swung the door open. When nothing happened, Ethan ducked in. After another second, Jamie nodded at her.

She returned the nod and braced herself for what or who was inside. AJ took a deep breath, an arrow nocked and her bow pointed for a shot as she moved inside and down a wide corridor. She kept low, her eyes searching for Ethan in the dim light. Beckworth followed on her left with Lando a couple steps behind on the right. Jamie and Fitz would remain outside.

The hallway opened into a small foyer, dark with the exception of two lanterns, one near the door and the other farther down the wall. Shadows filled the end of the room. Off to the right was a door that had to be the holding cell. Ethan was trying to pry the lock.

A rough-hewn table with several chairs took up most of the room. Another chair had been pushed against the wall near the lantern, under a chain with iron manacles. Fury ran through AJ at the sight of the manacles. She kept her bow raised and turned toward the shadows. A spark flashed, and without another thought, she twisted and loosed the arrow.

The sound of the pistol was deafening in the small room. A figure ran past AJ. Beckworth, she thought as the person headed for the man with the pistol. The sound of blades made her whirl to see Ethan fighting another soldier. Lando circled the room, searching for anyone else who might be hiding under the table or in the shadows.

When Lando stepped into the center of the room, he shook his head. By then, the metal sound of blades had stopped, and Ethan cleaned his sword on the shirt of the man lying dead on the stones. AJ raced to the door of the cell, glancing at Beckworth, who stepped away from the other guard. The arrow pierced the guard's right shoulder and blood stained his shirt where his heart was.

Beckworth smiled. "You do have a penchant for shoulders."

She shrugged. "Does he have a key?"

Beckworth crouched and checked pockets, finding a small ring of keys in the second pocket he searched. The third key worked, and when he stepped aside, she handed him her bow and quiver before facing the door. Her earlier fury melted to jangled nerves, wanting Finn to be inside but terrified at what she might find. Ethan and Lando stood next to her, neither making a move for the door. They would wait until she was ready.

AJ checked the lock and heard it click open, but when she pushed against the door, it wouldn't budge. With her shoulder pressed against the door, she put all her weight into it, shoving until she heard the door scrape across the filthy floor. Then she realized Lando was behind her, helping her. As soon as it was wide enough, she squeezed through to a dark room, the smell almost bringing her to her knees.

A dim light from an opening at the top of the far wall wasn't bright enough for her to see anything. She waited, listening while her eyes adjusted. After a minute, she thought she saw movement to her right, opposite the wall with the lit gap. She heard the rattle of chains, and she closed her eyes.

She prayed this was Finn because then she'd know he was alive. Lando filled the partially opened doorway behind her, holding one of the lanterns and spreading faded light across the cell. She cringed at the conditions this man had been kept in. Whether this was Finn or not, she'd kill the duke's son before this was all over. Beckworth's warning about killing someone hovered. She hated that she would consider it, and she hated Reginald for making her into that person. But the condition they left their prisoners was intolerable and unforgivable, and definitely worth a piece of her soul.

She took a step and then another. Her eyes, now acclimated to the dim light, allowed her to see the figure stretched along the floor on a threadbare mat covered with filthy straw. Six feet away was a bucket, and from the smell alone, she knew what it was for. She absently wondered when it had last been changed. When she stepped closer, she heard Lando step into the room, giving her more light. The rough outline turned toward her, his hands in front of his face as if the dull bit of light was too much for him.

She hurried forward, but before she got too close, she called, "Finn?"

Her voice cracked as if she hadn't spoken for weeks. When she caught the slight movement of his head turn toward her, she raced the last couple of steps, dropping to her knees.

He lifted his face toward the meager light. His hair hung to his shoulders, his three-month-old beard unkempt and crusty, his skin dark with filth. His eyes, at first dull, lit with an inner light, turning his eyes from black jade to the forest emerald she knew so well. "Oh, Finn, what have they done to you?" she cried and wrapped her arms around him.

11

———

When AJ had first rushed through the door of the lone cell, the smell had made her gag. She had to breathe through her mouth to avoid the worst of the stench. But it wasn't the stink of human waste, mold, and blood that chilled her bones. Underneath it all was the foul odor of infection.

Squashing her worry, she clung to him even as he tried to push her away. She refused to let go, and he was too weak to stop her. He was so thin. Hadn't they fed him? She glanced around. An empty bowl and a tin cup lay abandoned a few feet away. If there had been food scraps, rats had eaten it long ago.

She brushed away his hair. "What did they do to you?" His face blurred as she blinked away the tears. She didn't know what to do, where he hurt.

"Shouldn't be here." His voice was raspy, like a thirty-year smoker. "Shouldn't have come." He hacked a weak cough. "Too dangerous."

The cough worried her more than his thin frame. She smiled and kissed his dirty forehead. "Of course, I'd come." She cupped his face and gazed into emerald eyes she hadn't been sure she'd ever see again.

"I'll always come for you."

Tears slipped, leaving tracks on his smudged face. "Missed you." He tried to chuckle but coughed instead.

She held him tightly, and he tried to pull away again.

"So dirty."

He was. There was no doubt he hadn't seen a bath for the three months he'd been bounced from place to place. But even through the sweat, grime, and the odor of sickness, she caught the unmistakable, if slight, cedar scent that was all Finn. Nothing could diminish that.

"Give me a minute." She turned to Lando, who stood in the doorway. He backed out when she approached.

She stepped out of the room and took a deep breath of passably clean air. The smell of the cell had seeped into the main room, and she vaguely wondered if she'd ever rid herself of the stink. "I'm going to need help. He won't be able to walk."

Ethan glanced down the hall and nodded toward the far side of the room that had previously been in shadows. Another lantern was lit to reveal a narrow corridor she hadn't seen before. Beckworth leaned against the entrance to the passage. She could only assume another room laid beyond.

She glanced around, trying to organize her thoughts. "We need a key for the manacles."

Beckworth fished in his pocket then tossed the keyring to Lando.

AJ swallowed another gulp of fresh air and returned to Finn. She heard the laborious scraping sound of the cell door as Lando pushed it fully open.

She dropped next to Finn, waiting for Lando to unlock the manacles. The frayed nerves that had settled when she found Finn returned with a vengeance as she worried over his condition. Her chest felt as if someone was sitting on it.

Finn leaned his head toward her until it touched hers. "Count to ten."

She almost laughed as the tears returned, and she silently begged Lando to hurry.

Several seconds that felt more like long, agonizing minutes later, the cuffs clanked to the floor. Lando stripped away the bare blanket covering Finn.

She blanched when Finn cried out as Lando lifted him. The big man didn't hesitate as he held Finn against him and half-carried, half-dragged him to the door. After passing into the hall, Ethan fell in to assist, holding up Finn from the other side. Beckworth led the men toward the entrance in case Jamie and Fitz had found more of Dugan's men.

AJ raced behind them, a dagger out as she kept watch behind her in case Beckworth had missed anyone. When she heard the footsteps, she almost sighed. *Can't anything be simple for once?* She stepped into the shadows against a wall and faced whoever followed, taking a quick glance over her shoulder to see the men disappear with Finn down the corridor.

When she turned back to the main room and saw the figure approach, she half hoped it would be Dugan. No such luck. But it was almost as good. She recognized the man who'd chased them from the masquerade ball. Her breathing slowed, and she braced herself against the wall. The man hadn't seen her yet. He slowed when he got to the empty cell door, and though he peered toward her direction, it was no more than a quick glance before he ran into the cell.

AJ heard footsteps behind her, and they stopped just off to her right, still in the corridor. She didn't have to look to know it was Lando.

The sound of boots leaving the cell brought her focus back to the man striding toward her, sword out. She almost laughed. Before Lando had a chance to react, AJ stepped into the light.

The man stopped short, and once he had a moment to register who stood in front of him, he did laugh.

"And what are you going to do with that tiny dagger, little girl?" He sneered at her before he scanned behind her, but he must not have seen Lando.

"You have no idea how angry I am right now." She snarled the words and was as surprised as Dugan's man to hear the venom in it. "But here's what I'm going to do. I'm giving you an option to walk away and go out whatever back door you came through." After making the offer, AJ worried he might take her up on it. They'd just have to kill him later. As much as she wanted to just throw the dagger, she wasn't sure she could. He was so close; there was no way she could miss his chest. Even with the boiling rage filling every part of her being, Beckworth's warning about taking a life kept running through her head like a continuous newsreel.

He seemed to consider her words. Then Finn's voice filled her head. Patience. Deep breath. Focus on the mission. Suddenly, a calmness spread through her. The man must have seen something change in her expression because he raised his sword and charged.

AJ threw the dagger, aiming for the middle of his chest. The man kept running. She couldn't understand how she could have missed the target with how close he'd been.

The next part flowed in slow motion, though she knew it was all in her head and must have taken only seconds to happen. She heard Lando move out of the shadows. Dugan's man took several more steps. His eyes bulged with anger, defiance, and something that looked like surprise. He glanced down just before his legs went out from under him. She was yanked back against Lando's frame, the man's blade barely missing her as it dropped to the ground.

The guard rolled onto his back. His shirt was covered in

blood, his fingers clutching at the dagger that must have slipped between his ribs. His eyes grew large and he gasped for breath. Maybe she hit a lung.

Lando pushed AJ to the side and finished the man off with his own blade.

Would he have died without Lando's aid? Probably, if she'd nicked a lung. It would have just taken longer. She waited for the horror of what she'd just done. She thought of Finn and spat on the dead man instead.

Lando pulled her away. "You weren't thinking. You let your anger blind you."

She glared at him. "You mean I shouldn't have thrown the dagger?"

Lando shook his head as if he was talking to a simpleton. "No. That you did well."

She raised a brow and looked down at Dugan's man. "I don't understand."

"After you threw the dagger, you remained in your position like a target. If I hadn't moved you out of the way, he would have skewered you."

"Oh. Right. That was stupid." Pink-tinged bubbles formed at his mouth, and she watched as they slowly evaporated, leaving a dried film in their place. She could be in shock, but felt lucid. It was more an embarrassment that she'd done something right, before doing something really dumb.

She finally tore her eyes from the man and glanced at Lando, who was studying her, probably wondering if she'd turn hysterical. She gave him her most innocent and worried expression. "You won't tell anyone, will you?"

Now Lando looked confused. "That you struck home with what would have been a killing blow if I hadn't finished him?"

"No." Her anger flashed. "That I just stood there like an idiot after I threw the dagger."

Lando stared at her, and she shifted under his gaze like a dim-witted student that couldn't get anything right. Then he laughed. A gut-wrenching guffaw that made her grin, thankful she received a pass for courage if not for brains. He pulled her dagger from the man, wiped the blood from it, and handed it back to her. He put a protective arm around her shoulder and led her toward the outer door. "I won't tell a soul. Now let's move before the next shift of guards arrive."

Before they reached the door, Ethan and Beckworth ran in, pistols drawn and ready for a fight.

"It's over," Lando called out.

The men stopped, pistols falling to their sides. Ethan seemed to peruse AJ for an injury, but Beckworth's gaze fell on her dagger, blood still marring its shiny surface. The two gave a sparing glance to Lando, who had already sheathed his sword.

"What happened?" Ethan asked.

AJ approached the two men as she moved toward the exit and forced back the grin that would have turned into an uncontrollable laughing fit. She accepted the fact that she was probably in shock after taking a man's life. Lando might have finished it, but she had struck the first killing blow. And right now—she was okay with that. It had been self-defense. Her actions could be considered a single act of vengeance for Finn, but she'd offered the man a way out. He'd made the wrong choice.

"Dugan lost another man. Extra points for me." Her voice sounded emotionless, but she couldn't stop the slight twitch of her lips.

They ran past her to see what happened for themselves, but it no longer mattered. She wiped the dagger against her pants, removing as much of the remaining blood as she could before tucking it back into her shoulder harness. When the bright morning sun greeted her, she lifted her arm against the glare and scanned the clearing for where they'd taken Finn.

He was already mounted in front of Jamie.

She ran to him. "How is he?"

Jamie struggled to reposition Finn. "He's passed out and burning with a fever. We need to get him to a doctor."

She ran her hand over Finn's leg. The plan had been to return to Eleanor's. They knew he'd have been tortured, and Maire had healed Finn after his beatings at the monastery. But with the infection, his current condition could prove fatal. She bit her lip, considering their options. Lando broke her concentration when he handed her the reins of her horse.

"Change of plans." She mounted the same time Ethan and Beckworth exited the building and ran for their horses.

"Ethan." She turned her horse to face him. "We're taking Finn to Bart's. Get Maire and bring her."

He gave her a thoughtful appraisal before giving her an approving smile. "Good job, AJ. We'll see you in a couple of hours." He kicked his horse and was gone.

Beckworth glanced over at Jamie. "Stay behind AJ. Lando and Fitz will follow and watch our backs." He turned his horse without another word, and the team headed out.

They hadn't traveled a mile when they had to stop. Finn kept sliding off the saddle and, even with his thinner condition, Jamie didn't have the strength to keep his taller frame from slipping. They moved him to Lando's horse, and Jamie took the spot in the back with Fitz. Though they kept a steady pace from there, AJ kept turning around to check on Finn. Beckworth guided them over smaller trails to keep them off the main road. Where the trails allowed, AJ rode next to Lando so she could keep an eye on Finn. The six miles they had to cover seemed like sixty.

When they reached the gate that led up the drive to Bart's, AJ didn't bother waiting to see if Lincoln was about. She jumped off the horse and opened the wire gate herself. After closing the gate behind them, she was halfway up the drive before she heard Beckworth call out.

"We have an injured man, and we don't have time for pleasantries."

She glanced at Beckworth and hoped this wasn't the day Bart decided to visit his neighbors. The old surgeon wouldn't mind if they made themselves at home, but no one else had the required medical skills. She hoped Maire would remember to bring her duffel.

As they approached the clearing with the cabin, Beckworth shouted again, "I'm only going to request entrance once before we come in with pistols primed."

Lincoln flew out the cabin's front door. "Sorry. I had to make sure it was you. We've had too many riders pass close to the gate. Come quickly." He ran down the steps but stopped as Jamie and Fitz jumped from their horses to retrieve Finn. Lincoln turned around to hold the door open as they carried Finn in.

AJ ran behind them and heard Bart's surprised voice. "What the hell? Oh." She heard a shuffling before she entered the cabin. "Take him to the cot in the back room." He met AJ's gaze. "Why is it you always arrive with someone injured?"

"Bad karma." She followed the men, and when they placed Finn on the cot, she immediately started cutting his clothes off.

Bart added wood to the fire before settling a fresh kettle of water over it. "Is he wounded or just weak?"

"He has an injury, but I don't know where or what kind. I can smell it though." AJ got his pants off, and when Jamie peeled his shirt away, they both gasped.

Multiple stab wounds covered his chest, and several had festered, expelling foul-smelling pus. Age-yellowed bruises covered his torso from what appeared to be heavy beatings. Once he was naked, AJ noted the only recent injuries were two of the stab wounds. Based on the color of the bruises, the beatings appeared to have stopped a couple of weeks prior. They hadn't left him for dead, but she didn't understand the number of knife wounds. He was still being given water and food, or he'd have been dead by now. Anguish and fear almost froze her. He was near enough death as it was.

His eyelashes were caked with crud, and dried blood covered his mouth, chin, and upper chest. He must have spit up blood and had been too weak to wipe it away. Once AJ completed a full inspection for injuries, she covered his lower half with a blanket and found strips of rags. Not bothering to wait for the water to heat, she began dabbing around the crusted wounds, cleaning as much dirt and dried blood away as she could.

"Dagger wounds," Jamie exclaimed when enough of the dirt was removed.

"More promising than gunshot. Some aren't too deep, but they're all infected." The old man bent over the worst wound and poked at it, then pinched to let the pus ooze out. AJ almost gagged, and even though he was passed out, Finn squirmed from the pain.

The old man looked around. "I need more rags and a bowl to throw them in."

AJ obeyed, searching in cabinets and shelves until she had everything she needed. She noticed Jamie shifting from one leg to another in the corner. "Go help Lando with the horses. Then start a fire in the kitchen. I'll need to get some broth going."

Jamie didn't argue, shutting the door behind him.

Once they were alone, AJ hovered while Bart assessed the wounds. After he grunted several times, he stood and began pulling bottles and jars from a shelf.

"Be honest," AJ said, her hand holding Finn's. "What are his chances?"

Without glancing back, he shook his head. "Fifty-fifty." He partially turned to her before going back to work. "Maybe less."

75

12

Ethan and Maire arrived two hours later with Thomas and three of his men. Thomas had been angry that he'd missed out on the rescue, arriving shortly after the team had left for Atworth. But they were there now, and with the extra men, AJ had one less worry, leaving her to focus solely on Finn.

She sat vigil by Finn's side, wiping the sweat from his brow as the fever raged. She hadn't changed her clothes, and with the adrenaline long gone, she was bone-tired, but she refused to leave him. She assisted Bart in another thorough cleaning and bandaging of the wounds. When Maire entered the room, her face paled when AJ turned to her.

Maire sucked in a deep breath, squared her shoulders, then removed all the new bandages to evaluate the damage for herself. She felt Finn's forehead then called for Bart and Ethan. The look Maire exchanged with Ethan shook AJ to her core and confirmed her worst nightmare. Finn might not make it. He might never regain consciousness, never hear how much she loved him.

She pushed back her sleeves and placed another cool towel on Finn's forehead while she waited to hear Maire's assessment.

Maire whispered a few words to the doctor and nodded at Ethan. Without a word, he took AJ by the arm, lifting her and walking her to the door. When she realized they were kicking her out, she gripped the door frame and pushed back.

Ethan grabbed her by the waist as he pried her fingers from the door frame. She fought while he struggled to remove her from the doorway without sustaining injury from her well-placed kicks.

"AJ. Just give me time to assess the more severe wounds and discuss the treatment with Bart." Maire laid a hand on her arm, trying to calm her.

She didn't want to be calm. "You can do that with me in the room." She was afraid to go. Terrified that Finn would leave them. That he would be alone.

"You need to refresh yourself." Maire's sharp tone surprised her, and the fight went out of her. Ethan released his grip and stepped away. Maire refused to back down, knowing she hadn't won the battle yet. "Do you really want him seeing you like this when he wakes?"

AJ searched Maire's face for the truth. She knew she had to pull herself together, but all she could think about when she glanced at Finn was how scared she was. She would never forgive herself if he died. If she'd returned just one day earlier.

Maire grabbed both her hands and squeezed them tightly. "I won't lie to you." She squeezed AJ's hands again. "Look at me." When AJ did, Maire released her hold and her expression softened. "Finn is gravely ill but not without hope. Nothing dire is going to happen in the next several hours. Take some time to clean up." She glanced at the waiting men, then leaned in to whisper. "Let me do everything I would normally do and get Bart out of the way. Then we can discuss the medicine you brought with you."

"You brought it?"

"Of course. Now go, we're wasting time."

She shook her head until Maire cupped her face, forcing AJ to look at her. "You've barely slept this last week with your fears. You've been through a traumatic ordeal rescuing him." Maire nodded. "Yes, I heard about your fight with the guard. You're exhausted, filthy, and need food. If you promise to clean up, put on new clothes, and eat something, I'll have Ethan set up bedding so you can sleep next to Finn."

AJ glanced at Finn. His lips moved, but she knew from the time she'd been sitting with him that his words were unintelligible. She didn't want to miss anything if he woke.

"Those are my conditions." Maire's tone brooked no argument.

Deep down, AJ knew she was right, but it still felt so wrong. Pulling herself together, she lifted her head, and Ethan returned to rest a hand on her shoulder.

"Come on. Lando set up a place for you to take a warm bath." Ethan guided her out of the room.

She flinched when the door shut behind her, but she steeled herself with each step she took. She knew she was being irrational and tried her routine of counting to ten when she needed to cool down. When she glanced at Lando and Jamie with their dour expressions and looks of pity, she ran from the house. She knocked into Beckworth, who'd been coming up the steps as she raced down them.

"Hey, now. Where are you going?"

She stumbled on the last stair but caught herself before she fell. Glancing around, trying to get her bearings, she noticed the heavily worn path. She sprinted for it and heard Beckworth's boots stomping down the steps before someone called him back. She ran until she found the creek and didn't stop until she stood in the middle of it.

The water was like ice. The spring days were not nearly

warm enough to temper the cold yet. She didn't care. Instead of going back for the bath Lando had prepared, she fell down and stretched her arms and legs wide to let the freezing stream circle around her. The stream ran through the gaps in her clothing, prickling her skin until goose bumps erupted. She didn't feel it. She felt nothing. They'd wasted a week in her own time. They could have been back in this century weeks earlier, possibly before Finn received most of his injuries. She'd known time had been moving faster for him than for her. Knew she needed to hurry but had waited for Maire to finish deciphering that damned druid book.

She screamed. Loud and wounded. She slammed her fists in the creek, the splashes hitting her face with icy pellets. She punched at the water again and again. Her screams echoed through the trees, their newly formed leaves shaking in her rage, though even in her state, she knew it was only the breeze. Birds flew away before returning to squawk in protest of being disturbed. When she'd tired herself out, she dropped her arms and allowed the numbing current to wash over her. The stream was deep enough where she lay that she partially floated as the water sluiced around her.

When the numbness began to hurt her head, and her body shook violently from the cold, she struggled to sit, her wet clothing holding her down. She removed the outer layer until she was down to her chemise. With her clothes resting in the crook of her arm, she crawled out of the creek and dropped to the grass. The sun had passed its zenith, and though she could still feel its warmth, it wasn't enough to dry her.

The snap of a twig told her she wasn't alone. She said nothing as Lando placed a blanket around her, and she pulled it tight. After a few minutes, when her body had warmed enough and her teeth stopped chattering, she sat up and glanced at Lando. He stared at something, maybe nothing, on the far side of the creek, lost in his own thoughts and worry. Her stomach growled, and she heaved a sigh.

"Are you better now?" Lando asked.

She lifted her clothes. "My clothes are clean."

He nodded. "As are you."

She touched her face then opened the blanket long enough to see that she was indeed clean. Or at least, clean enough. "Two birds."

Lando raised a brow but said nothing. He returned to his faraway gaze.

"Sorry I was such a child."

"You have nothing to be sorry for. We all want to do the same thing. Jamie has chopped enough wood to last the next month. Ethan has chased everyone away with his constant pacing. Even Beckworth has been mumbling that he should have done more. We all worry in our own way."

AJ stood and stared at her wet clothing. She hadn't even thought to bring fresh clothes. She wrapped the blanket around her, and Lando picked up her clothes while lending her an arm. Her shoes squished with water as they walked back to the cabin, and she absently wondered how long they would take to dry. She had another pair of shoes, but they weren't as sturdy as the pair she'd brought from her timeline.

When they reached the cabin, she smelled freshly baked bread. The hearth was blazing, and the table had been set. Lando led her to a corner where a private area had been cornered off for her to change. Her duffel had been brought in, and she selected her plainest dress. She placed her wet clothing and shoes by the hearth to dry.

When she was brave enough to face the group, she turned toward the table where everyone had gathered. Lincoln had been busy. A simple meal had been laid out with stew, cheese, and bread. The men waited for her to join them before digging in. She glanced at the closed door before looking down at her meal, her bowl already filled.

"Where's Beckworth?" She asked as she noticed everyone present except him.

"He said something about not letting a perfectly good tub of warm water go to waste," Fitz mumbled through a mouthful of stew.

AJ hung her head as she bit into a piece of cheese. "Sorry about the bath."

"I'm only sorry Beckworth got to it first," Ethan grumbled.

The rest nodded in support but quickly refocused on the food.

AJ's growling stomach got the best of her and she tried the stew. They were almost done eating when a crash came from the back room.

Everyone stopped, and AJ had partially risen when Ethan laid a hand on her arm. She hesitated, needing to know what happened. She didn't have to wait long as the door flew open.

Maire filled the doorway, and sounds of a struggle made everyone stand. "AJ and Ethan. We could use your help."

13

———

AJ raced in with Ethan mere steps behind. She wasn't sure if what she found in the room should give her hope or force her back to the river to throw another frustrated tantrum. Finn was trying to rise from the cot while Bart struggled to hold him down. Finn appeared delirious. His sweat-drenched hair and sheet-white face accentuated the wildness in his eyes. He babbled unintelligible words. He might have lost a great deal of weight and been as weak as a newborn lamb, but he had enough strength to overpower the doctor.

Ethan pushed her out the way and moved the doctor to the side. He grabbed Finn's arms and easily pushed him back to the bed. "Should we restrain him?"

"Move to the other side so I can try to help." AJ knelt by the bed and soaked a cloth in the basin of water before laying it across his forehead.

In a low whisper and keeping her voice as steady as she could muster, she murmured words of comfort. "I'm here now. You're safe. But we need you to rest and let the medicine work. I love you. You're safe. I'm here." She kept repeating the words, replenishing the rag every few minutes. She wiped the rest of his

82

face, neck, and chest to cool his heated skin. After a few more minutes, he began to calm enough for Ethan to sit back, though he stayed close.

Maire brought over a foul-smelling cup.

Ethan wrinkled his nose, able to smell it from where he sat. "Good God, is he supposed to drink it or wear it?"

"Drink it. I'm hoping he won't fuss over the taste if he's unaware of his surroundings." Maire appeared to wait for AJ to step aside but, after reading AJ's glare, thought better of it and handed her the cup. "Just a few drops at a time until it's all gone. Ethan, be ready in case he balks at the taste."

Fortunately, Finn's mind was too befuddled to be concerned with the nasty smelling tonic and it went down without mishap.

"What will that do?" AJ asked.

"It should put him to sleep and help with the infection. It's mostly herbs and a powder Bart claims should reduce the fever. We can't guarantee it will work, but it's all we have." She gave AJ a barely noticeable nod.

"Ethan. Why don't you leave AJ alone with Finn for a bit? He'll sleep now." She turned to Bart, hands on hips. "I imagine you could use something to eat. Why don't the two of you go finish dinner, and I'll be out as soon as I clean up."

When the men left, AJ stood and hugged Maire.

"What was that for?" Maire pushed her hair back and turned for the counter.

"I know how difficult this is for you. I'm sorry my behavior added to it."

Maire picked through her tote-sized bag that held her potions and herbs and withdrew a toiletry bag that she handed to AJ. She glanced up, moisture evident in her worried gaze. "Tell me again how this works."

AJ understood Maire's unwillingness to talk about anything that touched on emotions. Better to work through them. She removed a tin box the size of a compact mirror from the bag. She opened the tin and set it on the table. "There's a sheet with instructions in the side pocket. I don't remember the dosage."

"Are these safe?" Maire's brows knit in concern as she searched for the paper. AJ would have thought she'd be more accepting of medicine from the future.

AJ nodded. "The pills are amoxicillin, a form of penicillin which was discovered almost a hundred years ago. I guess for you, a hundred years from now. Some people can be allergic to it, but my understanding is that it's quite rare. If he's allergic, we should see signs within the first hour. The symptoms should be listed below the instructions. If he shows any negative response, we just stop giving him the medicine. If he has a severe reaction..." She stopped when Maire grabbed her wrist. She pried Maire's hand away and rubbed the area. "Don't worry. There's something in the bag for that as well." She removed a second pouch and pulled out a syringe, needle already attached.

Maire read the instruction sheet twice then frowned at the syringe.

AJ suspected Maire required more convincing. "The syringe is filled with something called epinephrine, which should counteract any allergic reaction."

After hesitating for a moment then glancing at Finn, Maire reviewed the instruction sheet again, selected two pills from the tin, and moved to another table. She drew water from a pitcher before returning to crush the pills in a mortar. "How fast will it work?"

AJ bit her bottom lip. "It depends on how bad the infection is. Maybe a day or two before we see improvement. If he isn't showing improvement by then..." She couldn't finish the sentence and fiddled with the syringe.

Maire crushed the pill and added water, mixing thoroughly. She took the medicine to Finn but turned to AJ.

"Go ahead, I'll try to hold his head up." AJ sat next to Finn and lifted his head while Maire sprinkled a few drops on his lips. When his tongue slipped out to taste the moisture, she gave him the rest.

"Now what?" Maire asked.

AJ laid the syringe on the table next to the cot. "Let's wait and see if he has a reaction."

"And if he does?"

"The best place is a shot in his backside."

Maire's brow arched, then her eyes glittered. "If that should happen, and of course, we don't want that, but if it should, promise you'll let me give him the shot."

14

AJ and Maire took turns watching over Finn, though AJ rarely left the room. She slept on the pallet next to his cot at night. Finn experienced short periods of lucid moments, enough for his emerald gaze to lock onto hers, his lopsided grin saying everything that needed to be said. AJ spoke to him, even after he fell back to sleep. She updated him on what Stella and Adam had been up to and how far Jackson had gotten on his list of projects, which wasn't far, considering from his perspective they'd only been gone a week. Finn smiled when she spoke about her mother and her plans for a large party once they returned home. She broke the news that Helen had already dug up part of the inn's backyard in preparation for the new garden, which would be ready in time for the event.

During his semi-lucid moments, Finn rambled about sacrificial blood and enhancing the stones' power. AJ assumed his mumblings were related to the fever, but Maire just nodded with a strange expression before busying herself with her potions and herbs. Along with the doses of antibiotics, Maire continued her own regimen, focusing on sleeping potions, herbal poultices, and pain relievers like wolf's bane, known to AJ as arnica. Finn's fever broke the evening of the second day.

The following morning, Ethan forced Maire and AJ to join the team for breakfast while Finn slept. AJ hadn't noticed that Eleanor had arrived at some point during the last two days. The older woman, with Lincoln's help and ignoring Bart's interference, reorganized the cabin to make room for the expanding crowd.

This morning, Eleanor had produced a huge spread for breakfast. With news that Finn was out of danger, everyone's appetite matched their improved good humor. The men had grown restless in the two days they'd waited for word on Finn's recovery. Jamie chopped enough wood to carry Bart through the next two winters. Fitz worked his way through the farm, mending saddles, bridles, canvas tarps, and anything else requiring wear-and-tear mending.

In between games of chess, Ethan and Lando went through the farm fixing larger issues like roof repairs, door replacements, and re-siding one portion of the barn. Thomas split his men between Bart's and Eleanor's farmhouse, working on drills before they went on patrol.

AJ saw little of Beckworth during the small periods of time she'd left the back room. He still wore his three month's worth of beard, claiming it helped with his surveillance in Corsham and around the Waverly estate. Reginald had returned to the manor the morning of Finn's rescue but had left the following day. If his departure was related to Finn's rescue, no one could confirm it, and AJ didn't care. Her focus was on getting Finn well enough for travel. Taking him through a time jump in his current condition would likely kill him.

When AJ followed Maire and the smell of eggs, sausage, potatoes, and most importantly, coffee, she was surprised to see

Beckworth. He hunched over the table, overfilling his plate. His uncombed hair and puffy eyes surprised her.

"Were you up all night carousing?" AJ couldn't help tease.

He snorted. "While you're here babysitting an invalid, I was out gathering intelligence, and being quite sly about it all. Tell me, Mrs. Murphy, which of us is doing the more important work?"

"Touchy this morning." Jamie snickered between bites of sausage.

"Has your scurrying about like the town vagrant gained anything useful?" Ethan asked. He ate with one hand while he rested his other on Maire's arm. AJ noted that Ethan's outward show of affection didn't seem to bother Maire as she poked at her food.

Beckworth finished chewing a mouthful of food before sharing his news. "Enough to know that Reginald—and I presume Dugan—are due back this afternoon."

Everyone stopped eating at that.

"Are you sure?" Jamie asked.

Even Fitz stopped eating long enough to consider what that meant.

Beckworth nodded. "I don't know if they're returning because that was the original plan, or if something else happened to force him back. Either way—" he pointed his fork at Thomas. "I suggest moving your men here. I have no doubt Dugan will send someone to see if Eleanor has returned." He glanced at Eleanor with a sorrowful expression. "I'm sorry, dear. I think it's time to visit some friends again."

"Nonsense." Bart bellowed from his seat by the hearth, his bowl of porridge held precariously on his lap. AJ thought he'd fallen asleep. He'd been spending more time by the hearth, claiming the early morning chill bothered his legs. "She can stay right here if she'd like." He winked at Eleanor. "I like her cooking."

Eleanor waved a dismissive hand at him and clucked her tongue before returning to the kitchen to make another pot of coffee.

"We need to leave," Lando stated, and the men nodded.

"Is Finn well enough to travel?" Jamie asked.

AJ startled, thinking he meant time jump until Maire spoke.

"We'll need the carriage, but I think he's healed enough to make Bristol." She peered at the doctor. "Would you agree?"

The old man nodded. "Certainly better than staying here. Men have been snooping around off and on for the last couple of months, though none have broached the property."

"Not yet," Ethan said. "We should make sure all signs of us being here are erased."

"I can do that," Fitz mumbled over a full mouth and smiled at Lincoln. "The young lad will help. By this afternoon, the place will look abandoned."

"We have another problem." Maire's voice was so low, AJ was surprised anyone heard it. Everyone had, and they gave each other sidelong glances, knowing if Maire thought we had an issue, it related to the damn book or stones.

Her statement was followed by a group sigh of resignation. Yet no one asked the question, as if avoiding it would make the problem go away.

When no one responded, Maire took it as a sign to continue. "As some of you know, I've translated the majority of the grimoire—the druid book."

Maire pulled away from Ethan and crossed her arms over her stomach. She seemed to shrink in on herself.

"I've heard stories growing up," she began. "Tales about the druids. Stories that weren't meant to be shared with children because they were sure to give them nightmares." She shook her head and laughed. "And they did." Her smile was nostalgic, and AJ assumed she was remembering a long-ago time when her parents had still been alive. "The vicar, who the town believed to be a bit disturbed, would tell tales of the druids after a few cups of ale. He spoke of their rituals, their love of nature, the importance of trees, and their desire to help their followers. Unfortunately, the druids believed the health of the society came with sacrifice."

"Everyone knows you have to work hard for your good fortune." Fitz responded as if by rote, but he watched Maire with admiration, head in his hands, enthralled by her story.

"Not that kind of sacrifice." Maire glanced around the table. If she was concerned about no one listening to her, she certainly had their attention now.

"You're talking human sacrifice." Jamie broke off a hunk of bread and dipped it in gravy. "We heard such tales as well. I think it was to prevent us from sneaking out into the forest at night." He shrugged. "And it worked." He bit into the bread with another shrug that said he'd heard it all.

Fitz, looking a bit pale, nodded. "I think anyone Irish has heard the old Celtic tales of druids and fae."

"Here we go." Bart coughed, then he spat into the fire. "Superstition and pagan beliefs."

"Maybe," Maire agreed. "But that doesn't stop people from practicing the darker arts."

Ethan put an arm around her, and she leaned into him. She seemed to draw strength from him. AJ wasn't sure she wanted to hear any more. Maire's reluctance to share what she knew made AJ's skin prickle.

The pounding of a fist and the clink of a fork made a few people jump. Beckworth threw his napkin on the table. "Good God, are you telling us Reginald is performing blood sacrifices?" He shook his head, a sneer wrinkling his perfect face, beard and all. "Somehow, that doesn't surprise me in the least. What is it? Virgins? Or is he nabbing some poor wretch with no warm place to sleep?"

No one seemed to know whether to laugh at Beckworth's comments or take him seriously. When their glances eventually landed on Maire, the team grew deathly quiet while she stared at her plate.

Maire took in a deep breath and shared a strained smile, her hands rubbing imaginary wrinkles out of her dress.

AJ's prickles turned to ice. She couldn't remember a time when Maire didn't mind sharing her knowledge.

"From what I'd read in *The Book of Stones*," Maire continued, "it was believed that the druid who traveled into the future had been crazed upon his return. Based on the era and depending on how far into the future he traveled, it makes perfect sense the man wouldn't have been able to cope with the advances he might have seen." Her voice lowered. "Though other interpretations posed a different possibility."

"That the druid was locked away for his protection." AJ offered her two cents of recollection.

Maire nodded. "And that it was during this time the druid wrote his book, what he called *The Mórdha Stone Grimoire*." She played with her fork, scraping the tines along the wood of the table, back and forth in a gentle rhythm. "Most of the writing in the book jumps around from topic to topic, which could be from a man with so much to share that he writes it as randomly as he thinks it."

"Or the signs of a madman." Lando nodded at Jamie. "We've seen that once or twice on a long voyage." Jamie nodded in return.

"And that's the crux of it. At first, the druid didn't understand how he'd traveled to the future. He spent several years studying the stones, the torc, and the incantations." Her gaze met AJ's, and the look made AJ want to throw something.

Their job wasn't done here.

AJ could read Maire's thoughts as surely as if she'd spoken them aloud. What Maire was about to say was going to ruin any thought of getting Finn well enough to jump home to Baywood. And Maire had known this before they jumped back to rescue him.

"From what I was able to decipher, the druid traveled more than once by using the Heart Stone, and without the torc. Though he was able to return to his own time, he had no control over where he jumped to or what time period he landed in. At first, the druids worked together to improve the incantations. Then something went wrong. The writing became incoherent, but there seemed to have been a disagreement between the druids, perhaps fueled by fear. The experiments stopped, and all the stones and torc were taken from the druid before he was truly locked away."

"Because someone finally woke up and understood the dangers," Beckworth shouted, as irritated as the rest of the group appeared. "Instead of writing about all of this, they should have just burned the bloody book and dropped the stones into the deepest sea."

By the glances shared around the table, no one seemed to find anything wrong with Beckworth's argument.

"This is why I believe *The Book of Stones* was written," Maire continued as calmly as if Beckworth had never spoken. "The druids rarely kept written documents. The stories say it went against their doctrines. This sect believed the stones too important to not keep a record. But they were smart about it."

AJ leaned forward. "That's what you were talking about back at the monastery. They wrote in code, spreading the information through the book but not in any order."

Maire smiled. "Yes. There isn't any one place you can look for the incantations. Pieces are spread throughout the book—a few words here, another someplace else, all hidden by code and clues. That's why I think the incantations we have are still incomplete, making them less accurate for time travel, or that what we have was the best the druids were able to create.

"The problem is, they missed a stone. And, if I'm understanding the book correctly, the lone druid was simply left alone, not locked away. He continued his experiments. This next part is why I believe the tales about him going mad remained in the lore. He began using blood sacrifices to increase the power of the stone. However, he believed the only blood that could make a single stone work alone was with the blood of someone who'd previously time traveled."

"He used his own blood?" Ethan blanched and shoved away from the table to pace.

Maire nodded, her expression pinched. "No matter how many times I go over the last parts of the grimoire, I can't discern if he had any success. His writing becomes less lucid toward the end. I believe his self-inflicted wounds became infected, and he finally succumbed to the fever."

AJ dropped her cup of coffee, and she jumped up, looking for something to mop the coffee that flowed across the table and onto the floor. Eleanor ran over with a rag, but all eyes were on AJ.

Her temper flared. "That's what that asshole was doing to Finn. All those wounds. He'd been cut so many times—some obviously older than others. All of his ramblings. I thought it was just the fever, but now I understand what he'd been trying to tell me. They were using his blood for sacrifice."

Lando and Jamie had both risen in some attempt to calm her, but she turned away from the table to pace. *What the hell had they walked back into?* Beckworth was right. Everything should have been burned or dropped in the nearest ocean. The fact she wouldn't have met Finn danced across her thoughts. But what had their chance meeting cost? Thorn, Dodger, and Peele had lost their lives over the stones. Ratliff as well. How many others were lost through the centuries, and how many more before this was done?

Ethan walked into her path and grabbed her shoulders, giving them a brief squeeze before she allowed him to lead her back to the table. Ignoring the group and sorry for her outburst, she poured another cup of coffee and returned to her seat, keeping her head down, wishing someone would restart the conversation. Thankfully, Ethan filled the silence.

"I'm assuming what AJ says is true?" Ethan asked Maire.

"Aye. I think Reginald has enough of the translations to make the attempt. Though I doubt he's having any more success than the last druid."

"That's what he was originally doing in Hagersham." Beckworth tapped his chin. "There's an old church near there said to have Celtic or druid beginnings. It's not far from Bath, close to the old Roman road. Maybe he believes the location increases the power of the stone."

"Which is why he continues to change locations. An attempt to find a place more connected to the druid rituals," Lando suggested.

"And if we remove his blood source, he'll be left without anything to travel with," Jamie said.

Everyone turned to Maire. AJ and Ethan sighed in unison. They both knew that look.

"For the small stone, I would agree," Maire finally stated.

Lando shoved his plate away and folded his arms across his chest. Beckworth tugged at his sleeves then laid his head back to stare at the ceiling. Bart appeared to have fallen asleep again.

Fitz refilled his plate. When he noticed the others staring at him, he shrugged. "I eat when I hear bad news."

"And what is the missing piece you're so reluctant to share with us?" Beckworth asked, still staring at the ceiling.

"I mentioned earlier that the druid was able to return to the future with just the Heart Stone."

More grumbling before Ethan's words quieted the group. "That was why Ratliff traveled to Waverly and got himself killed."

Beckworth sat up. "You mentioned that before, when we were still in Baywood. I'd forgotten." He pointed to Ethan. "You and Thomas had stopped there to search for Maire before you traveled to the future seeking help from Finn and AJ." He drummed his fingers on the table, his brows knit. "The piece I don't understand is why Ratliff would have thought to seek me out after all that time." He looked to Ethan. "Did you mention Waverly when you spoke to him?"

Ethan scratched his head. "To be honest, I don't remember what story we gave him. Thomas might remember."

"I'm not sure it matters," Maire said. "I think Reginald knows the Heart Stone can give him what he wants, but by killing Ratliff..." She raised her hands before the conversation got away from her again. "I agree we don't know whether Reginald or Dugan killed him. I don't think they would have if they'd known Ratliff had the Heart Stone, but it might have been unintentional. Either way, I think we have enough information to believe Reginald knows who might have the Heart Stone now."

AJ instinctively squeezed her pocket, where the Heart Stone from her century resided.

"And why would they know that, Maire?" Ethan's voice was gentle as he laid a hand on her arm, and she grabbed it as if needing his added strength.

"This just keeps getting better," Jamie mumbled before turning away from the table.

"I found some papers in the east library," she replied.

"My old office?" Beckworth asked.

Maire nodded. "I think that was where Reginald's other translator worked." Her gaze scanned the group. "There were letters that spoke of a man called Langdon. It sounded like they were monitoring his whereabouts."

"Langdon? The Earl of Castleton?" Beckworth asked.

"Yes," Maire replied.

He stared at AJ. "I know him as well. He's a close family friend of the Ratliffs."

"And if Ratliff or his daughter no longer have the Heart Stone..." AJ began.

"Then this Langdon must," Ethan answered for her.

AJ squeezed the necklace in her pocket. "Which puts the Heart Stone and the first keeper in jeopardy."

15

───────

Unable, or simply unwilling, to consider the ramifications of Reginald getting his hands on the Heart Stone, AJ focused her attention on Finn. His fever was gone, but he'd fallen into a deep sleep. Not a coma, AJ reasoned, because he responded to certain stimuli. Bart insisted his body needed to recover. If he'd been surprised how quickly Finn's fever broke, he gave no indication as he hummed and fiddled with his medicines.

While AJ hovered over Finn, the rest of the team spent time preparing for travel and removing all traces of their time at Bart's. The day before their departure, Ethan knocked on the doorframe of the back room. AJ had fallen asleep across Finn's chest. She heard the knock which seemed in rhythm with Finn's heartbeat. Pushing her hair back, her first instinct was to check Finn. Still asleep.

"I didn't want to disturb you, but Beckworth is saddling his horse."

At first, AJ wasn't sure why she needed to know that. She nodded slowly, more to give her time to wake up than as a response to Ethan's statement. Then she understood.

"Did he say where he was going?"

"He's going to help Eleanor close down the farmhouse, and then Thomas's men will see her back. Beckworth mentioned something about town."

If she didn't go talk sense into the man, no one else would do it. "Give me a minute."

She waited until the sound of Ethan's boots drifted out the front door. "And how are you, my love?" She ran a hand over Finn's face before kissing his forehead, then lips. "I'll be right back."

Maire sat at the table, reviewing the grimoire and her translations. She glanced up and nodded her acknowledgment—she'd watch over Finn.

Ethan waited for her at the bottom of the stairs then followed her to the barn without a word.

Beckworth had saddled his horse but was still checking the straps. He turned his head but continued fitting the saddle.

"You need to come with us to Hensley's." AJ considered a gentler approach, but she didn't want to waste time with him when she could be sitting with Finn. Sometimes a swift kick worked better with Beckworth.

"Why in the devil would you want me to go there?" Beckworth appeared genuinely surprised by the request.

"Because you know Langdon. We'll need your insight."

"It's been years since I've seen him." Beckworth balked.

Ethan shook his head. "It's still more than any of us know." He glared at Beckworth. "Is there something you're worried about with Hensley?"

Beckworth turned his back on them as he fussed with the bridle. "Someone should watch what Reginald and Dugan are up to."

AJ stepped closer and laid a hand on his arm. "We know enough about their activities. But you're the only one that knows

Reginald. You know these men's instincts. Maybe not as well with Langdon, but how can we make plans regarding Reginald without you?" She thought about her next statement and decided to continue. "You're in harm's way if you stay anywhere near Waverly."

Beckworth's shoulders dropped, and she felt the tension release, but he didn't respond.

"Hensley knows you didn't betray us." AJ didn't think he'd respond to a softer approach. When he proved her right by adding his bags to the saddle, her anger flared. "All that talk, groaning on and on about how important Waverly is to you. Sounds to me like that was just a bunch of hogwash. If you wanted Waverly back bad enough, you'd be chomping at the bit to get to Hensley's and put a plan together." She paused for the briefest of seconds. "I guess you're not the man I thought you were."

That did it.

Beckworth turned on her so quickly, Ethan took a step forward until AJ grabbed his arm. Beckworth's face pinched with anger. He glared at her, then as quickly as it started, his face relaxed, and he barked out a laugh. "Damn, woman, if you haven't learned how to push my buttons."

"And it's a shame you catch on quickly. I was looking forward to taking a tree branch to your head to knock some sense into it."

Beckworth bristled. "You've been spending too much time with Bart."

Ethan shook his head. "Now that we've worked that out, let's see to Finn."

———

Finn's nose twitched. The scent of mint and chamomile made him think of late nights at home in front of the fire. AJ exchanged coffee for herbal tea when they met in the library to read. She preferred old literature or personal journals she discovered at estate sales. He enjoyed history books, gaining a better understanding of the centuries he'd momentarily lived during his chase for the Heart Stone. On occasion, he'd read one of the classics, or as he'd been doing of late, studying books on woodworking. With the new skills he developed remodeling the inn with Jackson and Isaiah, he considered trying his hand at making furniture.

He sighed and reached for AJ, but she wasn't there. In fact, the bed didn't seem right. It didn't feel like a bed at all. His nose picked up another scent—cloying and nasty. It reminded him of his sister's remedies.

Maire. She'd been missing.

Then the memories flooded back—Ethan returning to the future, Beckworth stalking AJ before he jumped back in time with her, his own jump, finding AJ. And the fateful masquerade ball.

He pried an eye open and began to rise, but the light was too bright. Arms pushed him down.

"It's all right, brother. Rest easy. Can you hear me?"

Brother. "Maire?" The word was barely audible to him. His throat felt constricted, but he managed a second word. "Water." He heard scuffling and prepared his body to be hauled up by Dugan's men. He braced for the cut of the knife as it sliced his skin so Reginald could collect his blood sample. His punishment used to end with a bruising slam to his side or belly, but they had stopped that part of the torture some time ago.

Recognition pierced the edge of his senses with the soft

tread of shoes on wood rather than boots on stone. His body relaxed, and he licked at the drops of cool water.

On his next attempt to open his eyes, the bright light stabbed into his head like dull knives. His cell had never been this bright, and the scent of Maire's treacherous potions confused his senses.

Then another pair of arms were on him. Her scent enveloped him. Not the smell of her favorite lavender shampoo, but of the woman beneath. He smiled. She smelled of something more than herself—horses and the light sheen of sweat after working with her daggers.

"AJ?"

He caught her quick catch of breath. Heard the mixture of worry and relief when she spoke. "Finn? Can you hear me? It's me. I'm right here. You're safe, and I love you." Her hands traced over his arms, stroked his face. He thought he'd been dreaming her words and caresses. Maybe not a dream.

"Where?" Damn. He was too exhausted to spit out a full sentence.

"We're at Bart's. We brought you here as soon as we found you."

Found me? "Who?"

Hesitation. Whispers. "All of us, Finn. We're all here."

He opened his eyes and was able to make out the blurry image of the face he didn't think he'd ever see again. Tears crept down the side of his head, and she wiped them away. Her smile offset by a wrinkled brow.

"You should drink some water, but only a small amount at a time. Okay?" She didn't wait for his nod though he tried. He couldn't lift his head, yet somehow it was rising, and he was fairly certain it wasn't under his own power. The sweet wetness met his lips, and he hungrily consumed all he was allowed.

"Give it a minute or two, then we'll try again."

His head was lowered. "How long?" He coughed and cleared his throat. The bit of water helped. "How long has it been?"

She ran a hand over his face, then his hair. "About three months."

He heard the catch in her throat and managed to lift his hand to brush away her tears. She caught his hand and kissed it before he could accomplish his task. "I'm so sorry it took us so long."

"Nothing to forgive. I love you, wife." Then he closed his eyes.

***

With Finn conscious and Dugan's men closing in on them, the team decided at dinner to leave the next day. Eleanor prepared a large breakfast to see everyone off and packed food for their journey. After lengthy good-byes had been completed, the caravan moved out. Promises of returning the coach had been met with Bart's gruff, "You know where it belongs," and a wave of his hand. Lincoln and Eleanor followed them down the drive, brushing away the tracks they left behind.

Thomas split his men so five led the coach, driven by Lando, and the other half followed behind. Ethan, Fitz, and Jamie rode alongside the carriage. Beckworth continued to demonstrate his singular nature. AJ was convinced he was reconciling being manipulated into joining them with his concern for the friends he left behind. For part of the trip, he rode a good distance ahead, claiming to watch for highwaymen, which was unrealistic with the size of their group. Other times he lagged behind, scanning for signs of Dugan's men. No one believed in the value of his actions, but no one challenged him.

Inside the coach, AJ and Maire were confined by limited leg space. Finn stretched across the opposite seat. A board had been added to widen the bench to accommodate his size. His upper body was propped up so his legs could fit without having to bend. Since he'd become conscious the day before, he spent most of his time sleeping until the morning of travel. He was too weak to walk, and it required the efforts of Jamie and Lando to hoist him into the coach. His wounds were healing, and his bruises, though still fading, weren't painful. His ribs, however, were a different story. They had barely healed from the abuse they'd taken from the French soldiers before Dugan's men had another go at him. But he could breathe easier. All he needed was time.

For the first couple of miles, AJ and Maire enjoyed Finn's company. AJ shared current events in Baywood while Maire bubbled with delight over the advancements in plumbing. AJ teased Maire about her long baths that became legend in the short week Maire had been in Baywood. But soon, the confinement wore at them, and Finn's increased grumbling over the coach's uncomfortable accommodations taxed both women. When Finn's face pinched, and his skin turned gray from the bumpy ride, a quick glance between the two women sealed their mutual agreement. Finn required more rest. For their sanity, if nothing else, AJ encouraged him to drink more water. Maire slipped in light amounts of an herb, touting their ability to reduce his pain, which, in a way, was partially true.

Finn slept until the coach turned into the drive of Hensley's estate, several miles east of Bristol. Dusk had settled, and lights blazed from windows and outdoor lanterns, providing a warm welcome. The coach had barely stopped when the front door burst open. Hensley and Mary rushed down the steps, their continuous banter that reflected the couples' charm encouraged smiles from the tired travelers. AJ had forgotten how much she enjoyed their company.

Footmen and liverymen surrounded the coach like ants, taking the reins of the horses and unloading luggage. By the time Lando and Jamie had assisted Finn out of the coach, the only people remaining in the courtyard were the visitors and their hosts.

Hensley shook everyone's hand and, when he got to Finn, took the man into a long embrace. "It's good to see you, old chap. I'm sorry we couldn't have found you sooner."

Finn's expression held deep respect for the man. AJ didn't know if he'd ever told Hensley how much the man meant to him. Seeing their warm smiles and how easily they fell into conversation, nothing more needed to be said.

After Hensley finally turned to shake Ethan's hand, he turned his attention to Maire, wrapping both of her hands in his. "It's so good to see you again, Miss Murphy. The two of you had quite the journey from what I hear. You'll have to tell us all about it."

While Ethan and Maire swapped pleasantries with Hensley, AJ turned to Finn, wanting to get him inside. She stopped short when she found he was staring at her. He leaned against the coach with Jamie and Lando hovering close. The other two men had been snared by Mary's chatter.

Finn's color had returned. His smile, more of a grimace, alerted her to his discomfort, but she felt a blush rise when she read the desire in his eyes. She wanted to throttle him, and she gave the group a quick glance to see if anyone else noticed. Not that she wasn't delighted to see he felt well enough to have those thoughts. She had a few of her own. But couldn't he wait until they were behind closed doors? He could barely stand.

When Mary stepped away from the men, she clapped her hands excitedly as she set her sights on Beckworth.

The entire courtyard quieted as the petite woman unleashed her full Mary charm on the unsuspecting man. AJ suppressed a laugh while everyone else slid sidelong glances to Hensley. At first, he seemed more bewildered than concerned before he reclaimed his typical stoic expression.

"Oh, you must be the viscount. It's a real pleasure to have you here." Mary rubbed her hands together. "We have a splendid room ready for you." She paused and stared up at Beckworth.

He fidgeted before tugging at his sleeves, though AJ had caught him lift his chin at Mary's reference to his title. Something he probably hadn't heard in some time.

"Do you plan on keeping the beard, or would you like me to send a man up to help you get rid of that?" Mary wrinkled her nose, and Beckworth's deep chuckle startled the rest of the group.

His smile would have charmed Medusa, and he offered Mary his arm while rubbing his scruffy beard. "Now that my surveillance has been postponed, I'm quite overdue for a hot bath and a shave."

Mary's gaze twinkled with satisfaction, and she called for a footman as Beckworth guided her up the stairs. Lando and Jamie followed, though somewhat slower as they assisted Finn.

Once they disappeared inside the house, AJ noticed Hensley frowning after them.

"Do you still distrust him?" AJ asked.

Hensley glanced down, at first not seeming to understand the question. Then he shook his head, a slow smile appearing. "A bit, I suppose. As long as I keep in mind Beckworth's sole purpose—to regain his title and estate—it keeps everything in perspective." He offered AJ an arm. "I must admit, I wasn't expecting him to be so suave. I'm afraid he'll lure Mary under his spell."

AJ snorted. "I'm not convinced who's under who's spell with those two. Beckworth can be a charmer when he wants to be. But I've seen the two sides to Beckworth and dozens more in between. He's devious and manipulative."

"You're not helping."

This time she laughed in earnest. "Underneath all that, the piece the other men either can't or refuse to see, is a man who grew up on the streets. He developed a certain code growing up that way. He's entirely loyal to his friends. If he earns your trust, and you give him yours, I don't think you'll ever have to worry."

"Easier said than done."

She squeezed his arm. "I never said it would be easy."

16

___

The manor was a flurry of activity. Maids and footmen rushed up and down the stairs, bringing hot water, towels, and tea service to each of the rooms. Mary directed AJ and Finn to their own room. After Jamie and Lando helped Finn into the room, Jamie wanted to assist Finn into bed. AJ assured them she could handle it and would call them if needed. She all but shoved them out the door.

Finn chuckled, then grimaced as he fell across the bed.

"I'm sorry. I wasn't thinking." AJ rushed to him and pulled off his boots. Then she crawled onto the bed and began removing his shirt. "Should I have let them stay to help you into the bath?"

An arm, stronger than she would have expected, snaked around her middle and pulled her close. "And miss having my wife see to my needs?"

His lips were chapped but heated as he delivered his first passionate kiss since waking. "I wasn't sure if I'd ever see you again. I'm sorry I made such a rash decision."

She placed a finger to his lips. "That's done. I'm just sorry it took so long to get back to you."

"You're the one thing that kept me going. I thought if I could just stay alive, someone would find me. Then I could find my way back to you."

"Finn." She leaned down until her forehead touched his. Her chest ached with how close she'd come to losing him. To never feel the strength of his arms tighten around her or savor the touch of his lips. To be left wearing his clothes just to cherish the last scent of him. She let out an involuntary whimper.

He squeezed her. "Everything is all right now. You found me." He kissed her forehead, and with a hitch in his breath, he pulled her next to him. "Though I'm not happy with the risk you put yourself in to find me. I'll need a few words with Ethan and Beckworth."

She sat back and ran a finger down his cheek. The dark circles distracted from the heat of his emerald gaze. His cheek-bones were more pronounced, and his lips curved with just a bit of tension she blamed on the remnants of pain. "You'll do no such thing. They had no choice in bringing me along. I would have found someone else to help if they refused."

"I've never met anyone as tenacious as you."

"You mean besides your sister?"

He grinned. "You could be twins."

"Which is why we work so well together."

"Aye. But you scare me when you risk so much." He pulled her in for another kiss, then his words caught. "I can't lose you."

She brushed away his tears while her own fell. "I couldn't stop thinking about what you've told me over and over." When he gave her a puzzled look, she touched his lips. "'I'll always come for you.' That goes both ways." When his gaze darkened in a way that made a tingle run through her, she was tempted to do more than snuggle.

A dining room full of people would be waiting for them. And while they might understand if Finn was too weak to join them, she knew Finn would crawl to dinner, just to prove he wasn't out of the game. She would ensure they had enough time later.

The task to bathe, bandage wounds, and dress Finn took longer than anticipated. Especially when he insisted on being clothed in proper evening attire. AJ had to admit, Finn's presence made him appear stronger than he was. Fortune had been with them when they found their duffels at Eleanor's farmhouse. The bags, which included the wardrobe Mary previously had made for them, had been left behind at Eleanor's after their quick escape from the ball. In addition to the clothing, they'd increased their weapons store.

After Finn had been dressed, AJ made him lay down until she finished getting ready. He was still pale. "Are you sure you want to go downstairs? I can have a tray brought up. They'd understand."

"No. I've been laying about for long enough."

She rolled her eyes but didn't argue. Though she could use some help getting him down the stairs. When she opened the door to find someone, she came to a stop. Beckworth leaned against the opposite wall.

"Sorry to intrude. I thought you might need some assistance with Finn."

She couldn't help but stare. His beard was gone, leaving the lower portion of his face a shade paler than his sun-kissed upper cheeks and forehead. Instead of the shoulder-length hair he'd purposely left filthy, his ash-blond hair had been washed and pulled into a queue, which sharpened the handsome planes of his face. But it was his clothing that put the viscount back in Beckworth. His breeches were a light tan and hugged his muscular legs before disappearing into his polished boots. The paisley blue of the waistcoat and solid-colored jacket matched the color of his eyes. He tugged at the light ruffles of his cream-colored shirt, and a slight smirk edged his lips.

"Will I do?" he asked.

AJ almost blushed after giving him such a thorough perusal, but it had been a long time since she'd seen him dressed so well. The last time she'd seen him in such splendor was at the monastery when they'd visited the duke. So much had happened since then, and as she studied him, the flicker of a shadow flashed in his gaze, giving her the impression he might be thinking the same thing.

"All the housemaids must be falling over themselves to get a look at you."

He laughed. "I do clean up well."

She winked at him. "And then some."

"Are you quite done flirting with my wife?" Finn's gruff question made AJ turn.

Fortunately, his smile belied his tone, but when she noted he was using the doorframe for support, she raced to his other side. "Are you sure you should be doing this?"

Beckworth moved in and pried Finn from the door. "Of course, he should. Now don't argue." He wrapped an arm around Finn and guided the unlikely trio toward the stairs. "Let's get you to the dining room with as little scolding from your wife as possible. I've had to listen to her harp for days."

"I'm not sure what else I can tell you." Beckworth sat in a George Heppelwhite shield-back armchair, his posture rigid. The only reason Finn knew the type of chair was from AJ's excited banter since entering the sitting room after dinner.

"I don't remember seeing those chairs the last time I was here. And Hensley owns two of them. Do you think he'd mind if we took one home with us?"

Finn could only smile as he shifted in his chair and patted

AJ's hand. He absently nodded in appreciation of his wife's love of everything antique, or more accurately, what would one day be an antique. Beckworth tugged at his sleeves, and though Finn had somehow associated that gesture with Beckworth's arrogance, he'd begun to see the affectation in a different manner.

Beckworth didn't lift his chin as if he were better than anyone else. Not as he'd done when in front of the duke. If Finn thought back to the dozens of times he'd seen Beckworth tug on his sleeves, he had to question if it wasn't more a nervous twitch, a sign Beckworth wasn't as comfortable as his stalwart appearance indicated.

"As with Ratliff, it's been years since I've seen Langdon." Beckworth paused to glance at AJ. If there was something that passed between them, Finn didn't catch it. It was more likely Beckworth was looking for emotional support. He turned back to Hensley. "But their two families go way back. The strong connection between their houses is generations old."

"Enough that Ratliff would trust Langdon with the Heart Stone?" Ethan asked. He sat on one of the sofas with Maire by his side. Finn smiled when Maire's hand rested on Ethan's arm. Ethan returned her occasional glances when he wasn't fully engaged in the conversation. Finn was happy to see Maire so content.

Beckworth relaxed as he considered Ethan's question, running his hands along the smooth wooden arms of the chair. After a long pause, he tapped his fingers on the wood, as if playing some silent melody before he nodded. "If Ratliff understood the importance of the Heart Stone, or perhaps had simply been told to protect it at all cost, then yes. If he thought he couldn't personally keep it safe, then I think Langdon would be his first choice."

"Why would he think the stone wouldn't be safe in the first place?" Fitz, dressed in the same worn clothes he'd been in the day before, looked out of place in Hensley's sitting room as he chewed on one of his nails.

The group quieted as they mulled the question over.

"Ethan's and Thomas's surprise visit in search of Maire." Finn doubted Ratliff had given the stone any consideration since receiving it from Sebastian ten years earlier.

Jamie shook his head. "How would he connect the two? He didn't know Maire was involved with the book or the stones."

Finn agreed. "He didn't know Maire at all. Didn't know Ethan or Thomas. Yet the two of them showed up on his doorstep, out of the blue, asking about a missing woman."

Ethan and Thomas exchanged a glance. Thomas, who leaned against a sideboard, his arms folded across his chest, contemplated their trip to visit Ratliff. "I believe the story we used was that we were to meet her in Peterstow. We mentioned she'd most recently been in contact with Sebastian, who she'd met on a trip to France." He rubbed his forehead. "I can't remember what else we said. Our story changed depending on who we spoke with."

"Ratliff's interest piqued when we mentioned Sebastian." Ethan picked up the story. "We never mentioned *The Book of Stones* or the Heart Stone." He grasped Maire's hand. "But we did share that she'd been assisting in translating some old Celtic text for their medicinal properties."

Thomas snickered. "He hadn't believed a word of it."

"Doesn't surprise me." Hensley sat in the matching Heppel-white chair, his hands clasped over his stomach. "I didn't know the man as well as Beckworth, even if it was years ago." He glanced at Beckworth with an easy smile. "But I've met both Ratliff and Langdon at a gathering or two in London. We enter-tained in different circles, but the short time I did spend with them, they seemed to lean toward the same political policies as the other men I work with. We once considered bringing one of them into the fold but never did."

"Why?" Beckworth asked.

Hensley shrugged. "We wanted men completely unassociated with us who could provide new information and not be tainted by what we already knew. Once you become involved in the intelligence business, it can be difficult to see things with a fresh eye, if you will. The network has several unsuspecting contacts we use for information gathering." When the group seemed surprised by his admission, he shrugged again. "Nothing but simple conversation over dinner or, more often, whiskey and cigars. Lips have been known to loosen over a game of Hazard." He gave Finn a wink. "We're always on the lookout for trustworthy men who might join our circle if the circumstance dictates."

Beckworth grinned. "Ratliff and Langdon would be perfect for that. Langdon is a Member of Parliament, and Ratliff had been close to the court. They were once powerful friends, and quite loyal to the throne."

Hensley nodded in agreement, his brow arching in a way that always made Finn nervous. He was already planning something. Either in assisting their current dilemma or, what was more common for Hensley, thinking six steps ahead. Finn turned his attention to Beckworth. How had Beckworth become acquainted with such high-placed men?

He felt a squeeze on his arm and glanced at AJ. She leaned against him. "How are you feeling? Do you need a break?"

"I'm fine. Tired, maybe, but we won't be much longer." Everyone was tired. It had been a long day, a late dinner, and they all should have retired early. But Hensley wanted to be brought up to speed as quickly as possible in case he needed to send posts. He gathered information like a packrat, gathering scattered bits of this and that to shape into something useful.

"So, Ratliff gets a visit from Ethan and Thomas, one of you mentions Sebastian, then he gets nervous. Is that what we're thinking?" Jamie finished the whiskey he'd been nursing and set the empty glass on a nearby table.

"Cautious, not nervous." Beckworth had slowly relaxed, easing past his discomfort with Hensley. "Ratliff was a bit like Hensley here, not one to easily shake. He'd been in the military and was difficult to beat at chess." He paused and gave Hensley an odd appraisal. "I assume you're a decent challenge at the game."

Hensley snickered. "I've been known to win a game or two."

Finn and Jamie exchanged quick looks, both knowing the man was near impossible to beat.

"Why did Ratliff go to Waverly?" AJ asked, turning to Beckworth. "If he hadn't seen you for years, why this attempt to reach you? Why didn't he send a letter first?"

Finn questioned the same thing. Not out of distrust as to what Beckworth might be hiding, just an interest in solving a mystery. The two of them, hell, all of them had come a long way with the displaced viscount. Finn knew they hadn't scratched the surface of Beckworth's past, but in the last few months, he'd proven his value and earned a certain level of trust.

Beckworth tugged on his sleeves, and Finn couldn't help but smirk. AJ's question must have hit close to one of Beckworth's secrets. "Let's just say I helped him out in a personal matter, affirming I was both resourceful and trustworthy."

Thomas snickered, which only made Beckworth laugh. "I do realize what an irony that is, but there you have it." He shook his head. "I can't tell you why he sought me out, but he probably assumed I still had ears in places he didn't. I ran in different circles. Circles that wouldn't be seemly for Ratliff to engage." His expression turned dour and the grip on his glass tightened. "He was a good man, and I'm sorry I wasn't there to meet him instead of Reginald." He cleared his throat and glanced at the group. "My guess is that his death was not intended. Reginald was probably trying to cover his tracks and made a mistake. He must have known he'd need Ratliff for the Heart Stone, or maybe he wasn't convinced the man had possession of it until after he was killed."

"How did they connect the dots to Langdon?" Ethan asked.

Beckworth thought about it but, in the end, just shrugged. "Couldn't tell you, other than anyone who's anyone in London would know the two were close."

Finn couldn't connect the pieces either. An overwhelming tiredness enveloped him.

AJ leaned into him, her voice low. "We're done here." When he shook his head, she ignored him. "You've overextended your-self." She began to get up, but he held her back.

"Just a few more minutes."

"No." This time she didn't bother with a whisper. She scanned the room before settling on Lando. "If you could help Finn back up to our room. I think we've covered as much as we can tonight."

"Quite right." Hensley's jovial smile and long appraisal made Finn feel like a five-year-old being sent to bed after dinner. "You've been through quite an ordeal. Your body needs time to mend, which provides me the opportunity to write a few letters. We should have additional information in a couple of days. In the meantime, enjoy our hospitality."

Finn stood on his own but had to admit the stairs would be daunting. And for no specific reason, his temper flared.

———

Lando deposited Finn on the bed, kissed AJ on the cheek, and closed the door quietly behind him. Finn glared at AJ, but she gave him a loving smile, ignoring his disgruntled mood.

"Can you help me with the ties?" She cooed as she turned her back to him.

Surprised she would think he had the energy to take the required two steps, he moved to untie her dress. Once she was down to her chemise, he ran his fingers up her back. She leaned into his touch for the barest of moments before stepping away. His irritation skimmed the surface until she bent over to pick up her dress. His manhood stirred, and he cursed himself for being so weak.

Irritated by his own foolish reaction to his weakened physical state, he bit out, "Do you have to prance about like that?" His outburst caught him off guard, but rather than apologize, he gave AJ a sour look and turned his head. He instantly regretted it, knowing she would either ignore him or give him a tongue lashing. He sat on the bed and worked at the ties of his shirt, but all he succeeded in doing was create a knot.

Strong, slim fingers batted his hands away as AJ took over, using her short nails to pick the knots apart. She didn't look at him, keeping her head down as she performed her task. When she pulled the shirt from him, he caught the twitch of her lips. His shoulders tensed and heat suffused his cheeks. She found him amusing.

When she moved closer to help with his boots, the hint of roses surprised him. "I thought you didn't like to wear anything that smelled of roses, even though you like them in the house." His voice was no longer edged with his pent-up frustration.

She shrugged. "I don't. But it seems to be Mary's favorite. She has bottles of it in every room." She gave him a whimsical grin. "And it reminds me of home." She pushed him back and helped with his pants. When he was all but naked, she stepped back, hands on hips. "Now, should we work on removing that whole 'I'm angry at the world' thing you have going on?" She'd used air quotes in combination with an eye roll.

He couldn't help but smile. "I'm not sure I'm ready."

She tilted her head, her hair swaying to graze her shoulders. "Hmm. There must be something we can do about that."

He wished there was. His arms and all other critical body parts felt like lead anchors, his energy completely zapped.

AJ pulled back the covers, and with a heavy sigh and several grunts, she settled Finn in bed. She removed the last of her clothes and climbed in next to him.

"You might as well have left your clothes on," Finn grumbled.

"Not a chance in hell. It's been months since I've felt your body next to mine. Skin on skin." She positioned herself so her body ran the length of him, her head nestled on his chest so she could hear the pounding of his heart. Close enough he could feel her heartbeat, and within seconds, his earlier frustrations faded.

"I know you're struggling with getting well, but you've only been awake for a couple of days. No one thinks any less of you. You're smart enough to know that." AJ planted soft kisses on his skin, the sensation sending tingles to lower regions.

What could he say to that?

He kissed the top of her head. "I've been an ass, but I couldn't seem to help myself."

"I know." Her legs tangled with his, and whatever anxiety remained flowed away. "You need a good night's sleep. In the morning, if you promise to follow my rules, we'll start sessions to rebuild your strength."

"Your rules?"

She nodded. Soft tendrils of hair shifted against his skin,

sending another round of heated sensations and forcing him to grit his teeth. His body was simply beyond the ability to move.

"Short sessions for the first couple of days with plenty of napping and lots of food. Then, with the assistance of your friends, we'll run you through a rigorous training schedule. You'll barely have the energy to make love to me each evening."

"And what makes you think I want to wait until the evenings to ravish you." He felt her shiver under his seductive tone.

She lifted up on one elbow, enough to tease him with a languidly sweet kiss. "If you can withstand the training we have planned for you, and you're still able to give me a good toss in bed twice a day, I'll swear to everyone that you're battle-ready."

"Now that's a worthy goal."

17

———

Ethan removed his boots and placed them next to the armoire. He poured a whiskey from a bottle he'd taken from Hensley's study and collapsed on the sofa. He stared into the low-burning flames. His life mirrored a man on an island—trapped with no place to go. A few short years ago, he knew his place. He'd been Sergeant of Arms for the Earl of Hereford. It was an honored position, considering he'd been a ten-year-old orphan on the streets of London when the earl had found him.

His early years hadn't been much different than Beckworth's. Yet Beckworth had worked his way to a titled estate through manipulation and connections—assuming he wrested Waverly back from his half-brother. What would happen when all this business with the stone and books were over?

Ethan stared into the glass, swirling the whiskey as if it were tea leaves that could divine his future. The earl would welcome him back to Hereford, but his life as the earl's guard was over. That position belonged to Thomas now, and he deserved it. The earl would find something for Ethan to do, and he was fond of Maire, but what kind of life would that be? The earl had no heirs. When he died, the estate would pass to his closest relative, leaving Ethan's future unpredictable.

Ethan worked well with Hensley, and the spymaster might find a spot for him in his network. It was a job that could open doors. Would it be suitable for building a stable home for Maire? For raising a family? Hell, the two of them had never spoken of a future. Her entire world focused on those damnable books.

The last few years had been difficult for Maire. She'd spent more time under someone else's yoke—first Beckworth and then Reginald. Ethan had only a handful of months with her. Without the books, would the fragile tie between them collapse?

He loved her. He never questioned his feelings before her last kidnapping. When she'd disappeared, he knew without a doubt what she meant to him. But were those feelings returned? She cared for him, but she was like the ethereal fairies of her homeland. Would she simply disappear on her own?

He drained his glass and set it aside. It was late, and he was overdue for a good night's rest, but he couldn't seem to move from his comfortable spot by the fire. He stretched out and turned to stare at the flames before finally closing his eyes, letting his dreams care for his future.

A horse neighed in a meadow. Birds trilled as they flew from tree to tree in the warm sunshine. A blanket had been spread out over the tall grass. Maire picked through a basket, setting out an assortment of treats—fried chicken, potato salad, grapes, slices of cheese, and a bottle of pinot noir from a local winery. The summer breeze tugged at the ends of her hair that had been tied with a simple blue ribbon, its length flowing freely down her back. Her eyes twinkled with joy when she found the choco-late-covered strawberries—one of her favorite treats.

In the distance, the blue of the sea almost matched the color of the horizon. Puffy clouds floated by, changing shapes as they slid along the coast. He sat next to her and pulled a wayward strand of hair from her lips before he bent his head to kiss her. Her lips were warm and inviting. He closed his eyes and wrapped her in his arms, releasing the ribbon until the blond strands fell around them like a satin curtain, shielding them from the world.

Her soft hair felt so real.

"Come to bed, Ethan." Her whisper was full of promise.

He moaned as her fingers untied his shirt then moved lower to release the buttons of his pants. "Wake up, darling. Come to bed."

His eyes flew open. Maire leaned over him, the curtain of her hair tinted by the golden glow of the fire. A bemused smile lit her face.

"What were you dreaming? Tell me it was of me. Of us." She brushed his hair back and placed a light kiss on his forehead, the tip of his nose, then his lips.

In a fluid motion, he rose, lifting her into his arms as he carried her to bed. She laughed before muffling the sound against his shoulder. She wore nothing but her nightdress and must have sneaked in after everyone else had gone to bed.

He set her on the bed and began pulling the bed covers down, but she stopped him. She grabbed the edges of his shirt and tugged it over his head. She kissed his chest before running her hand down his stomach. He caught her hand before she reached his pants, kissing it as she gave him a bewitching grin.

"If you insist on removing your own clothes, be quick about it. I don't think I can last another minute without feeling you next to me."

Ethan didn't require any further urging as he followed her command, all of his earlier concerns erased by the longing in her gaze. For the moment, he cared little about the future. His only thoughts were of the here and now. Once he was naked, he removed her gown, her soft giggles encouraging him. Before he could pull her close, she pushed him onto his back then straddled him. Once again, her long strands encased them, the fire still playing against her hair, but this time with a rosy glow.

Her smile was angelic, which didn't quite match the current situation that had risen between them. The smile turned wicked when she positioned herself to take him inside her. Heaven. Hell. Nothing mattered other than this beautiful woman who had stolen his heart without even trying. And for the moment, concerns for their future evaporated.

Before dawn, Maire stretched against him. He should be exhausted after the last few hours, but he felt more rested than he could remember. They entwined their fingers as they both stared at the canopy.

"This is the first time we've truly had to ourselves since the jump." Ethan kissed her knuckles.

"Aye. And I missed you. Missed this."

Ethan rolled to face Maire, her leg naturally moving over his. He wanted to ask about the future, but he didn't want to ruin the bliss of this moment, scared of what her answer might reveal. Maire was a woman who would be better suited for AJ's time period. She was intelligent, well-schooled with the Celtic language and herbs. She was high-spirited and knew her own mind. Though she loved London, she hated the rules of society that oppressed women, and growing up Irish had doubled down on her lower position in the eyes of most of the English. Her beauty, charm, and wit had helped her move past some of those issues and explained why Hereford suited her so well, as far from London as it was. And the earl never held to societal rules unless forced to.

"Tell me your favorite thing from the twenty-first century." Ethan had never asked, though he could think of several items that had excited her.

"Hmm. That's a difficult decision. You already know I couldn't get enough of the bathtub." She giggled. "AJ tells me it's also one of Finn's favorite things. The shower was interesting, but to lay in a bath and refresh the hot water by just turning a knob with your toes..." This time her laughter was loud and melodic. "Well, that's just heavenly."

Her brows furrowed. "Though I do like the automobiles and the feel of the wind in my hair, like when you drove us down the coast. Maybe the television. Though more for the idea of it than anything else. Or maybe electricity. It certainly saves from having to constantly search for a flint." She snuggled close, then jumped up, bumping her forehead against his chin, causing her laughter to start over. "Disregard everything I've said. I know exactly what my favorite thing was."

"Do tell." He rubbed his jaw. "The excitement could kill me."

"Ice cream."

"Ah." He smiled. "I have to admit that is a good one. I liked the strawberry best."

"Me too." She settled across his chest. "I'd ask your favorite thing, but I think I already know it."

"Do you?"

She nodded, and her hair tickled his skin. "Espresso."

He laughed. "What gave it away?"

"It might have had something to do with that monstrous machine you had in the kitchen. Though I think the one Adam had was larger."

He rolled her over. "We're not going to discuss espresso machine envy, are we?"

She ran a hand over his cheek, her eyes darkening. "We only

have an hour before the maids will be roaming the halls. I can think of more important things than talking."

Once again, any thought of a future beyond the moment scattered when Maire kissed him and pulled him into a hungry embrace.

18

AJ collapsed against the tree and wiped her forehead. Her shirt, soaked with sweat, clung to her body. At least she'd had the foresight to bring a sports bra with her this time. She sipped cool water from the skin and watched Finn and Ethan continue with their battle. Lando grunted as he joined her under the tree to cool down from the unusually warm spring day. She passed him the skin.

"You're improving, little one." Lando drank deeply before pouring some over his face. "This is the first time you've been able to escape my bear hug."

She grinned. "And how long did that take to learn?" Using a stick, she made circles in the dirt. "I'm still weak with my left-handed throws."

"That's not from your training. You need to use more of your left hand and less of your right in your daily tasks. That will strengthen your reflexes, not just your muscles. You need both hands to grip the dagger as if there were no difference."

"That makes sense. Harder to do."

He chuckled and pulled out his whetstone to sharpen his dagger. The sound of steel sliding against steel made them glance up. Finn advanced on Ethan. He'd pushed him back several more steps until Ethan switched his footing. Ethan swung his blade from the right, slicing toward Finn's left. Finn attempted a block. Ethan's swing was too powerful. Finn's sword dropped from his hand, and he fell to a knee.

"Yield." Finn slammed a fist into the ground before taking Ethan's hand to help him stand.

"Much better than yesterday." Ethan retrieved Finn's sword and handed it to him.

"Once more." Finn moved into position, his sword held at shoulder height. AJ could see the strain in his face as he used every ounce of strength to hold the sword straight.

Ethan shook his head. "No more today. It's AJ's turn."

AJ leaned toward Lando, keeping her voice low. "I guess Finn has the same problem as me."

"No. Finn fights equally well with either hand. It comes from years of practice and fighting."

"It's his ribs." She nodded with understanding. Finn's ribs had taken their fair share of abuse. First, with the French soldiers when he and Ethan had first arrived in France. Then Dugan's men had used him as a punching bag in between Reginald's blood sacrifices. Finn was lucky none of the ribs were broken.

"He'll heal. Ethan's right. There is much improvement from yesterday. I think the treatments you and Maire provide are helping."

"He hates them." As if to prove her statement, Finn stormed by with a scowl on his face. On their first day of training, he fully cooperated with the treatment and training plan. Now, three days later, he still followed everyone's instructions, but not without argument and moodiness.

Everyone was restless waiting for news from Hensley's posts, but spirits remained high. All except for Finn. He was courteous to his hosts, but he didn't participate in dinner conversations. When the men left for an early morning hunt, Finn grabbed his sword and walked off to the woods. He came back two hours later, sweaty and aching, which resulted in longer treatment sessions with AJ and Maire, and, of course, more grumbling.

He'd taken care of himself while locked up for three months, at least in the beginning. He shared his daily exercise routine with her, remaining vigilant in finding a way to escape. But Dugan was too smart and kept too many guards. The men were doubled when Reginald interacted with Finn, otherwise known as beat downs in AJ's world. Once Reginald began taking blood from him, Finn's circumstances changed. At first, the minor blood loss was quickly replenished after he ate. When the blood donations increased, Finn's food and water rations were cut back. With the filthy conditions he was caged in, an infection from his wounds set the stage for a natural downward spiral, zapping his strength and stamina.

In full recovery mode, all he needed was time, but he wasn't willing to wait.

Finn's training and treatment over the last three days had been broken into two segments. The weapons training was led by Lando, but Ethan, Jamie, and Beckworth all participated. The treatment, coined interestingly enough by Fitz, was all AJ and Maire.

Maire used her herbal knowledge to heal with ointments, tinctures, and, if anyone would believe Finn, magic spells and potions. AJ grinned, recalling Maire's tactics, which did nothing to dissuade the gossip. When Maire heard from Jamie what stories Finn was weaving, she began mumbling over the herbal remedies, specifically when they were added to hot tea, and always when Finn was within earshot. It seemed positively witchy with her old Gaelic words and steam rising from the cup.

By the end of the second day, Finn caught on to what she

was doing, which only soured his mood. AJ never realized how sensitive he was when the butt of a joke. He could normally take as good as he gave, but that was the problem. He wasn't dishing it out.

When AJ insisted on adding yoga as part of her treatment, he readily agreed. They practiced in their room, away from prying eyes and teasing from the men. However, for some reason, Finn thought yoga had been a code word for more intimate activities. When he discovered it wasn't, and he was forced to become a human pretzel, the arguments began. He changed his tune when she threatened to end all intimate contact until he could best any of the men.

When she added meditation sessions, she thought she'd lost the battle. He continued to fidget, his eyes roaming to the window. She pouted, and pulling on the memory from when she thought she'd lost him forever, she released the tears. He muttered under his breath until his mind and body succumbed to the silence.

He still complained through the sessions, but he at least followed everyone's orders. She knew her husband. Understood his inner struggle. He'd lost a good friend and several others the night of the masquerade ball. Then he was taken hostage, tortured, and starved. He'd been put in a position where people risked their lives to rescue him, only to discover their nightmare wasn't over. And him, weak as a newborn foal. That was more than enough to make someone introspective and grumpy.

The fact the training and treatment plan was working, and he was making tremendous progress each day, actually made him moodier.

Deciding to get to the bottom of his behavior before the men took it upon themselves to handle it, AJ patted Lando on the arm. "Thanks for the workout." She picked up her bow and quiver and followed Finn.

"Go easy on him," Lando called out.

She waved a hand to signal she heard him as she stalked after her disagreeable mate. Her determination increased with every step. Finn kept his head down as he marched to the manor, but AJ stormed after him with her chin up, eyes on her target. When she caught the glances of the men and their twitching lips, or how a few turned away before she could catch their wide smiles, she was satisfied they were leaving it to her to fix Finn.

She mounted the stairs to the second floor two at a time. Once again, she found herself wanting to slam a door in the Hensley's home, knowing it would be to no avail. Their doors wouldn't slam. That in itself egged her on to a discussion that was long overdue.

When she closed the door with the barest hush, Finn turned, somewhat surprised to see her. She squared her shoulders. It appeared the whisper of the door gave almost the same satisfaction as a slam. She grinned at him. It wasn't one of her more pleasant ones.

His brows drew together. "Stretches or mental clarity first?"

She refused to back down. He was trying to placate her. He wasn't sure why she was angry, but she had to give him points for being aware of her current temperament.

"Neither."

He sighed and stood straight, or as straight as the hitch in his left side would allow. Ethan had really challenged his weak side. Finn waited, his expression pensive.

AJ nodded toward the sofa in front of the hearth, where embers from the morning fire still glowed. "Letty brought tea. Sit."

Finn opened his mouth, then turned away and took a seat.

AJ dropped her bow and quiver by the door, set the dagger and thigh strap on the sideboard. She considered his body language before picking up the silver tea service. He positioned himself on one end of the sofa, half turned to where AJ would sit. She settled the tray on a table in front of the hearth and poured the tea. When she handed Finn his cup, she sucked in her breath at the tingle that passed between them. He stared at her, and she knew he'd felt it too. That lock of hair that always hung over his brow beckoned her to reach out for him. Not yet. His lips turned into his signature grin. The one that made that earlier tingle shimmer through her, as it was doing now. She pushed the sensation away.

After a moment, his grin faded, and he sighed. "Aye, lass. Let's get it done."

She didn't hesitate, keeping her voice calm. "Why are you so angry? If you were angry at one person, I could figure out why. But you seem to be mad at the whole world, and I don't know what to do with that. I don't know how I can help you." Somehow, she didn't weep, get upset, or show anguish. All she wanted was an answer. Something to allow her to take action.

He set down his cup and leaned toward her. "You're right that I'm angry." He brushed the errant lock back as he ran his hand through his hair. "But it isn't the world I'm angry with. It's me."

AJ set down the tea and scooted closer. She took his hands, running her thumbs over them. "Thorn's death wasn't your fault. No one saw the depth of Dodger's pain."

He shook his head. "I know all of that."

"Then what?" An ugly itch formed in her belly. Had she missed something? Was there more to his incarceration than they knew? Did he reveal something to Reginald or Dugan that could impact the team?

"Lying in that cell, day after day." He grinned and squeezed her hands. "You think I fight your meditation because I believe it has little value. But it was contemplation that helped me survive while I rotted away in that cell. The only thing I had was my mind and time."

She felt him shiver, but it might have been her because she'd felt a cold breeze at his words. At how lonely he must have been.

"This wasn't the first time I'd been locked away for several months. But I've never had so much to lose before." He gave her a wistful smile. "It was a mistake to come back. I can't be my sister's guardian forever. That might sound harsh, but we had a good life in Baywood. A home, good friends, each other." He stopped as his tone deepened with emotion. He hung his head.

AJ released his hands and raised his chin until he looked her in the eyes. She brushed a cheek. "You're wrong."

When he did nothing but hold her gaze, she continued, "We didn't have a good life. We live a wonderful life. Our home isn't gone. Our friends are waiting for us. But we have work to do here. Important work. Of course, we had to come back. That decision wasn't yours alone. The three of us made it. Hell, even Stella and Adam knew we had to return."

A slight spark nestled deep in his emerald gaze. A sign of hope. AJ pressed harder. "This time, we finish the job. Once and for all. And we make sure the history of the keepers gets its start, because without them we never meet. I'm not saying it will be easy. My God, we don't even know our next step. But we're all in this together. And no one blames anyone for whatever path we've already journeyed."

She raised his hands and placed a gentle kiss on each. "What matters is the road ahead of us."

Then he kissed her. His lips hot and determined. She felt the tension in his body release as he pulled her close. All her delayed passions—the ones she kept at bay until Finn fully healed—demanded to be set free. She didn't resist. Because this Finn, the one who parted her lips and moved a hand to a more opportune southern location, was the one that heated her blood and stole her heart. This was the man she remembered from before they'd left Baywood. The one who had married her in the bathtub.

She vaguely heard the tinkling of china as the table was shoved away. Her back hit the floor with a soft whoosh, and Finn held an arm under her head to protect it from the landing. He pulled the shirt from her shoulders, and she chuckled at his soft swear when he discovered the sports bra. He sat up, pulled her into a sitting position, and without a word, grabbed the base of the bra and stripped it off before tossing it unceremoniously across the room.

She giggled as she grabbed for his shirt, but he was one step ahead of her, already pulling it over his head. He must have found a second wind after losing to Ethan, because he had them stripped naked in record time. AJ couldn't stop her giggles through the whole five seconds of activity, or that was how long it seemed.

They were skin to skin with only the dying fire and their passion to keep them warm. Turns out, that was more than enough. She reveled in the weight of his body, the assurance he was real, and that their separation was truly over. She had him back—body, mind, and soul.

Later, as the shadows lengthened along the walls of their room, AJ stirred. Her head rested on Finn's chest, and when she pulled back to glance up at him, he was already gazing at her. He looked relaxed. Content. Maybe she should have skipped the yoga and taken Finn up on his more intimate inclinations sooner.

He smiled. "What are you thinking?"

She smirked. "I hate to admit it. But maybe we should have started this a day or so ago."

He pinched her chin. "Told you. Though, to be honest, I'm not sure it would have been as spectacular as the last few hours.

I have to admit, the yoga has helped both my stamina and flexibility."

"I would definitely agree on the flexibility," she teased with wiggling brows.

He kissed the tip of her nose then rolled them to the side. A glimmer suggested he was ready for more treatment. A knock made them both jump.

"What?" Finn yelled.

After a short pause, they heard a snort. "I hate to intrude on whatever a married couple does behind closed doors." Beckworth used his bored tone. "I imagine chess or something of the like, but I thought you'd want to know Hensley's received a couple of posts. He's called for a meeting."

After a moment of silence, another tap sounded at the door. "Ten minutes. And I so hope I didn't interrupt anything." His laughter taunted them as it faded down the hall.

"Why is it he's always the one coming to our bedroom door?" Finn grumbled.

AJ sat up and glanced around to see what damage they created. She found herself pleased, if not dismayed, by the fact they'd left no destruction in their wake. "He likes needling you. And it seems to work."

"Are you sure it isn't his infatuation with you?" He stood and gathered their scattered clothing. He wasn't jealous, but she could tell it irritated him.

"Even though I stabbed him twice, I was the first one to believe he could be trusted. At least where our mutual goals aligned. I was the first, and quite frankly, the only one that has forgiven his past deeds where the stones and the duke are concerned." She sighed. "Let's face it. He's just one more turn-of-the-nineteenth-century man who feels the need to protect a woman. It's in your genetic code and environment." She became the one to grumble as she tore her clothing from his grasp, thought better of putting them back on, and tossed them in a corner. She yanked a dress from the wardrobe and began dressing.

"There she is," Finn mumbled into her neck after grabbing her from behind to pull her against him.

"Who?"

"My feisty, modern wife. The one who doesn't take crap from anyone." Finn kissed her cheek before letting her go.

"I just love it when you get all mushy."

19

AJ followed Finn down the stairs, her hand in his, feeling as giddy as a teenager. Not giddy enough to miss the way Finn protected his left side as he swerved to sidestep a servant who could barely see past the stack of books he carried. He wasn't alone. A line of servants streamed from the dining room and trailed like ants down the hall. AJ pulled Finn against the wall. Before he could say anything, she grabbed his hand and followed a wide-eyed Fitz, who carried an armful of rolled-up parchment that looked like maps.

"What the hell?" Finn asked.

"Quiet. This is not something we want to get in the middle of." AJ tugged on him to keep up with Fitz.

"I don't understand." Finn moved in front of her when they approached the conservatory.

"I have a feeling this is something between Hensley and Mary." AJ stood on her tiptoes to see past Finn's shoulder and into the room.

Finn stepped inside and found a quiet spot along the wall. He pulled her close, so her back rested against his chest. "Then let's stay put until the whirlwind passes."

A long, unremarkable table dominated the middle of the airy room. Two housemaids spread tablecloths while several footmen prepared the sideboards that were soon filled with serving trays of light appetizers and a buffet-style coffee service. Mary flitted about as she assigned tasks, then stood back to scan her accomplishments.

Fitz dumped the maps on the table once the cloth had been laid, then glanced at Mary, his eyes glazed with the look of a man trying to make a fast escape. She nodded at him with a smile, and his posture instantly relaxed. Then, glancing around and seeing he was the only team member in the room besides AJ and Finn, he scurried out the door.

Mary clapped her hands and pointed to the hearth. A housemaid immediately began stacking wood to start a fire. The conservatory faced the west, and though the spring day had been warmer than normal, the evening would cool off quickly. Sunset was only an hour away.

A few minutes later, multiple boots could be heard as the team arrived, led by Jamie and Ethan carrying books and more maps. Maire followed with her own books and the stack of papers that looked like the ones she'd stolen from Reginald. Lando followed her, carrying inkpots and quills. Once Lando placed his light cargo on the table, Mary touched the sleeve of another housemaid, who proceeded to place the writing instruments evenly around the table.

Lando leaned against the wall next to AJ and Fin. "You were wise to delay."

"What happened?" Finn asked.

"Hensley had taken over the dining room. His study was too small for all of us, and he wanted a place to strategize. The sitting room didn't have sufficient tables and was too exposed if they received visitors. When Mary came in and saw the dining table piled with books and maps, she went into a frenzy issuing orders. Hensley became irritated until Mary pointed out they would need the dining table to eat and suggested they find a more permanent place to build his play models. He was still a little red in the face, but he couldn't seem to outthink a wise woman."

AJ tapped Finn's arm and gave him a sassy wink. "A good thing to remember."

When Hensley arrived, followed closely by Fitz, he didn't appear like the man Lando just described. He clasped his hands in delight, then kissed his wife on her cheek, which caused her to blush. She didn't say another word as she rushed the serving staff out, took one last scan of the room, winked at her husband, and followed the last housemaid out of the room.

AJ hoped she and Finn had the makings of whatever kept Hensley and Mary so happy, though she would have paid a few bucks to have seen the first part of this show.

"Let's all find a seat and get started." Hensley searched through the maps and, finding one he liked, handed it to Fitz, who immediately unrolled it. Hensley had brought a small box of tiny bronze statues to use as map holders.

Thomas, who either just arrived or had the good sense to stay out of everyone's way, entered the room and walked straight to the serving trays piled high with finger sandwiches and pastries. He placed several on a plate before taking a seat across from Ethan, who raised a brow.

Thomas shrugged as he stuffed a whole beef pastry in his mouth. After swallowing, he brushed off his hands and shrugged. "I missed lunch."

"I've asked Mary to hold dinner for another couple of hours." Hensley continued to pull bronze pieces out of their box. "If you can't wait, I suggest you take the time to gather some nourishment. But don't overdo it. Dinner will be a light affair, but Mary will expect you to eat."

Before Hensley finished the offer, Fitz jumped up, followed at a more leisurely pace by the rest of the team. AJ let Finn get a plate for both of them while she filled coffee cups for everyone. When she finished, she dropped next to Maire.

"I see my brother's anger seems to have abated." Maire gave her a wink.

They watched Finn as he gathered plates and laughed at something Ethan said. AJ sighed. "If it was always so easy." She glanced around. "Where's Beckworth? He's the one that told us about the meeting."

Maire shook her head. "I saw him leave while we switched rooms."

Hensley wiped his chin then clapped his hands. He gulped coffee, his gaze surveying the team as everyone settled into their seats. "Now that we have a more permanent room, we'll meet here each day right after breakfast and before dinner. More if circumstances dictate."

He rested his gaze on each individual before continuing. AJ had a feeling they wouldn't like what he was about to share. "Posts were sent to several individuals in the network, including the Earl of Hereford and Sebastian. Though I expect it will be weeks before Sebastian receives his, and even longer before he responds. That specific note was more to make him aware of the current situation. The posts were twofold. First, I needed to make the network aware of the druid's grimoire and this Reginald fellow, or at least provide more information than I had since the fiasco at the ball. Second, we need to confirm Langdon's location, and if possible, his schedule for the next month."

"Shouldn't we just contact him?" Ethan asked.

Hensley took a moment to consider his response, biting into a cheese pastry. "I'll get to that in a moment." He sipped coffee and rolled one of the bronze pieces in his hand. When he placed the piece in the middle of the map, AJ realized it was a chess piece. The entire piece was bronze except for the white crown. The white king.

"For those new to my enterprise, let me fill you in with what I can about the network. While connected to the Crown, we work independently of it. We are seen as first defenders who work behind the scenes to investigate, and when possible, prevent threats that could bring harm to the country."

"Preferably breaking up treasonous plans before they grow legs, and without anyone noticing." Finn sat up, noticing where Hensley placed the king. He picked through the other pieces then placed one in the center of the table—the black king—and knocked it over. "We'll assume we've already taken out the duke." When everyone nodded agreement, he placed a second piece on the map, across the river from the white king. It was the black bishop. "This is Reginald. Beckworth believes he's left Waverly again, this time for London."

"It's getting late for London's season." Ethan tapped his fingers on the edge of the map, then glanced at Hensley, "Langdon must still be in residence at his London home."

"That much we've been able to confirm." Hensley nibbled at a sandwich, looked at it, then set it aside.

AJ leaned over the table to get a better look at the map. The river was the Thames, and the white king had been placed where Parliament would be. The bishop sat on the outskirts of London, as if being an outsider. London was an expansive city, even in 1804. Reginald would be difficult to locate.

Hensley shifted in his chair, a worried expression quickly replaced by an excellent poker face. "We have confirmation from three reliable sources that Langdon plans on staying in London for at least one more month, possibly longer."

"Because of the war?" Ethan asked.

Hensley grimaced. "There are several rumors as to why. The

war is a reasonable consideration. That and, from what Mary heard, the family is planning a large wedding next season."

The group quieted, but AJ perked up. "His son's marriage to Elizabeth Ratliff."

Everyone turned surprised gazes toward her, and she shrugged. "The first keeper of the stones..." She noticed a few blank stares and realized not everyone knew about the keepers. "Sorry, those are the women who protected the Heart Stone through history up to my time. According to the names passed down from keeper to keeper, a woman named Elizabeth Langdon was the first keeper. It seems reasonable to assume that Ratliff's daughter Elizabeth, would be the bride. Beckworth said their family had been close for generations."

"We've come full circle." Maire tapped her cup then, as if an afterthought, she flipped through the stack of pages she'd taken from Reginald. "These are letters from Reginald and someone referred to as Gemini. They imply these men have access to Langdon's schedule. Reginald must have spies, possibly from someone within Langdon's employ."

"I agree." Hensley scratched his head, then his belly before glancing at Thomas. "This isn't the first time we've heard of Gemini. He's someone we've tried to identify for years. At some point, he may have had ties to the duke as a purveyor of information."

Jamie snickered. "Or someone with the right connections. Earning his keep by selling information he's overheard to anyone with enough money."

AJ considered Jamie's comment, then studied the man. She remembered the first time she'd met him as a brash young sailor on their journey from Ireland to England. Then his daring as a fledgling spy in France, finding mercenaries to turn against the duke. He'd matured so quickly in the short time she'd known him, though more than two years had passed for him. Finn had always been fond of him, and trusted him enough to captain the *Daphne Marie.* Now he was following in his mentor's path, becoming a critical part of Hensley's network. She was almost sorry she wouldn't be around to meet the woman who captured his heart.

Hensley nodded approval at Jamie's assessment. "We don't believe Gemini is motivated by any particular cause, other than the one to line his pockets. We believe he would go as far as selling information outside the country, which is why the network has been eager to uncover his identity."

"Or hers," Maire added. When glances turned her way, she shrugged. "You need to broaden your horizons, gentlemen. Gemini is quite likely a man, but you should never discount how much information a woman can gather in a single day."

AJ noted the quick glance between Finn and Hensley. Had they suspected the same thing, or were they just agreeing on Maire's insight? If she knew her husband, she'd bet on the former.

Hensley brought the group back to order. "We haven't been able to discern where Reginald might have gone, but I've provided descriptions to my contacts in London. The Earl of Hereford has extended Thomas and his men's continued aide in our endeavors. The earl has already returned to Hereford, but he dispatched two men back to London to investigate within his circle of influence."

"And the posts to Langdon?" Ethan repeated his earlier question.

Hensley sipped his coffee, then set it down. His brows scrunched together, forming bushy points over his eyes. "I'm not sure what to make of it. I sent posts to Elizabeth Ratliff and Langdon. I haven't received a response from either. Langdon, I might be able to understand. He's a busy man. But I would have expected a note from Miss Ratliff. I've since sent personal messengers to both parties."

He nodded toward Thomas. "Thomas spent yesterday and most of today between here and the Ratliff estate." He shuffled through his papers and picked out a slip of linen paper with a matching envelope. "This was written by the Ratliff's butler. The oldest of Ratliff's sons isn't in residence. The youngest is in the Royal Navy, and according to the butler, Elizabeth is traveling."

"Traveling? She couldn't have gone far with the war." Jamie wasn't the only one troubled by the news.

AJ wasn't sure why. Didn't people travel during war? Maybe not outside of England, but if people were still going to London for months of balls and parties, surely they traveled elsewhere. Although she had to admit the timing was odd.

Hensley seemed to agree with her silent sentiment. "The timing is questionable. Until we hear back from my messenger to Langdon and a few other posts I have out, we have little to go on. We know Reginald is watching Langdon. And Maire has shared the purpose of the druid grimoire and why Reginald took blood from Finn. Without Finn, he must turn his focus on the Heart Stone." He turned to Maire. "Would Reginald be able to time travel if he had the Heart Stone?"

Maire rested her hand on the druid's book. AJ hadn't realized she'd set it out with the other books and papers. "I don't believe so. The druid appeared to have been successful with the Heart Stone, but I don't think he needed blood for that, just the right incantation. But neither Sebastian nor I were able to find an incantation for the Heart Stone that allowed it to travel on its own. The incantations have mostly been for the smaller stones to find the Heart Stone or vice versa. For true time travel, one required the torc. The only reason AJ's Heart Stone works on its own is because it was altered. Two small pieces were chipped off, and the Heart Stone seeks its other parts.

"If the druid did, in fact, travel with the Heart Stone, then it would be possible for someone else, if they had the correct incantation. But I haven't found anything like it in the grimoire. The druid didn't begin his work with the smaller stone and blood sacrifice until after the others pronounced him mad and locked him away. Once he was imprisoned, I think the other druids continued their efforts with the stones."

She caught Finn's gaze. "If I could review *The Book of Stones* again. Now that we know what we're looking for, Sebastian and I might be able to find the answer."

"No." Finn, Ethan, and Jamie spoke the single word in unison.

Maire scowled, and AJ laid a hand on hers.

Hensley raised a hand to quiet the group. "I won't rule that out. But it would take near a fortnight to prepare a ship and attempt the voyage to the monastery. We don't have that kind of time. We'll table Maire's suggestion for now. What we do know, or have a strong suspicion, is that Reginald didn't get everything he needed out of the grimoire. So, his only other play at this point is the Heart Stone. Even if we believe he'd never figure out how to use it, the Heart Stone must stay its course through the keepers."

Everyone was in agreement.

At that moment, Mary rapped on the door. "I hate to intrude, but it's time to gather in the drawing room. I've kept cook too long in the kitchen."

"Quite right, Mary." Hensley stood. "We've done all we can for one night. We'll meet back here after breakfast tomorrow. And don't worry, you'll have plenty of time for training."

Before they left the room, AJ pulled Finn and Ethan aside. "Do either of you know where Beckworth went?"

20

For the next week, the team met in the conservatory twice a day as planned. New information trickled in, but most of it was worthless. There was no word from Langdon. Hensley received confirmation that Reginald and Dugan had left Waverly, but no one could confirm their destination was London.

Thomas sent men to Hagersham, an area Reginald had been known to frequent. The townspeople hadn't seen him or the dozens of men in his contingent for several weeks. Men were sent to other locations that Beckworth had provided, all with the same result. Unless Reginald had found an ancient Celtic sight farther afield, London seemed the only viable possibility.

The daily meetings became an endless litany of what-ifs that could have soured everyone's mood. Fortunately, the training sessions had turned into daily sparring matches. The result was less frustration and a form of bonding as the men looked forward to besting each other.

Finn's training was the only bright side to AJ's days. His left side was tender, but he continued to use his left arm until he was too tired to lift it. Ethan, Thomas, and Jamie rotated their sparring with Finn, each attempting to be the fastest to weaken him.

As each day progressed, forcing Finn to yield became more difficult.

On a particularly sunny day, AJ and Maire relaxed under an elm with their lunch. Maire had spent the week in the conservatory, pouring over the druid's book, searching for anything she might have missed in her earlier translations. When tired of that, she reread all the posts she'd taken from Reginald and others Hensley received. And learned nothing new.

When AJ had woke that morning to find a mischievous gleam in Finn's gaze, she knew something had changed. He took special care with his training attire, a light grin on his face as he carefully belted on his scabbard. While most of the men had grumbled at dinner the night before, Finn's mood was light and cheery. He was up to something. AJ suspected he'd grown tired of being the whipping dog on the practice field. The expression on his face after the resounding kiss he'd given her before waltzing out the door told her one thing—today was going to be a special day.

She selected her best day dress instead of her pants. Her muscles would thank her for taking a day off. On her way to the conservatory to find Maire, she ran into Mary. She spent several minutes explaining her plan.

Mary's gaze lit up and she clapped her hands. "What a wonderful idea. I couldn't think of a better way to break the tension. If dear Hensley doesn't hear something soon, I may have to send everyone out on a hunt." She pulled AJ with her as she hustled toward the kitchen. "I've even threatened a party." She giggled. "Hensley turned white as a ghost at the thought. With all the men we have here, well, you know, it would be difficult to explain. But he knows my garden parties start about this time."

AJ stifled a laugh thinking about the look on Hensley's face at the mention of spring tea parties. "I'm sure we'll hear something soon." She understood Mary's concern. If she wasn't able to entertain, as was her passion, neighbors and friends may start asking questions. Excuses could be made, but for how long?

She escaped when Mary began explaining the new plans for lunch to the kitchen staff. On AJ's way back to the conservatory, she ran into Hensley. After sharing her idea for the training session, she happened upon Fitz and a couple of Thomas's men. Satisfied she'd spread the word with enough people, her focus turned to Beckworth. She didn't know why, but her curiosity had been piqued the minute he'd left a week ago. She'd asked Hensley several times, but his answer was always the same— Beckworth was running errands. His rote responses only enticed her reporter's instincts.

AJ had to ponder her own concerns over Beckworth's welfare. At what point had he become her friend? She snorted. If he was a friend, wouldn't he have said good-bye before leaving? The truth was, they needed him. With all the men at Hensley's disposal, only Beckworth knew Reginald. Understood his inner workings. Maire understood Reginald's obsession with the stones, but would she be able to guess his moves? Doubtful. That was where they needed Beckworth. And, damn it all, she wanted to see him get Waverly back. She convinced herself it was solely for the benefit of the staff and the local town.

By the time she reached the conservatory, she worried if she'd literally have to drag Maire away from her precious books. But as soon as AJ discussed her plan, Maire leaped from her chair.

"Thank the heavens. I need out of this room." Maire slammed the grimoire closed, making AJ flinch. She picked up a shawl and all but floated to the door.

AJ found herself racing after her. "I thought you liked being stuck in there all day."

"Aye. At first. But if there's anything more to be found in the words of a mad man, it will take months of study."

"Then why are you still spending time there?"

"Because I feel guilty not trying. You and the men have weapons training."

"You could join us."

Maire's tinkling laugh filled the hallway as they reached the dining room. "I already know how to shoot. That's enough for me. Now let's see if the men left us any coffee."

Three hours later, Maire laid out their lunch as they watched the men participate in light sparring. AJ's plan hadn't specified any details. She'd told the men enough for them to fill in the blanks. All she could do is wait and see if everyone played their roles.

AJ had barely taken a bite of sandwich when she noted that a few men stopped fighting and found a place to sit down. More men continued to break away from the sparring, casually arranging themselves in a loose circle around the make-shift arena. AJ focused on the four remaining men—Finn, Ethan, Thomas, and Jamie. They'd gravitated toward the middle of the arena, their jabs and footwork nothing more than a long warm-up. If she hadn't been watching each of the men closely, she might have missed when Thomas nodded to Jamie. Jamie stepped away as Thomas turned to team with Ethan. Two men at the top of their game against a recovering Finn.

When Jamie glanced around, he noticed the ring of men. Hensley sat at a table with Fitz. The table was piled with food, and men stopped long enough to grab something before searching for a resting place. Then Jamie's gaze landed on AJ, and she smiled. He shook his head, grinning as he ran to the table, grabbed his own plate of food, and sprawled in the midst of Thomas's men.

The three men still fighting never took their eyes off each

other. Ethan and Thomas wore determined expressions. Finn's signature grin lit his face, and if she were Ethan and Thomas, that would have been a sign that something significant had changed. As they circled, their swords swung more frequently, their movements more precise. Finn led with his left, and as Ethan and Thomas took advantage, neither seemed the wiser. When they looked at Finn, they probably saw what they expected to see—a man who began the match as he had all week. A man who still favored his left side and would soon weaken.

The two men were so focused on working Finn's left side, they'd forgotten about his perfectly healthy right side. After some fancy footwork by Thomas, he lunged. Finn spun away, narrowly escaping the backside of Thomas's blade. Thomas had clearly been expecting to hit his target because when his blade hit thin air, it made him stumble.

Ethan smiled when Finn spun his way. He raised his sword to block the blow he was expecting to come from his right. Finn switched arms and hit Ethan in his right ribs with the backside of his sword. Ethan went down.

Maire jumped up as Ethan dropped, but she couldn't stop laughing at Finn's ruse. AJ could only smirk. Ethan should have known better. Finn was paying them back for getting lazy.

And he proved it by going on the offensive. The crowd cheered as Finn swung with all his might at his two friends. The clash of steel loud enough to echo beyond the shouts of the men. AJ noticed that even Thomas's men could be swayed to temporarily switch loyalties by excellent swordsmanship.

Ethan and Thomas could swing a sword with their left hands, but they didn't do it as well as Finn. Until now, they'd been sparring with their right hands to provide Finn with a tougher opponent. By starting with his left, then switching to his right, Finn increased his advantage over Ethan and Thomas, who were tiring. Switching to their left against Finn's stronger right would only bring a quicker demise.

To prove this point, Finn moved faster and increased his swings, using his entire upper body to bring the full force of his blows. If his ribs bothered him, he didn't let it show. Finn moved them across the field, getting past a sword once or twice to deliver a solid hit. After a loud grunt from Thomas and a curse from Ethan, they dropped their swords and kneeled.

Cheers erupted, and for the first time, the three battle-weary men noticed the crowd. They shook hands and lumbered to the food table. The men greeted Finn with handshakes and slaps on the back.

Maire had dropped back to the blanket, and she leaned over to hug AJ. "I couldn't have asked for a better sister-in-law."

A sense of pride filled AJ at how hard he'd worked to regain his strength and find his way. Her smile matched his own lopsided grin as he punched arms and returned handshakes. Finn was back.

"Bloody damn. I'm gone for a week and now he's everyone's favorite again."

AJ swiveled and glanced up.

Beckworth stood with hands on hips, a twitch of a smile on his face as he stared down at the two women. "Miss me?"

21

AJ paced the floor of their bedroom. Beckworth had been back for two days and the only result had been the cancellation of the team's twice-daily meetings. Hensley rarely left his study. Instead, men filtered in and out, and whatever occurred behind closed doors stayed there.

The frustration AJ had successfully kept at bay for the last two weeks breeched her barriers. "Maire and I both have a right to know what's going on. Why aren't we meeting anymore? Hensley must be receiving new information based on the number of men traipsing in and out."

Finn leaned against the wardrobe and tried to grab her on one of her passes, but she dodged him. He ran a hand through his hair. "You need to remember what century you're in. You know the men have respect for you and Maire, but Hensley is a man of this century. He hasn't time traveled like Ethan and me. He has his own way of doing things."

"He was all about open communication when we met in the conservatory. What changed that made him close it all down?"

"We haven't accomplished anything in those meetings for

days. Without new information, there's nothing to plan or discuss."

"And it's not just the men coming and going, no one is saying a word. There's like a cone of silence around a certain group while the rest of us sit in the galley."

Finn pushed both hands through his hair. "For heaven's sake, woman. Stop creating conspiracies where there are none. Isn't that what came between us the first time we were here?"

AJ stared at him before turning away. Was it the same? She didn't think so, yet it made her reconsider her anger. Everyone was on edge. Finn's victory in his mock battle with Ethan and Thomas had restored the men's purpose, as had Beckworth's return. With small groups of men coming and going from the manor, two days of silence had quickly restored the tense atmosphere.

"Let's not fight." He opened his arms. "We've been apart for too long. Come here."

She blew out a breath. How could she argue with that? She dragged her feet as she walked into his arms, but the minute they closed around her she felt the anger drain away. Though she beat a fist against his chest in one final act of defiance. "It's so unfair being a woman."

He chuckled. "Which is why I returned to your century rather than asking you to stay in mine."

She laid her head against his chest. "I can't argue your reasoning." He hugged her tightly then led her to a chair, pulling her into his lap.

"Is there anything you can share that I don't already know? What does the man do in that room all day?" AJ was beginning to think he was simply hiding from everyone. Even Mary didn't go into the study.

"He's going a bit mad himself. It's true he continues to gather information. The problem is that much of it contradicts other reports."

"What about Beckworth? Why was he gone for so long?" She'd been just as irritated with Beckworth. Anytime she asked him something, he would give her an annoying smile, tug on his sleeves, and make some excuse to leave.

The only obvious task Beckworth had performed was bringing Eleanor back with him. And, as with everything else, there had been no explanation. It wouldn't have required an entire week to travel to Corsham just to retrieve Eleanor. The town was only a single day's ride. Eleanor had been happy to see everyone, but she spent most of her time in her room, preferred to eat in the kitchen with the household staff, and was as tight-lipped as Beckworth.

"It's Beckworth's information that contradicts everything Hensley had originally gathered. Hensley is trying to get to the bottom of the discrepancy before calling us together."

"Then why doesn't he just tell us that?"

Finn chuckled, tightening his grip on her when she tensed with new frustration. She relaxed when he kissed her forehead and rubbed her back. "Because everyone understands Hensley will bring us together once he has more facts. You're frustrated because you're not in his study hearing everything. No one, not even me, knows everything Hensley is doing. But after years of working with him, I know not to question. He'll share everything he knows once he separates facts from ruse."

"This century is tough."

"It's not the century. I doubt Adam shares information with his clients until his team vets everything. It's not being a woman or being from two hundred years in the future that frustrates you. It's the reporter in you and your insatiable curiosity."

She leaned into him, the last of her walls crumbling at her

husband's damnable insight. She took his hands in hers and kissed them. "I hate it when you're right."

"I know." He stood, lifting her in his arms before tossing her onto the bed. "Enough about Hensley. I can think of something that will take your mind off your troubles."

———

The following morning, AJ and Finn came down for breakfast an hour later than normal. When they arrived on the first floor, they had to sidestep two footmen who carried a trunk toward the front door. Two housemaids followed toting bags while Mary hustled them along, pointing fingers and admonishing them with, "Careful, don't jostle that one," and "Heddy, I'll need you to see about lunch baskets once you're done here." They had barely exited through the door when Mary's voice floated behind her. "No, no, no. Not like that. Oh, wait, let me show you."

Finn pulled AJ out of the way as Thomas's men scurried past with more trunks. Two men had come from Hensley's study, four others from the direction of the conservatory.

"What's going on?" AJ asked, but Finn's puzzled expression matched her own.

"Let's find out." He grabbed her hand and dodged a servant carrying what appeared to be part of the table that had been set up in the conservatory.

After days of sheer boredom, the pandemonium raised AJ's spirits. Finally. Some answers. When they entered the dining room, however, the team was gathered around the table, eating and chatting as if no one noticed the bustling activity outside the room. Finn guided AJ to a chair and gave her a reproachful glance, which was meant to be a signal. AJ understood it as a plea to keep her mouth shut until after Hensley spoke.

She bristled but took a cue from Maire to be patient for a while longer. Unable to sit still, she didn't bother to wait for a footman and jumped up to pour her own coffee. After glancing around the table, she refilled all the cups before returning to her seat.

Hensley, who'd turned away from the table to speak with a footman, perked up when he saw AJ. He waved the staff away, sipped his refreshed cup of coffee, and cleared his throat.

"Now that we're all here, it's time I bring you up to speed on the last couple of days. I know some of you have been impatient not knowing what I've been up to." His glance brushed gently on AJ, who held his gaze. He smiled as if he was in on some private joke. "Unfortunately, all I can tell you at this time is that we're still not sure about anything."

Whatever expectations AJ had conjured up died, and she couldn't help but blurt, "You've got to be kidding me."

A few chuckles mixed with grumbles of irritation. AJ wasn't the only one tired of sitting around.

Hensley waited for the room to grow silent. "You're right to be frustrated. I'm not any happier than you. The contacts I've reached out to still claim that Langdon is busy with the war effort. At first blush, that would seem to follow his patterns since the war started. And we've had no other reason to believe Miss Ratliff isn't traveling."

He glanced at Beckworth, who gave a slight nod. "Many of you know that Beckworth has been gone for the last week. One of his missions was to bring Eleanor to us." He stopped and nodded toward the back of the room.

Everyone turned to see Eleanor sitting in a corner, a pleasant but stoic expression on her face.

"Beckworth also visited with his own contacts. For the last two days, I had hoped to discredit those revelations." He ran his fingers around the cup saucer, his mind seeming to have traveled elsewhere. Then he let his gaze fall on the others around the table. "If his contacts were correct, the information casts a more dubious reason for Langdon's apparent disinterest.

"Some of what I'd been told regarding Langdon being in war council meetings was true, but it seems his growing absence in the meetings has gained attention in the wrong circles. Word has spread that he's become more reclusive and has made two mysterious trips in the middle of the night no one can explain."

He stopped to let that sink in. AJ wasn't sure what this latest information meant but, by the looks of those around the table, many seemed troubled by the news.

"Reginald and Dugan didn't just leave Waverly, they seemed to have abandoned it." Beckworth tugged at his sleeves. AJ expected him to have been happier with the news. This was the moment he'd waited for. His time to reclaim the manor. Instead, he spared a glance at Thomas and shrugged. "Thomas's men searched for miles around Waverly, but no one has seen Dugan or any of his men. This would also include the town of Corsham."

"How do you hide a group of mercenaries the size of Dugan's?" Jamie's question had probably been somewhat rhetorical, but others shook their heads.

"We've searched all the areas he's been known to have his midnight gatherings. Twice over. But there's no sign." Thomas had stood as he delivered the last sentence, waving his arms, apparently as frustrated as Beckworth.

"They've gone to London." Finn said the words everyone had been thinking all along. Though there was still no proof, other than Reginald's apparent interest in the Heart Stone.

Hensley nodded. "That's still our best guess. Which makes Langdon's mysterious trips and disregard for his Parliament duties troublesome. There's no more we can do here. We need to be closer."

AJ sat up. "We're going to London?" She couldn't hide her excitement. She was beyond bored. If she had to run one more battle drill, she might actually loose an arrow on some poor soul. Just in the arm. Then there was London. She'd never been, and what a fascinating time period to experience it. When Finn squeezed her knee, she remembered this wouldn't be a tourist trip. She glanced at Maire and her guilt melted away.

There was a gleam in Maire's gaze. She had been to London the previous season, and it appeared she was eager to return. AJ doubted Maire's interest lay with parties, fancy dresses, and balls. Maire wanted to track down Reginald and ensure the Heart Stone was safe. London seemed as good a place as any.

"Yes." Hensley answered the question AJ forgot she'd asked. "I don't believe you've been to London."

AJ shook her head.

Hensley considered that. "That might give us a few avenues to explore. Finn and Ethan are both known in certain circles. It wouldn't be unusual for Finn to want to show off his new bride. And though the season is ending, there will still be a few aristocrats in London who will remember Maire. While you work the upper crust for information, Thomas and Beckworth will work their contacts.

"It will take a couple of days to get there, so I'd like to be on the road before noon. I've sent word to have my house opened, but only Mary and I will be staying there. However, you will all dine with us each evening so we can gather to resume our strategy sessions. For everyone else, Beckworth has arranged a safe house that is large enough to house everyone, including Thomas's men."

"I didn't think there were whorehouses large enough for all of us," Fitz exclaimed over a mouthful of biscuit.

After the laughter died down, Hensley gave Fitz a disapproving stare that didn't appear to faze Jamie's first mate. Fitz spread jam on another biscuit and winked at Beckworth, who didn't seem bothered by the comment. AJ hoped Fitz was wrong on Beckworth's idea of a safe house.

Hensley turned to Finn. "We've repainted the carriage you brought with you. Mary and I will travel in our own coach, along with Eleanor and a lady's maid. We must keep up our appearances."

"Fitz and I will head to Portishead. We'll meet you in London with the *Daphne*." Jamie glanced at Finn as if extending an invitation to join them.

AJ held her breath, then braved a quick glance at Finn. He was watching her, then uttered words she didn't realize she'd longed to hear. "I can't say I'm looking forward to a coach ride, but I'm not leaving your side."

He'd rather be with her than his old ship. Her heart did a little flip.

Hensley stood and checked his timepiece. "You have two hours to finish your packing and meet us in the courtyard."

AJ grabbed Finn's hand and almost pushed him up the stairs.

"What's your hurry?" Finn asked as she gave up pushing and tried dragging him along.

She turned and batted her lashes at him. "I don't know about you, but I only have about ten minutes of packing to do."

He gazed at her with a quizzical look, and she heaved a sigh. "When we get to London, we'll be tucked into a house that can't possibly be large enough to fit everyone comfortably. This could be our last couple of hours to be truly alone."

Dawning finally lit his emerald gaze, and he lifted her to race up the stairs. It required every ounce of strength to stifle her laughter until the bedroom door closed.

———

Thirty minutes before departure, Hensley called the team together in the library. His expression looked troubled, and his unflappable demeanor seemed chipped as he fell into his favorite chair. Stony silence gathered as Hensley stared at a letter he held in shaky hands. The only noise came from the hall where Mary ordered footmen and maids around in a vain attempt to whisper.

AJ glanced at Finn, whose mood had altered as quickly as Hensley's. Everyone appeared as clueless as she did with one exception—Beckworth. He stared into the distance as if distracted or completely disinterested in what Hensley had to say.

"Beckworth received a post shortly after breakfast. It was from one of his contacts he'd sent to the Ratliff estate." Hensley cleared his throat then repositioned himself, once again becoming the man everyone expected to lead them.

Beckworth never took his gaze from whatever held his attention. If he was listening to Hensley, he gave no indication. In fact, he seemed nothing more than a marble statue.

"One of the housemaids was overheard telling someone in town that Lady Ratliff wasn't traveling. About the same time that I began sending her my posts, a carriage arrived at the Ratliff estate with a large contingent of men. The manor was aflutter with gossip about who was in the coach. It was thought to be someone from court. Not even Langdon traveled with such numbers."

"Reginald and Dugan." Anger seeped in Ethan's tone, and he pulled Maire closer to him. She curled into him. Her time as Reginald's prisoner had to be replaying in her head.

"Do we know for sure?" Thomas asked. When others stared at him as if he'd been in a coma the last two weeks, he held up his hand. "I'm not saying it's not them, but households inflate their stories with gossip. Did she say anything about the coach? Or what the men looked like? Did they go into the manor as guests, or did someone sneak in, bundle up Lady Ratliff, and carry her out in the dark? We need to confirm the information."

"You're quite right," Hensley responded. "It fits with Reginald's previous actions, though much bolder than I gave him credit for." He glanced at Maire, but she had the same distant gaze as Beckworth. "I agree we need to confirm the information if we can. I considered sending you, Thomas, but Beckworth suggested another approach."

As if he'd been waiting for his cue, Beckworth cleared his throat. "If my contact understood the situation correctly, and the housemaid's story is more than an old wives' tale, I don't think Thomas will have much luck. My contact couldn't gain any further information from the local townspeople nor anyone from the Ratliff estate. It might be as Thomas says, nothing but sheer speculation. But if it is true, and it's being hushed, then I think any further questioning requires a more delicate approach." He turned his head and stared at AJ.

Though she didn't break eye contact with Beckworth, she could feel the intense gaze of their other teammates and the tightening of Finn's grip on her hand. She broke her gaze from Beckworth to find Maire sitting taller, a determined expression on her face.

"I wouldn't think of sending you." Hensley interrupted the silence. "I don't know what this means other than a probable connection to the Heart Stone. If we knew for sure who had it, these actions might make sense. It's even more imperative that I meet with Langdon, but a request isn't always granted. If it is, it could be days before I gain an audience."

"It appears we know where the good viscount has been for the last two weeks." Fitz scratched his beard. "But it's still rather nervy if you ask me."

"Or desperate." Maire's tone sounded bitter. AJ couldn't blame her. If Elizabeth Ratliff was put into a cell similar to Maire's, there would be greater repercussions. The Ratliff family was close to the King, and Reginald's actions could be seen as a threat to the Crown.

Finn stood. "Then we need to move. I assume you want us to head straight to Ratliff's estate."

Hensley nodded as the others stood. "You, Ethan, and the women will go to Ratliff's estate. Beckworth will travel with the rest of us to London to oversee final preparations for your arrival. Send word when you make London." He glanced around the group. "I think it's safe to say the stakes have risen. This is now a rescue mission."

AJ couldn't let it end like this. "If they took her, where would they go? Isn't that something we should be considering?"

Hensley smiled at her, nodding his approval or agreement, she wasn't sure which, though it made her feel better for asking. "And both Beckworth and I have men looking into that. We still think London is our best option."

AJ wasn't so sure, but that kind of thinking wouldn't get them anywhere.

"Reginald won't keep Lady Ratliff in the same conditions he kept Maire. He'll want to keep her close and well treated." Beckworth glanced at Maire. "I'm sorry, love, but Lady Ratliff's station alone, and her ties with Parliament and the court, made her a high-risk target."

Maire returned his smile. "I completely agree. If he's trying to get to the Heart Stone, which we believe Langdon to have, the stakes are definitely higher. And there's no better place to get lost than in London."

22

The carriages rolled away from Hensley manor at noon. The caravan stopped twice before making their way to the first inn on the trip, arriving late but still in time for a hearty dinner. Mid-afternoon of the second day, Lando turned Bart's carriage north with AJ, Finn, Maire, and Ethan. The rest of the team remained on the road to London.

The Ratliff estate was several hours north of London and would require another two days of travel. Lando kept a brisk pace, and Finn and Ethan spent part of the journey on their horses, giving the women more room in the carriage to nap. The sun had passed its zenith when the castle came into view. AJ couldn't think of another word for it. The formidable structure was three stories high and included four towers. Its gruff exterior was softened by a nearby lake surrounded by flowering trees. Expansive manicured gardens framed the estate, dotted with spring colors and shade trees. If AJ thought Waverly and Hensley's manors were lavish, this grand estate reeked of centuries of wealth.

"You remember what to do?" Finn asked as he assisted AJ from the carriage.

Maire rolled her eyes, and AJ nudged him. "I think the hour review last night and again at breakfast, followed by the additional thirty minutes at lunch, was more than adequate."

Finn glanced at Ethan for support, but his friend seemed to have taken a keen interest in the overgrown grotto that edged a section of the drive. "Sorry. I seem to have pent-up energy and no one else to order about." He kissed her cheek before turning the group toward the main door.

The door opened before they reached the top step, and a portly butler smiled down at them.

Finally. A butler with a friendly face. But after all her grumbling complaints about overly serious butlers, and now having come face-to-face with a pleasant one, she immediately knew anything he said would be a lie. Her dormant reporter skills kicked into gear with clear guidance to trust her old instincts.

She gripped Finn's arm and caught his slight nod, but she didn't feel any tension in him. He suspected deceit but apparently nothing more sinister. And nothing less than they'd anticipated. She supposed the smiling butler had thrown her off, as he'd hoped to.

"May I help you, sir?" The butler bowed his head when they reached the door.

"Yes, my name is Captain Murphy, and this is my associate, Major Hughes. We're on our way to London from Coventry and, since we missed the season, Mrs. Murphy," Finn nodded to AJ, "was hoping to see Lady Ratliff on our way. We assumed she would have already returned from London."

By using military titles, Finn left the impression the two men might be involved in the war effort. AJ glanced at Ethan, wondering if his military rank was real. He'd made offhanded comments before about previous battle experience, but AJ had never associated it with military service. There was probably a great deal more to Ethan she'd never questioned.

The butler paused. AJ assumed he was probably preparing his standard response. She gripped her wrap closer and leaned toward Finn, settling her hand on her stomach. The butler slid a glance toward her then focused on Finn.

"I'm afraid Lady Ratliff didn't return from London." The butler cleared his throat. "She traveled south to visit friends but didn't state when she'd return."

The same general story, though the details didn't track. That didn't mean anything, especially after hearing stories third and fourth hand. The butler's story would also be close enough to the truth if Elizabeth had been kidnapped. They were strangers to the butler, and he wouldn't provide any more information than he had to. AJ had no doubt he would say anything he could to protect his mistress and the Ratliff honor.

"Is Lord Ratliff here by any chance?" Finn's question was another test. Hensley had told them Elizabeth's eldest brother wasn't at the estate.

"No. He's still in London."

They had expected to be put off, and AJ wondered if Reginald had any more success. He might have arrived only to discover Elizabeth was truly traveling. He may have left empty-handed, but that was what they were here to find out.

Finn made a show of glancing at Ethan before looking down at the women. He squared his shoulders and addressed the butler in what AJ knew would be his manipulative tone. "I hate to impose, but we've been on the road since early this morning. The ride has been most unsettling for my wife." AJ tugged on her wrap again, forcing a grimace as she gently rubbed her stomach. "She could use a rest before we push on."

"I'm so sorry, sir. I didn't realize." He hesitated, and his mask of butler slipped easily into place, though his eyes darted about. He clearly didn't want them to stay, but he also didn't want word leaking out about the Ratliff house being inhospitable to guests. His smile returned. "It's almost time for tea."

"We don't want to be an imposition."

"Not at all, sir. The sitting room is this way."

The group followed the butler. Once they were seated, AJ breathed a sigh of relief. Stage one complete. Now came the hard part—tempting someone in the house to divulge their secrets. There was little hope they'd find anyone willing to talk, but there were other ways to get answers.

They'd barely been settled when a footman appeared. "Your horses are being cared for, and the coach will be ready at your request."

Finn had been hoping for that opening. "Can you have someone add more wood to the fire? The women are chilled from the ride."

The footman nodded and was turning to leave when he noticed Ethan's hand raise. "I say, do you think this might be a good time to check that wheel?"

Finn shook his head, as if in admonishment for forgetting something so important. "I was so worried about Mrs. Murphy, I completely forgot." He turned to the footman. "Do you mind if we check with our coachman?"

"Certainly, sir. I can show you the way."

"Wonderful." Finn turned to the women. "This might take some time. Enjoy your tea and rest. We'll be on our way soon."

AJ nodded demurely and gave a weak smile. Maire patted her knee as if agreeing to care for the poor invalid. AJ kept her head down to squelch the snort fighting to bubble out.

As soon as Finn and Ethan followed the footman out, two housemaids entered. The one carrying the tea service appeared to be a good twenty years older than the other. She placed the silver tray on the table in front of the couch and gave AJ and Maire a slight smile. Not rude but not completely welcoming.

Before she left, she gave the younger maid a stern nod. The young girl, who couldn't have been more than sixteen if AJ had to guess, knelt in front of the hearth to add wood.

"Well, what do you think?" AJ asked.

Maire glanced around the room as if looking for someone who might overhear, yet completely ignoring the maid as if she weren't there. She leaned closer though didn't lower her voice. "I think the rumors are true. Elizabeth has a wealthy suitor."

"Wealthier than the Langdons?" AJ noticed the maid lift her head as she slowly stirred the embers.

Maire shrugged. "If the stories are true, it must have been someone important to send a carriage with all those men."

A clatter came from the hearth where the maid had dropped a piece of wood. Both women glared at the girl who mumbled some apology as she returned to the fire.

AJ wished they didn't have to follow through with their ruse, but she reminded herself this was in Elizabeth's best interest. She fidgeted in her seat. "It's been days, and no one's heard a word from Elizabeth." AJ's tone filled with concern. "If you ask me, it's almost as if she was plucked from the estate by highwaymen."

Maire suppressed a chuckle, but the loud clatter of iron hitting stone made them both jump.

AJ let out a short cry. "Oh, my dress."

The housemaid forgot about the fire and ran over to the women. "I'm so sorry, Madam. I'm not usually so clumsy." Her grip on her skirts was so tight, AJ expected to see white knuckles. The girl kept her head down, peaking up through curly locks that had escaped her bonnet. Whether she was worried about reprisal from the housekeeper or the whereabouts of her mistress, it was too early to tell.

AJ made a show of wiping tea from her skirts. "Oh, Maire, do you think this will stain?"

Maire used a napkin to dab at the stain then glared at the maid. "Get some soda, quickly."

The maid raced out of the room.

"Something we said spooked her." Maire sipped her tea and took a bite of biscuit before the maid returned.

It didn't take long. The older woman returned with the younger maid in tow.

"I'm sorry if Miss Broadsworth caused you trouble. Let's see what we have here." The older maid knelt next to AJ to get a better look at the tea stain. She mumbled something then snapped her fingers at the young girl who held a bottle that looked like a large salt shaker.

While the maids went to work to clean the stain, Maire picked up the conversation as if the other two women kneeling in front of them weren't there. "You never quite know when to keep your mouth shut, dear sister. I seriously doubt anything sinister happened to Elizabeth. Although a rendezvous with a secret admirer will cause tongues to wag."

The older woman pressed her lips together, but the younger woman was already past her breaking point. Her eyes filled with tears she couldn't blink away. She all but threw the glass shaker at the older maid, stood on shaky legs, and rushed from the room.

"I'm sorry." AJ brushed the other maid away. "I think the stain is gone. We've already caused too much trouble. I've been out of sorts since leaving home, and I so hoped to speak to Elizabeth." AJ wasn't sure where she found the whiny tears, but sensing Elizabeth was in trouble appeared to be all the incentive she needed.

"It's no trouble." The woman picked up the soiled napkins and bottle of soda. "We all wish Lady Ratliff was back home."

The clearing of a throat made everyone glance toward the door. The butler frowned at the housemaid, but the woman gave him a defiant glare before lowering her head. "I do believe we got the stain out before it had time to set. Safe travels." Then she followed the younger maid's brisk path from the room.

"Your coach is ready." The butler glanced down at the wet spot on AJ's dress then seemed to relax.

Maire took a last bite of biscuit, sipped her tea, then rose, helping AJ to her feet. "Thank you for your hospitality. I'll be sure to let Elizabeth know when we see her."

This time AJ caught something in the butler's gaze, and her stomach heaved for real. Had it been fear?

For the first time, AJ never thought she'd be so happy to see the coach.

Ethan stayed a few paces behind Finn as they followed the footman to the stables. Lando was bent over one of the coach's wheels. Another man, dressed in the livery of the estate, squatted next to the wheel, studying where it connected to the axle.

"So, my good man, have you found the problem?" Finn strode over like some dandy while other men working in the stable hovered nearby.

Lando shook his head as he stepped away so Finn could get a better look at whatever the other coachman was doing.

Ethan couldn't hear them because he'd stepped back into the shadows of the barn. A horse neighed nearby, and another kicked its stall. One lad raked the aisle, but he darted glances toward the coach, probably interested in any activity that broke the monotony of the day. The barn carried the strong stench of manure, mingled with the scent of horse and old leather.

He studied the faces of the men, searching for someone who might be bribed. A broad-chested man, leaning against a far wall, with a battered hat and dirt-stained face, seemed a likely target. He was on his second scan of the crowd when a movement underneath one of the carriage horses made Ethan's heart jump to his throat.

A small boy, no more than eight, hunched near a horse. Ethan stayed in the shadows as he edged his way toward the boy. He was almost there when the boy, not aware of Ethan's approach, backed away from the men.

He'd taken two steps before he jumped, then squeaked, when Ethan clamped a hand on his shoulder. In a few short steps, Ethan steered the boy toward the far end of the barn. He glanced in the stalls and, finding an empty one, pulled the boy in with him before shutting the door.

The boy's wide eyes stared up at Ethan. After a minute of intense perusal, the boy stood taller and lifted his chin. "What do you want with me?"

Ethan couldn't help but chuckle. "Nothing nefarious, I assure you."

The boy glared at him.

"It means evil."

"I know what it means." The boy's snappish tone suggested otherwise.

Tough kid.

Ethan squatted so he was eye-to-eye with the boy. His first thought was to play on the boy's attachment to the lady of the house. He considered the boy, whose expression changed from defensiveness to curiosity. Ethan changed tactics. He narrowed his eyes, leaned in, and whispered. "Can you be counted on to keep a secret?"

The boy leaned forward as if in a trance. He nodded solemnly.

Ethan lifted his head then tilted it to the side as if listening for something. He turned back to the boy and hesitated.

The boy took a step closer, eyes growing as wide as when he'd first been pulled into the stall.

"My friend and I are on a secret mission for the Crown." Ethan waited, and the boy's head began to nod. "We've been following a group of men."

If it were possible, the boy's eyes grew even larger, lighting with excitement.

"We heard they might have come by this way." He waited a heartbeat before asking, "Have you seen any large groups of men?"

The boy licked his lips then turned toward the stall door. Satisfied they were still alone, the boy took another step. "Three days ago, they came." He glanced over his shoulder. When he turned back, tears filled his eyes. "They took our lady."

And there it was. He dropped a fist to the ground to keep from falling over, bending his head at the regretful news. After a deep breath, he pushed himself up, and avoided glancing at the boy while he wiped his tears. Ethan glanced out the stall door, but everyone had moved on to complete their daily tasks.

When the boy slipped into the aisle behind him, Ethan grabbed his shirt. Before the boy could struggle, Ethan dropped a coin into his hand. "Hold onto that until you really need it. Hide it someplace safe."

The boy rubbed it before tucking it into a pocket. "Was I helpful then?"

Ethan smiled and nudged his chin. "You might be the very thing that saves your lady." He turned, but before he took two strides, the boy called him.

"A coach and four. Black as night. No coat of arms." He looked down. "She didn't want to go."

"She'll be back. I give you my word." Ethan turned and almost ran to the coach. He hoped he hadn't just lied to the boy.

23

AJ stared up at the massive stone building and blinked several times. This wasn't what she'd expected. The journey from the Ratliff estate to London had been harrowing. After they'd driven away from the estate, they'd stopped to let Finn out. Since he knew Hensley better than any of them, he'd be the best one to track him down in London, and he could make faster time on horseback. Someone had to get to Langdon as quickly as possible. With confirmation that Elizabeth had been kidnapped, and if Langdon had the Heart Stone, Hensley had to prevent a trade at all costs. They would find another way to rescue the first keeper.

Lando had driven the horses hard to stay with Finn, but the increasingly crowded roads and lumbering coach simply wouldn't let him keep up. Such trivial things didn't prevent Lando from trying. With the first sight of London, AJ temporarily forgot their troubles. She'd had a quick view of it as they crested a knoll, and the vision had taken the breath from her. The city sprawled before her, and nothing could have prepared her for the pre-industrialized city that attempted to accommodate a growing population. The coach slowed to a crawl as they were caught in the congestion of street carts and other carriages. That was when the cloying smells of London caught up to her. The scents changed depending on which road the coach turned down—baked bread, sewage, unwashed bodies, freshly cut flowers. She finally scooted away from the window.

As the carriage carried them deeper into the heart of London, the cityscape changed to wider streets, more flowers and trees, and upscale residences. The people on the street dressed in finely tailored clothes, a far cry from the edges of London where worn and tattered clothing was the most a person could afford. Some things didn't change regardless of the century, there were always the rich and the poor.

When the coach stopped in front of the three-story mansion, she didn't know what to think. When Hensley had told them they'd be staying at Beckworth's safe house, she assumed some hovel in a downtrodden part of London. From what Ethan said, this residence wasn't in the heart of the upper-crust neighborhoods, but it was certainly within the boundaries.

The urgency of their situation reinserted itself when Ethan jumped from the coach before it came to a complete stop. A footman appeared from a side door and scurried over, holding the door so Ethan could assist Maire and AJ.

"Are you sure this is the right place?" AJ asked.

Ethan glanced up at Lando, who had set the brake and was climbing down.

"This is the address Hensley gave me." Lando waited by the back of the coach as Ethan's horse was led away, and two other footmen began removing trunks. "I'm not sure how the little man does it."

The group had started up the steps when the front door opened and Beckworth stepped out. He spread his arms wide in welcome, and his dapper smile appeared earnest.

"Welcome to your new residence. It might not have the warmth of Eleanor's or Bart's fine homes, but I think it will do for a couple of days." He paused, and his smile faded. "Where's Finn?"

Ethan blew past Beckworth and began pacing as everyone gathered in the foyer. "We have confirmation that Elizabeth was abducted. Finn came ahead to inform Hensley."

Beckworth frowned. "We expected that might have been the case. Hensley went straight to Parliament to track down Langdon." He clapped his hands, and a butler and two maids stepped out from a doorway. After a rushed introduction of the two lady's maids, Beckworth urged AJ and Maire to their rooms.

"I thought we'd have more time to settle in. Since we don't know what to expect, I suggest you go upstairs and let Cora and Nellie prepare a quick bath. Then rest until we hear news. Do you need something to eat?" Before AJ or Maire had a chance to respond, Beckworth shook his head. "Silly question. You've been in the coach for hours. Jergens." He glanced at the butler. "Arrange a tea service with sandwiches to be taken up."

AJ shook her head. "I think it's better if we wait down here until we hear more."

"Trust me when I say it will be at least an hour before we hear anything. And that's assuming Finn finds Hensley the first place he looks. You've been on the road for three days, and I imagine Lando wasted no time in the drive from the Ratliff estate."

"Beckworth is right." Ethan pushed Maire toward the stairs. "We have time. I'll go to Hensley's and see if there's any word. Until then, there's nothing to do but wait. Lando and Beckworth will be here to see to your safety." He turned to a footman. "Take me to my horse."

After Ethan left, Maire, always the patient one, followed the maids up the stairs.

AJ, on the other hand, hovered by the staircase while the staff hurried off to do Beckworth's bidding. She glanced at Lando first, who scanned the foyer before disappearing through a door that AJ assumed led to a sitting room. Beckworth leaned against the newel and waited.

She admired the entryway, noting the richly appointed furniture and fine artwork. She lifted a brow when her perusal landed on Beckworth. He wore a soft, dove-colored jacket, with a deep burgundy waistcoat that matched his pants. His black boots were polished to a fine sheen. She grinned when he tugged at the white-ruffled shirt.

"Should I even bother asking how you came up with such a fine house? Is it yours?"

He smiled back. "I have no need for a house in London. I usually stay at a gentleman's club when I visit. This"—he waved an arm around—"belongs to a friend I once did a favor for. He spends a great deal of time out of the country but retains a small staff to keep the place running. He's given me permission to use it when needed, as long as he's not in residence."

AJ studied him but had to admit, given all she knew of Beckworth, his story rung with truth. She considered the mystery that summed up Beckworth, knowing anything she asked wouldn't satisfy her. She simply had questions that would lead to more questions. When it seemed Beckworth would wait her out, she sighed.

"Fine. You're right, again. I'll go up and get the road dust off me. But I expect you to tell me the second you hear something."

He nodded. "No time for games. I understand."

Satisfied, she gave him a weary smile. The last three days caught up with her, and she used the banister to help pull her up the stairs, relieved to find Nellie waiting for her on the second-floor landing.

———

AJ leaned back against the sofa as she flipped through a book she'd found in the library. Her feet were tucked underneath her, and she'd become completely engrossed reading the archaic English. Only occasionally did she look up at the rustling of paper coming from the other side of the room.

Maire read through the stolen letters that spoke of Langdon and his itinerary. She'd reviewed them countless times at Hensley's, but the waiting had gotten the better of her. AJ would prefer to be pacing, but books could always distract her, if only temporarily.

The two of them had bathed, dressed in new finery, then found each other in the sitting room to stare into the empty hearth. A maid had suggested starting a fire, but AJ had shaken her head. An hour later, when they hadn't heard any news, AJ relented to lighting a couple pieces of wood.

Beckworth called for dinner, but it was a quiet affair with only the five of them. Thomas and his men had yet to arrive, and there'd been no word from Jamie. After dinner, Lando and Beckworth made a quick escape, leaving the women to their own devices.

The ticking of a clock and the occasional pop of a spark from the hearth's embers grated on AJ's already agitated mood. When the continual stirring of paper and scratching of a quill fried the last of her nerves, AJ leaped up and tossed the book aside.

"Maybe a walk in the back gardens would do us good. Lando can tag behind." AJ strolled toward the writing desk, but Maire didn't seem to be listening. Her head was bent low as she scratched away in the low light.

AJ tried again. "You could use some air." When Maire only mumbled something, AJ grabbed the quill out of her hand. "And stop straining your eyes."

Maire snapped her head up and glared. "I was in the middle of an important thought."

AJ froze. It wasn't Maire's reaction to what she'd said or done that bothered her. She was upset by her own actions, unable to control her anxiety.

Maire's expression grew slightly less irritated, but before she could say anything more, the front door burst open. Although they were a room away, the smell of horse assailed AJ's nose. When she heard several male voices, her gaze flashed to Maire, who was already standing. Before they were halfway across the room, Finn and Ethan strode in. They were followed by Lando, Beckworth, and Thomas. Other voices continued to murmur from the front door, and AJ assumed they were Thomas's men.

Finn swooped her into his arms, hugging so tightly she couldn't catch her breath. He released her and scanned her face, his expression relaxing when he saw she was all right.

"Where have you been?" AJ returned the quick perusal, but her frantic concern for Elizabeth overrode everything else. "We've been going out of our minds with worry."

"Let's move to the dining room first. I think Cook can put something together. I know a few of you haven't eaten in a while." Beckworth shooed everyone out of the sitting room, taking complete advantage of the fact he was the host in this domain.

Finn collapsed into a dining room chair and let his arms fall past the armrests. AJ noted the slight narrowing of his eyes, the pinch of his lips, and though he looked relaxed, he could spring from the chair in a flash. He was more than tired. She thought she'd caught a slight limp on his left side. His ribs must ache. He was healed, but after a two-hour ride to London and then racing around after Hensley, the ribs had taken some abuse.

It didn't stop him from finding a second wind to polish off every scrap of food put in front of him. Beckworth made sure his glass was always filled with fine wine. Whatever happened where Elizabeth Ratliff was concerned, the urgency must have passed because none of the men felt the need to discuss it until after they'd eaten. Though AJ and Maire had both tried.

"Okay." AJ finally pounded the table for attention, ignoring the glances from the footmen. "You've rested, you've eaten, and there seems to be a full cellar of wine. For all that's holy, please tell us what's happened to Elizabeth."

Finn laid a hand over her fist, and the warmth of it settled her. "You're right. We should have said something right away. Elizabeth is safe."

"Where is she?" Maire asked. When Ethan had arrived, they'd clung to each other as fiercely as AJ had with Finn. But as dinner progressed and with the men too focused on their meal to answer any of her questions, Maire became withdrawn and had put some space between herself and Ethan.

"She's with Langdon at his residence." Ethan's hand slid toward her, but he pulled it back, wisely waiting for Maire to make the first move.

Maire nodded, but her glance confirmed everything AJ had feared.

They'd been too late.

But AJ had to ask what the men were reluctant to state. "And the Heart Stone?"

The silence was all the answer she needed.

"I spent hours chasing after Hensley while he and Thomas were continually directed to the wrong places. Ethan found me on my second visit to Parliament. We didn't catch up to Hensley until a couple of hours ago at his manor."

"We wasted time going to the Ratliff estate." AJ gulped her wine, then took a second, long swallow. It didn't seem to help.

"It wouldn't have mattered." Finn ran a hand through his hair then pounded a fist on the armrest. He grimaced as he stood and walked with a slight limp to the other side of the room where a sideboard held several bottles of alcohol. He lifted a few before finding the one he wanted and poured an amber liquid into a glass. "Hiding the good Irish whiskey, I see." He lifted a glass to Beckworth.

"I wasn't hiding it. I always put the cheaper stuff in the back." But Beckworth didn't complain when Finn set a glass of whiskey in front of him.

Finn continued around the room until all the men and Maire had a glass. AJ refilled her wine glass.

"So, dear brother, why wouldn't it have mattered if we'd come here straightaway?"

"Because the exchange was made yesterday."

Ethan downed his glass. "Langdon hasn't told anyone, including the staff of the Ratliff estate. They're devising an alternate story."

AJ collapsed into her chair, all energy zapped, her bones felt like ooze. When would this end? Reginald was always one step ahead of them. She reached into her pocket, relief elevating her mood from utter despair to guarded pessimism when her fingers wrapped around the Heart Stone. Reginald's actions hadn't changed the fate of her Heart Stone.

Not yet.

24

———

The coach lurched through the streets of London. Hensley gathered wool as he stared out the window. It was unusual for him to be so quiet, but AJ knew he blamed himself for not getting to Langdon quickly enough to prevent the kidnapping or the loss of the Heart Stone. Or so Finn had told her. Hensley had appeared his jovial self when he'd first arrived to collect AJ and Maire. As they approached Langdon's London house, he seemed to turn introspective.

Maire had been withdrawn all morning. She never spoke of her six-month incarceration at Waverly, but she must have been thinking about it. They were on their way to meet Elizabeth Ratliff, another of Reginald's kidnap victims. Hensley said Elizabeth had been kept at an inn, and as rundown as the place had sounded, it wasn't the same as a dank cell.

AJ touched Maire's arm, waking her friend out of her own musings.

"I'm fine." Maire glanced at Hensley then pulled her bag closer.

"What did you bring?" AJ knew it was her herbs and potions, but if someone didn't say something before they reached their destination, she might have to scream to release the growing tension.

Maire blinked as if no one had ever asked that before. Then she smiled. "A bit of this and a bit of that. But you knew that already."

She shrugged. "What I think is that if we all keep such dour faces when we meet Elizabeth, she'll run for her room and never come out."

Maire sighed and released her hold on the bag. "Ethan said as much before we left." She blinked away the moisture filling her gaze. And for the first time, AJ realized she'd never seen Maire cry. And God knew, she'd had the right to on any number of occasions.

"He can be a wise man." AJ lifted a brow. "Almost as perceptive as your brother."

Maire's tinkling laugh made AJ smile. "You know Ethan is more astute than Finn."

"Let's agree they each have their moments."

"That is a wise conclusion."

"And what do you make of old Hensley?" His wistful tone touched her heart. AJ wasn't sure he was expecting an answer, but she gave him one anyway.

"He's the wisest of them all."

He responded with a weak smile before turning back to stare at the picturesque landscape. A drizzly day would have better matched the mood in the coach. AJ reached over and placed a hand on his arm. "And even the wisest of men aren't clairvoyant. No one could have anticipated Reginald being crazy enough to march in and take Elizabeth."

"Beckworth would have." Even with his argument, he seemed to relax.

AJ shook her head. "He didn't see it either until it was too late. So stop blaming yourself. We still have work to do."

Hensley sat back. "All this talk about wise men. We wouldn't be as far as we were without the two of you." He glanced to Maire. "The two of you are among the strongest people I know."

It was AJ's turn to blink back tears. He didn't say the strongest women. She sat a little straighter and nodded. There weren't any words for that appraisal.

The coach slowed, and AJ leaned across Maire to get a look at the Langdon house. Then she sat back. It was a mansion, set in the heart of London, with a massive garden. At another time, she might have been fascinated by all the wealth and power surrounding her. But it was at these moments that she preferred to be back in Baywood, tucked in their own monstrosity of an old inn, while wrapped in Finn's arms as they stared out to sea.

When she stepped from the carriage and stared up at the imposing three-story structure, butterflies swarmed her belly. It wasn't Langdon that worried her. Hensley would be keeping him occupied while she and Maire spoke with Elizabeth.

She'd never imagined this moment possible, and reaching into her pocket, her fingers clutched the Heart Stone. She was minutes away from meeting the first keeper. How crazy was that?

———

AJ hovered behind Maire, straightening her dress and pulling her shoulders back, trying to appear like an assistant to a natural healer. Langdon only approved of the women's visit because the family physician had no answer for Elizabeth's mental recovery other than a bottle of laudanum. Keeping the woman drugged wouldn't help anyone, and Langdon was smart enough to realize that. Not knowing what else to do, Langdon seemed to have grabbed at any assistance Hensley could provide.

She glanced at Maire and followed her lead, waiting patiently behind Hensley, hands clutched in front of her. Given the time while waiting, AJ let her gaze roam the antique furniture. Not only antique in her time period, but antiques in this century. She had taken a step toward one when boots could be heard on the marble floor.

The Earl of Castleton was a striking man with a full head of graying hair and matching goatee. His dark-gray jacket and pants reflected his somber air. He radiated confidence, but the dark circles under his eyes and sallow skin told the truth behind his stern welcome.

"I'm not sure this is wise, but with my son out of town with Elizabeth's brother, I'm not sure how else to help her." He gave Maire a thorough perusal before giving AJ a condensed review. "She's not sleeping, barely eating, and she has no desire to leave the house even to attend the gardens. I know it's only been a day, and it was all I could do to have her meet with you. But I want to be clear, I don't believe in magical potions."

He stared down at Maire, who didn't back down. Her smile radiated warmth and respect as she curtsied. "I don't either, Lord Castleton. I only use what can be found in the simplest of apothecaries. And while I think only time can help Miss Ratliff recover, I have some herbs that should help her sleep. All natural and without any opiates."

Langdon studied her a moment, then nodded. "If Hensley tells me I should trust you, then I will. God knows, I don't really have any recourse. My son will be home the day after tomorrow. Anything we can do until then. I know he'll be able to do something to lift her spirits. Just remember. That girl is like a daughter to me, even without her pending engagement to my son."

"Of course. No harm will come from anything I give her. And it might even help."

Langdon brightened at that, and his whole countenance morphed, changing from striking to dashing in an instant. But beneath his display of approval, AJ picked up a touch of duplicity behind his polish. Men of his stature didn't get where they were by playing nice. Somewhere under all that veneer lurked a very dangerous man.

"Come Hensley. Let the women to their tea. I believe we have a few items to discuss."

When the two men strode down a hallway, the butler ushered AJ and Maire through three richly appointed rooms until they reached a small drawing room where a fire blazed in the hearth. Furniture as impressive as what she'd seen in the foyer filled the space with charm. Delightful landscapes and brightly colored drapes added to the cozy, if not overly warm, atmosphere.

The butler announced them, bowed, and left the room. A housemaid rattled cups as she placed them on a small table in between a sofa and two chairs. In one of the chairs, a woman a few years younger than AJ huddled within its deep depths, as if the chair itself could protect her from the evils of the world.

She dressed in current London fashions, the deep shade of blue accentuating the woman's dark curls and alabaster skin so prevalent in the aristocracy. Yet there was no rosy glow in her cheeks, just the dark shadows under her eyes that revealed her sleepless nights. Her thin smile was practiced, almost pained. When the maid left, she struggled to sit up so she could reach the tea service. Each task seemed an endeavor, as if some invisible force weighed on her.

Maire took a seat on the sofa across from Elizabeth, and AJ sat beside her. "Did the earl tell you why we're here, Miss Ratliff?" Maire placed her bag next to her and began pulling out vials.

"Please, call me Elizabeth." Her words were as forced as her movements, but her smile seemed sincere. "I do hate all the politeness." Her gaze moved to a distant point, and she waved her hand. "Although, sometimes, it does help to maintain expected norms. The comfort of them."

"I suppose something can be said for routine." Maire set a mortar next to the line of vials then added a pinch of this and a pinch of that into the tiny cup. "They provide a sense of security, a feeling of the protection and safety we were raised to expect." When all the ingredients were in the cup, she crushed the contents. "But those feelings are false."

AJ shot a glance to Elizabeth. She hadn't expected Maire to be so forthright, and it surprised Elizabeth too.

"AJ, could you open that window?" Maire nodded toward the far wall where a curtain hid most of the window. Maire lifted her gaze to Elizabeth. "I hope you don't mind, but the room is much too warm, and it's stealing what little energy you have."

Elizabeth released a long sigh. "I tried to tell the house-keeper the rooms were too warm. I think they believe the heat will somehow exorcise the last few days away." Her eyes filled with moisture, and AJ took that moment to pop up, startling Elizabeth.

AJ drew back the drapes and filtered sun flooded the room. She opened the window and sucked in the cool air before turning to see Elizabeth drink the potion Maire handed her.

When she set the glass down, Elizabeth smiled at Maire. "I probably should have asked what was in that before drinking it."

"Probably." Maire shared her own smile while adding different ingredients into the mortar. "They're mostly herbs that will help calm your nerves. You might feel like a nap before dinner, and that's perfectly normal. I'm also putting a couple herbs together that will provide a deeper sleep. You should take this with tea an hour before bedtime. I'll leave you enough for the next couple of days. It won't be a cure, but it will help."

"Thank you." Elizabeth tapped a finger against the arm of the chair.

AJ glanced around the room as if some object might ease the discussion into the sensitive topic of Elizabeth's ordeal.

"We understand the people who kidnapped you were interested in a large gem referred to as the Heart Stone." Maire's bold statement made AJ choke on her tea. So much for subtle.

Elizabeth seemed to shrink into herself. AJ hated what she and Maire had to do—make her relive her worst nightmare. On the other hand, while Elizabeth might fight it, she would feel better talking through it.

"I'm sorry to be blunt, but we don't have much time." Maire kept her tone even, almost pleasant. "I believe you know a French monk named Sebastian?"

Elizabeth's eyes lit with fondness. "You know him?"

AJ and Maire both nodded, but AJ scooted to the edge of the sofa, eager to finally have something she felt comfortable talking about. "We spent time with him at the monastery, learning about the stone and its history. Sebastian mentioned that the previous prior had sent the Heart Stone to your father for protection."

"And it seemed to have gotten him killed." Elizabeth's bitter tone seemed to fuel the spark of defiance in her gaze.

"I agree." Maire waited for her words to sink in.

Elizabeth arched a brow and leaned forward. "You think he was truly killed for what he knew of the Heart Stone?"

Maire considered her response as she packed her vials. "I don't know if Lord Ratliff knew the history of the Heart Stone, but I think he believed it to be important enough to keep and protect. When our friends traveled to your estate in search of me, I think it sparked your father's curiosity about the stone."

Elizabeth turned to the fire, one hand grasping a locket AJ hadn't noticed before. Lockets were common in this century, and she hadn't thought much about it. Now she wondered if it had been a gift from the senior Ratliff.

Maire stopped her packing and held Elizabeth's gaze. "I think your father sought an old friend who had the ability to uncover secrets. But your father had no idea that his old friend had already been embroiled in the lure of the stone. He also had no idea that this same friend had been unknowingly replaced by some very bad people at Waverly."

"I knew it." Elizabeth stood, but she did it too fast. Most likely weak from lack of sleep and food, she stumbled before catching herself on the back of the chair. "His death seemed too coincidental."

"We believe the people that took you are the same people involved in your father's death."

If Elizabeth was shocked by Maire's accusation, she hid it well. She walked to the fire and stared into for several minutes.

AJ poked Maire and whispered, "A bit too much, don't you think?"

Maire shook her head and responded loud enough to ensure Elizabeth heard. "You see, I know a little something about your recent incarceration. I understand how it feels to have your freedom, your sense of security, and all you know taken from you."

Elizabeth stiffened. She played with the top of the fire iron. AJ wasn't sure if the woman intended to stoke the fires or beat her and Maire over the head with it. But the woman just rubbed a thumb over the glossy worn top. She eventually squared her shoulders and returned to her seat. She freshened the cold tea and placed a biscuit on each plate. "I understand there's something old at play here. Something that is the responsibility of men. Lord Castleton assured me he'd get to the bottom of it." She paused, and her hand shook as she sipped her tea. She turned a pleading gaze to Maire. "To be honest, I don't know what you're asking of me."

Maire set two vials of her mixed herbs on the table before packing the rest of her supplies. AJ expected Maire to keep going, but she didn't respond. AJ understood. Elizabeth would be glancing over her shoulder for months before this experience faded. What could they ask of someone who already gave too much? AJ reached for her inner pocket, almost as if she could feel the Heart Stone fading away. As if this solitary moment had changed the trajectory of the stone, removing it from its future path. What would that mean? Would she never meet Finn?

AJ stood and closed the window, the cool air having done its job. They had to reset expectations. Then she remembered a critical element. Elizabeth hadn't become the first keeper until she married into the Langdon family. They still had time to set this all straight.

She sat in the chair next to Elizabeth and reached out to pat the woman's arm, giving it a light squeeze before releasing it. "We're not asking anything. Not really. Someday, we'll recover the Heart Stone. At some point after that, someone will need to protect it, care for it, and, when it's time, pass it on for the next person to safeguard. You probably aren't aware of this, but both the prior and Sebastian suggested the stone be kept by women."

Elizabeth's calm exterior began to show signs of cracking again. AJ touched her arm again, forcing the young woman to focus on her.

"The reason is fairly simple," AJ continued. "Women are less likely to use the stone for devious reasons. Women are masters at keeping secrets. And who would question a woman having an elegant stone in her possession?"

When Elizabeth's eyes filled with moisture, AJ shook her head. "No one is asking anything from you now. It could be years before we find the Heart Stone." AJ hoped she hadn't just cursed them. "Just remember that the prior and Sebastian felt the stone was safest with the Ratliffs." She held the woman's gaze for a long moment, then smiled and glanced down at the tea service. "Now, let's eat the biscuits before Hensley returns."

AJ didn't know if what she'd said was enough. All she could do was plant the seed. When she glanced at Maire, her hopes soared with Maire's pleased expression that seemed to say job well done.

25

Beckworth, dressed in the simple clothing of a merchant, led Finn and Ethan through the brothel and upstairs to the second floor. Sounds of the working house could be heard behind the doors, and Finn shook his head at how easily Beckworth transformed from viscount to street hustler whenever the situation required.

AJ and Maire had left to visit Elizabeth Ratliff shortly after lunch. The coach had barely turned the corner before Beckworth advised Finn and Ethan of his afternoon plans. Beckworth had hired a modest coach to drive the three of them to the Covent Garden district. A location teeming with whorehouses. An area Finn had been familiar with in his first years working for Hensley.

When they reached the last door at the end of a long hall, Beckworth tapped three times, paused, then tapped twice more. The scrape of chairs, shuffling of feet, and grumble of male voices made the three men take a step back. When the door opened, a forehead and two eyes appeared.

"What?"

"It's me." Beckworth glowered.

"It's about time." The forehead disappeared, and the door opened wider.

Beckworth shouldered his way in, and Ethan followed. Finn hesitated then glanced down the hall. A mere slip of a brunette wearing nothing but a gossamer gown that barely covered her backside tiptoed out of a room. She gripped the arm of an elderly gentleman who wore nothing but his long drawers. They scurried past two doors before the young woman tapped on the third door. Another brunette poked her head out, and giggling, pulled the two visitors inside before slamming the door shut.

Finn shook his head, and not seeing anything suspicious, followed Ethan. The room, being at the end of the hall, had two windows, one on each of the two corner walls. A man stood by each window. Two other men sat at a small table with a bottle of whiskey and four mugs.

The bed, the main feature of the room, was mussed, and the blonde woman lounging in it wore a gown similar to the woman in the hall. The only difference was the color. Where the other woman had been dressed in a soft blue, this woman's gown was a vivid red that matched her ruby-painted lips. She leaned against a thin headboard, and oddly enough, was hard at work stitching a shirt. Her focus was so intent on her task that she barely took note of the men who walked in.

Beckworth strode to a window, nodded at the man, then peered out before moving to the next. He spent a full minute at each window, surveying the streets below.

When he seemed satisfied, he sat next to the woman and smiled at the men at the table. "So, Billy, what do you have for me?"

Beckworth patted the woman's leg. She smiled at him and pushed her foot toward him. He picked it up and stroked it as he watched Billy.

"You said you'd pay."

Beckworth studied Billy, who refused to utter another word. After another few seconds, he sighed and glanced at Finn. "When are people going to start trusting me more?" He reached into his pocket and tossed a coin bag across the room, which Billy caught in one hand.

"We've recently been crossed by a few men we thought we could trust. It's standard practice now."

Beckworth thought about it then returned to rubbing the woman's foot. "I understand. No hard feelings."

Billy released a deep breath and relaxed into his seat. Finn shot Ethan a glance. His friend's expression told him he'd also noted Billy's shift. The man was boastful but a little scared of Beckworth. Good to note.

After giving his response some thought, Billy leaned over the table. "There have been a lot of men roaming the Strand. Men we haven't seen before, walking in groups of two to three."

Beckworth shrugged. "It's a bad part of town, lots of men walk in groups."

"It's more than that. These men, they stand out." Billy seemed to struggle for the right words.

"They seem organized—focused. If they were our men, I'd say they were planning a mission." The comment came from one of the men at the windows. He spoke but never took his gaze from the job. "They try to fit in. Some do okay, but others..." He scratched his scruffy beard. "It just makes them stand out more."

"That's it." Billy nodded and snapped his fingers. "They look like they belong, but if you watch close enough, it's like they're biding their time for something."

"Do you know where these men are staying?" Beckworth asked.

Billy shrugged. "We've seen them in and out of several boarding houses."

"If it's Dugan's men, there are too many to put in one or two places." Ethan's offhanded comment made the two at the table swing their heads in his direction.

Finn, who leaned against the wall next to Ethan, noted that the two men at the windows never wavered from their duty. These were well-trained men, not easy to distract, even standing in what appears to be a safe room. He began to take the information seriously. Beckworth appeared to have a competent group of informants on the streets searching for Dugan's men. And they'd found them, faster than Hensley could. Hensley had contacts on the streets, but they couldn't always be trusted, and their information had proven to be shoddy at best.

Billy waited for Beckworth, who had nodded at Ethan's comments but seemed to be performing his own assessment. He laid the woman's left foot aside and picked up her right foot, his hands tender as he slowly massaged the length of it. She continued with her sewing as if this was how she typically spent her afternoons. Maybe it was.

After several minutes of silence, Billy offered another tidbit. "We've tried to take note of their faces. It's hard to tell sometimes, you know, one man from another. But if we had to guess, there are at least twenty different men. The problem is that they seem to team with a different man each time they go out. I'd followed one bloke. A right big and scary man, but a few of them are like that. This one has a pocket watch. Takes it out all the time. That's how I always know it's him." He set his gaze on Ethan and Finn. "He's with a different man almost every day."

"If it's only a couple dozen men, then Dugan has half of his men in town, some here hiding out on the Strand while the rest guard Reginald." Ethan stood and strode to the window. One of the men stepped to the side, keeping his focus on the street below. Ethan stayed back as he stared out the window. "He probably has the rest outside London, but someplace close in case they're needed."

"Do you have any men at the docks?" Finn asked.

Beckworth shook his head. "No. But now that your ship has arrived, it's probably a good idea." He looked to Billy. "Do you have anyone you can spare?" When Billy stared at him, Beckworth rolled his eyes. Finn wondered if Beckworth had picked the behavior up from AJ.

"You'll get paid the standard rate." Beckworth patted the woman's foot and set it down, grumbling, "I don't know why I always have to repeat myself on the topic."

Billy nodded with a sheepish grin. "I can put two men on it. Tell me the ship's name, and we'll see if anyone takes interest."

Beckworth glanced at Finn.

"The *Daphne Marie*." Finn didn't hesitate. It wasn't as if they were hiding her.

"Done," Billy said.

"Now we just need to know where Reginald is hiding," Finn said. "He has to be close."

The second man at the table pushed his chair back and tapped the table twice. He waved at Billy then pointed at his eyes and made a gesture with his fingers.

"Yeah, I was getting to that." Billy glanced at Beckworth. "Hugo has been following a group of men. You know, to see what they do all day. Most of them walk the streets and stop for ale. But occasionally, he follows a group who leaves the East End for Hyde Park."

Finn stood straighter. This tidbit might be the golden egg.

"Go on," Beckworth urged.

"They've been seen entering one of the homes through a back entrance. An old brownstone, number 35 Basil."

Ethan slammed a fist on the wall. "We have him."

"Do you have anyone on the house?" Beckworth asked.

Billy shook his head.

Beckworth reached into his coat and tossed another pouch

to Billy, who deftly caught it, though he looked surprised. "You've done well. In addition to the men at the docks, I need someone to monitor the house."

Billy glanced at Hugo. "Sounds like a job for Luisa."

Beckworth laughed. "I thought she settled down, babes and all."

Billy nodded with a wide smile that displayed wide gaps between the stained teeth. "She did, but she gets bored. Her sister moved in with a couple babes of her own. Luisa takes the odd job to make ends meet. Nothing risky."

"Then she's perfect." Beckworth gave Ethan and Finn a wink. "If Reginald is there, Luisa will find out. She's one of the best."

Billy and his other men nodded agreement, the two at the window still focused on the street. Then one of the window watchers said, "He's here."

Billy jumped up. "Hate to run, but we have another job going."

Beckworth stood and slapped Billy on the shoulder. "Good job, chaps."

As one, the four men silently filed out of the room. Finn watched from the door as the men hustled down the hallway. Two turned right and disappeared toward the main stairs, but the other two continued on to what Finn assumed was another way out of the building.

When Finn turned around, Beckworth had taken a seat at the table. He picked up a mug, dumped the meager contents into the washbasin, then poured himself a whiskey. After a sip, followed by a grimace, he smiled. "Now that my task for the day is complete, why don't you saunter back to your womenfolk and leave me to my own devices."

As if she'd been waiting for those very words, the blonde tossed her sewing aside and rose from the bed. She was tall, and her gauzy gown showed off a curvaceous figure. She strolled across the room to stand behind Beckworth before leaning down to kiss his ear.

Ethan shook his head and walked out the door.

"That was good work." Finn leaned against the door frame and crossed his arms across his chest.

Beckworth shrugged but didn't say anything.

The woman tugged at Beckworth's jacket, and he leaned forward to let her remove it. Grinning and glancing at Finn, she tugged at Beckworth's shirt.

When Beckworth noticed Finn hadn't moved, he grumbled. "In addition to the two women posing as lady's maids, I already have someone monitoring the safe house. And I have two men who will follow the women wherever they go, regardless of who you have tagging along. AJ and Maire will never notice them."

Finn grinned and nodded at the woman. "Have fun."

He closed the door behind him as Beckworth shouted, "I'll be at Hensley's for dinner."

Ethan had stopped halfway down the hall. "Everything set."

"The women have protection."

Ethan relaxed for the first time since walking into the brothel. "I hate to admit it."

"Let me stop you right there. Anything you say in this place will get back to him. The last thing Beckworth needs to hear is how damn indispensable he's become."

The two men laughed as they took the stairs. When they stepped outside, Ethan sniffed his jacket. "How did you plan on explaining to AJ why your jacket smells of a brothel?"

26

———

Hensley's London house, another testament to Mary's sense of style, was half the size of their Bristol estate. The rooms were still large enough to entertain, and Mary selected the library for Hensley's meeting room. Several pieces of furniture were moved out to make room for a long table and simple chairs. The remaining side tables were cleared of ornamentation so they could be used for food and drink service.

The room buzzed with activity as members of their inner circle arrived and joined others in heaping their plates from a buffet of roasted pork, baked fish, and glazed potatoes mixed with other root vegetables. A second sideboard held meat pies, fruit pastries, breads, and cheeses. AJ was surprised to see ale being served. Hensley never allowed anything stronger than coffee or tea during his meetings. She had no idea what this change meant, but after pacing the mansion and gardens all afternoon while men gathered in Hensley's study, she filled a mug with ale, hoping it would settle her anxiety.

Hensley, followed by Finn and Ethan, entered the room and stacked a pile of papers and journals at the head of the table before gathering a plate of food. He nibbled while he organized, seemingly alone in his world. Yet, AJ noticed his overt glances and knew he was listening to most of the conversations around him.

Finn brought her a plate and squeezed her knee under the table. He recognized her mood, and taking the smart approach, decided to keep her fed with as minimal discussion as possible. She almost smiled when he refilled her mug. When other team members noticed Hensley paying attention to their small talk, they took their seats until the room quieted.

In Hensley's own purposeful way, he drank from his mug of ale, wiped his chin with a napkin, then surveyed the group before him. "Let me start with the events of the last two weeks from Langdon's perspective. He received a letter from an anonymous source about two days after Finn's rescue. Without going into details, the insinuation was clear that Langdon's best course of action was to turn over the Heart Stone. A date, time, and location were provided."

"That explains his seclusion," Jamie said.

"Yes. And three days later, when he was to exchange the stone, he sent other men in his place in hopes of capturing the person."

"Dugan's too smart for that." Beckworth sipped his ale and tore a hunk of bread apart, dug out the middle, then tossed both decimated halves on this plate. His earlier good humor had vanished, leaving AJ to wonder if Dugan was supposed to have been the bread.

"I'm afraid you're right," Hensley continued. "No one arrived at the meeting place. Though it was more likely they were there, saw the ambush, and left. Langdon thought he'd chased them away, but three days later, he received another letter. This time it was an admonishment for Langdon's deceit. No other request for the stone was made."

He stopped, chewed a slice of roast, then washed it down

with ale before shuffling through papers. His eyes scanned the room while he reviewed a particular page. "You have to keep in mind that Langdon had no idea what was so important about the Heart Stone, though he knew it had some value. Langdon is a wise man. He knew there was something strange about Ratliff sending him the stone shortly before his untimely death. A death Langdon, as well as Elizabeth, thought to be suspicious." He laid the paper down and leaned back, his hands folded across his stomach. "It was another four days before he received the note advising that Miss Elizabeth Ratliff was now their guest."

"What took so long? And why didn't someone from the Ratliff estate inform Langdon?" Thomas's question received agreeing nods from the other team members. AJ had to admit the question seemed warranted, but the fear she'd seen in the maids' expression while at the Ratliff estate would stick for some time.

Hensley only shrugged. "It was unfortunate timing."

Which, AJ summed up, seemed to be the entire theme where the stones and books were concerned.

"The Ratliff butler did send a note to Miss Ratliff's eldest brother, who was in residence in London. However, he had just left for a short trip to Dover with Langdon's son. Although, I'm not sure what they could have done, other than what we'd already been doing. But Langdon didn't share our insight as to who was pulling the strings. Terrified for his friend's daughter, and as it turns out, his son's betrothed, he complied with the new instructions. And, as you know, we were a day late in preventing the exchange."

Hensley glanced at AJ. "I took AJ and Maire to visit Elizabeth earlier today. She won't discuss the kidnapping, but Langdon was able to determine she only saw two men, and they wore masks when they brought her food."

"Elizabeth is still quite traumatized." Maire had moved food around on her plate. AJ didn't know if her lack of appetite had to do with remembering her own incarceration at the hands of Reginald or that she was full from lunch and two tea services before the meeting. "I was able to give her herbs to help her sleep, but she clearly wasn't ready to discuss her ordeal. Unfortunately, she also wants nothing to do with the Heart Stone, which she sees as the reason for her father's murder."

"I thought she was the first keeper?" Ethan asked.

Finn reached for AJ, and she squeezed his hand. Did he wonder if she would vanish from their midst if the Heart Stone didn't follow the path it was meant to take? She had to admit, until the Heart Stone was safe, it would be her foremost concern.

"She is the first keeper," Maire agreed. "And with AJ's words of encouragement, she still will be." She winked at AJ. "Who knows? Maybe it was AJ who started the keepers with a mere suggestion."

When positive comments were thrown her way, AJ became uncomfortable with the attention. She'd only tried to keep Elizabeth from making a fateful decision while still traumatized by events. Hensley tapped the table to quiet the group.

"Are you sure Reginald can't use the Heart Stone?" Beckworth asked Maire.

Maire shook her head. "I don't think so. I found nothing in the grimoire that explained how the Heart Stone would work on its own. Only *The Book of Stones* would have that information, though I never translated anything that spoke of it." Grateful sighs floated around the room. "I suppose Dugan might be aware of the incantations."

"Doubtful. Dugan never involved himself in the stones. Though, he's probably sorry for that now." Beckworth's mood seemed to be improving as he popped the last of a meat pie in his mouth.

"But we need the Heart Stone." AJ watched the others. Surely, they understood that, and the tension building along her spine eased when everyone nodded.

Beckworth downed the rest of his mug, squelched a burp, then smiled at the group. "Then it seems a good turn of fortune that we know where Reginald is."

Everyone gaped at him except for Finn and Ethan. So that was what they'd been up to earlier. Hensley wasn't surprised either, which explained the afternoon discussions in his study.

When the room erupted, Hensley once again beat on the table for silence. "When I explained the situation with Langdon..." Hensley held up his hand before anyone could speak. "I didn't tell him anything about the books or time travel. I simply said the stone was of historical value, originally sent to Ratliff for protection during France's political and economic plight. I also told him we suspect the person who took Elizabeth was the one responsible for her father's murder. Langdon has guaranteed his full support for our efforts to catch Reginald." He paused until he had everyone's full attention. "We must catch Reginald with the Heart Stone in his possession. Without that, we have no proof that Reginald was behind the kidnapping. There's also no evidence connecting him to Ratliff's death. However, if he's caught with the Heart Stone, Langdon will have free rein to force other confessions from him."

"We might know where Reginald is, but how do we know he'll have the stone with him?" Jamie's question wasn't far from AJ's own. He'd hidden the druid's grimoire well enough. The Heart Stone could be anywhere.

When everyone in the room turned to Beckworth, he grinned, always happy to be the center of attention. "I think it's time for a family reunion."

27

"I'm not going to discuss this." Finn slammed the wardrobe closed then put on his waistcoat.

"Wouldn't it make more sense to have one or two people on a roof in front of the club? In case you need some type of cover?" AJ persisted as she poked loose tendrils back into the elaborate hairstyle her lady's maid had concocted. She was ravishing, especially with her cheeks rosy from agitation.

"What you really mean is that you should be up on the roof dressed like one of Beckworth's street kids with a fully stocked quiver."

"What if Dugan storms the club?"

Finn stifled a chuckle and managed to keep a solemn expression. He didn't trust Dugan any more than she did. But if this meeting was nothing more than a diversion, Dugan's focus wouldn't be on him and Beckworth.

"We'll be in the heart of London in the middle of the day. If they have plans, it will be carried out by a discreet group, not a large force. That is why you and Maire need to be someplace else. Somewhere public."

He pulled her to him and held her tight, breathing in the

earthy scent of heather that reminded him of Ireland. "You don't smell of roses anymore."

"Maire lent Nellie some of her oils." She squeezed him tighter. "I hate it when we're not together."

"We have a plan. It's a good plan." He stepped back and held her gaze. "I have to know you and Maire are safe while we meet with Reginald." He ran his fingers over the loose tresses that preferred to stray. The burgundy dress was one of her finer ones, and when she dressed like this, all he wanted to do was spend the afternoon removing one article of clothing at a time until he had her naked and panting. He blamed most of his intense desire on the months they'd been apart, but if he was honest, he'd have to admit to having the same urge if they'd been apart for only hours. And he had no doubt he'd feel the same way in fifty years.

Her eyes narrowed, and she stepped away. "I know that look."

She couldn't fool him. He'd seen the same heat flushing her cheeks.

"If the entire team wasn't waiting for us." Then he decided they could wait five minutes more. He tugged her to him, and she answered his kiss with a passion that had them both breathing hard.

AJ took the first initiative to breakaway because his mind had gone fuzzy. "You've messed up my hair." She stuffed tendrils back in place, but her grin told him everything he needed to know.

A knock preceded Maire's call, "The carriage is here."

"Game time." Finn patted her backside, and when he turned, she patted his.

"Good hunting."

He winked as he opened the door and gave his sister a surprise kiss on the cheek before hustling down the hall.

When he walked through the front door of the safe house, the team was waiting.

Fitz perched atop Hensley's carriage, and Finn had to do a double take. The stocky sailor had been dressed in impressive livery, and his beard had been trimmed. Based on his sneer, it wasn't by choice, but he nodded at Finn before returning to stare out over the horses. Mary and Eleanor looked out from the windows of the carriage. Mary waved at the men while talking nonstop to Eleanor, who smiled and nodded.

Jamie and Lando sat astride their horses with two of Thomas's men. They would escort Hensley's coach, and all four appeared eager to be off.

Thomas and the rest of his men paired with a few of Beckworth's street informants. Half of the teams were stationed at various points along the path Hensley's coach would take toward Hyde Park. The other half had been stationed around the meeting location. Beckworth had identified several areas where Dugan might make a move. It was highly unlikely Reginald would approve of something so daring in the middle of the afternoon, but it would be foolish to underestimate their boldness again.

Beckworth stood next to the carriage, holding the reins of two horses. "She wanted to hide out and shoot arrows at someone, didn't she? Maybe at Dugan on his way up the steps to the club?" Beckworth asked.

Finn wasn't sure whether to growl at him or laugh at how easily everyone could read his wife. He grabbed the reins and decided to ignore the man.

Beckworth laughed. "I know she doesn't believe me. But by dinner, we'll be celebrating our success."

"You're not getting cocky, are you?"

"Never. I've always been able to read my mark. And I've been watching my brother for years. Trust me when I tell you, we'll be smoking cigars and drinking that Irish whiskey you're so fond of."

"We won't accomplish anything if we have to listen to you bluster, little man." Lando's grin at the chorus of laughter seemed to offset his impatient stare, though his horse continued to prance in place.

"How many times must I ask you not to call me that?" Beckworth muttered.

Before anyone responded, the front doors opened. AJ and Maire stepped out, and the men seemed to have forgotten what they'd been laughing at. Finn certainly had. The women, dressed in Eleanor's tailored handiwork, would put any noblewoman to shame. But he might have been biased.

AJ grimaced at the coach, and Finn couldn't help but smile. She used to hate riding horses, but after enduring long miles in a coach, he understood the longing glance she gave his horse. He helped both women into Hensley's coach, but not before planting another kiss on AJ's cheek. Ethan made it to the coach in time to give Maire a long hug and a kiss on the forehead.

"Oh, my dears, you both look stunning." Mary's voice rang out as she grabbed their hands. "It's such a beautiful day for a ride through Hyde Park."

Finn leaned into the coach and smiled at Mary. "And if Hensley didn't say it earlier, you're looking quite fetching yourself."

Mary beamed and slapped his hand with her fan. "You've always been such a rogue."

Finn's signature smile lit his face. "I'll take that as a compliment, madam." Then he turned serious as he glanced at Maire. "You have the book?"

Maire patted the skirts of her dress. "Sewn into a special pocket." She winked at AJ.

"I told you women were the more devious." Ethan had poked his head through the window.

When all the women nodded, Finn refrained from shaking his head. He tapped AJ's hand. "You have your dagger?"

"We have everything. Heart Stone, grimoire, dagger, Maire has her pistol, and..." AJ patted something lying along the bench near her feet. The object was covered with a piece of canvas the same color as the coach interior.

Finn's brow rose, and AJ whispered, "A bow and quiver, just in case."

He stepped back, and Ethan slapped him on the back. "Five men, and the women armed to the teeth. I almost wish Dugan would try it, except I wouldn't be there to see it."

"You and Beckworth need to be off before you're late." Maire sat back, turning to look out her window, clearly ready to get on with it. "And we need to get off this street."

Finn closed the door, winked at AJ, then stood back and stared up. Mary was right. Not a cloud in the sky. He only wished he were the one taking AJ for a drive through the park. He patted the backside of a coach horse as he glanced up at Fitz. "Stay on open roads if you can so you don't have to sit idle. And keep to the crowds once you're in the park. If Dugan does have something planned while we're meeting with Reginald, he won't want many witnesses."

"Don't worry." Lando's usual jovial expression had been replaced with a fierce resolve. "Beckworth already has men inside the hotel where they'll have lunch. The women will be well guarded and, if Dugan has any plans to snatch them while you're meeting with Reginald, his men will be hard-pressed to find them."

Fitz ran a finger under his collar, pulling on it as if the gesture would make it easier to breathe. "Can we be off now?" He mumbled something else before clicking his tongue and shaking the reins. The carriage took off and, once they were out of earshot, the rest of the men laughed.

Ethan mounted his horse and scanned the street. "I'll follow you for the first couple of blocks before joining up with Thomas's men at the club."

Finn and Beckworth mounted. They studied the street and people as Ethan had.

"Do you think Dugan has someone here watching all of this?" Finn asked Beckworth.

Beckworth shrugged. "Maybe. Though I have two urchins keeping an eye out. They know this street well and haven't signaled any concern."

Ethan eyed Beckworth. "You have children doing your work for you?"

Beckworth laughed. "Don't worry about them. This type of work is their specialty. And they're getting paid handsomely for it. Their families will be well-fed for a week or more just on today's harmless task." He gave Ethan an odd look. "And you might remember that street urchins are invisible."

Finn thought he saw a shadow of acknowledgment pass over Ethan, then it was gone.

Ethan just nodded but held Beckworth's inquisitive gaze.

Beckworth smiled before turning his horse in the opposite direction of the coaches. "Then let's be off. I'd hate to be late for drinks with my brother."

28

Finn glanced up the steps of the gentleman's club. Beckworth had a sense of humor, he'd give him that. The club was Finn's old stomping grounds and happened to be the same place Beckworth frequented when he'd been given the title Viscount Waverly. The two of them had met on these very steps as adversaries, while Dugan transported AJ and Maire, with some difficulties, to Southampton to board a ship for France.

Reginald made his first mistake by agreeing to meet at this club. He'd given them the home advantage.

"Old times. I just love nostalgia." Beckworth glanced around and dismounted, handing his horse to a footman.

"You have an odd sense of what amuses you." Finn smiled at the young footman before handing him the reins and a few coins.

Beckworth, apparently unable to contain his mirth at the irony, placed an arm around Finn's shoulders and gave him a few shakes. "Oh, how quickly things change." He released Finn, tugged at his sleeves, then ran his hands together. "Let's get in there before too many people recognize me."

The men mounted the stairs, and the doorman's face lit with

recognition when he spotted Finn. "Well, if my eyes aren't deceiving me. It's good to have you back, Captain Murphy. It's been a long time, sir."

The man almost gushed with excitement, and Beckworth shook his head. Finn placed a crown in the old man's hand. "It's been too long. And how's Agnes and the children?"

"Doing well, sir. So kind of you to remember."

Finn patted the man on the back before walking through the opened door. The club wasn't busy during the middle of the day, though it wasn't empty either. They strode past the gaming tables on their way to the bar when the maître d rushed over to greet them. "Captain Murphy. Lord Beckworth. So good to see you both again. We have your room ready, and..." He shifted his glance toward Beckworth. "The staff has been arranged."

Beckworth nodded, and Finn spared another crown. "Thank you, Phillip. As always, you've seen to everything."

The man pocketed the coin with a brief smile then led them past the bar and down a narrow hall to a private room. When Finn entered, he noted a table for six to his left. On the opposite side of the room, two chairs and a sofa were positioned around a fireplace that glowed with embers. Well-polished side tables, bookshelves, and paintings of hunts completed the room.

"This is perfect." Beckworth rubbed his hands as he surveyed the room.

Finn nodded at Phillip, who bowed his head and closed the door on his way out.

Beckworth sprang into action rearranging the six chairs at the table. He dragged two against the wall. The other four were left where they'd originally been placed, but he spread them out so the setting appeared more natural. He sat in one of the chairs that faced the wall, laying his arms on the table. After a moment, he moved to a chair on the opposite side, squirmed as if he was settling in, then nodded with a satisfied expression.

Finn leaned against a sideboard, watching Beckworth with some bemusement. "Can I ask what you're doing?"

"It's just a little something I picked up watching old movies with the sisters."

For a second, Finn didn't understand who he was talking about until he remembered Beckworth's jump to the future. "You've never talked about the sisters. How did you get them to take you in?"

"It wasn't by choice. I dropped into their driveway like an old rag, completely delirious from being stabbed then tossed about in the fog." He gave Finn a wry smile. "That woman of yours was quite deadly with that bloody dagger long before her intensive training."

Finn could only smile in return. He didn't think any amount of training could have made AJ stab someone unless she was pushed. And Beckworth had a special skill that made people want to stab him.

"Anyway," Beckworth continued, "they nursed me back to health. They were two lonely old women who needed one more project."

Before Finn could ask more, a waiter entered with two servers behind him. One of the servers glanced at Beckworth, and Finn thought he saw the barest hint of a nod. A friend of Beckworth's hired for extra protection.

Two decanters were placed in the middle of the table, one of wine and the other of whiskey, followed by a platter of cheese, bread, fruit, and meat pies. Beckworth grabbed one of the pies then pointed at the whiskey, holding up two fingers while he chewed.

The waiter nodded and poured two glasses of whiskey, setting a glass in front of Beckworth. He placed the second glass on a small silver tray and walked to Finn.

Finn accepted the glass with a smile and a nod. Once the

waiter and the servers left, he raised a brow. "I'm still not sure what you're up to."

Beckworth waved to the chair next to him. "Sit in this one. I'm testing a theory of what is called psychological intimidation." He glared up at Finn. "For the love of God, you're as bad as that woman of yours. They're just chairs." When Finn hadn't moved yet, Beckworth shook his head with an exasperated sigh. "After all this time, you still don't trust me."

Finn thought about the question. Did he trust him? If he did, why continue to needle him? In all honesty, he wasn't sure if it had anything to do with trust or just a routine the two of them had fallen into.

"It seems old habits die hard."

Beckworth laughed. "Well, at least you're honest." He ate a handful of grapes followed by a chunk of cheese.

The two men fell into a discussion regarding which was the better game—Hazard or Faro. Finn was arguing the merits of dice, their one glass of whiskey gone and a third of the food eaten, when the knock came.

"Showtime," Beckworth whispered.

29

———

When the door opened, Phillip entered, turning to allow four gentlemen to follow him in.

This was the first time Finn was able to study Reginald in daylight. Their previous encounters had always been in bleak cells. While the likeness to Beckworth was uncanny, Finn doubted he'd ever have a problem distinguishing the differences between the men. It had nothing to do with the slight scar over Reginald's upper lip or the fact he was thinner than his brother. His overall presence was a shadow in comparison to his half-brother. The duke must have been disappointed.

Finn scowled when he met Dugan's gaze. The animosity between the two of them was almost palpable, and Finn was positive the temperature in the room had risen a few degrees.

Beckworth ignored the hostility and graced the visitors with a congenial smile that Finn knew was as false as the stilted smile Reginald managed to squeeze out in return.

"Welcome, brother." Beckworth held out his hand to the two remaining chairs at the table. "It's been a long time since we've shared a meal. I couldn't remember if you were a whiskey man or preferred something more like wine."

Whether he meant it or not, the offer came across as a test. If Reginald asked for wine, it would appear he wasn't quite the man the rest of them were.

Dugan pulled out one of the chairs for Reginald and nodded at his men, who took the chairs Beckworth had placed against the wall. Finn noticed the chairs were placed far from the single exit.

Reginald sat as Phillip poured two more whiskeys and refreshed Beckworth's and Finn's glasses. When Reginald reached for his glass, he had to raise his arm to reach it. Beckworth's expression never changed and seemed to ignore Reginald's heated glare. Finn fought to hold in a chuckle as Dugan sat, ignoring the glass of whiskey. Though Dugan was taller than everyone in the room, he had to lift his gaze to meet Finn's eyes. How long had it been since Dugan ever had to look up to someone?

Now Finn understood Beckworth's game and had to admit he was impressed. Beckworth had arranged for shorter chairs before they'd arrived, allowing Finn and him to look down on their opponents. One simple change in logistics explained why Beckworth had always been a formidable foe. He was more of a strategist than Finn had given credit.

"Now that you've played the loving host, let's not mince words. I have a timetable." Reginald only spared Finn a small glance before meeting his brother's patient smile. He shifted in his seat. "I see you're still running with the riffraff."

Beckworth snorted and nodded at Dugan. "As are you."

Dugan didn't move, but Finn caught the frustration in the man's quick glance at Beckworth. If they hadn't been in a gentleman's club where guards would be close, Finn had no doubt Dugan would have tipped the table over to get to Beckworth.

"Tell me, brother." Beckworth leaned over the table. "What

right do you have moving into Waverly Manor? The estate never belonged to the duke."

Finn stiffened. They weren't here about his damn estate. He thought of kicking Beckworth under the table until he saw Reginald's face begin to mottle. Had he meant to get his brother mad?

"You didn't seem to be using it. And from what Dugan tells me, Father helped you gain that title. That's a good enough inheritance for me." Spittle flew from the man's mouth, forcing Beckworth to sit back.

"And the only thing keeping it for you is your dog." Beckworth gave Dugan a look that made the man seem as small as a beetle.

Dugan, to his credit, ignored the barb.

Finn laid a hand on Beckworth's arm. "The issue of your estate can be cared for in good time with a word to the local magistrate."

That drew the other men's attention. Finn smiled. "But that isn't what we're here about today, is it, gentlemen?"

The two brothers sat back and glared at each other. Then Beckworth flashed his evil viscount smile. "You're right as always, Captain Murphy. We have a trade to discuss."

Though surprised by Beckworth's use of his retired title, Finn held his expression as he laid out the trade. "So, let's get this done. None of us want to be here any longer than necessary. You have the Heart Stone, and we have the *Mórdha Stone Grimoire*. The book, though an historical treasure, is of no value to us. And we want the Heart Stone returned to its proper owner."

Dugan shifted in his chair, probably chafing to stand and regain his imposing stature. But he was well-trained, and knowing he couldn't intimidate from the current seating arrangement, took a different approach. He pushed his chair back and rested a leg across his knee, as if he knew the conversation was about to get interesting. It also had the effect of restoring some of his dominating presence.

Reginald eyed his brother, his lip curling in disgust. "Since it would be foolish to ask how you knew I had the Heart Stone in my possession, I'll simply ask why you really want it. I doubt it's for chivalrous reasons as you claim."

"Then we'd have to have that boring discussion as to why you need the grimoire." Beckworth already seemed bored. He ran a finger over the lip of his whiskey glass, the contents untouched. He appeared to be considering his words, his expression sad when he finally spoke. "I've never known you to meddle in the dark arts, brother, regardless of our father's bent ideas. However, if you think a book filled with a mad man's ravings will be worth your time and effort, then have at it. We don't care about the book. But the Heart Stone has sentimental as well as historic value."

Finn studied Beckworth. Where was he going with this? Telling Reginald about the Heart Stone and associating it with the possibility of monetary value seemed a risky approach.

Reginald scratched his waistcoat as he studied Beckworth. "You know nothing about the book. When did you become so knowledgeable in Celtic lore to assume it has so little value?" Reginald focused on the book, not the Heart Stone. After their years of separation, maybe Beckworth still knew how to push his brother's buttons.

Beckworth waved his hand in a dismissive gesture. "You know we're the ones who rescued the women from your dungeon months ago. Let's not beat about the bush. And since the man you tortured for blood sacrifice is sitting at this table, we'll just move on to the important matters. Maire has transcribed the entire book. She's found nothing but the scribbles of an old man locked in a dark cell for too long."

Finn flinched at Beckworth's confession that Maire had transcribed the book, but Reginald was smart enough to already know that.

"And you expect me to believe you on your word that the book is nothing but nonsense?" Reginald blew out a breath and leaned back in his seat. He absently scratched his waistcoat before turning to Beckworth. "It doesn't matter why I want the book. But instead of the Heart Stone, I'll pay you a tidy sum." He grinned. "Shall we say as a finder's fee?" When Beckworth and Finn simply stared at him, Reginald tried, quite unsuccessfully, to hide his irritation. He forced another sigh, as if what he was about to offer greatly pained him. "And I'll consider moving out of Waverly."

The silence grew until it felt like a heavy hand pressing on Finn's shoulder.

Then Beckworth laughed, almost doubling over in his mirth. Finn stared at him with the same puzzled expression as the other men. Trying to figure Beckworth out would be a lifetime's exploration.

"Oh, brother." Beckworth attempted to speak but fell into another short fit before he cleared his throat. He tried to look apologetic, but Finn doubted anyone believed it. "After all this time, you still know nothing about me. Because you think I'm no better than the rag you wipe your shoes with, you think I have no intelligence. And that has always been your mistake."

Finn caught Dugan's side glance at Reginald. Dugan might hate Beckworth, but he'd known him for years while they'd both been in the duke's service. He knew Beckworth was more than a pretty face who could pass for the duke's true heir.

Reginald lifted his chin. "You can't hide what this game is all about. Getting your precious manor back."

Beckworth reached into his pocket and pulled out an old timepiece. He rubbed a thumb over its engraved silver casing before tucking it away. "We have other places we need to be. So let's stop pissing over some piece of land with, I must say, quite a lovely garden." He glanced to Finn as if including him in an important topic. "I've always had a soft spot for well-cared-for gardens." He turned back to Reginald. "We know the book says nothing of the Heart Stone. Whatever magic you think you can produce has to do with the smaller stones, and we know you received one from Father."

Reginald's brow rose, and he glanced at Dugan.

"Oh, Dugan didn't say anything. He wouldn't." Beckworth nodded to the big man as if passing him a compliment. Dugan blinked. "Father was missing two small stones the last time I saw him at the monastery. I know where one is, but I have to assume the second one was given to Dugan to pass along to you."

Reginald rubbed his side, his eyes darting to a corner of the room before resettling on Beckworth.

"I mean..." Beckworth stopped to wave his hand around. "How else would you know anything about them?" He stared around the table, Finn included. "I'm sorry, but can anyone give me another explanation?" He waited a beat before blowing out an exasperated harrumph. "So, there you have it. The Heart Stone does nothing for whatever game you think you're about. The book has no meaning to us other than an interesting trip down someone's delusional journey. Let's set a time and place to make a trade. Last chance before we move on to other priorities." He waited another second before his expression matched the edge in his tone. "Like chatting with the magistrate about proper ownership of Waverly."

Beckworth sat back, clasped his hands over his stomach, and waited.

Finn wasn't sure what Beckworth was up to, but he seemed to know how to handle his brother. If he was bluffing, and Reginald called him on it, they might have just lost any chance to retrieve the Heart Stone.

Without warning, Reginald pushed his chair back and stood, surprising Dugan, who immediately stood, hand moving to his sword. Dugan's men, who'd grown bored, stumbled to follow suit.

Finn began to rise, but Beckworth stayed him. He relaxed into this seat but kept a hand on his sword.

Beckworth said nothing as he held his brother's gaze.

Reginald smiled and brushed his waistcoat. "Westminster. Tomorrow at noon." He nodded at Finn. "Just the two of you. If we see any of your men, the deal is off." He turned to the door, the other men walking backward as they followed. Then Reginald turned. "And my offer regarding Waverly is off the table. I'll take my chances with the magistrate." His smile was cold as ice as he turned and left the room.

Dugan followed behind him. The last two men, keeping their hands on their hilts, backed out before closing the door behind them.

The room quieted as Finn listened to the clomping boots fade down the hall. He glanced at Beckworth. A tic pulsed along his jaw, but that was Beckworth's only outward indication of his anger. After another minute, he seemed to wake from wherever his mind had taken him. He sat up, drank the glass of whiskey that had been sitting in front of him, and poured another.

He lifted his glass. "I'd say that was a rounding success!" Finn touched his glass to Beckworth's, and as one, they downed the amber liquid in one swallow.

"He seemed to know how to push your buttons regarding Waverly," Finn tested.

Beckworth grunted. "You have a sister. After years of separation, would you know how to get under her skin?"

Finn nodded. "Aye. She'd know how to push me if it had been twenty years."

Beckworth eyed him as he poured another round. "Be honest. You thought Reginald had me at the offer to give Waverly back."

It seemed silly to lie to the man after all they'd been through. "Aye, it gave me pause."

"Reginald can be hard to rattle. But he never responded well to needling, especially where Father was concerned. He always hated the constant reminder that Father never considered him good enough. Typical of the old man with both of his sons." Beckworth shook himself. "Besides, I already have men moving into Waverly. If Reginald tries to return, he won't find a welcome reception."

"There's only one problem. We don't know where Reginald is keeping the Heart Stone."

Beckworth's eyes twinkled. "Oh, but we do. He had it with him just now."

"How do you know?"

"Did you notice him constantly poking at his waistcoat?"

Finn nodded. "I thought it was an affectation." Had they only known Reginald would have the Heart Stone with him, maybe they could have brought more men and taken them by surprise. But there would have been too many people in the club who would have gotten hurt.

Beckworth nodded. "He'll keep the Heart Stone on him from now on, or very near. No farther than his bedside table if I were a betting man."

Finn smiled at him. "But you are a betting man."

Beckworth winked. "That I am."

30

AJ perched on the edge of her seat and fretted over the men as the carriage rolled away from Beckworth's safe house. When they entered a crowded Hyde Park, her worries melted away, overtaken by the ornate carriages, stylishly dressed pedestrians, and dozens of noblemen and ladies on horseback. Mary was the perfect tour guide, not only pointing out the sites but sharing names of different individuals as they passed. It didn't take long before AJ was lost in the earls, lords, and ladies this or that, but Mary was enjoying her position. AJ made a point not to spoil her good time. If all went as planned, this would be AJ's last day in London, and she had every intention of soaking up what she could.

Maire became the woman AJ first met at Waverly. Though she'd been confined under Beckworth's roof for almost two years, she hadn't been burdened by the stones. She laughed at Mary's colorful gossip and asked questions about places she recalled from the last time she'd been in London. The dark memories of her recent incarceration were shoved aside, at least for now.

After an hour of sightseeing, they stopped at a coffeehouse.

Surprisingly, or not, Mary ran into two ladies from her garden club who joined them for lunch. At first, AJ worried she'd have nothing to share in the conversation, but when one of the women mentioned meeting Chippendale, AJ became lost in the moment.

Two hours later, a disgruntled Fitz drove them back to Hensley's. None of the men were back, so Jamie posted guards at the front and back doors to monitor the streets. All was quiet.

The women gathered in the drawing room. Mary focused on her needlework and regaled AJ and Maire with updates on the other people they met at lunch and the late-season parties she'd been invited to. Maire and AJ grinned at Mary's nonstop chatter while they played chess. When AJ couldn't concentrate anymore, she taught Maire Go Fish. They laughed so hard that Mary stuffed her needlework away and joined them.

They were all giggling as they slapped cards down when Finn and Ethan entered the room.

"Here you all are. We thought you'd be huddled by the front door, peering out the windows." Ethan gave Maire a kiss on the cheek just as Mary called out, "Go fish." He gave Maire a wounded look before glancing to Finn. "I believe the women forgot all about us."

"So it would seem." Finn kissed AJ, his hand rubbing her back.

The warmth of his hand as it slid down her back made her forget the cards in her hands. "We had a lovely ride through the park. Though I doubt Fitz will be speaking with any of us anytime soon."

"Oh, I think he's recovered," Mary said. "He's in the kitchen devouring Cook's meat pies with an endless supply of ale. I wouldn't let him complain too long."

Maire studied the men. "You're in a good mood. I assume the meeting went as planned."

Finn nodded. "If the next phase goes as planned, this will be our last day in London."

Mary laid down her cards and jumped up. "I must see to preparations. We'll have one last party this evening." She hugged both women. "What a grand day we had. Now, try to return by seven. We'll have a late dinner, and rooms will be prepared for afterward." When a housemaid entered to check on refreshments, Mary grabbed her hand and hustled her down the hall.

"Let's take our leave." Finn led them to the front door. "Jamie and Fitz need to return to the *Daphne Marie*, and the rest of us could use a nap before our long evening."

When they arrived at Beckworth's, the butler advised the group the viscount had been called away. AJ went straight to her room and let Nellie help remove her dress and take down her hair.

Once her hair was back to normal, she shooed Nellie away. She was still removing other layers when Finn entered. She gave him a quick glance before returning to her task, fussing with the ties on her petticoat. She did a double take at Finn's expression as he crossed the room in three long strides, picked her up, and tossed her over his shoulder.

She giggled. "Stop. I'm not done." After he dumped her in the middle of the bed, she caught the heat in his gaze. "How did the meeting go?"

"Later." His growl made her forget everything as he quickly untied her petticoat and, with a practiced hand, removed all remaining pieces of clothing. She attempted to help him undress, but it was clear he wasn't in the mood to slow down.

They were still making up for lost time. His kiss on her neck made her shiver. When he moved down to a breast, she arched into him, running her hands through his hair. He wasn't in the mood for much foreplay, and she could work with that. When they joined, there was nothing in the world but the two of them.

Two hours and two rounds of passion later, she could barely lift her head to rest it on Finn's chest. If Dugan wanted to have an advantage, now would have been the time. She snorted at the thought.

"What was that for?" Finn asked. "You're not making fun of my lovemaking, are you?"

"Hardly." She hated to bring it up but needed to know. "How was the meeting?"

Finn went over the details, including Beckworth's trick with the shorter chairs. "I never truly understood his ability to strategize. I always assumed the duke directed his actions."

"There are always two sides to a person." AJ stretched then pressed the length of her body against him.

"Or three or four in his case."

"So, what's next?"

Finn clasped his hands behind his head and stared at the ceiling. "We have a lovely meal with good friends. Afterward, we say our goodbyes and move at midnight."

"Will Hensley be ready?"

"Aye. It's not Hensley I'm worried about."

"Dugan?"

She felt his nod and scooted closer.

Finn turned, wrapping her in his arms. "Don't fret. We stay alert and stick to the plan."

She didn't want to mention that something always seemed to interfere with their plans. "I just wish we were on our way already."

He kissed the top of her head. "Soon enough. Let's get what sleep we can. It's going to be a long night."

31

—————

Mary's party began as a melancholy evening for AJ. This would be the last night she'd see these friends who'd fought together, cried together, and would somehow succeed together. Her pensive mood disappeared once the men began sharing tall tales during dinner. She'd heard most of them before, but they sounded more outlandish than the last time she'd heard them. And that made her laugh twice as hard.

After dinner, everyone gathered in the drawing room to play card games and chess. When the group began gravitating toward the hearth to discuss the evening to come, Mary took that as her signal to retire. She hugged everyone, tears in her eyes, as she said her goodbyes. If all went well, everyone would be gone when she woke the next day.

AJ listened to the men for a while longer, but even with her growing anxiety, she could barely keep her eyes open. She needed an hour's rest, and midnight was approaching. She took Finn's hand and led him upstairs to the room Mary had prepared for them. Maire and Ethan follow them up, their soft voices vanishing when Finn closed their door.

She changed out of her dress and tucked it and her petticoats into her trunk. Finn dragged it into the hall where it could be retrieved by the footmen. Once they left for home, Maire could take what dresses she wanted and donate the others.

"Where are the rest of the men sleeping?" AJ crawled into bed, curling onto her side to watch Finn undress.

"Most of them are too restless to sleep, the others will use the sofas or the floor."

"Will Jamie and Fitz leave on the *Daphne Marie* tonight?"

Finn nodded. "And Lando too. Although this mission has the blessing of Langdon, Hensley thinks it would be wise for everyone to leave London by morning. Although Beckworth has talked Thomas into harboring at the safe house for a day before leaving for Hereford in groups of two." He slid next to AJ and pulled her close. "Now sleep. I need you bright-eyed in an hour."

————

She'd barely closed her eyes when Finn nudged her awake. The scent of coffee filled the air, and she thought maybe Finn had taken them through the fog as she slept. Wouldn't that be the easy way out? When she pried open an eyelid, a silver tray service called to her from the sideboard. Her legs, heavy as sodden logs, refused to move. One more hour of sleep would make all the difference.

Finn poured a cup and walked toward the bed. She smiled, ready for the coffee that was sure to waken her dead limbs. When he stopped and leaned against the far post before taking a sip, she quirked a brow. "You'll have to get up if you want a cup of this." He drank more and grinned. "I think it's the best I've tasted so far."

She threw a pillow at him before dragging her body out of bed, making a beeline for the coffee. Finn massaged her shoulders while she sat at the dressing table and brushed her hair.

"You're nervous." He kissed her temple. "Take a deep breath."

She did, then leaned into his massage. "I'll be better once we get moving."

He chuckled. "It's good to be nervous. It keeps you on your toes."

"It's not the nerves as much as the butterflies. I feel nauseous."

"That's normal too. Now drink another cup and get dressed." He stroked her shoulders before kissing the left one. "I think I'll miss the smell of rose perfume." He dodged her swat then grabbed his jacket. "We should go downstairs. It will take the edge off to be with the others."

AJ dressed in her pants and shirt, tucking her dagger in a pocket. When she picked up the necklace, she ran her fingers over the chip in the Heart Stone. Had Lily, the last keeper, somehow protected this Heart Stone by taking pieces of it to make earrings? Was it enough to protect Finn from disappearing from the future if they didn't steal back this century's Heart Stone? She kissed the wedding band that seemed to cling to the large stone before tucking the necklace into another pocket.

When they left the room, AJ noticed their trunk was gone, already loaded in Bart's coach along with their weapons store. Ethan and Maire were already downstairs talking with Hensley and Thomas. Soon, the rest of the team joined them, and, after Hensley's quick recap of the plan, they walked as a group to the waiting carriages.

They weren't expecting trouble once Reginald was caught, but the men had created alternate plans should something unexpected happen. Fitz and Lando would both take the box seat of Bart's coach. One to drive, the other to handle the muskets and pistols, of which Lando would have two of each. If they got into trouble, they wouldn't have time to reload, so AJ and Maire would be in the carriage, ready to provide cover fire.

Hensley attempted to assuage their fear with the notion that the constables and Langdon's presence would prevent Dugan from attempting an armed response. While AJ appreciated Hensley's words of assurance, no one else seemed to believe Dugan cared one ounce about the Bow Street Runners, the current London police force.

Finn and Beckworth mounted their horses and followed Hensley's coach toward the Mayfair district. Beckworth's informant had confirmed Reginald's residence at the Basil Street address earlier that day. Thomas and his men followed Hensley and would move into position once they got closer. Their sole task was to provide an extra layer of protection for their team. The Runners and Langdon would be on their own.

Jamie and Ethan would follow Bart's coach, which would be driven to a point just southeast of Reginald's residence. If Finn and Beckworth succeeded in retrieving the Heart Stone, they would meet up with Bart's coach. From there, they would drive into the darkness of Hyde Park and jump home.

As Bart's coach lurched forward, AJ positioned the quiver where she could easily grab arrows. Maire primed two muskets and two rifles. She also prepared four pistols in case the fighting got close or if Lando and Fitz needed them. The mission was a simple raid of Reginald's home, but no one took Dugan for granted anymore.

The streets were quiet. Once the women completed their tasks, AJ watched the city pass by as hooves beat a steady staccato on the cobbled street. Dim light filtered through the darkness from the oil street lamps. An occasional glow flickered in a house, candlelight from a night owl.

When the carriage stopped, Ethan opened the coach door. "We have at least an hour before anything happens but stay sharp. Jamie and I will stay close, but one of us will ride around the block every fifteen minutes."

When he closed the door, AJ and Maire lowered their curtains halfway, leaving enough space to monitor the alley and buildings. Fitz had parked in an alley, just a few yards from the main street. With the darkness, if someone was watching, they wouldn't be able to see the women.

AJ and Maire huddled close, sharing two blankets between them to ward off the chilly spring evening. She touched her bow, the smooth wood a gentle reassurance. Her ears strained for sound, but other than the light scrape of leather on wood that increased with the sway of the coach as the horses settled, everything was eerily quiet.

Maire squeezed her hand. "It won't be long."

AJ hovered deeper into the blanket. "I think this is going to be the longest hour of my life."

32

———

Hensley's coachman set a fast pace through the shadowy streets of London. The sound of hooves echoed off the buildings, and Finn was grateful for a clear night. A foggy London would be a dangerous place for tonight's mission. He swept his gaze from left to right in continuous motion as he trailed the carriage with Beckworth. If he hadn't been watching so intently, he might have missed the boot sticking out of the dark alleyway or the scurry of a youngster as he dashed from door to door. Were they Beckworth's informants or curious street people? He thought he caught Beckworth nodding at someone, but he wasn't sure. Thomas's men, if they were close, were well hidden.

The coach slowed as it entered the upscale neighborhood of the Mayfair district. After turning down several smaller streets, it turned into an alley and parked behind two other coaches and a group of men. Finn guessed they were a block or two from Reginald's residence, but he didn't know the streets as well as Beckworth.

Beckworth brought his horse next to Finn's. "I need to see the front of the house."

Finn nodded, but he waited until Hensley left the coach and was walking toward the men before he turned his horse to follow Beckworth. He found Beckworth at the end of the next alley. His expression, Finn was sure, would have been red with anger in the light of day. He recognized Beckworth's scowl.

"What's wrong?" Finn asked as he moved his horse to the corner of the building. He didn't need to hear Beckworth's response. Several men, most likely the police, scurried up and down the street, racing from shadow to tree in an attempt to be unseen. But there were too many of them. And rather than move slowly, which would be more difficult to spot, their quick movements were almost as obvious as a spotlight.

"All it will take is one of Dugan's men to glance out the window. The minute they see men darting about, they'll run." Beckworth's statement only confirmed Finn's earlier thought.

Beckworth dismounted and paced back and forth. On his second pass, he stopped and stared into the shadows of the building across the street. He tapped his left shoulder with his right hand, almost as if he were brushing away errant dust. A signal? Finn wasn't sure until a small figure slid through the shadows with more grace than any of the men still dashing about.

When the tiny lad reached them, he smiled up at Beckworth. "Yes, sir."

Beckworth crouched so he was eye level with the boy. He leaned in and whispered something. The boy nodded and took off down the street toward Reginald's residence, cutting through the neighbor's shrubbery.

Finn raised a brow.

Beckworth shrugged. "Insurance."

Without another word, Beckworth mounted his horse and led Finn back the way they'd come. Hensley was still speaking with Langdon, and Finn noticed the signs of an argument. He knew from Hensley's rigid posture, his head bent as if in deference to the man speaking, that his mentor was angry. Rarely did Hensley rant and rage. His anger was quiet, and when Finn glanced at Beckworth, the man was pacing again.

An icy foreboding slithered up his spine. An itch that told him they'd need another plan. A sixth sense quite similar to the one he'd felt when he'd searched Reginald's bedroom at Waverly with Beckworth and Maire.

Hensley walked away from the group of men and returned to the coach where Finn and Beckworth had tied their horses.

Beckworth didn't wait to lodge his complaints. As soon as Hensley was within earshot, Beckworth laid into him. "Did you see all the men scurrying about the street as if the May Fair was still in full swing?"

When Hensley reached them, he grabbed Beckworth's shirt and pulled him toward the coach. "Lower your voice." He released Beckworth. "I'm afraid it's worse than that," Hensley grumbled, clearly as angry as Beckworth. "Langdon had planned on using the Runners, but communications were crossed, and the magistrate sent men from the local precinct instead."

Finn shook his head. The Bow Street Runners were London's elite police force. They would have made a better choice if Langdon insisted in taking the lead. But either way, he or Beckworth had to get to Reginald first. If that was possible anymore. "And what is our role?"

Hensley leaned against the coach, and, for the first time, Finn noted the dark circles, the thinning hair, and sallow skin. His friend was tired and showing signs of age. He should have noticed it long before now, and a sadness took hold in the knowledge that, after tonight, he'd probably never see his friend again. He would ask Ethan to watch over him. To keep him out of the action. Mary would be lost without him.

Beckworth's angry retort shook Finn out of his musing. "We came all this way just to look at the bloody stone to confirm its authenticity?"

His voice was more a screech, and Hensley glanced behind them to see if Langdon or any of the police had heard them.

"We could have done that in the morning." Finn kept his tone calm. "It wasn't Langdon's idea. This was the magistrate's doing."

Beckworth flailed his arms about in frustration, but he lowered his voice when he spoke to Hensley. "Sorry, mate. I can see you're as upset as the rest of us. But, at this point, I'd be surprised if Reginald is still in residence."

Hensley sighed. "I suspected the same, but we'll know soon enough. They're getting ready to go in."

The three of them joined the larger group but kept to themselves as they waited on the opposite side of the alley. The police had formed two groups and were stationed at what appeared to be two houses down from the target residence. The view from the alley was clear, but from Finn's perspective, it was difficult to tell how close to the residence they actually were.

The police began to move as running footsteps approached from behind Finn. He reached for his sword, but Beckworth stayed his hand.

"He's a friend."

The man stopped and planted a hand on the wall to steady himself as he caught his breath. "Sorry, sir." The man continued to heave, and Beckworth laid a hand on the man's shoulder.

"Take slow, deep breaths." Beckworth glanced at Finn and Hensley. Another shoe was about to drop.

After a second, the man stood on his own. His clothing was

tattered but clean. He was in good shape from what Finn could tell, and he must have run a distance to be so out of breath.

The man shook his head. "Johnny said the big man has left. He had a score of men with him. We've signaled the other watchmen, or I'd have been here earlier."

"And?" Beckworth waited patiently, though he tugged on a sleeve.

The man peered over their shoulders, possibly noticing the police for the first time. If they bothered him, he didn't show it. "They appear to be headed for the docks."

"Damn." Hensley's tone was a mixture of anguish and defeat.

The sound of something striking wood drifted down the street, followed by shouts. The police were pounding on the door for entrance. All nice and legal, but would do nothing to prevent someone from sneaking out through the back garden.

"Did they put men at the back of the house?" Finn asked.

Hensley shook his head, then turned to look down at a slip of a boy who tugged at Beckworth's pants. No one had noticed his approach.

Finn finally understood Beckworth's use of the children. In AJ's time, it would be unthinkable to use children in such a fashion. And he'd understood Ethan's appalled view, but these children lived a different life. They were put to work early in factories and stores. Many went hungry. Like the man who'd just brought them news of Dugan, the urchin's clothing was old and many times repaired. But the filth wasn't from not being washed on a regular basis. Streaks of sticky red jam on the front of his shirt where he'd wiped his hands after eating a pastry and mud on his knees from crawling through fences were markers of any boy his age, regardless of the era.

Beckworth knelt in front of him again. "What's up, young master?"

The boy smiled, and Finn noticed the missing front tooth.

"Harry was on his way to you. Says a fancy-dressed man was helped into a coach with six riders. They left not ten minutes ago."

"Good job." Beckworth fished in his pocket for a coin and handed it to the lad. "You're done for the evening." The boy tucked the coin in his pocket and started to back away, but Beckworth caught his jacket. "You be sure both your mum and sister get something to eat." The boy nodded with a solemn expression. "Good boy, now off with you."

Within seconds, the boy disappeared.

"They have a ship." Finn hadn't considered that. Had that been Reginald's idea from the beginning? Or had the threat of a magistrate to determine Waverly's rightful owner make him change his plans? A glance at Beckworth made Finn think the latter.

"If he doesn't expect to get the grimoire back, he'll need to make do with the Heart Stone." Hensley seemed to have caught a second wind. His features brighter now that the game was back in his hands. The police and Langdon would come up empty. "From what Maire has shared with us, he'll either need an incantation or the torc for the Heart Stone to have any power."

Beckworth considered that. "Reginald wouldn't have any idea how to do that."

"But Dugan would." Finn hated this. Hated what he'd have to tell AJ. "If they're heading for the docks, they'll be going to the monastery."

Hensley's grim expression said he agreed. "I'd prefer to have them stopped before they left England. But if not." He didn't have to finish the statement.

"What will you tell Langdon?" Finn was glad he wasn't the one to speak with the earl.

Hensley harrumphed. "The truth. That the police made a mess of it."

Finn raised a brow.

Hensley lifted his chin and squared his shoulders. It wasn't until he brought himself up to his full height that Finn realized Hensley had been shrinking into himself with each snippet of bad news. "If you bring me the Heart Stone, Langdon will let all other matters drop."

Beckworth gave Hensley an odd smile. "And Reginald?"

Hensley stared at Beckworth for what seemed like minutes before glancing toward Langdon. He returned Beckworth's mad grin with a smirk. "I'll leave it to your best judgment."

Beckworth nodded with a light in his eyes that should have made Finn shudder. But whatever Beckworth had in store for his half-brother wouldn't be nearly enough.

Finn grabbed Hensley's arm and pulled him in for a hug. "This will be the last we see of each other, my friend."

Hensley held on tight, and Finn found himself blinking rapidly. This was the man who'd given Finn a purpose—a fresh start in life. He was the second father any man would be proud of. "You'll always have a home should you ever need to return."

Finn hugged him just as fiercely. "I doubt it will happen, but it's good to know you'll always be here."

Their hug ended too soon, and when Finn stepped back, he saw Hensley was working hard to keep his own tears in check. "It's been a pleasure working with you. Once we have the Heart Stone secured, I'll make sure it finds its rightful place." He glanced to where Langdon now paced. "It might be a couple of years from now, but the keepers will have their start."

Hensley turned to Beckworth. "And don't be a stranger when you return. I have a feeling we could do some good work together."

Beckworth waved him off. But the spark in his gaze told

Finn, and most assuredly Hensley, that he didn't think it was that bad of an idea.

The men stared at each other for another moment, then Finn nodded to Hensley. "We need to go."

Hensley shook his hand one last time. "God speed, my son."

33

———

AJ startled and woke, wiping a small amount of drool from her lips. She'd nodded off again. That was twice since she and Maire began their watch vigil. If you stared at the shadows long enough, they shifted. Whether it was a person or her imagination was anyone's guess. The nauseous feeling returned, and hovering in the coach was becoming an unbearable confinement. If she only had a thermos of hot coffee. She snorted. Her first stakeout—eighteenth-century style.

"What's so funny?" Maire asked. She stretched and leaned out the window, probably to let the cool night air wake her.

"I think I've been staring at too many shadows." AJ repositioned herself. "Isn't it taking them a long time?"

"It hasn't been an hour yet. They'll be back soon."

The words were barely out of her mouth before the sound of hooves drowned her out. They were coming fast. The women grabbed their weapons at the same time Lando pounded on the roof.

"They seem to be in a hurry." AJ was wide awake now. She crouched, bow and arrow in hand.

Maire rested the rifle on the window. "I don't see anything.

Wait. Two riders."

AJ raised her bow.

"It's Ethan and Jamie." Maire's voice sounded relieved.

A moment later, Ethan leaned in through her window. "We have word from one of Beckworth's men. Reginald and Dugan are on the run. They're headed for the docks."

"Is that who's coming?" AJ asked. More horses were headed toward them.

Ethan stepped back to look, but Lando would have signaled if there was a problem. He shook his head and leaned back in. "It's Finn."

Four horses stopped, and Finn almost leaped from the saddle. Thomas and one of his men took positions to watch the street. Beckworth nodded to Jamie before turning his horse and racing off in the opposite direction.

Finn leaned through AJ's window and gave her a quick kiss before telling the group the events at Reginald's residence. "If they're headed for the docks, they have a ship."

"There must be a hundred ships in port." Ethan rubbed his jaw before running his hand through his hair. A typical sign he didn't know what to make of the situation. "Maybe it doesn't matter."

Finn grunted in agreement, but Maire was the one who put their thoughts into words. "Because we know where they're going."

AJ sighed. Of course. It only made sense they would end up where they had before. "The monastery."

"Aye. Beckworth is riding ahead to ensure we have a safe route to the ship. We need to move fast. It will be a harrowing ride." His gaze met AJ's, and he grinned. "Quite the honeymoon we're having."

She kissed him. Hard and fast before sitting back, her own grin matching his. She was pretty sure she was either in shock or had simply gone mad, but a laugh gurgled its way up. She stifled it to a snort. "It does have the magic of being unique."

Finn and Ethan stepped back and mounted their horses. Finn turned his horse in a circle, scanning the shadows if she had to guess. A figure stepped out of a doorway and pointed to the left. Finn nodded and led the way. Fortunately, the coach had been facing the correct direction.

All they had to do was get to the docks. It was the middle of the night in the heart of London. This should be the easy part.

———

The carriage sped through the narrow streets. Once again, the heavy pounding of hooves on the cobblestones would wake anyone within a hundred yards of them. The coach lurched to one side as they took a corner, barely slowing down. AJ tumbled and slammed into Maire, who pushed her upright and back toward her window.

AJ forced her fisted hand to release the arrow. She would poke someone's eye out. Probably her own. The ride to the dock was as terrifying as Finn predicted, and she swallowed the rising bile. At least she wasn't bored anymore.

The ride seemed to be never-ending, and she'd been bracing for the sound of a musket since they left the safety of the alley. When they turned the next corner, AJ grabbed the edge of the window, her fingers digging in as if she were hanging from a boulder on one of her climbs, but this time she stayed upright. She glimpsed one of the riders behind them—Jamie. He road low and kept looking over his shoulder. The briny smell of dead fish and the increased chill in the air from the river forced a sigh of relief. They were almost there.

The sound of a musket split the night air, clear as a bell above the sound of horses. Another shot rang out. Moments later, responding fire barked from above, the sound echoing through the coach. She guessed it must have been Lando as the smell of the spent powder reached her nose.

The coach increased speed, and AJ fought harder to hold on. Additional horses caught up to the coach, but AJ couldn't tell whether they were friend or foe until she noticed a familiar face —one of Thomas's men. The explosion from Maire's rifle was deafening. She turned in time to see Maire drop the rifle and pick up a musket. Maire braced her legs against the opposite bench and let her body sway with the movement of the coach.

AJ couldn't brace the same way and still use the bow. She dropped to her knee and pushed back against the seat, her other leg braced awkwardly against the opposite bench. Ignoring the discomfort, she nocked an arrow and braced an elbow against the window as she sighted a target.

With the shadows and intermittent light, it was difficult to see anyone, so she focused on the areas where men might be positioned—doorways, alleyways, and the roof of buildings. And the latter was where she spotted the spark from a flintlock. The man stood on a low roof and appeared to be reloading a ball into the muzzle.

AJ tracked him, getting a feel for the bounce of the carriage. She had little time before the coach moved out of range. When the coach swayed to the left, she loosed the arrow. The man jerked back, but whether from her arrow or someone else's shot, she'd never know. She nocked another arrow.

The ship had to be close.

———

Finn kicked his horse and glanced to his right. Thomas kept pace with him, looking over his shoulder to the coach some twenty yards behind them. The coach barely fit through the narrow alleys, and Finn didn't want to get too far ahead of it. He had no false illusions that Dugan had left men behind to slow them down. Beckworth's informants had moved to strategic positions to guide their way to the docks. Hidden in the shadows every few blocks, they stepped into the light long enough to point the way before blending into the darkness.

Two calendar years had passed since he'd been in London, but with the time jump, it had only been six months. He knew the town and most of its backstreets. But with his constant surveillance for Dugan's men and Beckworth's indirect route to the docks, he had to admit he wasn't sure where they were in relation to the ship. When their path twisted down an alley then broke out into a wider thoroughfare, the strong scent of the Thames tickled his nose, and he knew exactly where he was.

From the left, a dozen horses raced toward him. At first, he thought them Dugan's men until he saw Beckworth wave to a young boy, another one of his street urchins. Beckworth must have some of Thomas's men with him. They were close now, only several more blocks before reaching the ship, but they were far from safe.

The first shot reverberated off the stone buildings, the sound thunderous in the alley. It was followed by another. Finn glanced over his shoulder for a split second to see Lando turning to fire at someone on a roof. The street combusted into a multitude of shots, and to his right, a man dropped in a doorway. Unsure whether it was one of Beckworth's friends or Dugan's men, Finn rode on. The only thing that would save them from the ambush was the speed of their travel. If they slowed, they'd be easier targets.

Up ahead, a man appeared out of the shadows and grabbed a man raising a pistol. He jabbed something into the man's side before releasing him to sink to the ground. Then they were gone. Finn waited for the blinding heat of a ball to pierce him, but nothing came—yet. When he glanced back again, he spotted an arrow fly from the carriage, but they were moving too fast for him to see where it landed. He clamped down his growing fear for AJ. He had to trust the women knew what they were doing.

The coach slowed long enough to take a turn down a steep street leading to the dock where the *Daphne Marie* waited for them. Halfway to their destination, a group of men waited. They raised their muskets, but only two men got a shot off before they were ambushed from behind. Beckworth, and the half of Thomas's men he had with him, raced ahead to engage while the other half of Thomas's men, who'd been hiding along the docks came up behind Dugan's men. The coach never stopped as it crashed through anyone not smart enough to jump out of the way.

Lando fired again, and if Finn counted correctly, that was his last musket. In confirmation of his thought, Lando drew his sword and jumped from the box moments before the coach pulled even with the ship. Lando leaned into the coach and shouted something before running back toward the group of men.

Fitz jumped down as soon as two men appeared to grab the horse's bridles. Finn turned his horse so his back was to the coach. He fired at a man who raced from the shadows toward the men holding the horses. The man dropped before he made it ten paces. He glanced back up the street where the fighting slowed. Finn gauged Dugan had left almost a third of his men behind. If it wasn't for Beckworth's informants steering them to the ship, the outcome might have been quite different. Though they weren't out of it yet.

He scanned the area and noted the sailors running down the gangway, their pistols raised as they ran for the coach. When they surrounded it, Finn dismounted and tied his horse to the carriage. Fitz barked for men to get the trunks before he turned to engage a man who'd slipped through the lines.

Finn opened the carriage door to find AJ and Maire still holding their weapons, their eyes wide with a mix of fear and determination. He gave AJ a swift kiss, happy to see both women unharmed.

"Put everything back in the duffels, but keep a pistol with you. I'll be back in a minute." He slammed the door shut and ran toward the group of men but stopped after a few short steps.

The few men left turned toward the ship, their swords still out but lowered. The fighting was done. Ethan and Thomas were still on horseback. They rode close with a third horse between them, a man slumped over the neck of the horse. When they passed under a light, Finn's heart clenched.

Jamie.

"Fitz." Finn's voice boomed above the residual noise, and the man came running. He arrived as the horses stopped next to Finn.

While Ethan and Fitz helped lower Jamie to the ground, Finn yelled over his shoulder to the sailors surrounding the carriage. "Get Michelson." A man immediately ran for the ship.

Finn scanned the area, but the shooting had stopped. Thomas's men mingled with the sailors as they moved to circle around Jamie's prone figure. Then AJ and Maire were there.

"You need to get to the ship. It's not safe here," Finn told AJ. As usual, she ignored him to move closer.

When they rolled Jamie onto his back, several of the men winced. Blood soaked his shirt.

"Gunshot or sword?" Fitz asked, his voice steady though Finn saw the man's hand tremble.

"Shot. Someone on the roof, I think." Ethan stared at Finn.

Maire squeezed next to Jamie. She pulled at the shirt, but it was so matted, it stuck to his skin. Finn searched his sister's face, and when she locked her gaze on his, she shrugged. "I need to see how extensive it is. But he's already lost a lot of blood."

Several sailors pushed through the crowd of men, one of them Michelson, the closest thing the ship's crew had for a doctor.

"Get him on the ship. His cabin," Finn barked.

Before the men could pick him up, Jamie roused and reached out to Finn. Finn grabbed the hand, which was cold, bloody, and of little strength. Jamie's head turned. He couldn't seem to focus, but then his eyes cleared as his darting gaze froze on Finn. "The ship is yours."

"No," Finn immediately responded. "Fitz will care for her until you heal."

He tried to shake his head but couldn't. "Ship in danger." His hand fell away.

"He's right, boss." Fitz held Jamie's other hand but turned his stern expression to Finn. "We have to get through the narrows and who knows how many blockades before we reach the monastery. I'm better served as your first. You know that."

"We need to go," Ethan urged.

AJ squeezed his hand. "Just until Jamie's well."

Finn stared at the crowd. Fitz was one of the best sailors Finn had the pleasure to sail with, but he never wanted the responsibility of captain. Jamie and Fitz were right, he was the best choice. When AJ squeezed his hand again, he smiled at her and nodded.

In an instant, all else faded except the safety of the ship, its crew, and its passengers. "Get Jamie on the ship. Raise anchor and set sails. Rig them for speed, gentlemen."

His voice hadn't carried far, nor had it been loud, but men scattered. Four men lifted Jamie, and Maire followed them. Ethan and Thomas shook hands before Ethan raced after Maire.

Thomas shook Beckworth's hand before turning to Finn.

"How many did you lose?" Finn asked.

"Two. Three others are wounded but should survive."

Beckworth shook Thomas's hand. "Take your wounded back to the safe house. Stay inside for a few days until this all blows over and your men are healthy enough to ride." Beckworth waved toward a building, and a young boy scurried to him. "This is Winston. He'll lead the way."

"Thank you." He gave Beckworth a long perusal. "I didn't think I'd find myself liking you."

Beckworth laughed. "Don't worry. It won't last long."

Thomas gave him a rare smile before shaking Finn's hand. "Do you want us to go with you?"

Finn shook his head and placed a hand on Thomas's shoulder. "You and your men have done more than we could have ever asked for."

"For the safety of the Crown, and whatever the earl asks of us. God speed, Murphy."

"Give the earl our thanks."

Thomas lifted the boy onto his saddle and mounted behind him. Without another word, he rode out, his men following as they took a small side street and disappeared from sight.

Finn glanced at Beckworth. "I expect you'll be wanting passage."

Beckworth smiled. "I have a score to settle."

"And Waverly?"

"I've tied up loose ends, and the rats have been cleared out. This time it will be safe until my return."

"Your men and urchins?"

"They've been paid well and have already disappeared into the shadows. As have several of Dugan's men, but they'll be too busy licking their wounds and hiding from the police."

"Then let's get aboard."

34

AJ studied the men as they moved about the ship. She didn't know the time, but dawn was still a few hours away. Fitz, easily recognizable in the dim lantern light, watched the men work the rigging. Finn studied the sails, shouting out commands as he guided the *Daphne Marie* down the Thames to the Channel. He'd once told her he disliked this river—overcrowded with ships and always a slow sail back and forth to open waters.

The ship was anything but slow now. She'd heard Fitz's warning about setting all the sails, but Finn had shaken his head.

"If Dugan's ship was ready to sail, he's already put too much distance between us. We're lucky to have caught a bit of wind. If there's a chance we can make the monastery before him, we have to try."

Fitz had no argument for his captain's reasoning. He'd performed his duty as first mate, providing a valid concern to his captain. He never questioned the order again.

AJ wanted to check on Jamie but decided to wait until the men settled into their tasks. Maire was with Jamie, and there would be nothing more to be done until she had him cleaned up and assessed the damage. The chilly air became unbearable as the ship picked up speed. She huddled in a bed of spare canvas that was out of the wind. She wrapped her arms around her legs and rested her head on her knees.

Twenty minutes later, Lando called out, "Port side, Captain."

Finn and Fitz both turned to their left. When Finn moved to the railing, AJ popped up to see what caught their eye. The only thing to see was the open area along the wooden boardwalk. And maybe the empty berth was sign enough in an otherwise crowded dock. Men moved about the pier, but they were too far away to make out faces. AJ took the opportunity to step next to Finn. He never took his eyes from the dock, but he sensed her presence and wrapped an arm around her.

"Do you think that was where Dugan had a ship waiting?" she asked.

"Maybe. But it's not unusual for a ship to be leaving now. We're almost at high tide. But if it was his ship, this is good news."

Lando grunted in agreement.

Finn glanced up at the sails. "Tighten up the foremast topsail, gentlemen."

Fitz barked an order for the men to trim the sails.

"It's good news because we might be faster and can catch him?" AJ scratched her nose and wished she had the binoculars that were packed in her trunk.

"As long as he doesn't have more cannon than us." Lando pulled out his spyglass and, leaning against the railing, scanned the dock.

Finn laughed. "Only you can dampen my spirits, old friend." He slapped Lando on the back. "What do you see in that glass of yours?"

"Not much." Lando kept his hand steady as he swept from left to right and back again. "Wait." He stopped and waited, then his lip turned up in a sneer. He handed the glass to Finn. "Twenty paces from the warehouse on the left."

Finn raised the spyglass and spent a moment finding the mark. "That confirms it."

"How do you know?" AJ asked, feeling like an idiot with all her questions.

"Their clothes." He passed her the glass.

Her experience working in the crow's nest allowed her to easily track to the spot where three men stood talking and smoking, if the tiny red glows were any indication. She'd recognize the uniform of Dugan's guards anywhere, having watched them long enough while hiding in tree branches.

"So now we know Dugan had a ship waiting after all." AJ handed the glass back to Lando.

Finn rubbed her back then glanced down at her. "You're cold." He kissed her forehead. "It would be better if you stayed below for now."

AJ nodded. "I want to check on Jamie."

She caught his worry and squeezed his hand. "It wasn't your fault."

"I know." He cupped her face and gave her a longer kiss. "We could use your help with the galley. Something quick and warm for breakfast. I need Cook's help up here." He took hold of her shoulders, his expression serious. "Try to get a nap if you can."

She nodded, leaving him and Lando at the railing as she made her way belowdecks.

———

The galley was quiet as AJ scurried through it on her way to the captain's quarters. When she knocked and heard Ethan's responding call, she opened the door to a battlefield horror. The room stank of blood and vomit. Two lanterns had been placed close to the bed where Maire sat tending Jamie. The sleeves of her dress had been pushed up to just under her elbows and were streaked as red as her arms were. AJ had no doubt the front of her dress was in worse shape. A pile of bloody rags filled a bucket, and Jamie's stained clothing had been dumped next to it.

Ethan, sitting on a stool on the other side of the bed, leaned over to watch Maire work. He was in the best position to restrain Jamie if he woke. The pain from Maire digging around in his wound would be unbearable.

AJ stepped closer to see what Maire was doing. "How's it going?"

"I've had a difficult time getting the ball out, which has made the wound larger." Maire grunted then dropped something into a pan that made a metallic sound.

AJ peered over Maire's shoulder. A misshapen ball rolled to one side of the pan before slowing to a stop in congealing blood. "Is that the only one?" AJ didn't know much about bullets in her century, but she knew some could fragment, creating massive internal injuries. But she thought shot of this century would stay intact, and the evidence before her seemed to prove her assessment. She remembered Adam discussing flintlocks with Finn. The shot itself wasn't necessarily what killed a person, unless it hit a vital organ or the person bled out. The slower death came from infection caused by other materials like dirty bits of a shirt that remained behind.

Maire began threading a needle to stitch the opening. "AJ, could you see if there's some whiskey in the galley? Ethan couldn't find any in here."

AJ was almost out the door when Ethan called, "Bring the bottle." She held back a smile. A nip of whiskey might be what she needed to stop the chills threatening to overtake her. The whiskey was in the storeroom where she'd seen Jamie stow it the last time she'd been on board.

When she returned and handed Maire the bottle, she asked, "Should I warm some water?"

Maire shook her head. "I don't think it will matter." She poured a healthy amount of whiskey into a bowl of clean water then handed the bottle to Ethan. "Can you find any more clean rags? I want to rinse out the wound, and I'd like to keep the bedding as dry as we can."

AJ glanced around and determined the towels had all been used. She threw open trunks until she found Jamie's shirts. She grabbed three of them and raced back to Maire, who nodded at Ethan.

He'd just taken a long swallow of whiskey and set the bottle on the ground. He scooted his chair closer to Jamie and waited. Maire poured a few drops of the whiskey and water mixture into Jamie's wound then sat back. Jamie shifted and began to roll away before Ethan pushed him back, forcing his shoulders down.

Maire drenched the wound as AJ did her best to soak up the draining red liquid. Jamie continued to struggle, shifting his hips and kicking his legs. Ethan couldn't hold his legs and keep his shoulders in place, so AJ threw the shirts down and jumped on his legs until his struggles lessened.

"The worst is over. At least for a while." Maire picked up a needle and thread.

AJ picked up the shirts, tossing them toward the stack of Jamie's soiled clothes. Then she stood behind Maire, ready to jump on Jamie's legs again. She couldn't imagine him sleeping through the stitching.

When Maire began stitching the wound, AJ offered a suggestion. "Don't stitch the wound all the way closed. Leave a small opening so the wound can drain."

Maire lifted a brow. "I didn't realize you had medical training."

AJ nudged her shoulder. "Our family has had its share of accidents." She glanced at Ethan before speaking to Maire. "I still have antibiotics left. We should get them started. Then I'll feel better about you closing the wound in a couple days if it's still warranted."

Maire considered AJ's direction. After a minute, she nodded. "I agree."

If Ethan had anything to say, he kept it to himself.

Maire's stitches were quick and neat, and Jamie reacted with only a groan or two. AJ smirked. Maire's excellence with stitches must have come from all those months at Waverly with nothing to do but needlework.

Once Maire began bandaging the wound, AJ glanced around the room. "I'll take the towels out and start cleaning the room. Where's Michelson?"

"Finn needed him, and he couldn't do anything more than what I've already done."

"Makes sense to me. Do either of you know where our trunks are?"

Ethan pointed toward the door. "They should be in the galley."

That would make sense. AJ hadn't bothered to look when she'd raced through, focused on Jamie and finding the whiskey. She nodded then picked up the bucket of bloody rags. She hefted the bucket through the galley and placed it on the floor near the stairs to the deck. The trunks sat against the far wall of the galley. AJ located two additional lanterns to lighten up the room.

She dug through her trunk to find the antibiotics then set a pot of water to heat. When she returned to the cabin and handed Maire the drugs, she gave Jamie a concerned glance. He was asleep, or more likely passed out, and his skin was deathly pale. She grabbed the bucket of vomit, lugging it upstairs to dump. The rest of the bloody clothing joined the bucket of rags before they were taken upstairs. Fitz directed her to the best place to carry out her tasks. The next hour was spent hauling water back and forth from the galley. After the clothes and rags were washed, she hung them to dry. She refilled the bucket with newly warmed water and took it to Jamie's cabin to begin cleaning the floor.

Maire moved to the galley with her box of herbs and antibiotics to concoct her magical brews. Ethan took the bucket and rag from AJ and shooed her out of the room. After laying out her herbs, Maire added two drops of an oil to a warm bowl of water and asked AJ to take it to the cabin. With the room freshly cleaned, the soft aroma of lavender and chamomile slowly replaced the earlier stench.

Jamie's face was still pale from the loss of blood, but he appeared to be sleeping peacefully. Ethan had returned to his stool and was reading a book.

She put another kettle of water over the fire to make porridge and coffee. The stores had been filled while the *Daphne Marie* had been at port, so AJ added cheese and day-old bread to the breakfast menu. When everything was ready, she dragged herself upstairs to find Lando.

"Breakfast is ready."

Lando glanced up from his task. AJ wasn't sure what he'd been doing. She wasn't familiar with the tools he held in his hands. She was going to ask when she noticed his unspoken question.

She squeezed his arm. "He's resting. The ball's been removed and the wound cleaned. Maire is working on tinctures. He's in the best of care."

Lando gulped in air like a fish out of water. Then he nodded and began relieving men from their duties to eat.

AJ searched the deck for Finn and found him at the bow, keeping an eye on the river as dawn approached. She wanted to stand by his side, but he would be reviewing strategies and considering contingencies. He deserved the time to do what he did best.

But she wasn't ready to leave, so she leaned against the rigging and watched her husband. One hand braced on the railing, his hair blown back by the wind. His back was straight, his head held high as he focused on whatever was coming.

She grinned.

Captain Murphy was back.

35

———

The *Daphne Marie* approached the mouth of the Thames as a gentle fog rolled in from the Channel. By the time they reached open waters, the air had grown thick with the dawn's silver mist, forcing Finn to reduce sails. The next two hours were run silently as lead lines were monitored and sailors became spotters, waiting for sight or sound of another ship.

Finn grew frustrated by the delay even though he knew Dugan's ship would have no better luck in the fog. He worried about Jamie. The last time he'd seen AJ, which had been before the fog, she assured him that his young friend was sleeping and there was no sign of infection. All they could do was wait, and he inwardly thanked AJ for the hundredth time. Without the antibiotics, he doubted he would have survived his injuries. And now she was quite likely saving Jamie's life as well.

He'd always been known for being a patient man when required. But this time, he itched to be moving. With his growing temper in check, he made another pass around the deck. He double-checked the rigging and the sails, issued an occasional order, and patted men on the back for their good work. Jamie had mastered Finn's training. His crew worked well together. Many of the men had been commissioned by Finn when he'd been captain of the *Daphne*, but he saw an equal number of new faces. Of those, he had to nod in appreciation of Jamie becoming his own man with his own way of doing things. The *Daphne Marie* couldn't be in better hands.

When the weak spring sun began to break through the fog, he issued the orders to unfurl the sails. The mist disappeared quickly, and his earlier frustrations faded with it. The ship picked up speed, and Finn could sense the relief of the men as they continued their normal tasks.

The warning whistle sounded three hours later. Finn spun around to port, searching the horizon. Lando was next to him in an instant, his glass scanning the water before he handed it to Finn.

"Three points off the port bow. Two ships." Lando braced his arms on the railing as Finn took in the scene.

They had barely put the Dover narrows behind them without sight of any Royal Navy. Though this close to English shores, they had more to worry about from the local British patrol who monitored the coast.

A flash of fire followed by smoke was soon accompanied by the blast of the cannon as the sound finally reached them. A warning shot between the two ships. Finn was about to hand the glass back to Lando and call an order to maintain a westward heading when he caught sight of the flag on one of the ships.

"Of all the luck." Finn swore under his breath. "It's the *Gypsy Runner.*"

Lando took the glass from Finn. After several minutes, he tucked the glass into his coat. "It looks like a patrol ship who's caught her. The *Gypsy* is running heavy. I don't think she'll be able to outrun it."

Another whistle blew, and Finn glanced up to his lookout. He pointed in the same general direction as the two ships. Finn leaned into Lando. "Get AJ and tell her to bring her glasses. Hurry."

He yelled for Fitz, who was beside him in a heartbeat. "Parallel their course and match their speed."

"Aye, Captain." Then he was off, shouting orders followed by an occasional whistle of his own.

Finn considered his options. The most obvious, they could stay their course. He had one mission—Reginald, Dugan, and the Heart Stone. But his instincts as a captain tugged at him, forcing a riskier evaluation of options. Valentin, the *Gypsy*'s captain, had recently smuggled him out of France in his race to get to England and find AJ, and they had a long history of having each other's back.

Feet raced across the deck, and her hand clutched his arm. Her simple touch grounded him. "What can I do?"

"I need to know what's going on. We have two ships preparing for battle and a third closing in."

AJ handed him the glasses, and he tucked them into the pocket of his coat before grabbing a ratline. Though it had been several months since he climbed the sails, his feet guided him easily as he reached the top of the foremast topsail. He braced himself and, not bothering to check if anyone watched him, studied the scene with the binoculars.

The *Gypsy Runner* didn't appear damaged and looked to be trying to escape, but Lando was right. Her cargo holds must be full based on how low in the water she rode. The smaller ship would have no problem catching her. They appeared to be equally matched with guns, but Valentin's ship wouldn't be able to maneuver as well.

Then he saw what his spotter had seen. A third ship, still some distance off, was making for the *Gypsy*. Based on the sails, it was another British patrol. Were the English just that lucky, or had they been following the *Gypsy*?

Damn.

Finn descended to find Lando and Fitz waiting for new orders. AJ worried her bottom lip, squinting to make out what little she could in the distance. When she glanced at him, her expression told him everything he needed to know. She trusted in his decision.

"There's a third patrol boat, still a ways out, but heading our way."

Finn glanced at his two mates and long-time friends. Their avid expressions erased his earlier doubts. He grinned wide, blood firing through his veins as the old excitement built. "Let's go see if Captain Valentin could use a hand."

Fitz wasted no time, turning to yell, "Come about. Port side." He ran off, shouting loudly before using his whistle to direct his orders.

Before Lando turned to leave, Finn grabbed his shoulder. "And keep our other flag handy."

Lando smiled and nodded before moving off to do his captain's bidding.

AJ stepped close and wrapped an arm around his waist. "I know I don't have a say in ship's business, but you're doing the right thing."

His heart hummed at her words. He had no business getting the *Daphne* involved, not with AJ and Maire onboard. Dugan was out there somewhere, and with the earlier fog, his ship could be in front or behind them. But he wouldn't be able to live with himself if he let the *Gypsy* be boarded, or worse go down, without providing assistance to prevent it. There were some things a man couldn't walk away from. All it would take is one well-placed ball, and the *Gypsy* could make a break. If she got farther to sea, the patrol wouldn't follow.

But he was taking a large risk. In order to make a difference, the *Daphne* would have to get close enough to become a target.

He gave AJ a sound kiss. "You might not have a say, but your support means everything to me."

Her fierce brown eyes, those eyes that told him she was battle-ready, met his. "I only wish my talents could be put to better use."

He laughed. "If only a nocked arrow or a swiftly-thrown dagger would be all that was needed."

She punched him playfully. "I meant my climbing skills."

"I'm aware." Then his grin faded. "We might have the need of you and Maire's other skills."

She nodded, her expression as grim as his. "I'll get water going, and we'll prepare for casualties."

"Sometimes luck just isn't with us."

"Maybe. But here's something that might help. Jamie has woken a couple of times. Not for very long, but enough to give Maire hope that he might be through the worst of it. He just needs to rebuild the blood he's lost."

His mood suddenly bolstered, he gave her a quick kiss and a swat on her backside as he turned her toward the hatch leading back to the galley. "Now that is exactly what this man needed to hear."

"And one other thing." She drew his head down to hers and kissed him softly. "We're together. And that's all the luck we need."

"God's blood, I love you, wife."

She hugged him then ran down the stairs as he turned to the crew.

"Our good Captain Jamie is on the mend. Let's be sure we get his ship to France."

Cheers went up as word spread, and Finn thought the men worked a little faster with the news.

He scanned the ships again as they began to draw near. Now, if the good news would hold.

———

Aj sprinted down the stairs. When she entered the captain's cabin, she stopped cold at the sight. She might have jinxed the ship with her premature evaluation of Jamie's recovery.

Maire hunched over him, bathing his forehead with water. Ethan's lips were drawn tight, his shoulders straining as he held down the struggling man.

"Is it an infection?" AJ couldn't keep the fear sneaking through the question. There was a small amount of antibiotics left, but she'd wanted to keep it on hand. They were still a long way from home.

"No. He's in pain. Hand me the mug from the table. It should ease his discomfort." Maire spoke gentle words to Jamie until AJ handed her the mug. "Can you hold his head up?"

AJ squeezed past Maire and sat next to Jamie. Ethan shifted him so his upper body sprawled across her lap. She cradled his head in her arms, chanting soft words as Maire worked the potion past his lips. The hint of honey and a bit of brandy tickled her nose.

She snorted. "You never gave me honey and brandy in those nasty concoctions you made me."

Maire smiled as the last of the drink went down. "You have no idea what I fed you while you were unconscious."

When Ethan smothered a laugh, AJ considered a rebuttal but decided it was in her own best interest to shut up.

"What's the commotion topside?" Ethan relaxed his grip on Jamie, who'd passed out, either from the pain or exhaustion.

"We're out of the fog, but the *Gypsy Runner* is under attack." She hesitated, then squared her shoulders in support of Finn's decision. "Finn's turned the ship to assist."

Ethan jumped up. "I think I'll be of more use upstairs now

that Jamie is sleeping again." He gave Maire a swift kiss before racing out of the room.

Maire shook her head, rinsing out the empty mug in a basin of water. "I think he's been waiting for an excuse to go up."

"Men aren't the best for sitting next to a sickbed."

Maire laughed. "That's the truth."

AJ slid from the bed and laid Jamie's head on the pillow. He murmured something before his breathing deepened.

"How bad is it?" Maire asked as she ground herbs in a bowl. When the herbs were sufficiently mashed, she sprinkled different herbs and continued the process.

"One British patrol ship, but another is heading our way from the east."

"Then we better prepare for casualties. Finn used to keep medical supplies in the stores. They were usually in the back. Can you see if Jamie still keeps them there? And we'll need plenty of water and alcohol. Gather everything you can and keep them organized in the galley."

When AJ reached the door, Maire called out, "And find a basket of some sort. We'll need it for carrying supplies to anyone who can't be brought below."

AJ shut her eyes for a moment, remembering the storm the *Daphne Marie* had weathered when they'd crossed the sea from Ireland. This could end up being so much worse. But if they ran and left the *Gypsy Runner* and its captain to their own fate, Finn would be haunted by never knowing what happened. And if anyone on the *Daphne Marie* was injured or lost his life? The decisions of a captain were incredibly difficult. The choices sucked. Had he made the right one?

She stumbled into the galley as the ship lurched sideways. The bulkhead kept her from landing on the floor. Shouts and whistles converged topside as orders were given. Fitz and Lando had been quick to follow Finn's orders to help the *Gypsy Runner*.

She'd heard the whoops of agreement from the crew. They didn't question his decision. They would rather save another ship than turn their back on it—even at their own peril.

———

"Prepare the guns." Finn kept his focus on the two ships as the *Gypsy* turned to starboard, leading the patrol ship away. Finn would try to come in from behind and attack while Valentin kept the British occupied. Smoke billowed from the *Gypsy*'s port side, the ball landing short of its target but managing to spew water onto the patrol ship's starboard side. He scanned beyond the two ships, the binoculars providing a clear outline of the third ship closing in. With any luck, the *Daphne* would be on her way west before they arrived.

Finn heard the scrape of wood as the gunports opened. "Take a mast. Let's just slow them down."

"Aye, aye, captain," came the returned call from the master gunner.

"What can I do?"

Finn turned to see Ethan running toward him, ducking to the left to dodge a sailor.

He slapped Ethan on the back. "Have you been in a ship battle?"

Ethan nodded. "Once."

"Find Fitz. He'll need help with the lines."

Lando came up as Ethan ran off. "What are your plans?"

"I want to slide up to the patrol on her starboard side and try to keep the *Gypsy* ahead of us. I'd rather the second patrol ship doesn't get a good look at us. We just need one good shot."

Lando nodded.

Finn raised the binoculars. The *Gypsy* had taken a hit on her port quarter, but it wasn't enough damage to slow her down. If

Finn didn't get there in time to slow down the patrol, another well-placed ball or two would be enough to put the ship in her grave. The patrol might chance a boarding to save the cargo, but that would put their men at risk. He also knew Valentin. He would give them a hell of a fight before allowing the ship to be boarded.

The *Daphne* had closed the distance, and Finn heard the shot of the gun as soon as the sparks flew. The patrol fired at the same time. Splinters flew from the *Gypsy*, somewhere farther up her port side. A yardarm cracked as canvas fell.

The patrol took a hit to their starboard side, and men scrambled on the deck. But the sails remained intact as they kept pace with the *Gypsy*. Finn tightened his grip on the railing. They had to move faster. As if the sailing gods had answered his prayers, the *Daphne* lurched forward and shifted position until she was on the patrol ship's starboard quarter.

"Fire as they bear," Finn yelled.

The order was called.

Fire flashed as the cannon spewed a ball. It fell short.

The deafening sound of the next gun smothered most everything else. The ball brushed the side of the ship as the *Daphne* inched past the patrol.

The shots needed to go much higher but remain true to their current line. The ship dipped to starboard as the cannon fired. This one hit its mark.

The crack of wood came seconds before the foremast buckled. Men yelled as it fell, scurrying to avoid the weight of the debris.

The *Gypsy* had turned to run with the first shot from the *Daphne*'s cannon. The second patrol ship was still too far away to help.

"Stay this side of the Gypsy. Let's stay hidden as long as we can." Finn kept his glasses on the first patrol ship. She was turning, her guns now pointed toward them. The ship had a clear shot if they could keep any accuracy.

"Get those sails trimmed. We need speed now," Finn yelled, just as the spark of ignition flashed from the patrol's gun port.

Finn braced himself as the ball found its target.

36

AJ was leaving the storeroom when the first cannon fired. The sound reverberated as the ship shuddered beneath her. She dropped the first-aid supplies and braced herself against sacks of flour. She waited. When nothing happened, she picked up the supplies but had barely walked into the galley when the next blast from the gun made her jump. She tossed the supplies on the first table she stumbled into.

She'd stopped listening to the shouts from above, mainly because they were muffled, and when she did make out the words, they made no sense to her. This was the first time the *Daphne Marie* used her cannons while she was aboard. She glanced around and decided to move anything breakable to the floor.

The next blast didn't seem as loud, but the smell of gunpowder seeped through the bulkheads. She remembered the layout of the guns that were kept midship. They must be firing down the line, moving farther away from her. Not knowing how much time she had, she found the basket Maire had asked for. She shoved in salves, ointments, and what appeared to be medieval suture equipment. She tucked the basket between the stack of duffels and their trunks.

The ship turned, and the pitch caught her unaware. When she tried to grab a table, she misjudged the motion of the ship, and her chin slammed against the edge. Her teeth chattered, and she laid where she'd fallen as she tried to catch a breath. Preparing for the worst, she moved her jaw around. It hurt like hell, but nothing was broken.

She crawled to her knees and was pulling herself up when the ship rolled. A loud crack of splintering wood was followed by screaming. The thundering thud of something hitting the deck rumbled through the ship. She thought she heard more orders, but the screaming was all that reached her—loud and incessant. Maybe it was her own.

All the bandages, rags, and bowls she'd meticulously laid out flew across the floor as the ship bolted upright. Another blast of cannon from the *Daphne Marie* was felt more than heard. It jarred her bones. She dove under the table to protect herself from flying debris.

The experience was reminiscent of the storm she'd weathered on their sail to Ireland. She'd found herself huddling in the galley back then as well. But the last time she'd stank of vomit. She admitted the seas had been rougher than now, but she'd like to think she'd gotten her sea legs. She might be crouched under a table, but it had been her decision. For safety. She wouldn't do anyone any good if she was unconscious from something hitting her in the head.

And rather than wait for quiet to descend, she proved her seaworthiness by crawling out from under the table. She could still hear the screaming and was half-thankful it hadn't been her own. Then she ran for the captain's cabin.

Finn grabbed a ratline to stay upright as the ball hit a yard. He turned to give an order to clear the deck, but Fitz had already called out. He must have seen where the ball was headed. Men scrambled, but he couldn't see if everyone had gotten clear before the timber hit the deck with a resounding boom, part of the sail dropping with a thud after it.

"Fire."

He wasn't sure if his order could be heard belowdecks, but a minute later, another burst of a gun sent a ball flying toward the patrol ship. The master gunner had been able to reload the first gun.

Flying debris hit him on the shoulder, and he grunted as he stumbled, but he kept hold of the line. His focus stayed on the patrol ship. Even though the *Daphne* had been turning to starboard to make her run, their ball hit the opposing ship on its foredeck.

A moment before the *Daphne*'s ball struck, smoke billowed from the patrol ship's gunports.

Finn yelled an order to trim the sails, anything to gain some speed. He doubted anyone could hear his order, but he didn't think it was necessary. Anybody who was still able would know they had to run. There was nothing to do but hold on and let the men do what they did best.

The ball from the patrol ship fell short, doing nothing but spraying water over the bulwarks. Finn felt the ship catch the wind as it completed its turn to starboard. He rushed across the deck, leaping over debris and men, keeping his eye on the patrol ship. He had a moment to glimpse the *Gypsy*. She was ahead of them, and the *Daphne* followed. When he refocused on the other ship, he could see it had slowed.

He turned to survey his ship. Men lay strewn across the deck. A group of men worked at pulling someone out from under the fallen yard. He analyzed the decision he'd made to help Valentin rather than continue on with the mission. Men had been lost today, most likely on all three ships. War. It was an ugly thing. And while Valentin was a smuggler, he worked for Napoleon's war effort.

What of his earlier choices? Like his first decision to go on Beckworth's unfathomable journey, which had Hensley's full support. Not one of them thought a simple stone and a few Celtic words would transport someone to another time. Maybe that was why that one had been easy to make. Then his last-minute decision to bring AJ back in time with him. He wasn't sure he could call that one a decision either. The pull to bring her with him hadn't come from his analytical mind. He'd known even then that she was his future. That she had already claimed his heart.

When Ethan found them again, seeking help to find Maire, Finn had been caught between his new life with AJ and the loyalty he felt he owed his sister. But AJ had never questioned whether they would go back. And to Finn, it somehow proved their life together had always been fated. So he didn't question his decision this time to help a friend. It was who he was.

They had made mistakes, but they'd always succeeded. And this chase wasn't just about him and AJ. The stones and books were a danger to everyone. He glanced at the *Gypsy*. He and Valentin were meant to make the crossing together. When the *Daphne* reached the monastery, the team would take back the Heart Stone. Then he and AJ could go home.

Until then, the ship required his attention. Men were already on the lines surveying the damage. Finn hauled himself up a ratline and began climbing, wanting to see how bad it was for himself.

37

———————

When AJ flew through the door of the cabin, Maire lay halfway across the bed, trying to pull Jamie back in. AJ rushed to the other side and, using her shoulder for leverage, heaved to push him back in place. After several minutes of pushing and pulling between them, she collapsed next to the prone man while she caught her breath.

"Thank you." Maire wiped the sweat from her forehead. She glanced around the room then bent to collect her packages of herbs and bottles of potions that had fallen to the floor. Only one bottle had broken, and the scent of lavender overpowered the room. She stuffed the remaining items in her case.

"I'll go up and see what damage there is." AJ pulled a blanket over Jamie, who'd managed to sleep through the whole event. His forehead was cool. Still no fever.

Maire picked up her case and followed AJ out of the room. "I'll come with. Let's grab bandages and a bucket of water. Based on the screaming, I'd say we have injured men. Let's focus on stopping any bleeding first. Anything more will have to wait until we're safe."

AJ grabbed the basket she'd stuffed next to the duffels and

266

worked her way around the galley, picking up the scattered supplies. She'd felt the ship pick up speed, and the sounds of cannon had ceased. Orders continued to be shouted, but most of the screaming had subsided. When she reached the deck, she blinked through the defused sunlight at the debris strewn across the deck. The scent of gunpowder was thick, and the dissipating smoke from the cannon discharge hung in the air.

Fragments of images played out as if in slow motion. Men scurried to the rigging, jumping over injured men who writhed and moaned. Others lay motionless, only moving with the roll of the ship. A large wooden beam, probably a yardarm, had landed on someone, and men worked to lift it off the man.

A ripped sheet of canvas blew lazily in the wind where it had been torn from the beam that had fallen. Men swung from ratlines, trying to cut it loose. The rest of the sails were taut, kept trim by the men she'd seen at the rigging. How much would it slow them down with one less sail?

Once the initial shock passed, she frantically scanned the deck for Finn. She found Fitz standing by the main shroud, his face turned up, eyes squinting against the sun. She followed his gaze and found the familiar figure of her husband working his way down a ratline. He must have gone up to check the damaged sail that seemed unwilling to be cut free.

Maire tugged on her skirt, reminding her of their current task. The first injured man they found had wood splinters in his legs and chest. Maire knelt to care for him. AJ moved on to the next man, who appeared to be unconscious. She couldn't find any physical injury and checked for a pulse. Faint but steady. When she ran a hand over his head, she felt the lump. There was nothing she could do for now. If he had internal injuries, he was beyond any help she or Maire could provide.

She didn't have nursing skills, but she'd seen enough medical shows on television to know the importance of triage.

Maire had mentioned almost the same thing in her comment to care for the bleeding first. So, she ran to each man and quickly assessed what she saw. Anyone who seemed able to move on their own, she directed to the galley.

Her path led to the men who'd been working to free the trapped man. When she walked up to the group and peered over a shoulder, she grimaced. She recognized the lad. He'd been on the ship when they'd sailed from Ireland. She pushed her way through the crowd and knelt next to him. He didn't have a pulse. She checked under an eyelid. It didn't take a medical degree to see he was gone. Tears blurred her vision as she placed a hand on his chest and kissed his forehead. She shook her head to the other men, who bowed their heads.

"You did all you could." She placed a hand on one man's shoulder before turning to search for others that could still use her help.

Finn dropped to the deck. They'd lost one topsail. Another yard was damaged and wouldn't bear the strain of a sail for long. After he ordered the men to ease the sheet, he returned to where he'd last seen Lando. When he found him trying to stand, he rushed over, brushing debris from him. Lando made it to one knee before collapsing to a sitting position.

"Easy there." Finn pushed Lando down when he tried to stand. "Sit for a minute. Fitz has everything under control."

Ethan, who'd been moving debris out of the way, arrived at the same time as Finn. He knelt next to them and lifted Lando's chin. "He looks a bit dazed. I'd let him rest. If he's not able to stand on his own soon, Maire will need to see him."

Lando pushed his hand away with a growl. "I'm fine."

"I'm sure you are. But you'll do no one any good stumbling

about the ship. Now stop whining and just sit. Fifteen minutes." He turned to Finn. "I've been helping with the wreckage, but is there something else you'd rather I do?"

Finn stood and surveyed the deck. "Have you seen AJ?"

"She's with Maire checking on the injured."

Finn nodded, one less thing to worry about. "I need to keep an eye on the patrol ship. Can you check with Maire and see if she needs help moving the injured? Then you can finish sorting through the wreckage with Lando."

Ethan patted Lando's back before striding off in search of Maire.

Lando tried to rise, but Finn pushed him back down. "Stay where you are. Those are my orders. Understood?"

Lando glanced away, clearly not happy about it. He didn't wince, so Finn took that as a good sign.

"Fifteen minutes doesn't seem like a lot to ask to make sure you're all right."

Finn took the grunt as a positive sign then turned to survey the other ships. He'd caught a glimpse of their positions when he'd checked the sails. Nothing had changed since. The *Gypsy* had moved ahead of the *Daphne*, her gunports still open as she shifted course to the southwest, moving farther away from the English coast. The first patrol ship faded behind them, its own condition not much better than the *Daphne*. The second patrol ship had turned to assist the first. They were out of danger for now.

The *Daphne* followed Valentin's course change, flanking the ship as they moved farther into the Channel. He scanned the ship with the binoculars and was surprised to see Valentin on the quarterdeck peering through his own glass. When the captain turned his gaze to the *Daphne*, he lifted his arm in a lazy wave. Finn waved back. It appeared Valentin owed him once again.

"Are we out of danger?" Lando rested his head against the bulwark, his face to the sun.

Finn grinned. "When are we ever out of danger?"

Lando grunted, but this time with a bit of a smile. "You'll get no argument from me."

They both turned when light footsteps approached. AJ's shirt and pants were stained with blood, her expression grim. She immediately hugged him, and he held her for a long moment, relishing the feel of her warmth. He ran his hands over her, at first to ensure she wasn't injured, but mostly to prolong having her in his arms.

When he finally pulled away, she was crying, but she wiped her face and took a deep, shuddering breath. "We lost Reilly."

Finn closed his eyes. Reilly had been a good man, just a boy when he'd first joined the crew. He would need to post a letter to the man's mother and ensure she received extra payment for her son's service. "He's the only one?"

"So far. There are two others who have more severe injuries, but Maire thinks they have a good chance. Ethan and I were able to get them below. I heard Lando took a hit to the head." She squatted next to Lando. "Look at me."

Lando stared at her with a hint of a smile. Finn almost rolled his eyes. Neither he nor Ethan could get the big man to listen, but with a few simple words, Lando instantly obeyed her. After a minute, AJ nodded. "I'd ask how bad your head hurts, but something tells me you won't be truthful." When Lando opened his mouth to object, she shook her head. "Don't bother. I forgive you. Now let's see if you can stand on your own."

She stood and stepped back, giving him space.

Finn stayed close in case the man stumbled. Lando grabbed the railing and dragged himself up to a standing position. He braced himself as he glanced around. He bent his head this way and that. Shrugged his large shoulders and took a few steps. "I'm good."

AJ patted his chest. "That you are." She turned to Finn. "I hate to ask, but Jamie's awake and Ethan's struggling to keep him in bed. Maire's trying to give him something to make him sleep, but he refuses to drink it. She needs to spend time with the other injured men, and I'm still needed up here. Considering the shape of the deck, I imagine Ethan's time could be better spent."

He took her hand and pressed a kiss to it. "I'll take care of it." He glanced at Lando. "Keep an eye on the *Gypsy* and the patrol." He glanced up. "And see about getting our nest back."

———

Finn raced down the stairs, eager to see Jamie but not sure what to tell him about his ship. He stopped short when he found himself surrounded by injured men. They were spread throughout the galley. Fortunately, most were awake, and they huddled in groups of two or three, their voices soft.

Starting with the man on his left, he circled the galley, stopping to speak with each man where he could. Two of them had broken limbs and were groggy from large doses of alcohol if he understood the empty bottles of whiskey correctly. An open crate with more bottles sat in a corner. Jamie would be more upset about the loss of Ireland's best whiskey than the state of his ship.

The rest of the men suffered from head injuries or wounds from splinters. If the ball had hit midship rather than flying over and taking part of a yard with it, the number of injured or dead would have been far greater.

He found Maire bandaging one of the men Finn didn't know. He laid a hand on the young man's shoulder, his eyes glassy from shock and a good bit of whiskey. The man didn't speak, but he grasped Finn's arm, his grip tight.

"Good job, mate." Finn kept a smile on his face, his tone warmed with a touch of his Irish accent. "Stay strong. My sister will have you good as new by the time we make France."

"Thank you, Captain." His gaze darted past Finn toward the short passageway that led to the captain's cabin. "How is he, sir?"

"I'm on my way to check on him, but I hear it's near impossible to keep him to his bed."

The sailor grunted, either from pain or in response to Finn's statement. Maybe a combination of the two.

When Maire finished wrapping the dressing, Finn took her aside. "Will they all make it?"

She glanced around. "Most of them will be topside by tomorrow. One was impaled in the shoulder by a large splinter of wood. I'm not sure if I got all the fragments out. I'm worried about infection."

"Are there any more of the antibiotics?"

She nodded. "But there is another man that might benefit from the medicine. I don't think there's enough for both."

"Check with AJ. Maybe we can split the dose between them."

She glanced to the same passageway the sailor had. "I don't want to give Jamie any more alcohol, but he's refusing the tonic. He needs to stay in bed until we reach France."

"I'll take care of it." He kissed the top of her head. "Thank you for everything you're doing."

She surprised him by hugging him. "You did the right thing for your friend. Don't burden yourself with guilt."

He chuckled. "And when have I done that?"

She pushed him away, a knowing smile almost producing dimples. "An old argument, brother." Then her expression turned serious as she returned to her wards, picking up a shirt and ripping it into rags.

He paused outside the cabin, sucking in a deep breath before pushing through the door. He'd expected to find a haggard man, too weak to sit without assistance, delirious with the need to return to duty. That wasn't the man staring at him from the bed. Jamie was clear-eyed, though still pale. He leaned against raised pillows and laid down the book he'd been reading. A chess set had been placed by his bed, and a game appeared to be in progress. If Finn had to guess, that was the first evidence that Beckworth was still somewhere on the ship.

"I was expecting the weak lad I found stowed away on my ship. Sick as a dog from the rough seas."

Jamie grunted. "That was only because I'd been locked away in the trunk for too long."

Finn laughed. "We were lucky to find you alive at all."

Jamie grinned, but it quickly turned into a grimace, and he laid his head back.

Finn surveyed his old cabin. Not much had changed. The personal items were different. If his quick glance at the bookcase was accurate, some of the books had been replaced with others better suited to Jamie's tastes. An age-battered table had been cleared for Maire's potions. A jolt of nostalgia suffused him, but not of his sailing days.

His memories were of a particular brunette with intoxicating, sable-colored eyes who owned his heart. He'd been angry the first time he'd found her peering into his cabin. His inner sanctum. She'd been anxious about her intrusion into his privacy, seeming unable to step back for fear of running into him, and she'd been so feisty moments before. He'd been close enough to smell the lavender in her hair, an incredible intimacy falling between them. Had that been when he'd first fallen in love with her? A short couple of weeks later, they'd spent their first evening together, making love in this very cabin.

"Have you broken my ship?" Jamie tried to sit up, but after an agonizing minute, he fell back. Irritation mixed with pain crossed his face before he managed to cover it with a questioning stare.

Finn pushed his lustful thoughts of AJ aside and cocked a brow. "I thought you gave her back to me."

Jamie paused, then catching Finn's mischievous expression, relaxed against the pillows. "Only until we make France. If we make France."

"Aye. You're right on that count." He ran a hand through his hair. "There was a friend in need."

Jamie's nod was almost imperceptible. "How bad is she?"

Finn shrugged. "The topsail yard took a ball and we lost the sail. There's other minor damage. It will slow us down."

"And now Valentin owes you another favor?"

"You knew it was the *Gypsy?*"

"A bird told me."

Finn nodded. "And the favor owed is to you, my friend."

Jamie considered what that meant then smiled. "Aye. I can live with that."

Finn sat on the stool next to the bed and squeezed his friend's shoulder. "I thought you could. Now, your job is to rest. I have to admit, you look better than I expected for taking a ball just a day ago. But you're weak as a newborn lamb. And you have stitches that could easily tear. Our trip will be slower, but the weather has cleared. I don't expect any more trouble."

"Do you know where Dugan is?"

Finn shook his head. "I would say he was ahead of us, but with the fog, it's possible we slipped by him. If I knew the ship he hired, I might better guess how quick they'll cross."

"But they'll be faster than us now."

"Aye. Which is why I only have a few minutes to check on you and the other men. We need to reset sails to gain as much speed as we can." He nodded toward the chessboard. "I'll come back tonight and give you a go."

When he stood to leave, Jamie grabbed his arm, but he was too weak to get a firm grasp. "Remember what you taught us. Always have an alternate route."

Finn nodded. "Don't worry, lad. I haven't forgotten. This old girl will see us to safety." He picked up the cup from the side table and passed it to Jamie. He'd recognize one of Maire's concoctions anywhere. "Drink this down. No argument." His stern tone had little impact on Jamie, but he drank it down, frowning at the taste.

"Now catch up on some reading. I'll make sure someone keeps you properly updated on our progress."

Jamie nodded, his eyes already drooping. Finn doubted it had anything to do with the drink and more to the exertion of having a visitor. He was at the door when he turned back. Jamie was still watching him.

"Do me one favor?"

Jamie waited, smart enough not to agree to anything before hearing it out.

"Do what my sister asks."

Jamie's impish grin returned. "I'll do my best, Captain."

38

For the remainder of the day, the crew scurried to clear the deck and repair damages in addition to their normal duties. Finn helped with the new rigging, but he didn't have to. Fitz drove the men with a firm hand, moving them from one task to another before Finn had to ask. The young man had the same flair as Jamie for sailing. He might be a bit rough around the edges and too eager for a fight, but he knew how to run a ship. Finn had no doubt Fitz would have his own command one day, if he ever desired one. Not everyone wanted the responsibility that came with being a captain.

Finn glanced off the port side, where several miles away, the *Gypsy Runner* kept pace. The *Gypsy* had taken two hits, and though she lost part of a mast, she was a larger ship and carried more fore-and-aft-rigged sails. She maintained speed with the *Daphne*, her course steering them westward, riding a little ahead but always a constant vigil. Based on his calculations, Valentin was staying on a narrow course, balancing with being closer to France yet remaining out of sight of the Royal Navy. Not an easy task. Since Finn hadn't sailed the Channel during this war, he'd have to trust Valentin to see them safely across.

Satisfied with the men's work, he stepped away in search of AJ. He'd caught glimpses of her long hair now and then, and being dressed in her pants, it was sometimes the only thing distinguishing her from the younger lads. Currently, she was nowhere to be seen. He assumed her own duties kept her busy belowdecks. She'd assigned herself all the dirty work—cleaning bedpans, emptying buckets, washing out bloody rags and clothes. When those chores were completed, she focused her attention on the injured men. Maire saw to their health, and AJ replenished their spirit. Several had already returned to duty, and she was like a mother hen, checking their bandages while drumming up conversation about their family and laughing at their bawdy jokes. The men tolerated it, but they couldn't hide their lingering smiles after she'd moved on.

Finn stood on the bow and surveyed the ship. These were the moments he missed—the men working with purpose, the sound of the canvas, and the slight shift of wind that forced him to bark an order to trim a sail. This had been a good life. But it no longer fit him.

He lifted his gaze to the sails and noticed the nest had been fixed. Someone was already in it. His brows furrowed when he noticed those long brown strands rippling in the wind. AJ. He would have laughed if fear didn't grip him. He understood the advantage of having her in the nest. But if Dugan, the Royal Navy, or a French patrol showed up, the nest was the last place she should be.

A hand rested on his shoulder. "She'll be fine. She knows to come down if she signals an alarm." Lando sat on a barrel and tossed Finn an orange.

Finn leaned against the rail and rolled the fruit in his hand. "And how much longer will you be sailing around instead of settling down?"

Lando spat out a laugh. "You'd rather pester me than discuss what we'll do with Dugan once we catch him."

"I think we both know Dugan won't be leaving the monastery. That's assuming we're lucky enough to avoid the Royal Navy and the French patrols. We won't be able to outrun them." He peeled the orange, tossing the rind into the sea.

"The Gypsy is still with us, and we can fly the French flag if we need to." He finished the fruit and licked the juice from his hands before wiping them on his pants. "I'm betting on your Irish luck to see us to the monastery to finish our task."

"I'm not sure how much of that luck is left."

Lando stood and again laid a hand on his friend's shoulder. He nodded toward the nest. "I think it's still with you, my friend." He stepped back and rubbed his hands together, his eyes twinkling with mischief. "So, let's focus on our run to France and how to take back the Heart Stone." His smile widened. "And maybe later, I can relieve you from a portion of your purse with a poor man's game of Hazards."

———

When dusk settled into the deeper hues of violet, AJ hauled the bucket across the deck. The evening air was warmer than the previous night, and the crew, exhausted from the day, collapsed where they'd been working rather than find their berth belowdecks. She ladled stew into bowls and added a slice of bread and hunk of cheese. With the evening came time for all but a few to rest.

The ship rolled and creaked, the sails catching the barest hint of wind. A single ray of light reflected dimly across the open expanse of sea, where the *Gypsy* continued her protective watch. The sliver of moon provided little light, but she could see well enough from the lanterns scattered around the deck.

AJ doled out the last of the stew and washed the bucket. Unable to find the energy to return to the galley, she shuffled to her favorite spot near the forecastle and dropped onto a canvas sheet. She unwrapped the package from her pocket and stared at the cheese, bread, and orange. If she closed her eyes, she could almost smell the crab po'boys from Joe's and taste the crispy french fries begging to be dipped into the best tartar sauce on the Oregon coast. She covered her dinner and set it aside.

They should reach the monastery tomorrow evening. Finn hoped to catch Dugan before they made land, but with a busted yard, that wasn't going to happen. So, instead of worrying about finding Dugan on the open water, she worried about Sebastian, who had no inkling of the threat about to arrive. Finn hadn't mentioned a plan, and he'd been busy with repairs, but AJ doubted he wasn't considering his options. Beckworth had been all but invisible since boarding the ship, though she'd seen him come out of Jamie's cabin a couple of times. She assumed he was Jamie's mysterious chess partner. Beckworth wasn't the type to stay idle. He had to be preparing something for his brother.

Too tired to think anymore, she pulled her wrap tight and turned on her side. An hour or two and she'd be good as new.

Strong arms and the slight scent of cedar woke her from her dreams. She tried to sit up, but the arms pulled her against a hard chest. "How long have I been out?" She gripped his arms and leaned her head against Finn.

"About four hours."

When she tried to sit up again, his hold tightened. "Hush. You needed the rest, and it gave me the opportunity for a couple hours myself." He kissed the top of her head. "And we've had little time for ourselves."

AJ stopped fighting and nestled deeper into his embrace. "How is everyone?"

"All is well. Most of the men are asleep. We found Fitz snoring over the lines he'd been retying. Everyone deserves a good rest."

"I hope that includes Maire."

"Ethan is seeing to that. They're bunking in the captain's cabin."

"And I assume that's not just for Maire's sake."

He chuckled and kissed her temple, an errant hand resting on her breast. "Aye. Jamie is still chafing to be up. I'd have the men bring him up in the morning, but I'm afraid that would only encourage him. I can picture him crawling across the deck to check a line."

"You could always tie him to something," AJ mused.

Finn laughed. "That would be a fine thing for a captain."

AJ didn't want to broach the subject, but she was curious if he longed for his old command. "Do you miss the ship?"

She waited for the tensing of his body, that little sign that suggested he wasn't prepared to have this conversation. That he might tell her something she didn't really want to hear. Though he hesitated in answering, his body remained relaxed, his strong fingers brushing her arm in slow rhythmic strokes.

He bent his head, his soft whisper tickling her ear. "I miss watching you climb the rigging like you were born to sail. I miss watching your fascination at the navigation table when I lay in a course. I miss the feel of your body when we make love in our own cabin."

She intertwined her fingers with his then brought his hand to her lips. "Those are sweet words."

"And the truth. Do I miss the days that the *Daphne* was my home? I miss it like anyone would miss their youth, their adventures." He shifted so he could turn her to face him. His expression was bittersweet as he ran a finger down her cheek. "Do I long for a lonely cabin with no one to share it with? Would I prefer having a ship full of men over a family? Do I miss seeking out each horizon, wondering if I was on the right path?" He cupped her cheek. "I have no regrets, sweet lass. I only have you, wherever that leads."

She pulled his head down to kiss him. It was meant to be a light kiss. A kiss of agreement. A kiss of contentment. But their exchange deepened as his words sank in. As comforted as they made her feel, she'd always known the truth of them. All of her worrying back in Baywood, her fears that he missed his own time, his ship, and his way of life—they'd all be unfounded. They'd been nothing more than her own insecurities. Her own niggling doubt of ever achieving her own happy ever after. They weren't home yet. But then she knew the truth of that as well. Home was wherever Finn was. The century didn't matter. She'd go wherever he went, just as he would follow her.

She curled into his chest. "You're all I'll ever need." And his deep sigh of contentment washed over her as she fell asleep in his arms.

39

AJ woke to Finn's bark of commands and the pounding of feet on the deck as men scrambled to change the rigging. The wind direction had changed, the morning sun filling the sails, urging them on to France. At some point, Finn had covered her with a blanket, and she'd hugged it close as she watched the men. No one questioned the additional orders given by Fitz and Lando.

Once the sails had been set and the major bustle was over, AJ left the safety of her haven and made her way down to the galley. Most of the men would have eaten before the wind changed, and those that hadn't would have to wait until the next shift. That gave AJ time to grab leftovers.

The last two of the severely injured men remained on the far side of the galley. They were on the mend but not strong enough to return to work. The same was true of Jamie, who was healing well but was still too weak to get out of bed on his own. When he did manage to stand, sweat dripped from his forehead and he'd collapse after a couple of steps. While Ethan continued helping with ship repairs, Jamie was left on his own. Maire threatened to tie him to the bed if she kept finding him crawling around on the floor. Then Beckworth stepped in. He assumed the task of keeping Jamie company, which included helping him back to bed after his failed attempts at staying upright, bringing him food, and playing chess.

After grabbing a cold biscuit, AJ popped in to check on Jamie. He was out of bed again, but this time he clung to Beckworth as they made an awkward stroll across the cabin. Beckworth put a finger to his lips, apparently wanting to keep Jamie's new exercise routine quiet.

She backed out of the cabin and returned to the galley. Hands on hips, she surveyed the room only to discover Maire had everything under control. Not surprising, but it left her with nothing to do. They were half a day from their destination. The *Gypsy* continued her course off their port side, but the *Daphne Marie* wouldn't be safe until she made port and her missing yard could be replaced.

AJ returned to the deck and watched the men work, feeling completely useless, until a movement from the sails caught her eye. A sailor was climbing out of the nest. Finn had refused to put her in the rotation for lookout duty, but it couldn't hurt to try again. Maybe she just needed a different approach. She searched for Lando, and after his brief discussion with Finn, which could have been classified an argument, she now leaned against the rough boards of the newly repaired nest and sucked in the tangy salt air.

Her task as spotter gave her plenty of time to consider the inevitable showdown at the monastery. She worried about Sebastian, and though Maire wouldn't admit to the same fear, she'd become more agitated the closer they got to France. Would Dugan follow orders to harm an old man just so Reginald could get his hands on *The Book of Stones*? Of course, he would. Her anxiety would lessen if she could catch a glimpse of Dugan's ship on the horizon. Not that she'd know what his ship looked like. She peered through the binoculars anyway. Nothing. Not even the Royal Navy or the French patrol.

When she wasn't obsessing over Sebastian, her thoughts returned to the Heart Stone and the jeopardy it was in. She didn't want to consider the ramifications if the stone never traveled through history. Would she just disappear from this timeline? Would they jump through the fog, only to discover on the other side that Finn was gone forever? His future rewritten? It was maddening. And the more she thought about it, the more restless she became.

Suddenly, the nest seemed too small, and a sense of claustrophobia overtook her. She could count on one hand the times this sensation had claimed her. And she didn't like it. Her body itched with nervous energy and frustration. The urge to flee was overwhelming, and her first instinct was to scurry back to the deck.

She stood and closed her eyes, swaying with the motion of the ship. The wind blew her hair back until the strands floated on the air, drying the sweat that had formed along the back of her neck. She gripped the edge of the nest and lifted her face to the sky. Her shoulders relaxed under the caressing warmth of the sun. She inhaled deeply. Again. Then once more as a lightness filled her. This new awareness didn't erase the dread but seemed to have tucked it away—for a little while. She suspected she'd need those darker urges to reemerge when they reached the monastery and they faced Reginald's defenses.

She opened her eyes and turned full circle. The coast of France could be seen on the far horizon. She embraced the sight, taking note of the color of the sea, the sharp details of the sails against an azure sky, and committed it all to memory. The scent of the salty air, the feel of the ship beneath her. Someday, two hundred years from now, she'd make Finn bring her back to sail across the Channel so she could compare the views. For now, she'd take each moment handed her, each day a new opportunity. There simply might not be a tomorrow.

———

Finn ran his hand along the new plank, satisfied with the repair. He moved along the railing, performing general maintenance, needing to be doing something, when the alarm rang out. He couldn't see the nest from where he worked. By the time he'd taken his first steps to get a clear view, the whistle blew again. He lifted his hand to shield his eyes against the glare of the sun as he glanced up. AJ pointed toward the *Gypsy*.

Finn raced to port side. Lando was already there, the spyglass raised as he scanned the horizon. When Finn approached, Lando turned and shrugged. He couldn't see anything yet.

When Finn glanced back to the nest, AJ was halfway down the ratlines, moving quickly.

"There's something out there. The *Gypsy* must be blocking our view." Finn took the glass from Lando but had no better luck finding what caused the alarm.

When AJ reached his side, she handed him the binoculars. "I don't think you'll be able to see it from here. I barely caught a glimpse, but it's there."

Tucking the binoculars in his waistband, he kissed the topped of her head and climbed the closest shroud. He stopped halfway up where he could see beyond the *Gypsy*'s sails. Several men paused in their work, waiting for orders. Other men continued to work the sails, capturing as much wind as they could until the captain said otherwise.

At first, Finn didn't see anything. But he knew something must be out there. They were all on edge, but he trusted AJ. If she said something was out there, it was out there. He shifted the binoculars to the *Gypsy*. Though the ship paralleled the *Daphne*, she was a good distance away. He could barely make out Valentin on the quarterdeck, his spyglass looking east to southeast. Aye. Something was there.

Finn climbed higher until he was almost to the nest. He only required a few seconds before he spotted what AJ had seen. Two ships, coming their way. Damn. He couldn't help the sense of pride in AJ's keen eyes, even if it meant trouble for them. The ships were still too far away to confirm their registry, but it was a fair guess they were French patrol.

Lando had already raised the French ensign, a flag that signaled the *Daphne* wasn't British, but that wouldn't be enough to stop a boarding. Nor would it stop them from using their guns if the *Daphne* showed signs of running.

He twisted toward the bow and scanned the horizon. The shores of France were close, but they still had to sail down the coast, past several smaller ports, before continuing to the large bay where the monastery perched on the cliffs. The winds would shift by then, slowing their speed. They'd have to make the bay before the French ships were close enough to see where they'd gone. At the moment, that didn't seem likely.

The *Daphne* wasn't carrying much cargo. Even if they were boarded, Finn doubted the French would do anything other than slow them down. He could use an excuse of asylum, but it would still slow them down. Possibly forcing them to dock right next to Dugan's ship. That wouldn't do.

Finn scanned the *Gypsy* again and noticed a new yellow jack flying below the French ensign and the blue merchant jack. The yellow flag would signal to the other vessels there was a health issue onboard but nothing contagious. The patrol, in theory, should lead the *Gypsy* to the closest port. Jamie wouldn't be happy to learn they would be cashing in on Valentin's debt so soon. He tucked the binoculars back in his waistband and climbed down the ratlines.

When he returned to Lando and AJ, Fitz had joined them, waiting for orders.

"Two French patrols hidden behind the *Gypsy*."

Fitz swore.

"If we can't see them, they can't see us." Lando glanced through his glass one more time before stuffing it back in his jacket.

"Agreed. And the good Captain Valentin put up his yellow jack."

"Did he now?" Fitz's mood took a swift uptick. He rocked back and forth, his gaze blurring as it often did when he was thinking. He turned toward the bow as Finn had earlier. "Slightly starboard until the *Gypsy* turns?"

Finn slapped him on his back. "Exactly."

AJ tugged at his sleeve. "I don't understand."

He put an arm around her. "The French patrol can't see us behind the sails of the *Gypsy*. The patrol ships are a good distance away, but I'm sure they've spotted her. Valentin will stay the course until we get closer to shore. If he doesn't change course, they'll still want to get close, but the yellow jack, which signals there's some type of health concern on board, should stave off any boarding."

"But they'll see us as soon as they get close to the *Gypsy*."

"Aye, but by then, the *Gypsy* will have turned for port, and we'll continue our run west. At least one patrol will follow the *Gypsy*, possibly to challenge the yellow jack. If both ships follow the *Gypsy*, we have a good chance of slipping past them."

AJ's eyes were huge, but as she studied his face, her pinched lips relaxed and her shoulders eased. She bent her head to his chest. "We're so close."

He kissed the top of her head. "And thanks to your sharp

eyes and Beckworth's binoculars, you've given us a fighting chance to escape a boarding."

He turned to Fitz and Lando. "I need to speak with Jamie. You know my orders."

He turned AJ toward the stairs to the galley. When they reached the lower deck, he led AJ toward Maire. "I'm going to need both of you to stay here. The next few hours will be busy for the men, and they'll be ravenous by the time this is over."

"And I imagine Cook will be up top." AJ bit her lip, nodding in thought. "I'll find something hearty to feed them."

"Where's Ethan?" Maire set down bandages and a small bowl of a thick golden ointment.

The sweet smell of honey and chamomile made Finn wince. Maire had used the same ointment to treat his knife wounds after his short imprisonment. It would be some time before he could smell the combination and not remember his treatment by Reginald and Dugan. The memory would fade faster if they were both dead.

When he realized the women were staring at him, he shook his head. "Sorry, I need him on deck. He's good with the sails, and we'll need him when we make our run for the monastery." His sister nodded, but frown lines marred her smooth skin. "Don't fret. There won't be any more guns. If the patrol gets close enough, I'll let them board. I'd rather not take the time or the risk. They could force us to dock at the closest port."

"Wouldn't that be where Dugan would go?" AJ whispered.

"Aye. But let's not get ahead of ourselves. The ships are still far away. We have a good chance they'll never spot us."

"Wouldn't it be better if I went back to the nest and kept an eye on them?" AJ asked.

"I'll feel better if you're down here. There's enough to keep you and Maire busy."

"And out of your way." Her response wasn't angry, but she

couldn't hide the disappointment. She wanted to be in the thick of it. But he really did need her down here, and not just so he wouldn't have to worry about her. He turned to his sister. "I need to speak with Jamie if he's awake."

Maire nodded. "He should be. I heard him and Beckworth arguing."

Finn lifted a brow, and she released a short laugh. "It's not what you think. They've been playing cards, and Jamie probably caught Beckworth cheating again."

"Jamie should know better. But I'll have Beckworth stretch his legs and get some air while he can." He'd been surprised that Beckworth had kept to himself, staying out of the way until his help was needed. But his nature wasn't one to sit idle for so long.

When Finn moved into the small hallway that led to the captain's quarters, AJ grabbed his arm. He hadn't heard her behind him, and he took a breath before turning around, expecting a fight. She would have some outlandish reason why she should be topside, preferably burrowed in the nest.

Instead, she surprised him by reaching up to run a hand over his neck before pulling his head down to hers. Her lips were warm and insistent. And he gave in to her. Her tongue tangled with his in a passionate kiss that stirred his blood. He snaked an arm around her waist until their bodies formed a single unit. He ran his other hand through her hair as her arms wrapped around him. All thoughts of the patrol ships, the *Gypsy*, and what he wanted to speak to Jamie about slipped from his mind. Nothing existed beyond this woman. His woman. His wife. How had he gotten so damn lucky?

She was the first to break the kiss. Finn was grateful because he wasn't sure he had the self-control to do it himself. She smelled of sunshine and crisp wind. He brushed her breast with his thumb and smiled when the shiver ran through her.

"You've taken all thought from me, lass." He kissed her brow then the tip of her nose.

Her lips twitched as she seemed to stare straight into his soul. Her dark-honey eyes were tinged with a ring of green that, for AJ, indicated either anger or passion. He had no doubt what caused the flash of green at this moment.

"Good. My job is done." Her grin appeared, and she gave him another swift kiss. To his dismay, no tongue this time. Then she patted his backside before scurrying back to Maire.

He grabbed the handle to the cabin and stopped when heard Beckworth's cry of surprise and Jamie's responding snort of laughter. He leaned his head against the door and forced himself to suppress the silly grin AJ had left him with. After a full minute, he knocked once before entering. When the men glanced up to say something, they both stared at him.

Beckworth chuckled and looked past Finn. "Where's that woman of yours? Do you two have need of the cabin?"

Finn's gaze hardened. "I need a moment with Jamie. This would be a good time to get some sun."

Beckworth continued to study Finn, then looked down at his cards. "This is the best hand I've had all day."

"Now," Finn growled.

Beckworth laid the cards down and raised a brow at Jamie before standing. "Good luck, mate." Before he passed Finn, he slowed as if he was going to make another comment but seemed to think better of it. He shut the door behind him.

Jamie put the cards away as Finn approached. "I heard the alarm. French patrol?"

Finn nodded. "But that's not why I'm here. I need you to tell me everything about your smuggling operation with Sebastian."

———

y the time Finn finished his discussion with Jamie and returned to the deck, the *Gypsy* had moved farther away. She still blocked the *Daphne* from view, assuming the patrol didn't have someone in the nest, though their glass wouldn't be as good as the binoculars. Fitz had modified their course, steering them toward the coast but with a slight angle west. The shift was enough for the ship to stay hidden behind the *Gypsy*, yet still allow them to catch the wind and put more distance between them.

Finn nodded at the men, slapping a few on their backs as he strode to the quarterdeck. He braced his legs and crossed his arms across his chest, his focus split between the encroaching shoreline and the *Gypsy*'s movement. An hour passed as Finn watched the other ships grow smaller, though not fast enough for his liking. He barked an order when he sensed a change in the ship. The *Daphne* had slowed. Within five minutes, the sails shifted and the ship picked up speed. A calmness settled over him as he listened to the wind and his ship.

His ship.

He shook his head. She was his for now, but he knew without any doubt this would be their last adventure together. And though he was bringing her in battered, he would see her safely to port. It had always been an unspoken agreement between them. Neither of them had ever let the other down.

A sharp order from Fitz brought him out of his short retrospect. A few minutes later, the ship changed course again. The *Daphne* sailed along the coastline, and Finn yelled several commands until he knew the ship had her legs. She was free to run. Finn turned back to the *Gypsy*. She had turned, keeping her length perpendicular with the shore. Her sails shifted, preparing to heave to. Valentin had picked his spot to wait for the patrol, and he'd turned his ship to give the *Daphne* cover as she made her escape.

He moved aft to monitor the situation. Lando stood next to him, his glass on the ship. Thirty minutes later, Finn raised the binoculars. The patrols were almost on the *Gypsy*, but neither seemed to be giving her wide berth. If they'd seen the *Daphne*, they either didn't care about the smaller ship or didn't think it was worth the chase. Valentin's ship rode low in the water, which meant full cargo holds and a share of the profit.

Finn patted Lando's shoulder. "I think our luck has returned. Let's discuss Dugan."

40

───────

The *Daphne Marie* bobbed at anchor inside the inlet, a few nautical miles from the monastery. Finn leaned against the railing and watched the sun sink into the horizon. The men were restless with a combination of exhaustion and anxiety. After the excitement of evading the French patrol, the crew was ready for whatever came next.

Finn had a few ideas, but for now, they hid in the cove, waiting for the cover of darkness. They could have made a run for the monastery, but without knowing if Reginald and Dugan had arrived or how many men they'd brought, Finn couldn't take the chance of being spotted. He was counting on the element of surprise.

A hand rubbed his arm before a bowl appeared in front of him. His arm slid around AJ's waist, and he leaned down for the kiss she placed on his cheek.

"Stew?" Finn took the proffered bowl and barely chewed the first bite of meat and vegetables before swallowing. He hadn't realized how hungry he'd been.

"We have time, and I think Cook wanted us out of his galley.

Besides." Her gaze twinkled with laughter. "I think the crew was tired of my porridge and hard tack."

"Aye." Finn managed between spoonfuls. When he finished, he stared down at the remaining juices. AJ handed him a chunk of bread. He smiled gratefully and used the crusty end to eagerly clean the bowl. "You think of everything."

She took the bowl from him then handed him a skin. He took a sip, expecting water, and gratefully sucked down the ale. When he'd taken his fill, he handed it back to her. "You are too good to me."

She set down the bowl and skin, wrapping her arm around him and laying her head against his shoulder. "If I was properly doing my wifely duty, I'd force Jamie from the captain's cabin and have my way with you."

He chuckled and squeezed her close as they watched the horizon. "I know of other places where no one would disturb us."

Her laugh was light-hearted, but he heard the pent-up emotions beneath. They were both high on adrenaline, and AJ was as eager as the men to finish the game. But for the two of them, they were close to going home.

"Do you think Dugan is already here? Would he be brazen enough to sail right into port?" Her arms tightened around his waist.

He wished he could say something to soothe her, but that wouldn't be what she wanted. She'd want the unvarnished truth. "From what Beckworth has told me of his brother, Reginald has more than enough money to grease palms to receive at least a partial immunity. Whether they made it here before us"—he shrugged—"they would have faced the same fog leaving the Thames, and could have run into the Royal Navy or patrol ships. But, aye, I think they're already here."

"I can't believe we're back here again. Where we thought we'd finished it the last time." She traced patterns on his arm, something she did when they lay in bed together, making plans.

"This time, we see it through. We always suspected the druid's book was out there somewhere. Now we have it. Once we get the Heart Stone and send it back to Hensley, it will find its rightful place with Elizabeth." He felt her stiffen and wished there was a way he could convince her he wouldn't fade from time. "Trust that it will work out." He released her, turning her to face him. "We were meant to be together. And we will go home together."

She held onto him like a drowning woman, and he knew she was close to tears. What else could he promise her?

After a few minutes, she cleared her throat. "Sorry." The muffled word was barely recognizable. She stepped back and ran her hands over her face, getting her emotions under control. "I trust that you'll get us home." She cupped his cheek. "I'm okay now. I just needed a minute." She gave him a gentle kiss, picked up the bowl and skin, and tugged at his shirt. "Come on. Jamie can't sit still. Maire and I both think he could use some fresh air, and we need your help getting him up the stairs."

Jamie was stronger than anyone expected. While everyone had been occupied with getting the ship across the Channel, no one had paid much attention to Beckworth. He and Jamie had been doing more than playing cards and chess. Maire had mentioned she thought Beckworth was helping Jamie walk around the cabin, but none of them had known how long or often Beckworth had been assisting the younger man.

Although Jamie could walk across the galley to the stairs, he required help from Finn and Lando to get topside. Jamie didn't arrive on deck in time to see the sunset, but there was enough light for him to assess the condition of his ship. He glanced around, studied the broken yard and the makeshift sail, then nodded with a slight smile of approval. He took a deep breath then turned back to the stairs where two of his men helped him back to the cabin.

"He looks well." Lando stepped next to Finn.

"Aye. He just needs time." Finn looked around at the skeleton crew left on deck. Most of the men had been sent to their bunks to get rest. "Where's Fitz?"

"I sent him down for sleep an hour ago."

"Then why don't the two of us sail the *Daphne* to the monastery?"

Lando's hearty laugh flowed across the deck. "Like old times." He slapped Finn on the back and turned to the crew. "Enough lying about. Prepare the sails and weigh anchor. It's time to finish this."

A strong cry of approval rang out as the men scurried to get the ship underway. The shout must have woken some of the others, and they began to appear on deck. Finn glanced at the fading horizon, the darkness claiming its turn. This would be his final sail on the *Daphne*. While the trip would be brief, mixed with apprehension and a sense of loss, he was eager to return to his new life in a different century.

———

F inn watched Lando ease the ship into the bay and moor near a slip of sand barely visible along the darkened shore. A long staircase that began at the narrow edge of the beach stretched up the rocky cliff to the monastery. Three-quarters of the way up, a small outcropping led to the old iron door—a secret way into the underground tunnels of the monastery.

The crew maneuvered a dinghy into the water, preparing to transport people to shore. AJ, Maire, and Ethan gathered around Finn. He sensed their eagerness to be on land, yet a larger question remained. Would the iron door be unlocked?

Beckworth shoved past a group of men laying out lines and stepped between AJ and Maire. He glanced up at the cliffs, and Finn followed his gaze. From this angle, the monastery perched on the ledge like a shadowed behemoth, lights gleaming from within. "Jamie says the door has always been unlocked when he arrived. Sebastian never told him how he knew when to unlock it." Beckworth tugged on his sleeves and chuckled. "The monk would only say it was divine intervention."

"He probably has monks watching for signs of a ship." Ethan had donned his sword and probably had a pistol hidden in his jacket.

"There's only one way to find out." Finn nodded at Fitz, who had directed the lowering of the dinghy.

Without another word, Fitz pointed to four men, and they disappeared over the railing. A few minutes later, the smaller boat made its way across the short distance to the shore. Two men would remain with the boat while Fitz led the other two up the stairs.

Thirty minutes later, Fitz climbed back on board the *Daphne*. He was shaking his head as he made his way to the waiting group.

"Door's locked."

Not completely unexpected but disappointing just the same. Finn glanced at Maire. Her lips compressed into a thin line, and she turned away from his gaze. She was worried about Sebastian, and it seemed she had reason to be. If Sebastian had been able, he would have known they were there and had the door unlocked for them.

"We need to send someone in." Ethan's grumble summed up Finn's own thought on the matter.

The iron door had been the only entrance not watched by Dugan's men.

"Maybe Sebastian didn't have anyone watching because

they're not expecting another ship." AJ bit her lip, her hands resting on her hips, her brows furrowed as she studied the cliff.

"Maybe," Finn agreed. He didn't like it, but he had no other choice. "AJ and I will go up."

"No." Ethan's response was quick but firm.

Finn shook his head and expelled a long sigh. Before he could voice his argument, another voice interrupted them.

"I agree with Ethan." Beckworth leaned against the rail, his tone almost bored.

The last thing Finn needed was people arguing his decision. He didn't like it any better than they did. He glanced at AJ. Her mood had changed, and she was almost bouncing on the balls of her feet, eager to get going. This was the moment he wished she was more like the demure women of this century. Then he noticed his sister and the stubborn set of her chin. Maybe they weren't all demure. The decision, however, came down to one critical element.

Finn stood his ground. "AJ is the only one that knows the tunnels well enough."

"As I said before, I agree." Everyone turned to stare at Beckworth, and he laughed. "You weren't expecting that. Good. But I should be the one going with her."

Finn snorted. "You must have been dipping into Jamie's stash of Irish whiskey if you think I won't be the one going with her."

"And that would be a mistake."

"How do you figure that?"

Beckworth sighed, and Finn could have sworn he rolled his eyes. "I'm almost Reginald's twin. If he's in the monastery, he hasn't been there long, surely no more than a day. No one will be able to tell us apart."

"Unless you run into Dugan," Ethan suggested.

"True. But the odds are small and worth the risk."

AJ squeezed Finn's hand, and he reluctantly looked down.

He didn't want to admit Beckworth was right. Didn't want her out of his sight, sneaking around Dugan. His breath caught at the thought of her tossed into another dark cell. She touched his arm, stroking it softly as if taming some feral cat.

"You'll hardly know I'm gone." She locked her gaze with his, not letting him turn away. "We'll go in through the kitchen. It will take us a little longer to skirt around the monastery, but once inside the tunnels, it won't take me long. I'll raise a lantern from the top of the stairs. When you see it, start sending men up."

She'd already worked out her plan, probably had it all figured out knowing the iron door would be inaccessible. He paused, but not due to any indecision on his part. She and Beckworth were right, but he couldn't seem to stop staring at his beautiful wife, willing to run into danger. And not just for the Heart Stone. She was worried about Sebastian too. They all were.

He ran a finger down her cheek and gave her his lopsided grin. "You should change into a dress. If they do see you with Beckworth, they might think he brought you from town."

AJ moaned. "This just keeps getting better."

Beckworth snickered and put an arm around her shoulder. "I couldn't agree more."

41

AJ stared up the weather-battered wooden staircase, unable to see the top from the base.

"I'll lead." Beckworth pointed at her, "You're in the middle. Fitz will have our back." He watched her, waiting for her nod of readiness.

She stretched her head to the left and then to the right, releasing the tension. With her arms raised, she finished a quick routine to limber her muscles. She grinned when Beckworth gave her an amused look.

"After you." AJ swept an arm toward the staircase, a polite smile on her face. The sound of the waves against the rocks made her think of Baywood, and she closed her eyes. She could almost hear the gulls. The sound of heavy boots on the creaking wood snapped her back, and she waited for the third man to run by before the next man waved her forward.

Before they'd climbed into the dinghy, Finn had insisted that Fitz and a five-man team go with them. They would stay hidden in darkness and monitor the men at the front gate. No engagement unless absolutely required. AJ sucked in air as she watched the boots of the man in front of her pound up the stairs. The heavy breathing of the men surrounded her, urging her on.

Her thighs burned by the time they reached the halfway point, but she could see the outcropping ahead. By the time she stepped onto the rocky ledge, she could barely catch her breath, and her heart hammered like a freight train. She insisted on checking the iron door. How foolish would they feel if they risked their lives sneaking past the guards only to discover Sebastian had unlocked the door? Beckworth agreed. She smiled at the small victory. Her sound argument about Sebastian getting the door unlocked was only part of her reason to stop. She couldn't ignore the momentary bliss of resting her legs.

She tugged on the door and wasn't surprised to find it locked. Before she could take time to lean against the door for another minute's rest, Beckworth pulled her away.

He pushed her toward the last remaining portion of staircase. "We're almost there. You can rest when we get to the top. I promise."

He lied.

Beckworth kept the group moving at a light jog for a quarter-mile by road, which took a circuitous route. But the smoother surface was safer than attempting a goat trail in the dark. They didn't need someone spraining an ankle. Luck was on their side that the moon hadn't risen yet. When it did, the thin crescent would provide only the dimmest of light, giving them an advantage when sneaking up on Dugan's men.

When the monastery came into view, Beckworth turned left and ran for a couple hundred yards before dropping down behind a straggly bush. The men squatted in a circle around her, everyone breathing hard as they scanned their position before settling their intense focus on the front gate.

Torches had been lit and placed in sconces on the wall and in tall staffs placed in an arc around a tent and a handful of men. With all the firelight, Fitz's team would disappear into the darkness. Another stroke of luck.

"Do you think this is all the men Dugan brought, or are the rest inside?" AJ whispered as she landed on her backside, her legs shaking from the strain. She massaged them in between slow stretches, wishing she'd spent more time running in their last week of training.

"Dugan doesn't do anything small. The rest of them are probably in the inner courtyard."

The inner courtyard was beyond the main entrance, which was two wide doors that opened to allow carts through. Once inside the doors, several wooden doors led to different parts of the building and skirted the interior yard. A small, second-floor balcony overlooked the courtyard. The duke had made his grand appearance from that vantage point the last time AJ had been there. He'd been a pasty, overweight man who enjoyed looking down on others.

Beckworth pointed at Fitz. "This looks as good a place as any to settle in."

Fitz's gaze narrowed, and he scratched his chin, his beard already unruly after its forced grooming several days before. "I'd rather move up to the rise. We'll have a clearer vantage point but still be close enough to get to the front door quickly if we're needed."

Beckworth glanced up the rise and nodded. "Good choice." He rose and tapped AJ. "Let's go."

He ran off, and AJ scrambled to follow. She almost tripped when she first stood, her legs moving slower than the rest of her. Once her legs had a chance to stretch, she kept pace with Beckworth. He returned to the road and followed it toward the front doors, but before reaching them, he slowed and grabbed her arm.

She attempted to pull away as he turned right into the outside courtyard. Men sat around a crackling fire, but Beckworth blocked her view, preventing an accurate count. When a guard noticed their entrance, Beckworth yanked her to him and wrapped an arm around her shoulder. He hugged her tight as he dragged her along. Before they'd taken ten steps, AJ found herself pressed against the wall, her cheek scraping against its rough stone surface.

She pushed back, her arms flailing before Beckworth covered her with his body. She sucked in a deep breath before his hand clamped over her mouth. Unable to break free, her instincts screaming to stomp his foot, she resisted the urge and relaxed.

"Keep struggling," Beckworth whispered.

She played along. Based on the laughter and bawdy comments, Beckworth's ruse was working. So much for gallantry. She tried to peer over her shoulder, but Beckworth didn't budge. When she tried to bite his hand, he dropped it.

"How many are there?" She sucked in air, though he still held her pinned against the wall.

"About a dozen, maybe a few more." Beckworth ran a hand down her side. "Just another minute, then I'll drag you to the side door. From there, we should be close to the kitchen."

She nodded.

"Continue to struggle but not as much. Make it look like you've resigned yourself to your fate."

She snorted. "That will be the day."

He chuckled as he released his hold on her and stepped away, his quick movement so unexpected, she almost fell. Before she could, Beckworth grabbed her upper arm and resumed tugging her to the door. She kept her head down, focusing on each step as she shuffled behind him. The catcalls and grunts coming from the men made her wish she'd brought an automatic rifle through the jump. She'd be happy to blow them all away while screaming, "Say hello to my little friend."

Before she knew it, Beckworth shoved her inside a door and slammed it behind them. They were greeted by a silent hallway. She leaned against the wall and waited for her heart to stop pounding.

Beckworth scowled when he glanced at her. He reached out a hand to touch her cheek. She batted his hand away, then noticed the smear of blood on his fingers. She rubbed her cheek and winced, remembering scraping her face against the wall.

"Finn will have my hide for that." Beckworth's eyes narrowed as he continued to stare at the injury.

"He'll understand."

He snorted. "It won't stop him from taking a swing."

She smiled. "True. Just suck it up for the team." Her nose told her the direction of the kitchen. "Let's get to the kitchen before Dugan or your brother show up."

"Excellent idea." He bowed and let her lead the way.

The staff was busy preparing supper. The monks would have eaten by now, so AJ assumed Reginald was keeping with the formality of a late dinner expected of most aristocrats. No one glanced up as she and Beckworth skirted the activity, but before they left the kitchen, AJ spotted a familiar face. Try as she might, she couldn't remember the young girl's name.

When the girl looked up from the dishes she'd been cleaning, her eyes went wide at seeing AJ. Shock turned to hope, and it broke AJ's heart. It was AJ's turn to drag Beckworth, and she led him to a doorway that led to another hall. "Stay here." When he began to protest, she placed a hand on his arm. "I trusted you to get us past the guards. Now it's my turn."

He nodded and waited by the door, glancing down the hallway to ensure no one was coming.

AJ smiled as she rushed to the girl. "You remember me?"

The girl nodded.

"We came to help, but I need to get to the tunnels."

The girl glanced at the kitchen staff. One or two raised their heads but said nothing. They kept an eye on the two women as they continued their work. When the young maid returned her gaze to AJ, she nodded again.

"Where's Sebastian?" A pit opened in AJ's stomach, her heart clenching at the tears that sprung in the maid's gaze. No. They wouldn't have killed him. They couldn't. He was the only one with the answers they needed. But then she remembered Ratliff. Who knew what Reginald was capable of doing? Dugan seemed too controlled to do anything rash.

"They locked him in a cell. No one is allowed to visit him."

A huge wave of relief flooded AJ. Sebastian was still alive.

She grabbed the girl's scalded hands, still wet from the dishwater. "I'll make sure he's safe. Don't say anything about me being here. And when you hear the fighting start, run and hide."

When the girl just stared at her, AJ gave her a shake. "Do you understand? Have everyone hide so no one gets hurt."

For the first time, the start of a smile lit the girl's face, and a look of determination replaced her earlier fear. Her back straightened. "Oui. Go with God."

AJ wasn't sure God was with them. If he was, they wouldn't be sneaking around the monastery, but she nodded before turning away. When she reached Beckworth, she tugged his sleeve and moved past him, racing on silent feet to the second door on the right. Without pausing, she swung it open and stopped a few steps down, waiting for Beckworth to close the door.

Torches had been lit along the passageway, giving AJ plenty

of light as she led them down the stairs, following the route she remembered when she'd helped Finn return to the fight. Had it only been four months since their battle against the duke's men? Finn had barely been able to stand upright from the beatings he'd endured, but he'd refused to stay hidden while everyone else fought. As badly as he'd been injured, he'd still been able to catch and kill the duke. Pushing thoughts of Finn aside, she turned down a short hall and stopped at the only door.

"There are probably a dozen rooms they could have taken Sebastian, but this was the cell where they kept Finn."

The only light in the short passage came from the torches along the main hallway.

"I remember. Stay here." Beckworth backtracked and returned with a lantern. "I noticed this at the base of the stairs." He struck a flint and the lantern blazed to light. He turned to the door. "Shall we?"

AJ faced the door and stared down at the handle and tried it. "It's locked." That should have been expected.

Keys rattled, and she turned to see Beckworth pick them off a nail next to the door. He moved her aside as he unlocked the door and opened it. He stepped in first, raising the lantern and stepping aside for AJ to follow.

She couldn't quite get her feet to work. She assured herself that Sebastian was in there and was all right. At the same time, she was afraid of what she'd find. He couldn't have been in there long, but Dugan may have already begun the torture. The smell of mildew and damp earth filled her nostrils. At least it was too soon to carry the scent of human waste and blood.

She held up a hand to cut the glare from the light, then froze. Sebastian sat on a stone outcropping that formed a small platform. Finn had mentioned that was where he'd slept in between beatings because there were fewer rats. She shivered, glancing at the floor, then realized the action wasn't from the thought of rats. The temperature in the cell was chilling.

Sebastian smiled and nodded his head when he appeared to recognize them. When he didn't stand, AJ scurried over to him.

"Are you okay?"

"It's a blessing to see you again, my dear. I'm only sorry I wasn't able to greet you properly." His thin wisps of white hair swirled over his head like a gossamer nest. A trail of dried blood marked his bottom lip where it had been split open.

"They hurt you." Her indignation made Sebastian smile wider.

"A misunderstanding."

Beckworth grunted. When Sebastian finally glanced his way, the monk stared openmouthed. Then his brows relaxed, and he nodded as if to himself. "I remember when you were here the first time. You could pass for your brother, at least from a distance." He gave AJ a quick glance. "I'm glad to see you've made new friends."

"I need to open the iron door so Finn and the rest of the men can get in."

Sebastian nodded.

"Come with us."

"No," Beckworth stated flatly as Sebastian shook his head.

"Why not?" But the answer came to her before either said a word. She sighed. "In case they come to question him." She didn't want to leave him.

Beckworth moved back to the door. "They won't do anything until after dinner and cigars. By then, they should be too busy with us to worry about Sebastian." He glanced out the door before turning back to her. "We need to hurry."

She touched the monk's shoulder. "Maire will be so happy to see you."

His eyes lit up. "I knew I'd see her again. We have much to discuss."

AJ just nodded. She didn't like the grin on his face. The last thing they needed to hear was that something else endangered the future. She gave him a quick kiss on his cheek then followed Beckworth out the door. Once Beckworth had locked the door and replaced the keys, AJ turned for the main hallway and stopped dead in her tracks.

42

———————

Finn stared at the strip of beach where the stairs led up the side of the cliff. The inky darkness all but erased the bleached-colored sand. He glanced up. The moon, or what there was of it, would be out soon. Then his gaze shifted to the point on the cliff where the outcropping should be. There was still no light from AJ.

He'd sent two boatloads of men to the shore. Finn had considered joining the last team, but he wouldn't be able to see the top of the cliff from the base, or so Jamie had advised. And he wanted to be the one to see the light regardless of how irrational it sounded. The dinghy now bobbed next to the *Daphne*, waiting in the darkness with him.

A shuffle from behind made him turn. Jamie, with Lando at his side, inched his way across the deck, stopping to talk to the men. Finn had spoken to his friend right after the dim figure of AJ had disappeared from sight with the rest of the men.

When he'd entered the cabin, Jamie was busy reviewing the inventory. Ledgers, their covers stained with age and drink, lay sprawled across the bed. Rolls of charts, a dozen or more, had been stuffed into a bookshelf. The books had been pulled out and stacked haphazardly against the bulkhead.

Jamie glanced up, a smile on his face, when Finn closed the door. He'd been writing something but set the ledger and quill aside before closing the inkpot. "I would've thought you'd be in the monastery by now."

"The door was locked."

Jamie nodded. "I thought it might be. That doesn't bode well for Sebastian."

Finn dropped into the chair closest to the bed and ran a hand over his jaw. "No. It doesn't."

Jamie gave his mentor a long look. "I assume you sent AJ."

He nodded. "And Beckworth."

"That's a good choice. Most will assume he's Reginald."

Finn studied his friend. To him, Jamie had always been that young lad who'd first stowed away on the *Daphne* all those years ago. But he was his own man now and had captained this ship for two years since Finn had been gone. Jamie had shown his intelligence the first day Finn had met him. He learned quickly, and the last two missions had proven just how cunning he was. And he proved it again when he grinned at Finn.

"Is the problem that you don't trust Beckworth, or you don't like sending her into danger without you?"

"We've been apart more than we've been together these last three months. And we all know Dugan."

"They won't hurt her if they can find her. Once she's in the tunnels, she'll be safe."

"Aye. I know. We should hear from them soon. In the meantime, since we don't know what to expect, this seemed like the best time to return the *Daphne* to your capable hands."

Jamie's brow rose, his earlier good humor slipping away. "She's not quite in the same condition."

Finn gave him a sheepish look. "She'll be like new in the next couple of weeks." He paused. "And it couldn't be helped."

Jamie relented and leaned forward to reposition the pillows. "I would've done the same thing. And Valentin owed me a debt, if only for a day."

"Valentin is a good man." He grinned. "But saving us from a boarding by the French isn't quite the same as taking a ball from the British. He still owes you."

Jamie considered that. "Aye. The French could have been handled. There would have been something in the hold to see us on our way. With nothing but a loss of a couple hours."

Finn grimaced. "You wouldn't be thinking of handing over that case of Irish whiskey?" Jamie wouldn't be pleased when he discovered Maire had used most of the case for medicinal purposes.

It was Jamie's turn to grin. "I know your sister used up almost a full case, minus the three bottles Beckworth was able to save. But no one knows where I've stashed the other two cases."

Finn threw his head back and laughed. God's blood, but it had been a long time since he'd laughed like that. He patted Jamie on the shoulder. "It appears you learned well, and I've had nothing to worry about."

"I learned from the best." Jamie rubbed his jaw. "And Lando has his own way of teaching me a thing or two."

Finn grunted. "That he does." He stood. It was hard to walk away from this young man. But if all went well this evening, he'd still have time to say his final goodbye. "The *Daphne* will be good as new in no time. She always finds her way."

"She knows how well-loved she is."

Jamie's last words before Finn had departed now rang in his ears. But his thoughts weren't of the *Daphne*. He returned to the quarterdeck to continue his vigil. His thoughts were jumbled as he waited for AJ's light. His patience had grown unbearably thin.

No one had spoken to him for the past twenty minutes. Men stayed several paces away in case—in case what? In case he blindly struck out at something? He almost laughed at the thought, though he'd be willing to plant a fist into the forecastle decking if he didn't mind giving the men one more thing to fix.

A flicker.

There one minute, now gone. Had he imagined it?

Another glow. Gone. Then it reappeared, stronger than before. One second passed, then another. Finn waited an entire minute.

"Let's move." Finn was the first one down the rope ladder and into the dinghy.

A few minutes later, Ethan joined him, followed by Maire. Lando sent two more men down the ladder before jumping into the boat. The waiting oarsmen turned the dinghy toward the shore and began to row.

When the boat arrived onshore, Finn ordered the oarsmen to continue bringing over two more loads of men. They'd already assigned those who would stay behind to guard the ship and those who would fight. It hadn't been an easy decision since most wanted to fight.

He took the stairs two at a time but slowed as he neared the outcropping. Ten men, dressed in dark clothing, hunched together on the ledge, axes and poorly maintained swords in their hands. The light from a lantern showed a long stream of men trailing up the stairs where it met the road. He couldn't guess how many. He frantically searched for AJ and then Beckworth, but all he saw were strangers. They didn't appear to be anyone Dugan would bother with.

He reached for his sword, but there were too many of them. Finn doubted the additional crew from the *Daphne* would make it a fair fight. Based on the strangers' weapons, the crew could overpower them with skill, but the sheer numbers could be a problem. The boots of the crew trudging up the stairs drew close, and he grudgingly gripped the hilt. Before he freed the blade from its sheath, the men on the landing parted.

AJ strolled down the aisle they made for her. Her wide and loving smile released the band that had tightened over his chest.

Then she was in his arms, and he gripped her close, breathing in the scent of her, the strands of hair soft against his cheek. She pulled out of his embrace and gave him a quick and tender kiss.

"I found some friends."

A man followed AJ through the path the men had opened. When he stepped into the light of the lantern, Finn recognized him. It was Luis, the cart driver who moved cargo for Sebastian.

Luis, an old broadsword in his left hand, held out his right hand. His handshake was firm, his gaze lit with determination.

"It's good to have you back, Captain Murphy. We feared we would have to fight on our own." He spread out his arms as he motioned toward his men. "We're not as well trained as the men who hold the monastery, but we are willing."

Finn studied the men on the landing. He was surprised to see that most were solidly built men—some old, some young, farmers and laborers. All with the same fierce conviction on their faces. They might not have the same skills, but it appeared they had the numbers, and they weren't just fighting for the monastery. If Reginald moved into the monastery as the duke had, the town's smuggling operations would be over, and they'd face economic hardships that were so often the results of a long war.

"Good to have you."

"Luis heard about Dugan's ship arriving and that a coach was being hired to take someone to the monastery. After the episode with the duke, he decided to take a couple men and check-in with Sebastian. They've been hiding in the tunnels until more of the townsmen could arrive." She hesitated. "Although there's a slight disagreement with the plan." AJ stepped back, her expression telling him it might not be as slight of a problem as she suggested.

Finn studied Luis. "How so?"

The younger man's face flushed with excitement that would have been easy enough to read without the assistance of the crescent moon. Within the glow of the lanterns, it seemed zealous.

Before Luis had a chance to speak, AJ lunged for Finn. At first, his hand reached for his sword, expecting a ruse from the men. Then he felt her tugging at her bow and quiver that he'd slung over his shoulder before leaving the ship. At least she had her priorities, though blissfully unaware that the grab for her precious weapons almost sparked a fight. He gave her an indulgent smile as he handed her the weapons.

She gripped the bow and quiver firmly in her fists then glanced back to Luis and Finn. She appeared to be waiting for them to continue their discussion, as if she hadn't interrupted what might have been a build up to a confrontation. Maybe it had been a ruse after all. One of her own making in an attempt to cool tempers. Sometimes his wife's actions were hard to decipher.

Whether planned or not, Luis's momentum had been slowed, and he glanced at the ground before raising his gaze to meet Finn's. "We're here and ready to fight. Not sit around while they eat the monastery's food and drink their wine."

"We agree with you. But our priority is to collect a missing artifact. That takes precedence over everything else."

"Even Sebastian?"

Finn nodded. "He would agree himself, and I think you know that."

Luis turned away, his knuckles whitening as they fisted the sword in his left hand.

"You said it yourself. Your men aren't skilled, but that doesn't make them useless."

Luis stood a little straighter when he faced Finn again, though he didn't appear convinced they'd be included in anything important.

"We need to work together, or we'll lose a lot of people on both sides." Finn nodded toward the townsmen. "These men have families. Let's regroup in the tunnels and determine a plan that will see the Englishman routed, your smuggling operations back on track, and get your men back home."

Finn stepped back and waited for Luis to consider his options. He sensed Lando and Ethan at his back, but he suspected Luis understood the stakes. The younger man glanced at his men, and though their desire to route the invaders from the monastery never wavered, the tension eased, and the men lowered their weapons.

Not waiting for an actual response, Finn strode toward the iron door. "Let's move men inside. We need to get them off the stairs, especially anyone that might be seen from the road."

"There are several empty rooms where the men can stay." AJ walked next to him until they reached the door. "There's also a hidden room where we can make plans."

"Work with Luis and Lando to get most of the men in the rooms. Mix them up so the men from the ship and town get to know each other." Finn pulled Lando and Luis aside, his first question for Lando. "You know where this planning room is?" When Lando nodded, Finn continued, "Good. Once you have everyone settled, I want both of you to bring two of your best men and meet us there."

Lando and Luis moved the men quickly as they followed AJ into the tunnels. As the crowd on the landing and stairs began to thin, Finn pulled Ethan and Maire aside.

"We must have more men than Dugan." Ethan had pushed Maire close to the door but out of the way of the men still trailing into the tunnels.

"Maybe." Finn watched his sister. She'd taken a few steps closer to the door to speak to the men before they entered the lower floors of the monastery. "But the townsmen are no match for Dugan's skilled fighters." Then he shrugged. "Maybe the sheer volume will be an advantage."

Within twenty minutes, the landing had been cleared. AJ returned to lead Finn, Ethan, and Maire to the planning room. Lando had left four other men—two from the ship and two from town—to guard the door.

As he followed AJ's torch, men's voices leaked from beneath the damp wooden doors of the storage rooms. Luis waited for them at an intersection. Several yards farther, AJ stopped next to a stone bench. A door that didn't look like a door was partly opened, and she started to step inside when Finn pulled her and Luis aside.

"Where's Beckworth?" Finn asked.

"He's watching over Sebastian." AJ launched into a quick review of what she knew. "There were a dozen men at the front doors to the monastery. Fitz is holding position on the rise. Another two dozen guards are in the outer courtyard. Sebastian was in a holding cell, but other than a bruise and split lip, he hadn't been harmed. Beckworth stayed to make sure nothing else happened to him."

"A change of plan." Finn pointed at Luis. "I need Beckworth with us. I'll need four of your best swordsmen to stay with Sebastian until we finalize our next steps. If anyone comes for Sebastian, take them out. I don't want anyone sounding the alarm. The men will eventually be missed, but it will give us more time." He paused as he considered the situation. "Then I'll need another group of ten men to meet up with Fitz. Have them go back out the iron door and come in from the road. You'll find Fitz on the rise. Move slowly so he doesn't shoot any of you. Their one mission, besides helping if fighting breaks out, is to prevent anyone from leaving by the road. We don't want anyone escaping."

"I'll need to lead the men to Sebastian." AJ stepped next to Luis, and Finn nodded. "Get back here as quickly as you can. I want to have plans in place before Reginald and Dugan finish dinner."

After Luis and AJ raced down the passage toward the storage rooms, Finn entered the secret room to find several torches and lanterns already glowing. More than a dozen chairs circled the scarred, wooden table that stretched the length of the room. Two men from the ship and two from town were already conversing as they waited.

It didn't take long before AJ, Luis, and Beckworth joined the small group. Finn shook his head at AJ. At some point between taking Luis's men to Sebastian and returning, she'd found time to change back to pants. Her fancy shoulder harness firmly in place. She set her bow and quiver next to her chair within easy reach. His deadly little soldier.

Ethan didn't wait to launch into their problem. "There could be at least another dozen guards or more camped in the inner courtyard."

"I'd count on it," Beckworth added.

"We need to know for sure." Finn leaned back in the heavy wooden chair, and he ran a finger along the wood of the table. He glanced at AJ, who was honing her dagger. When he glanced across the table at Lando, he was doing the same thing. Peas in a pod.

"We can do that for you." Luis nodded to his two friends. "Francois's wife is a housemaid at the monastery. She can find out from the other staff how many and where."

"Everyone should coordinate with someone in the kitchen." AJ never looked up from her task. "No one seems to be spending time there other than to give orders. And it's the closest to the door leading to the lower floors."

"Easy enough to do." Luis grabbed Francois's arm before he reached the door. "Have your wife gather the information, but you stay hidden on the stairs that lead to the tunnels. If you get into trouble, lead the guards to the holding cell where they're keeping Sebastian."

Francois grinned, and it was a grin that made Finn glad the man was on their side.

"Before you go," Beckworth called out, "find out which room Dugan is staying in. I have a guess, but let's be sure."

"What about Reginald?" Ethan asked.

Beckworth snorted. "My dear brother will be staying in the same room our father did. Second floor, make a right, last set of double doors." No one questioned him.

"Reginald and Dugan are our primary targets." Finn didn't want the bloodshed from their last encounter at the monastery if it could be avoided. If they cut Dugan down, Finn suspected most of Dugan's men would either try to run, or they'd simply drop their swords.

"We'll need a diversion." Lando's quiet voice kept tempo with each strike of his dagger on the whetstone.

Maire sat up, and for the first time, Finn noticed the leather bag that carried her herbs. "I still have valerian root and something Bart shared with me. There isn't enough time to knock the men out, but they won't be very agile of foot or with sword."

"Are there enough barrels of wine or ale for the job?" Lando asked.

Luis nodded. "There are several barrels of wine in one of the storage rooms." He shook his head. "We'll lose a great deal of money."

"Consider it covered." Finn grinned at everyone's surprised expressions. "Hensley sanctioned the mission. I think England can spare a few pounds toward its success." After the laughter settled, Finn considered the number of men and how they were dispersed. "We'll need at least three barrels."

"Dugan doesn't let his men drink while working." Beckworth scratched his chin. "But if I were to walk behind the men with the barrels, and simply give a nod or two, they may consider it an official approval."

"You would have to get too close. Someone in the guard might suspect you're not Reginald." Ethan's comment quieted the room, but Beckworth didn't seem concerned.

"I'll wear a robe. Reginald seems to have become fond of them with his druid gatherings. I'm guessing most of the guards have seen him dressed up in a robe at least once. I'll show just enough of my face for their minds to put the rest together."

"How long will this take?"

Maire shrugged. "At least a couple of hours from when you start pouring the wine. Maybe less, but I'd prefer caution. I only know how quickly the potion acts on injured men." She smiled at Finn, and he gulped. So that was what she'd dowsed him with that made everything spin. He almost felt sorry for the guards.

"If we time it right, we could be passing out the wine as Reginald and Dugan are starting their last course." AJ tucked her whetstone and dagger away. "The men handing out the wine can also confirm the number of guards."

"Afterward, we split up." Finn wasn't sure they'd be happy with the teams he'd already decided on, but they would each be satisfied once their task was completed. "Beckworth and Ethan will go after Reginald and the Heart Stone." Beckworth's feral grin confirmed he was on board. When Ethan nodded in agreement, Finn let out a sigh. Ethan could work out his anger with Reginald for Maire's kidnapping and imprisonment.

"Maire, I need you to take Sebastian to his room and stay with him." When her eyes flashed in defiance, he quickly added. "I think the pistols will be better than the rifle, but you should keep two of them with you just in case." His words seemed to calm her.

"I'm his protection?"

Finn couldn't help but grin at her surprise. "Yes. And the two of you have a great deal to discuss. I don't see why you can't do both as long as you stay focused on your primary mission—keep Sebastian safe." When she nodded, he was left with the most difficult assignment, but he turned to Luis first. "I'll need you and your men to keep a light presence throughout the monastery. Keep most of your men spread out but hidden. Their task is to keep watch over the guards. If one or two become unruly, take them out and hide the bodies."

His gaze landed on AJ, her shoulders tensed, her lips thinned. He didn't hesitate. "I need you at the iron door."

She didn't say anything, but she didn't look happy. He figured she was mentally calculating his reasoning, and by the scrunching of her forehead, she was having a hard time seeing it.

"You already have men at the door." She waited, but when Finn didn't respond, she gave it more thought. "That's the only path to the ship." She shook her head. "I still don't understand."

"The men at the door can fight, but I need someone who understands more of what's happening to decide whether we need more men brought up from the ship, or if we should be telling them to weigh anchor."

Her eyes widened until Finn thought they might pop out of her head. "You're putting me in charge of making that decision?"

He nodded. "I think you've been on the ship long enough to make the call. You can ask the men for advice, but it will be your decision."

She glanced across the table. "What about Lando?"

"I need him with me. We're going after Dugan."

Her eyes glistened, but there was nothing he could do to calm her fears. She had every right to be worried. They all did.

Beckworth jumped up, tugged at his sleeves, then rubbed his hands together. His expression was full of mirth. "Perfect. I do so love a good raid in the wee hours of the night. Now, I must find a well-tailored robe, preferably in white."

44

Sebastian eased into the chair, a slight puff of air escaping his lips when he leaned back. His usually bright eyes were dulled by exhaustion, the dark circles emphasizing the deep crevices at the corners of his eyes. Blue veins showed under his pale skin, and AJ wondered if it was an effect of hypothermia.

Maire wrapped a blanket around him, then followed it with another. "You should have told someone how cold you were."

"I just need a good cup of tea, and I'll be back to my old self again."

"Just another minute." AJ poured hot water into a serving pot. A soft explosion of scents intoxicated her nostrils, and she breathed deep. She found a mug and waited for the infusion to complete. "I'll share a cup with you, then I need to get to the door."

"Have they passed out the wine yet?" Maire gave Sebastian his tea after stirring something into it. He didn't question her actions before taking his first sip.

"About an hour ago, I think." She snorted. "I'm not sure Beckworth needed to prance about in his robes. From what Ethan said, the men didn't need much coaxing. Maybe Dugan's deprived them for too long."

They chatted for another ten minutes before AJ stood. She would have preferred to stay and talk all night, but she sensed the need to get into place. She pulled the harness over her head and checked to ensure the daggers were secure. She reached into her pockets and confirmed her personal dagger, the Heart Stone, and her wedding ring were tucked away. When she slung her quiver over her shoulder, Sebastian stood, the blankets falling to the floor.

"Where are you going?" Maire asked as she picked up one of the blankets.

"It's time for us to go as well."

AJ stared at him for a moment then glanced at Maire. They had just reviewed the plan with Finn, and no one mentioned Sebastian or Maire leaving the room. Maybe Sebastian injured his head when he'd been hit. "Where are you planning to go? This is where you're supposed to be."

The monk shook his head. "The best place I can be is upstairs. I need to watch over my people."

"Your people are fine." Maire placed one of the blankets over his shoulders.

Sebastian patted her hand then removed the blanket before folding it and placing it on the table. "There's a small office next to the kitchen. It's out of the way and has a second door that leads to the herb garden. Everyone on the staff knows to look for me there." He reached for the door but gave Maire a sharp look when she reached out to stop him. "You can bring your weapons and guard me from there if it makes you feel better."

Maire tapped her foot and glanced at AJ, who just shrugged. What were they going to do? Tie him down? Sebastian had a mind and will of his own. And a back door was always a good idea. There were plenty of places to hide in the dark if they had to go out that way. Whatever they were going to do, they needed to do it now. "Sounds like he has it worked out. It would be best to get in place before the dinner is over."

AJ waited until the glow from Sebastian's lantern faded down the passageway. She made sure the entrance to Sebastian's secret lair was closed then followed the tunnels to the outer door. The brisk air nipped at her cheeks. The men greeted her with husky grunts, and she walked to the stairs and gazed down at the *Daphne Marie*. It took several minutes before her eyes adjusted to the darkness and the ship's image cleared. There wasn't a flicker of light, only the faintest glow from the moon. The ship was visible, but you had to be searching for it.

She returned to the men and sat down near the entrance to the tunnels. The ground was frigid hard, and she wrapped her coat tighter. She had traded her dress for the coat with one of the kitchen staff, and though the coat was a bit ragged, what there was of it was warm.

Now came the wait.

———

Sebastian led the way, only stopping when they reached the doorway that led to the main hall. He poked his head out and, after a moment, raced down the hall to the kitchen. Maire's footsteps were silent as she followed him, cursing under her breath. It was useless to ask him anything, and the noise would only attract unwanted attention.

They passed the opened archway into the kitchen then stopped in front of the next door on the right. Sebastian tested the latch and it opened easily. He disappeared inside and Maire followed, glancing up and down the hallway before quietly shutting the door.

Sebastian had already lit a lantern and was lighting a second one. "There should be a few sticks of wood to start a fire. I had a pitcher of water in here this morning before the duke's son arrived. Mary isn't very quick to change it. Ah, yes, here it is." He fumbled in a desk drawer and pulled out a small tray with tea and cups. "If you can put the water on, we'll be settled in."

Maire continued to follow his orders. The weight of the druid's grimoire in her pocket reminding her they needed to talk, but first, they needed to get settled. Once the fire was lit and the kettle was warming, Maire set out the teacups. She'd given Sebastian the druid's book, and he sat near one of the lanterns reading a page or two before flipping to another random section. When she placed a mug of tea in front of the monk, he closed the book and rubbed his eyes.

"I'm afraid my eyes can't absorb any more in this light. They aren't as young as they used to be, child. Tell me what you think of this book. Was the druid as mad as everyone claimed?"

Maire sat down and held the mug with both hands. Steam rose from it, and she passed the cup under her nose to catch the aroma before testing the first sip. "My current opinion is that he was quite sane when he began. It's possible he was on to something with his early testing of the small stone. By the end, either his obsession over the stones and time travel got the best of him, or the isolation did. His last chapters make no sense. I've tried several translation keys to no avail." She set the mug down and leaned across the table. This time, with Sebastian's aid, a more thorough translation could be performed. "Maybe you can sense a pattern in his later writings that I missed."

He avoided her gaze. There was something he wasn't telling her. She opened her mouth to ask, but something made her stop. She wasn't sure why until she heard the sound again. Sebastian turned toward the door.

Maire yanked a rifle from the duffel and moved to the farthest table, dragging the duffel with her. She'd primed both rifles and muskets before leaving the ship. Her pistols had also been prepared, and she laid one on the table next to the other firearms. She picked up her favorite rifle and aimed it at the door.

The soft knock made her jump. She wasn't expecting that. She nodded at Sebastian, who stepped toward the door. When he opened it, a young girl, no older than fifteen, popped in with a tray of food. Maire dropped the rifle to the table.

"We smelled the fire in the hearth, and Cook thought you could use something to eat now that you're out of the dungeon." The girl placed the tray on the table, gave the weapons a quick glance before ducking her head and sneaking a peek at Maire through her bangs.

"That was kind of you." Sebastian grabbed a hunk of cheese, nibbling on the end as he surveyed the other items.

The young maid, who Maire thought might be Mary, shuffled toward her. "There should be enough for the both of you. And the kitchen staff wanted to say they were happy to hear you were back, m'lady."

"It's just Maire, and thank the staff for me. I just wish it was better circumstances."

"Yes, m'lady, I mean Maire." She curtsied, which made it all the more awkward. "Oh, that reminds me. The guards were served their wine an hour ago. Laney, that's one of the stable boys, he says he saw a couple of them stumbling around. Word is, there are men on the move to the viscount's chamber."

45

Beckworth dashed down the hall, Ethan close on his heels. They'd been hiding in a storage room filled with dusty trunks of old books and ledgers, some dating back centuries. The official records of the monastery. They'd spent half their time rummaging through the trunks, but other than trivial notes of life in the abbey and a note Ethan had found on the monks' opinion on the best use of whey, there wasn't anything interesting enough to pass the time.

Before they'd found the storage room, Ethan had monitored the disbursement of wine. All the men had donned monk robes and Ethan had done the same. As Beckworth had predicted, they found one of Reginald's druid robes with other dirty clothes waiting to be laundered in the morning. At first, Dugan's guards had questioned their good fortune when the barrels of wine were rolled out. When Beckworth appeared like a phantom in the dark, a portion of his face clearly visible, they couldn't pour the wine fast enough.

Ethan braced for an alarm to be raised. When they left the barrel with the guards and moved onto the next group at the front doors, the men reacted the same way, and Ethan began to relax. Until they moved to the inner courtyard. The staff hadn't exaggerated. Two dozen men lounged in small groups. These were hardcore mercenaries, and when Beckworth appeared in his white cloak, the men weren't impressed. These guards weren't scared of Reginald as the other men appeared to be. That meant only one thing to Ethan. These were Dugan's most trusted men, and the most deadly. Ethan grew cold when the captain of the guard took the first cup and swirled it around. Then he sniffed it. Ethan wasn't sure if the man was a wine snob, as Stella called it, or if the guard suspected foul play.

Ethan released his breath when the man nodded and cups were distributed to the men. Beckworth tossed the robe to a townsman as they made their way to the storage room. Before the man ran off, Ethan asked him to find someone who knew all the exits out of the inner courtyard. They would need to keep these particular men contained as long as they could.

Now, over an hour later, as they ran toward Reginald's room, no alarm had been sounded. The plan was working.

Beckworth stopped at an intersecting hallway then glanced back at Ethan. "Are you still worried about the guards?"

"The men in the inner courtyard are going to be a problem."

"Probably. But we would be foolish to think we'd rid the place of vermin without some bloodshed. Trust that the others are doing what you asked. We have our own problems." Beckworth peered down the hallway then turned and led them in the opposite direction. When he stopped at the next hallway, he whispered. "Remember, Dugan will have guards posted outside Reginald's room."

Ethan ran a hand through his hair and stared at Beckworth. As if he hadn't been standing right next to the man when the housemaid told them there were three guards outside his brother's bedchamber. Rather than respond with something caustic, which would only encourage Beckworth, he simply nodded. Though it didn't do much good.

Beckworth grinned at him before glancing up and down the hall, and without hesitation, bolted down the hallway.

The entrance to the secret passage was down the hall from the door that led to the outer courtyard, which was the door AJ and Beckworth had entered earlier that evening. Ethan drew his sword when the sound of boots approached from another hallway. He lowered the tip when one of the ship's crew rounded the corner. The man's voice was barely audible but loud enough for Ethan to hear that the outside guards who were still awake had been stumbling. Then the man melted into the darkness of the hallway.

"Ready?" Beckworth asked.

When Ethan nodded, Beckworth opened the door, leading them into a room that appeared to be a cloak closet. That made some sense if the door that led outside was just down the hall. Beckworth shoved cloaks and robes aside to reveal the back wall. He muttered as he felt around the edges of the wall until a click echoed in the room. It was followed by a quiet whoosh as a door popped open. Beckworth pushed on it, shone his lantern inside, then stepped through the opening.

Ethan followed, rearranging the cloaks before shutting the door behind him. Beckworth held the lantern so Ethan could see the narrow set of stairs that led upward. They took the steps slowly, and when they reached the end, Beckworth set the lantern down, searched for the mechanism to open the door, then extinguished the light.

"Here we go," Beckworth whispered as he moved into the next room.

The first step wasn't all that tricky. The door opened into an empty dressing chamber, and with Reginald fast asleep, he wouldn't be worrying about his wardrobe. Ethan hoped this wasn't a night for druid gatherings.

The dressing room was quiet, but that couldn't be said of Reginald's bedchamber. Hushed murmurs floated around the chamber. Ethan pressed closer to Beckworth, who had stepped partway into the room. Soft light from candles flickered, casting undulating shadows on the wall. Then a giggle.

Beckworth glanced at Ethan with wide eyes. Ethan wasn't sure if Beckworth's expression was one of dismay or disbelief. He had the same reaction. Obviously, neither of them had given any consideration that Reginald wouldn't be alone.

Finn stretched until his feet hit the wall. He leaned back against the staircase railing, the balusters digging into his back. He and Lando had been sitting on the stairs for well over an hour. They had followed AJ when she led Maire to the cell where Sebastian was being held. A cell Finn had experienced firsthand. He'd spent a few days in there as a guest of the duke and Dugan.

Finn and Lando had continued on after leaving AJ and Maire. They followed the tunnel to the staircase that led to the main floor. One of the housemaids met them in the hall and took them to another staircase that led to the cellars where most of the wine was stored.

Now, they sat halfway down the stairs, a lantern on a lower step, away from the door. There was more than enough light for Finn to study his friend.

The big man faced him, leaning against the wall, his head back, eyes closed. Lando had the uncanny ability to sleep at any moment and could wake at the slightest sound. It was a skill he'd honed over the years. He tried to teach Finn, and it worked on occasion, but only when the stakes weren't high. Finn's stress levels were off the charts at this particular moment.

He tried to sit straighter so his legs would have more room.

"You could never master silencing your inner spirit." Lando spoke low, his words nothing more than a grumble.

"I'm getting too old for this." Finn gave up and moved up a step so he could sit, his legs perched on a lower step.

"In a few hours, you'll be home."

Home. Baywood. He'd spent three months in that dismal cell, wondering if he'd ever see the inn again. Now, the possibility was within his grasp. It always had been. AJ and he could have left at any time, but at what cost? The only way they could plan a future and know the past couldn't touch them was to put this matter of the stones and book to rest. They were so close.

"And what of you?" Finn asked. "How much longer will you sail with Jamie? Why don't you find that woman of yours and settle down?"

A deep chuckle rose, and Lando peered through a partially lifted eyelid. "I admit I've been giving it more consideration. You will be going home soon, but our mission won't be over until the Heart Stone is placed in Hensley's hands."

"Which means another Channel crossing."

Lando shrugged. "We'll sail farther west and head to Bristol. It should be safe enough."

Safe enough didn't really mean safe, but for the men of the *Daphne*, it would seem a pleasure cruise compared to what they were used to.

Lando's hand shot out, and he put a finger to his lips. Someone was in the hall. Finn hadn't heard it, but he knew better than to question his old first mate. After the wine had been handed out and the kitchen cleaned, the staff were to go directly to their rooms and remain there until morning, regardless of what they heard. Some had mumbled their disagreement, wanting to be included in defending the monastery. In the end, they heeded the fair warning.

When the footsteps stopped outside the door, Lando extinguished the lantern. A soft rap sounded. After a few seconds, another knock. This time Finn heard the person move away.

"Let's go." Finn stood and waited for Lando.

The door opened quietly, and after a quick check of the hall, Finn stepped out and made a right, his long strides rushed but not running. He passed three rooms, the soft glow of dying embers providing enough light to see that each room appeared empty. When they reached the foyer, they passed the main staircase leading to the second floor, stopping briefly to listen for guards.

Hearing nothing, they continued down another hallway to the servant's stairs, which led up to their rooms on the third floor. There were rooms on the first floor for the monks in service. The second-floor rooms were for the prior of the abbey and other higher-ranking monks and guests. This set of stairs had a landing on the second floor, which provided access to a narrow hallway between the wings.

When they reached the second floor, Finn took a tentative step toward the main hallway. Reginald's room would be at the end of the hall to their left. He stuck his head out and peered into the darkness. If the guards were down there, he couldn't see them. He hoped that meant they couldn't see him.

Finn turned right until he stood in front of Dugan's bedchamber at the opposite end of the hall from Reginald's room. He'd been surprised when the staff confirmed Dugan kept no guards at his door. But then, who would be stupid enough or crazy enough to disturb Dugan? Other than Lando and himself, of course.

Based on Lando's steady breathing, he must have taken a position across the door from Finn. The hallway was too dark to make out Lando's features, but he reached for Lando's shoulder while he settled his hand on the hilt of his sword. He tapped his finger on Lando's shoulder, and on the third tap, Finn opened the door.

A fire burned low in the hearth, and Finn swept his gaze from left to right. The chamber appeared empty. Felt empty. He took a tentative step through the door, then another, Lando directly behind him. Once they passed the threshold, Lando shut the door but didn't latch it.

The drapes around the bed were partially open, but the light from the fire cast too many shadows to confirm if it was occupied. Finn approached on silent feet. He stopped two steps from the bed and used the tip of his sword to pull back the drapes.

Empty.

He glanced around the room, searching for someplace Dugan could be hiding. The expansive room had few amenities, and of those, none were large enough to shield someone of Dugan's size.

Lando strode out of the dressing room and shook his head. "Maybe he left to relieve himself."

Finn shrugged. "Let's wait in the dressing room."

They waited fifteen minutes before Finn got that itch. The one that said something wasn't right.

Where the hell was Dugan?

46

─────────

Maire placed the two muskets back in the duffel but left the rifles and pistol out until she could coerce Sebastian to follow her back to the tunnels. She settled into her chair, tapping her fingers on her mug of tea. She was beginning to understand Ethan's need to pace.

"We should be going. Let me package some food to take with us." She watched Sebastian as he picked at his meal. It must have been hours since he last ate. There hadn't been any tray or plate in the cell, and she doubted the guards focused on housekeeping. Sebastian had been locked in the cell most of the day without food or water, yet he picked at his plate as if he had all the time in the world.

"Do you believe the druid traveled to the future more than once?" Sebastian's asked as he continued to nibble on a sausage.

Maire sipped her tea. After her last visit to the monastery and witnessing the damage Dugan could inflict, Sebastian should know how bad this could get. Two dozen townspeople had joined them this time. Farmers and merchants who were no match against skilled mercenaries. The monk had been just as stoic when the team fought Dugan's men the last time, but the

335

two of them had been locked away in his secret chamber that the duke had never been able to find. Now, they weren't more than twenty feet from the kitchen. Maybe his mind wasn't as clear as it used to be.

"Maire? Are you all right?"

She glanced up and barked out a short laugh. "I could ask the same of you. You heard that it's about to begin."

He nodded, and his gaze darted around the table. "The grimoire?"

"Aye. I put it back in my pocket."

He continued to nod while he chewed a piece of cheese. "Good that you're keeping it close. I'd like to read more of it once I have more light. You didn't answer my question about the druid."

She leaned over the table and grasped his hand. "It's time to go, Sebastian."

He squeezed her hand and smiled. "I suppose you're right. It will begin soon."

Maire pulled her hair back and began to push away from the table when stomping boots echoed in the hallway.

Sebastian looked up, a dreamy look on his face. "They're here."

Maire picked up the rifle just as the door was yanked open. Her eyes grew wide with horror.

Dugan.

He seemed just as surprised, and while that pleased her, and she wanted to relish the sensation a moment longer, she squeezed the trigger without taking the time to sight it.

The ball splintered the wooden door frame, missing Dugan but forcing him to dive out of the way. He didn't stay down for long. The man was quick for his size, but when he came at the door again, Maire didn't hesitate with the second rifle.

She had the rifle trained on the door. And though smoke

from the last shot filled the room, she spotted Dugan through the haze when he moved into the doorway. She fired with the same result as Dugan dove in a different direction.

Not having enough time to grab the muskets, she pulled out her pistol. The sound of running boots made her race to the doorway. She caught a glimpse of his cloak as he ducked around a corner.

If she hadn't been surprised at seeing Dugan, she would have taken more time on her first shot. Then she noticed the drop of blood on the floor. Well, that made her feel better. She followed the trail of blood halfway down the hall. Not enough of it. He might have gotten hit with splinters.

Maire raced back to the room, thankful Sebastian was standing while wrapping up his bread and cheese. "I just need a few minutes to reload." Once the rifles were primed, she packed them in the duffel.

She hefted the duffel on her shoulder, checked her pocket for the grimoire, and picked up her pistol. "We need to get to the tunnels before he sends men back for us."

Sebastian nodded and left the room, but rather than leading her toward the door to the tunnels, he turned for the kitchen.

Maire grabbed his arm. Was he confused? "Where are you going?"

"Not back to the tunnels."

"Are you mad as the druid? We need to hide."

He shook his head. "Not again. Never again. I hid with you before. At the time, it seemed the wisest thing to do. This time, I can help."

She shifted the duffel and followed him to the kitchen. "How can you help? Dugan has his mercenaries everywhere."

When they arrived in the kitchen, he led her to a door on the far side. She assumed it was a storage room and wasn't disappointed when they entered. The shelves were filled with bags of flour, rows of canned foods, and bins of root vegetables. He walked to the back where other sacks of grain had been pushed aside, leaving the back wall clear. He knocked on the wall.

"Another secret passage?" She could live here for decades and never find them all.

"Of a sort. It was added after the duke was removed. This was one of our larger storage rooms, but we added a wall. Just in case."

The monk was full of surprises.

He knocked a second time. What she thought had been a crack in the plaster opened to reveal the camouflaged door. Hidden inside were two men, the one who opened the door and another who huddled around a lantern. He stood when he saw Sebastian.

"It's time." Sebastian turned and shooed Maire back to the kitchen. She dropped the duffel, the weight digging into her shoulder, and waited for an explanation.

The two men followed Sebastian out. They were tall men, more lanky than brawny, but they carried bows, their quivers slung over their shoulders. Archers. She raised a brow at Sebastian, who seemed to be quite pleased with himself.

"So, what's the plan?" She had to ask since Sebastian probably wouldn't volunteer the information.

"Have some patience, child. We don't want to be too late, but we'll be safer if we take the long way around." He'd taken a few steps when he stopped to watch her heft the duffel. He pointed at the men. "Will one of you help Maire with her bag?"

Beckworth and Ethan hovered in the dressing room, the noises from the bedchamber more than Ethan wanted to hear.

"This seems the best time to surprise him," Ethan suggested, his voice low.

"It seems almost a shame. I really didn't think the old boy had it in him to find anyone willing." Beckworth seemed genuinely shocked. "All right. You grab the woman, and I'll take Reginald."

"We could just announce ourselves." Ethan raised his sword. "We are armed."

"And odds are Reginald will have a pistol by his bedside." Beckworth eyed him. "You're not squeamish about naked women, are you?"

Ethan stood a little taller. "That's not the point."

Beckworth chuckled when a boom sounded from somewhere in the monastery. When the second shot followed, neither man wasted any time.

Reginald's head had shot up at the sound, the woman underneath him starting to crawl away. He turned his head in time to see the two men racing toward him and barely had time to shout, "Guards."

Ethan ignored the door, which remained closed. Maybe the guards hadn't heard the call. More likely, all three had gone to investigate what had surely been gunfire. If that was true, the guards would be back soon, but well after Reginald was dealt with. Thank the heavens for small miracles.

He caught the woman by the arm as she pulled on a robe, and he yanked her away when she grabbed for more clothing. They barely missed getting slammed into the wall by a fleeing Reginald. Beckworth had been right. Reginald had leaped for the pistol on the bedside table, but seeing that Beckworth was almost on him, he backtracked. Reginald had rolled off the bed toward Ethan and the woman, grabbing a sword from the floor.

The clash of steel as the two brothers came together echoed in the room. The woman screamed. Ethan considered taking her to the dressing room to flee through the passage. But how many people knew of the passage? There would be a great deal more after the woman told everyone of her harrowing escape.

Better to push her out to the hall. Surely the guards would let her pass. The woman began struggling, swinging her free arm around to clock him in the head. He caught her flapping arm and moved her out of the way as Reginald forced Beckworth across the room, his blade swinging in wide arcs as if determined to remove his brother's head.

Ethan dragged the woman to the double doors and flung one open, prepared to surprise the guards with the flailing hellcat. There was no one there. As he suspected, the guards had moved farther down the hall, where, lucky for him, Finn and Lando had engaged them. By the time he managed to pull the enraged woman toward the staircase, one of the guards was down, the other two not faring very well.

The woman broke free from his grasp and raced down the stairs on her own, her partially opened silk robe flying behind her. At least with the robe she got something of value for the evening.

He turned just as a guard crashed into him and they both went down. The guard rolled him over and punched him in the jaw. Irritated by the events of the evening, Ethan instinctively punched back. They rolled again, and when the guard brought his arm back to wind up for another blow, Ethan slid a knife into his side, then shoved the man off him.

Finn reached out a hand. "I see you've found the party."

Once on his feet, Ethan turned in search of Beckworth. The brothers' fight had moved into the hallway. Reginald used practiced, almost choreographed sweeps and lunges as he forced Beckworth into a defensive posture. A bloodstain marred Beckworth's left sleeve.

Finn slapped Lando on the back. "Let's go. The other guards would have heard the shots."

Lando led the way down the stairs, and Ethan watched Finn trail after the big man. Ethan wanted to follow, but he had to stay and make sure Reginald was down should Beckworth fall.

He was useless, unable to join the fight with Finn, and nothing to do but watch Beckworth and Reginald fight. It was clear who the better swordsman was. Even with Reginald's precise, classroom form and smooth swings, Beckworth was lighter on his feet and never stopped moving. From lunges to parries, to his short jabs and forceful blocks, Beckworth had the edge. Which made Ethan question why he remained on the defensive. Beckworth should have been able to cut Reginald down by now.

"Will you stop playing and finish him off," Ethan growled over the sound of steel. "We need to get downstairs and join the real fight."

Beckworth ignored him as he continued to let Reginald force him down the hall.

"Tell me, dear brother..." Beckworth's tone was sticky sweet. "What happened when Sir Ratliff came to Waverly?"

Reginald sneered. "I met with him in the drawing room. Even wore one of your insufferable jacket and waistcoat ensembles." He spat in distaste. "But he'd barely been offered a drink before he called me out as an imposter. Knew after my first awkward hello I wasn't you. I had no idea you were friends."

"He always was a smart man."

"And who could have guessed you'd have friends in such high places."

"You've always underestimated me, brother."

Ethan wasn't sure why Beckworth kept calling him brother, but Reginald appeared to fight with more furor each time he heard it. Beckworth was wearing him down.

"A mistake Father seemed to make as well." Reginald's night shirt was wet with sweat. It stuck to his chest and arms. His eyes blazed with a cold fury. "I told him a street thug knew nothing of loyalty or family."

"Perhaps if I'd been raised as his son and your brother, I would have felt more attachment."

"As if we'd ever take in a bastard."

"So why did you kill Ratliff, or had that been a mistake?"

"Oh, no mistake. He would have created problems for me. With his position in court, he could have persuaded the magistrate to force me from Waverly." He shrugged before he lunged, stabbing at nothing but air. "But I wasn't the one who killed him. I let Dugan have that pleasure. He does seem to enjoy it. It wasn't until after Ratliff was dead that I discovered he might have the Heart Stone. Imagine my dismay."

Beckworth seemed to have heard enough. His stance changed and he leaned forward, his swing picking up a more intense tempo as he went on the offense. Or would have, if he'd seen the fallen guard before tripping over him. He twisted and landed on his back.

Reginald didn't hesitate, striking faster than Ethan would have guessed. Beckworth seemed to know where Reginald would strike, and he rolled in the opposite direction, but not before the sword sliced into his left arm.

Beckworth growled as he jumped to his feet. And then he was merciless. His movements swift, his footwork precise, his back straight as he pushed forward, effortlessly blocking Reginald's sloppy strikes. He pushed Reginald back toward the bedchamber, and Ethan followed.

Ethan momentarily thought of Thorn and wondered who would have won in a duel with Beckworth. A momentary stab of sadness hit him in never knowing.

The first pierce of flesh was on Reginald's right shoulder.

The same place AJ had stabbed Beckworth—twice. Was that a symbolic strike for AJ and her short-lived imprisonment? The next swing of the blade swiped across Reginald's midsection, and he let out a sharp yelp, wincing at the ensuing pain. They disappeared into the bedroom, but Ethan caught up in time to see another flash of steel as it came down on Reginald's sword arm, almost severing the hand, but Beckworth pulled back. Quick thinking to not let the sword get lodged in bone. And the strike had been enough. Reginald dropped his blade and pulled his arm to his chest, the blood splashing his nightshirt, and arcing through the air to spray across the floor.

Beckworth wasn't satisfied. Reginald scrambled back, his gaze darting to the dressing room. Ethan, sword raised, didn't hesitate and sidestepped to block any exit Reginald thought he might have. Eyes wide, trapped with nowhere to run, Reginald fell to his knees, his good arm held out in supplication, his other arm hanging limp at his side.

He looked sad and defeated, but Beckworth didn't seem to have any pity left. He stood over the man and used the tip of his sword to slice a thin ribbon of skin on Reginald's left shoulder.

"Have mercy on me, brother." Reginald's voice was shaky, his forehead creased in pain, his hair slick with sweat.

Beckworth laughed.

"I'll leave immediately for Austria. You'll never see me again."

Beckworth glared down and, after a moment, his hard features lightened.

Ethan stared in astonishment. Beckworth didn't believe his brother, did he? Family ties could be blind at the oddest moments.

"I want to be sure I get this straight, brother. After lavishing me with nothing but years of abandonment and scorn, you travel to England and steal my home. You kill a good friend, then kidnap another. Rather than keeping her in a gilded cage, you dumped her in a cold cell and treated her no better than garbage. Yet, you expected her to unravel the musings of a mad man for you. Then you imprison two more of my friends and kill two others. To be honest, I'm having a hard time keeping score."

"I'm sorry. If I could take it all back, I would."

Beckworth retreated two steps and seemed to consider his brother's apology. "Maybe. If you told me what you did with the Heart Stone."

At first, Reginald's eyes glistened with hope, then whatever he'd been thinking vanished. His gaze darted to the bed before he glanced toward Ethan and the dressing room.

"Just as I thought. You've always kept your most precious toys close to you."

Ethan would have expected something quick, but Beckworth placed the tip of his sword on his brother's chest, over his heart. Reginald tried to stand, but the last slice on his left shoulder must have damaged muscle because he didn't seem capable of putting weight on his only good arm, and his legs were too weak from the earlier fighting. He fell backward as Beckworth pushed the blade in. Reginald lay on his back, mumbling. Beckworth stood over him, leaning in as he pushed the blade, ever so slowly, deep into his brother's chest. There wasn't so much a scream as a grunt of pain and a gurgle. And then nothing as Reginald stared blankly at the ceiling.

Beckworth waited a couple of heartbeats before withdrawing his sword. He stood, staring down at his own likeness. "Eerie, isn't it. Looking at death wearing your face."

Ethan wasn't sure how to respond to that. "We need to go."

Beckworth nodded. "I'll be right behind you."

But he was still staring down at his brother when Ethan ran from the bedchamber.

47

―――――――

AJ plucked at a loose string on her shirt. She was bored, cold, and feeling completely out of the game. Finn's decision to keep her away from the fighting made sense. He didn't want to have to worry about her, and he had been right; she couldn't fight in hand-to-hand combat. And she'd swallowed his line about being the one to make the call on whether the *Daphne Marie* should stay or go. He could have asked any of his crew to make that call, but he'd given the honor to her. And his trust did mean something, assuming the fighting ever made it this far.

She glanced at the four men. Two stood, one sailor and one townsman, each gazing off in a different direction. One watched the sea, the other the stairs leading to the road. The other two had their eyes closed, either catnapping or mentally preparing for what might come. None of them were restless, and she took strength from them while trying to keep down the bile from her pent-up worry.

Between the early morning hour and her previous rush of adrenaline, her energy waned. Her head fell back against the rock wall, her eyelids fluttering closed. She woke with a start when the men rotated their positions. As the men resettled, AJ relaxed, one hand clutching her pocket where the Heart Stone still bulged her pocket, her wedding ring a slim outline next to it. Her thoughts were jumbled and unsettled, and she breathed deep to recenter herself.

The crack of musket fire shook her from her trance. The two men who'd been resting jumped up, and AJ followed suit. Another blast drew their attention to the top of the cliff. The gunfire had come from the front of the monastery. The battle had begun.

After ten minutes, the gunfire ceased, but all that meant was that the fighting had moved to closer combat. Or maybe it was over. The guards would have been drowsy from drugged wine. It was possible.

The men had returned to their original stations when the sound of clambering boots forced them to face the stairs again, hands on the hilts of their swords. Someone was rushing down the stairs. More than one person. She couldn't tell how many but guessed a handful as the pounding grew louder. Her hope that it was Fitz or other crewmen vanished when one of the sailors pulled his sword, and the townsman raised his ax, holding it across him with both hands, his legs moving back and forth, shifting his weight as he prepared for battle.

AJ glanced around, searching for the best place to position herself. The fighting would be too close for her bow, but she could try to use her daggers. But that wasn't her job. Not yet. She squeezed back against the rock wall as two guards leaped from the staircase to the landing. Rather dramatic, but she didn't have much time to question the maneuver before two more guards attacked. At least the men were evenly matched. She'd thought the townsmen wouldn't be able to fight, but they were holding their own. As the guards pushed toward the iron door, AJ grabbed the lantern that had been sitting along the wall, and dashed for the stairs, barely missing a guard as he backed into her.

She ran down a few steps before stopping. The fight had moved back toward the edge of the landing. From her current position, she had a clear view of both the landing and the stairs leading to the road. She turned and stared down at the bay. The slim sliver of moon provided enough light for her to make out the shadow of the *Daphne Marie*. Suddenly, the decision on whether to signal the ship weighed heavy.

The men were focused on the fight in front of them. Blood stained shirts, and the heavy grunting grew louder as each man used brute strength to push the enemy back. She glanced up the stairs. Was that the sound of more men on the wooden steps? It was difficult to tell with the clanging of metal swords and axes, the grunting, and the taunts.

It was decision time—send the signal for the *Daphne Marie* to weigh anchor and leave or send more men. The blast of more musket fire made the call for her. She lit the lantern and used her whole body to swing it back and forth in the darkness. The lantern, the light blinding her night vision, swung four more times. She counted out loud to ten, her voice gravelly and shaky, before swinging the lantern five more times.

She waited. After a moment, an answering light flashed from the ship. The ship responded with five swings of a lantern, followed by a short pause and five more swings. She breathed out a long sigh. It was done. More of the crew would be coming, joining those already on shore waiting for the signal.

The vibration on the stairs made her glance up. Movement of shadows from above gave her a new problem. They could be more townsmen, but the hairs on the back of her neck convinced her she'd be disappointed. If she stayed where she was, she'd be caught in the middle of the fight.

She ran up a couple of steps, scanning the landing. A

townsman was down, but so was a guard. It was impossible to tell if they were dead. Even so, there was no way to safely skirt the remaining fighters to get to the iron door. But it wouldn't have mattered. Someone had already shut it. Probably to prevent any of Dugan's men from going in.

She couldn't go up. She could go down, the crew would let her pass, but it felt like running. Dugan must have discovered the door at some point, or maybe Sebastian had let it slip. The heavy sound of multiple boots running down the steps told her they had underestimated how many men Dugan had, or the potion in the wine hadn't carried a lasting effect.

Distant gunfire echoed from what might have been the outer courtyard on the other side of the monastery. From her position, she couldn't accurately pinpoint where it originated. Between the open sea and the rocky cliff, the true location of sound was distorted. She stared across the expanse of cliff. It was a long way to the other side of the monastery.

She inched closer to the railing and leaned over, giving her eyes time to readjust to the darkness after the brief glare from the lantern. She'd only seen the cliff in daylight once from a position in the monastery when she'd looked down at the bay. The entire cliff had been impossible to see, but the top portion was nothing more than a brush-covered hill that turned to rock as it dipped out of view. The rock had appeared to be cracked and rough. From her position on the stairs, that impression held true at this lower level. The rough surface of the wall would provide plenty of pockets and holes to position her hands and feet.

The men from the ship were almost there, their heads bobbing as they stormed up the stairs. They would arrive just in time to engage the men racing down the stairs, who she could now confirm were Dugan's men. Another decision.

Without any thought other than to get out of the way and get to Finn, she clambered over the railing, landing on a large boulder, her bow getting stuck for a moment. The thrum of the bowstring gave her a start. Thinking she'd broken her bow, she sighed with relief when she felt the firm line still intact. She pulled the strap from the quiver through the bow and positioned the bow so it hung smoothly from the quiver. Then she tugged the quiver strap over her head and one arm, allowing the quiver to lay against her back. She bounced on the boulder, feeling for her new balance with the added weight. She turned left and right, getting a sense for how the quiver would swing as she climbed. When the crew was close enough to spot her, and she was satisfied the quiver felt no different than a backpack, she stepped out to the first foothold, her fingers finding easy purchase on the stony wall.

48

───────

Finn followed Lando down the stairs to the main foyer. His mind raced as he considered where Dugan might have gone. The logical course would be to check on his men, or maybe he went to the stables, or maybe he decided on a midnight stroll. Any of the choices was a possibility. One thing was fact—he couldn't let Dugan get away.

He focused on that single thought. How many ways to leave? By horse or by ship were the only choices. And he'd put AJ right in the middle of the last option. If Dugan knew the crew of the *Daphne* was split between the monastery and the ship, he might consider seizing the ship. That would mean Dugan would have to know how to get to the *Daphne*. Finn couldn't think about that. He had to trust that AJ and the men he'd left at the iron door would make the best decision.

By the time he reached the bottom of the stairs, he was planning the best route to the stables when a guard staggered through the door from the inner courtyard. Blood marred the front of his tunic, but he appeared more drunk than injured. Finn knocked him in the head with the hilt of his sword, and after the man landed on the floor, he pulled him to an alcove.

"We stop and fight?" Lando asked.

"We should at least take a look. Dugan has to be searching for his best way out."

"The ship?"

Finn nodded. "It's a possibility. Especially if he thinks we brought most of the men to the monastery."

"Even if AJ doesn't signal Jamie to leave, he would keep the dinghy at the ship. Dugan would have no way to get to her."

"Maybe. But I'm tired of underestimating the man."

Finn moved into the courtyard first. The scene was reminiscent of their last battle at the monastery, but with fewer men. The torchlight added macabre shadows on the wall, which made this fight eerier. For men under the influence of doctored wine, the guards fought well against the townsmen. Many of the guards moved slowly, a few staggered as they lunged and parried, but the call to fight appeared to pull them out of their haze.

Lando jumped into the fray, and Finn followed. Once he'd engaged a guard, Finn immediately noticed the difference. The guards were slower, their only advantage was their sheer strength and will to survive. And that might be all they needed. Finn had pushed his adversary as far as the middle of the yard when the front doors burst open.

More guards spilled in, followed by more townsmen and then Fitz's team. Either Maire's potion didn't work, or they hadn't given it enough time.

Lando moved off to assist two townsmen in trouble.

Finn pushed his way out the front doors and ran into Fitz.

"Captain." Fitz spat into the dirt, then wiped his mouth with his sleeve. "Dugan." He was breathing hard, his tunic smeared with fresh blood. He pointed in the direction of town. "He had a group of men. They were moving toward the outer staircase."

Toward the iron door, the ship, and AJ. "I'll take care of it. Try to keep everyone in the courtyard."

Fitz nodded and ran inside, his battle cry echoing behind him.

Finn turned toward the worn path that would lead to the stairs. He was tempted to grab one of the torches but decided to follow the trail in darkness. He'd gone twenty feet when men with a lit torch raced over the short rise. He stepped into the shadows and waited. When they were almost on top of him, he recognized faces from the ship.

Michelson, the ship's part-time doctor, led the group and stopped short when he saw Finn. "A group of Dugan's men were headed for the beach."

"Didn't we leave you on the ship?" Finn asked.

He nodded and waited for a breath. "The signal was given to send more men."

AJ must have given the signal. "AJ?"

"Someone said they saw her on the stairs when they arrived, but she was gone by the time I arrived. The iron door was closed. She must have gone that way."

"Was Dugan there?"

Michelson shrugged. "Not that I'm aware of. But most of the guards were beaten back and they returned this way."

"I saw him, sir."

Finn glanced down at one of the ship's younger recruits. "And you're sure it was Dugan?"

The lad stood taller. "Big man with two scars across his face?"

"That's him."

"He gave orders to another man and then headed in this direction." He pointed toward the front of the monastery.

Yet, he hadn't been in the inner courtyard or outside, and Fitz never saw him. If he hadn't gone through the iron door and didn't make it back to the front door, he either had horses waiting on the road to take him to town or there was another entrance into the monastery he wasn't aware of. And no one mentioned seeing horses.

"All right. Fitz could use your help in the courtyard."

The men followed Finn back inside. Not much had changed, and though the men appeared to be battling hard, there were few men on the ground. He had to assume the townsmen were only willing to spill blood if they had to. Before Finn had a chance to engage someone, gunfire exploded.

The fighting halted as some men ducked to the ground and other men searched for the source. Eventually, all heads turned up to the second-floor balcony. Finn wound his way through the stalled fighters, moving closer, his awe growing as he stared up at the delightful sight of Sebastian.

To his left, two men, somewhere in their later years but still strong enough to work a plow, leaned over the railing. Each man held a bow, arrow ready, as they tracked the room from person to person. To Sebastian's right, Maire lowered her pistol, smoke still rising from it, and pointed a rifle at the crowd.

Sebastian had everyone's full attention. Though his voice was light, it was steady, and the men moved a little closer to hear him. "Sorry for the interruption, but your fighting is finished for the evening. This monastery has seen more than enough bloodshed."

Finn pushed his way through the last group of men. They stared at their closest neighbor as the rest of the room did. Confusion and doubt on their faces, each determining if anyone else would obey the command from the diminutive monk.

"Sebastian," Finn called.

The monk's dour expression lightened when he found Finn in the crowd. "Captain Murphy. So good to have you back. I thought I might be seeing you one last time."

Finn grinned. He knew the fighting could break out again,

even with the arrows and rifle trained on the men, but he had to find Dugan. He'd let Lando and Fitz work things out with Sebastian. "And I'm pleased to find you're doing well. I apologize for the mess." He spread his arms wide, having no problem with taking the blame. "I was curious to know if there were any passages between the trail that leads to the outer stairs that might bypass the front door."

Sebastian considered the statement, then nodded. "The monastery has many passages. Some obvious, others..." he trailed off. "But yes, there is a side door on the far side of the building that enters into a long hallway that runs behind the rooms attached to this inner courtyard. There is an additional exit that leads to the main hall between the sanctuary and the monks' quarters."

Finn nodded as an arrow was loosed and a man grunted. Everyone turned to see a man, who must have been moving toward the door, dropped on one knee, an arrow protruding from his left shoulder.

The archer had already nocked another arrow.

"I'm sorry, young man. I might not have made myself clear. No one is to leave the courtyard at this time. Would someone be kind enough to close the front doors?" When no one moved, Sebastian continued, "The gentlemen on my left are quite excellent with the bow. They were both archers in the King's army. And while you might think that was a long time ago, you would be mistaken to think their aim is any less true."

Sebastian scanned the group and nodded. "You might also note the young lady to my right. A rifle may not seem appropriate since it requires time to reload, but you can be sure her first shot will find its mark. Now, I ask again, will someone shut the doors?" Fitz and another crew member closed the doors and placed a wooden beam in the braces to prevent them from being opened from the outside.

Sebastian nodded his thanks. "I suggest you might want to sit and get comfortable." No one moved, but with a nod from Finn, the crew from the *Daphne*, swords still drawn but lowered, sank into a sitting position and laid their swords across their laps. The townsmen followed next. When no one else moved, the men on the balcony trained their arrows on those left standing, and Dugan's guards dropped to the ground.

"And someone should see to the young man's shoulder." Then he turned his clear gaze on Finn. "And, I believe Captain Murphy, you were searching for someone."

Finn nodded and glanced at Maire. Her expression was fierce, but before he responded to Sebastian, she winked at him. She was enjoying this.

He directed his request to Sebastian. This was his monastery. "Yes, if I could continue that pursuit."

The monk nodded. "I would also ask you to select a few men to secure the outer courtyard."

"As you wish." Finn gave him a slight bow and searched for Lando, noticing for the first time that Ethan and Beckworth had joined them. Beckworth just smiled. Reginald had been taken care of. "Find Lando and whoever else you need to get control of the courtyard. Check the stables. We need to ensure no one can get to a horse. If Dugan wants to leave, he can damn well walk."

Finn gave Sebastian a nod then raced for the door to the foyer. When he stood in the empty hall, he stopped. Which way? For some reason, he glanced up to the second floor. If nothing other than to assuage his concerns, he stormed up the stairs. He had to confirm Dugan didn't circle back. Though Dugan didn't seem the emotional type, his loyalty to Reginald's mother might override his common sense.

When he reached Reginald's bedchamber, he barely glanced at the fallen man, whose blank eyes clouded over as he stared at nothing. He checked the dressing room, but the door to the passage was firmly closed. That didn't mean Dugan hadn't returned, found his master dead, then fled through the dressing room. But that didn't feel right.

He turned to rush back out the way he'd come, but stopped halfway to the double doors.

Dugan waited for him in the doorway.

———

AJ slammed into the hard slate wall, her fingers gripped the edge of the rock like hawk talons. She pressed down on her toes, steadying her fragile hold on the ledge, and closed her eyes as she waited for the quiver to resettle on her back. Her breaths heated the cold roughness of the stone against her cheek. She winced as the stone rubbed the fresh scratch she'd gotten earlier from being pressed against another wall.

The climb had begun moderately challenging. Her plan had been to creep upward as quickly as she could in hopes the cliff tapered off into the brushy terrain she'd remembered. But a quarter of the way up, she found a small ledge that ran horizontal to the wall. It was no wider than her foot but, in rock climbing, and with the solid holds this cliff provided, it might as well have been four-feet wide. She took her time, but it was still faster than climbing, and her luck was still with her. The ledge angled upward. Not by much, but it was better than going down.

She was halfway to the courtyard when she reached a spot where the ledge had broken off. The ledge continued after a four-foot gap. Too far for her to reach without releasing her grip on the wall and leaping for it.

She looked down and then up. Wasn't it just her luck there were minimal footholds? Nothing but sheer rock stretching into the darkness, well below the candlelight glowing from the monastery windows. The fight had woken everyone. She should retrace her steps, but backtracking would take too long. And it hadn't escaped her notice that the wall surface had become smoother the farther she traveled. She'd been searching for a safe place to climb for the last fifteen minutes.

She gazed in the direction she'd been heading. The moonlight cast more shadows than light. If she stared at a single spot for too long, the shadows seemed to move. She scanned the wall quickly with climber eyes. The ledge on the other side of the gap appeared solid. There was no evidence of crumbling rock or broken shards. The wall itself appeared promising. Bumps in the surface of the cliff hinted at footholds. The question was, promising enough to attempt a jump?

The impulse to glance down was strong, but she ignored it. She lifted her head and let the cool sea breeze remove the sweat from her face. The crew had seen her slip over the railing and begin her climb. If she didn't make it to the courtyard, at least Finn would know what happened to her. The thought made her frown. If they didn't find her body, with the Heart Stone in her pocket, Finn would be stuck in this century. As odd as that sounded, and as much as it should hurt, the thought actually irritated her. He would be heartbroken. He would blame himself. Without her, he'd have no reason to go back to the future. He wouldn't even have the *Daphne Marie*.

And the thought of it all pissed her off. That wasn't going to happen. She was a rock climber. She felt strong. Her legs weren't shaking, her muscles were alive—and ready. Without spending any more time thinking about it, she planted her feet, waited until the quiver nestled along her spine then leaped.

Now, she gripped the wall as if her life depended on it—which it did. But she'd made it, she had a solid hold, and her heart rate was slowing. She could try climbing now, but when she scanned to her left, the ledge continued for another fifteen yards, still slanting upward.

She followed the ledge for another ten feet as the number of holds above her increased. When she noticed how close she was to the brush-covered slope, she grinned. Almost there. She selected the best route, based on what she could see of the holds, and started up. The strong odor of sage tingled her senses. As she grew closer to the brush, the metallic sound of swords drove a new panic. She'd wasted too much time. For a reason she couldn't explain, a strong urge told her to hurry.

She began her scramble, her focus on the line of brush and where the top of the courtyard wall should be, still shadowed in darkness. In her haste, she didn't test an edge before bearing her weight, and her foot slipped. As she grabbed for a more solid handhold, the quiver swung around. Her balance shifted as her other foot lost its edge.

49

———————

Finn lifted his sword and charged Dugan. They met in the middle of the room, swords crossing. Dugan, all brute force, pushed him back. Finn feinted and allowed Dugan to pass by him, pivoting to meet Dugan's blade again as the man turned and raised his sword in a powerful upward arc. Their swords met, and both men tested their strength against the blades, each pushing for the advantage. Dugan found an ounce more energy and shoved Finn backward.

Dugan sneered, the scar that ran down the left side of his face blazed pink from his exertion. The scar tissue not yet tempered by time like the scar that hid within the creases of his forehead. He stepped back and lowered the tip of his blade. "And so, we find ourselves here once again."

"For some reason, you keep betting on the wrong side."

He shrugged. "There's only one side."

Finn considered pursuing the statement, but it didn't matter what drove Dugan. Money, loyalty, or just for kicks, it was his soulless morality that made him dangerous and, in Finn's opinion, irredeemable.

Most of his life, Finn had fought with a sword. Life at sea

could be harsh, and the world of Hensley's espionage and secret missions were just as deadly. But he'd met each challenge with a zest for a fight, saving those he could, harming only those that forced his hand. He'd never faced anything more important than this fight. AJ and the home they made together meant everything to him. Their future depended on this time period not encroaching any further than the here and now. To that end, this man had to go. He knew too much, had killed too many innocents. Now that those he was most loyal to were gone, he'd be willing to sell information to the highest bidder.

"How did you find out about the staircase?" Finn didn't particularly care, but after Dodger's betrayal, he'd rather know if they had another snitch on the team.

"Quite accidentally. One of my men thought he saw someone sneaking away, and after following them, discovered a trail. Unfortunately, we only found the staircase shortly before the first gunfire. If we had known of its existence sooner, we would have been waiting for you. I told Reginald we should have pushed the monk more. But after the unfortunate death of Ratliff, he lost his balls in making decisions. He wanted to take his time, not miss anything. He was a fool to have waited."

Finn charged again without warning, surprising Dugan, who spun out of the way. He wasn't fast enough, and the edge of Finn's sword cut across his left shoulder. Dugan danced away with deft grace for such a large man. Finn went on the offensive, attacking with fierce determination as he lunged and feinted, the tip of his blade scoring several hits. Nothing deep. Dugan moved too fast to receive a full strike, but little spots of red appearing on his shirt proved the man did, in fact, bleed.

Once again, Dugan seemed to find a deeper pool of energy, and he pushed back. His swings more reminiscent of a broadsword, each strike like a hammer as it came down. Finn had to use two hands to fend off the attack. Then with one final push, Dugan forced Finn back out into the hallway.

The blade had come too fast for Finn to keep an eye on his feet, and they tangled in a piece of clothing when he stumbled backward. Had that been a chemise?

Instead of taking advantage of Finn's momentary vulnerability, Dugan turned and ran back to the bedchamber. Finn glanced over his shoulder and could make out the shapes of two men reaching the second floor. Finn ignored them. If Dugan was running, it couldn't be guards. He struggled to his feet then dashed after Dugan, who must be running for the hidden passageway. He would have known about it when the duke lived here.

When he reached the room, Dugan wasn't in sight. The man couldn't have made it to the dressing room that quickly. Finn barely cleared the doorway when a wardrobe slammed into him. Caught unaware, he lost his balance as the heavy wooden furniture collapsed over him.

———

Sweat poured off AJ's brow, the pain in her fingers excruciating, but she grunted through it as she dug her fingertips into the rocky crack. She was sure the moisture that slicked her fingers was blood rather than sweat. The gap she'd caught herself with was sharp, but she held on as she searched for an edge.

She raised her right foot, moving it around, searching for any foothold. She closed her eyes and pictured where she thought the crack would run down the face of the rock. Her biceps shook from the strain as she pulled her foot up higher. There. Something. Then her toe slid into a hold, and she gathered every bit of strength she had in her leg to push up. Holding on with her right hand, she reached for the bare root of a straggly bush, hoping the root ran deep. Once she had hold of it, she tugged. When it seemed strong enough to bear her weight, she pried her right hand off the crack, hoping she wasn't leaving part of her skin behind and grabbed the crack farther up. She winced as her hand made contact.

Fissures in a rock wall could run the entire face of a cliff, but many times they were sporadic. Their existence depended on the type of rock and other geological changes in the topography. This crack seemed to run far enough up that it should take her to the vegetative cover that danced enticingly out of her reach, a mere twenty feet above her.

Her hands felt raw, but she found the next foothold and took a moment to lean into the wall, allowing her legs to bear her weight. She wiped one hand at a time on her pants before reaching up to continue her climb. Time seemed to be an enemy. In the back of her mind, she heard the gunfire diminish to be replaced by the smooth sound of steel before that sound began to fade. Concern for Finn and the rest of the team burst through her, spreading anxiety and dread. The multiple sensations spurred her faster. With numb fingers and wobbly legs, she crawled over a small lip. The terrain flattened into a shallower slope.

She didn't waste time resting as she scrambled for the four-foot-high stone wall that ran alongside the cliff next to the outer courtyard. Before peering over it to see what faced her, she stopped long enough to pull the quiver and bow over her head. She forced long, cool breaths in and out of her lungs, her body restoring itself with each inhale. After quickly slipping the bow from the quiver, she grabbed an arrow and slid the quiver back over her head again. She raised her head over the top of the wall just enough to study the situation.

Torch light filled the outer courtyard. To her left, small

pockets of fighting continued. Several men lay on the ground, most moving, a few releasing screams of pain or low groans of misery. Others made no motion at all. Near the stable, on the far side of the courtyard, the familiar figures of Lando and Ethan moved through the flickering light.

To her right was the garden. Nothing going on there. Still hidden behind the wall, she headed that direction, hoping to locate Sebastian and Maire, who should be in the tunnels. She was almost to the garden when she found a darkly shadowed area. A perfect place to get over the wall without being seen. As she dropped to the ground on the other side, Dugan ran out of the outer door that led from the kitchen to the garden.

Finally. Something was going her way. She stopped and dropped to one knee. She nocked the arrow, her fingertips screaming at the new assault, but she pushed through the pain and raised the bow until her target was in her sights.

Finn had little time to react when the wardrobe hit him. He'd turned his back to it, hoping to take the brunt of the weight, but it was heavy enough to knock him off balance as it crashed over him, knocking him to the floor. The breath rushed out of him. The wardrobe had landed across his legs and part of his back. He pushed up until his biceps shook, but he couldn't gain enough height to get his legs under him. After another minute, he fell back to the floor, grunting as a fresh lungful of air was forced out.

Dugan was stronger than Finn thought. Although tipping over the wardrobe was easier than trying to lift its full weight off him, assuming he didn't suffocate first. He pushed up again, if only to get air in his lungs. His blade lay a few feet away, but even if he could reach it, it wouldn't get him out of his current dilemma.

Then the weight of the furniture lessened. Deep grunts brought satisfaction as the wardrobe was lifted off him. He'd forgotten. There had been men coming up the stairs.

"Captain, are you all right?" He recognized the voice of Stephenson, one of his gunners.

"Aye." The response sounded more like a wheeze. "Just help me up."

When Finn was standing again, he almost fell when he put weight on this left foot. Stephenson caught his weight.

"Give it a minute, sir. Is there anything else hurt?"

Finn leaned away from the crewman, forcing his foot to take his weight. With his weight on his right leg, he swung his arms around. His old rib injury flared back to life, but the dull ache was tolerable. His right shoulder felt a pinch. As he continued to work out twinges, he gradually shifted weight to his left leg, each attempt less painful.

"Here you go, Captain." The second crewman, a face he remembered but not the name, handed Finn his sword. He was one of Jamie's men, but he still addressed Finn as if he captained the ship.

"Thank you for the rescue. Other than my ankle, I'm good." And to prove it, if more for himself, he split his weight between both legs. He'd be fine. "Clear the rest of this floor and the one above. Make sure no one is hiding and there's no one who needs aid."

The men nodded as Finn marched toward the dressing room. With each stride, his left ankle improved until he was running down the stairs.

When he broke out into a hallway, he had to stop to get his bearings. The door to the outer courtyard was to his right. He raced to it and pulled it open, quickly scanning the courtyard. It was filled with fighting men, but they were in small pockets throughout the yard. There was no one running away. Dugan had maybe three minutes on him. No more than five. But enough time to disappear.

He focused on the stables. Lando and Ethan stood in front of the entrance. Dugan wouldn't have bothered. He had to be somewhere in the monastery.

Dugan couldn't go through the inner courtyard to the front door. Sebastian had that locked down. He might try sneaking out the way he came in. His only other options were through the kitchen or the tunnels. The tunnels would be the better choice, but Dugan wouldn't know the way to the iron door, not without a guide. And other than Sebastian and AJ, Finn didn't think there were more than one or two others that knew the secret. Finn had traversed the passage a couple of times but still required AJ to get him through. There were too many intersections, most leading to dead ends.

The kitchen exit would give Dugan more options. Finn ran that direction, but when he raced through the kitchen, all he found were a few of the staff huddled against the far wall near the washing tubs.

"Did a large man come running through this way?"

As if they were connected by the same puppet string, they shook their heads.

Damn.

He didn't slow as he raced into another hallway. When he glanced to the right, he saw remnants of splintered wood on the floor. He moved cautiously toward the debris that seemed to be what was left of the doorjamb. The small office was lined with shelves filled with a mixture of books and pantry items. A ledger lay open, and he thought he caught the light floral scent of his sister mingled with gunpowder. Whatever happened here had happened earlier in the evening. Or was it morning now?

He exited the room in time to see Dugan coming through the door that led to the tunnels. Did he think Sebastian was still in his cell, or had he been searching for something else? He hadn't been down there long enough to have been searching for a way out.

Finn ran toward him, and Dugan, hearing his approach, glanced up.

Dugan almost smiled before he raised his sword, then turned and ran. Momentarily surprised by Dugan's reaction, Finn chased after him. This time, Dugan ran toward the door that led to the secret entrance he'd used earlier to sneak back into the monastery. If he hoped to find his guards at the front door or the outer staircase, he'd be disappointed.

As they closed toward the front of the building, Dugan steered toward the right until two townsmen, their axes resting over their shoulders, turned the corner. They were burly men, with beefy forearms, and when they saw Dugan, the muscles in their arms flexed as they pulled their axes to rest against their chest, a hand braced on both ends of the well-worn leathered handles.

Dugan slid as he veered toward the left and raced past the front entrance. The man could run all he wanted. The net was beginning to close. They ran from one hallway to another. Dugan had lived here for a while, and though he never discovered the secrets of the inner passageways and lower tunnels, he would know the rest of the monastery quite well.

Finn recognized the hallway as soon as they raced out of the library. He expected Dugan to make for the door to the outer courtyard, but he must have known there'd be no escape there. He'd be spotted instantly, and without a horse, he had no place to run.

Dugan ducked into the kitchen, and Finn paused at the threshold to catch his breath. The ribs that had been a dull ache earlier spasmed with each breath. He glanced at the same group of kitchen staff that hadn't moved from the last time he'd been through. How long ago had that been? Ten minutes? Longer?

One of the younger maids lifted a shaky hand and pointed to the small door that led to the kitchen's garden. This was it. He could feel it in his bones.

———

AJ tracked her arrow as Dugan slowed. He placed his left hand on his hip, his body partially bent as if he was trying to catch a breath. He'd been running. Hard. He turned and brought his sword up. AJ was about to loose the arrow until she realized whoever had chased Dugan had caught up to him.

She lowered her bow and stood when another man flew out the door, stopping short and raising his own sword.

Finn.

Relief. Anxiety. Excitement. Fear.

The emotions overwhelmed her, and she stumbled back. Her legs were mush, but she forced herself forward. It was like walking against a strong tide, and she couldn't move any faster.

Finn advanced on Dugan, and he wasted no time in swinging his sword in a wide arc. Dugan easily blocked it. The battle began. Finn fought as hard as he had when he'd sparred with Ethan and Thomas after his recovery. He had something to prove. A task to complete. Yet, his movements weren't fluid, and he held his left arm too close to his body.

He must have recognized it himself, as had Dugan, who continued to strike in that same area. Finn's ribs must be hurting. Had he injured them again? Or were the events of the evening taking their toll?

Finn sidestepped one of the garden beds and switched his sword to his right hand. Now that Finn had shifted his body,

Dugan would have to find another soft target. AJ had watched Finn train many times. Dugan would be hard-pressed to get to his left side unless Finn wanted him to.

Finn moved in, pushing Dugan back toward the stone wall where the shadows were thicker. AJ pumped her legs faster, trying to keep her eyes on them. Seconds later, they danced back into the light. This time, Finn was on the defensive. Dugan landed a perfect strike, and AJ forced herself to not shut her eyes.

"No." But no one heard her scream.

Finn had turned to the side, but he wasn't able to completely evade the tip of the blade. He stumbled backward, flexed his right arm, then fell to one knee.

Without thinking, AJ braced her stance and pulled up her bow, the arrow still nocked. She stared down the length of the shaft until she spotted Dugan. She loosed the arrow, aiming for his upper shoulder. Without taking her eye off the scene, she reached for another arrow and nocked it.

Before the first arrow had left the bow, Finn had regained his footing. Dugan had taken a step back, partially turning toward her. Which was why AJ's arrow missed its mark.

When Dugan had turned, the arrow missed his shoulder and pierced his chest, right above his heart. He lurched to a stop and glanced down, then he raised his head to scan the vicinity, as if pondering where that arrow had come from.

Suddenly, she had no problem closing the distance. As she approached, Dugan's legs went out from under him, and he landed on his backside before tipping back, the arrow straight and true as it pointed toward the heavens.

Finn stood over the man and only glanced up when AJ was a few short steps away. When she reached him, he pulled her into a crushing embrace, keeping an eye on the fallen man.

Dugan wasn't dead yet. His eyes worked to focus on the couple standing over him.

"I'm sorry. I meant to hit his shoulder, but he turned at the last second." AJ stared at Dugan, her only regret was that she had killed him, robbing Finn of his revenge.

Finn rubbed her arm and kissed the top of her head. "It's okay. It didn't matter which of us did it."

"As long as it was done?" she asked.

"Aye. As long as it was done."

Dugan lifted his head but couldn't hold it up. He fell back, dark red staining his lips. He coughed, spattering red droplets over the front of his shirt and waistcoat. His words slurred. "It doesn't matter." He sucked in a breath. "Others know. They'll never stop searching for the stone." He laughed, but it was more a choke. Then he turned his head, his blank eyes somehow peaceful as they stared at AJ.

She wanted to scream. But that would've only fed his satisfaction—had he been alive to hear it. But he hadn't been the type of man to give deathbed confessions. He'd rather curse them by dying and giving nothing away.

Finn knelt next to him and shocked her by plunging a knife into his side. "For Thorn. And all the others."

Then he stood and met her gaze. They both understood what Dugan's last words meant. They knew what had to be done.

50

AJ and Finn stood on the landing outside the iron door, staring down at the *Daphne Marie* as daybreak grew near. Parts of the staircase had been damaged in the fighting. Fitz and Lando had surveyed the broken steps and determined the stairs were sturdy enough to support the crew's return to the ship. Repairs would be required before Sebastian's smuggling operation could resume.

The crew had assisted the townsmen in restraining Dugan's surviving men, which were quite a few. The men's momentary adrenaline rush at the start of the battle drained quickly as they expended energy. In the end, the soporific wine had tipped the scales in reducing the death toll. The townsmen would watch over the prisoners until the French army could retrieve them. Sebastian would send word to the local garrison at first light.

After Dugan's death, AJ and Finn met with Sebastian and Maire to begin their survey of the aftermath. They wouldn't know the true number of dead until after daybreak, but from their quick tally, their side had lost two sailors and three towns-men. Then AJ and Finn followed Fitz to the ship to say their goodbyes.

Now they hovered on the landing with Lando and Beckworth.

Lando scraped the rocky ground with his boot and glanced over at Finn. "So, this is the final goodbye?"

Finn had his hands in his pockets, his head turned toward the bay, a light breeze tousling his hair. "Aye. I don't think I'll be back this way again." He turned and reached out to shake Lando's hand.

The big man took his hand and pulled Finn in for a hug. The two men gripped each other for a long time before stepping back. There was a moment of sadness that seemed to pass between them before Finn gave him a full grin.

"You need to find that woman of yours and make an honest woman of her."

"Forever with the advice." But Lando's smile had returned, and he reached for AJ.

She held on longer than Finn had and whispered in his ear. "You know how much I love you, right?" When she felt the nod of his head, she sniffled. "And I'll miss you so much."

He stepped back and gave her a stern look. "Don't stop your practicing. I don't care how safe this future of yours is supposed to be, you can never go wrong with having a dagger by your side."

Finn groaned. "That was the last thing she needed to hear."

Beckworth laughed. "I don't know. After living in your future, I dare say I'd keep a weapon or two handy."

The laughter died quickly as the four of them stared down at the ship.

"You'd better be off. You know how stern the captain is about departing on time. And you'll lose your tide soon." Finn turned to Beckworth. "You never said where you found the Heart Stone."

"Turns out my brother was predictable to the bitter end. I

found both the Heart Stone and the smaller stone in the drawer of the bedside table." Beckworth retrieved a velvet bag of deep burgundy from his pocket, just large enough for the Heart Stone. "I gave the smaller stone to Sebastian. I promise Hensley will get this one." He met AJ's gaze. "Now that I have Waverly back, I think it's time to renew my acquaintance with the good Langdon family. Between Hensley and me, you can be assured the Keepers will find their beginning."

"I can't thank you enough for that." Finn reached out his hand. "Or for taking care of AJ when I couldn't."

Beckworth pocketed the velvet bag and took Finn's hand without hesitation. "You might have noticed she can take care of herself."

"You both know I'm standing right here," AJ quipped, but happy to see the two had forged a friendship.

"Besides." Beckworth tugged on his sleeves. "You did help in returning Waverly to me. A deal well struck."

Finn stepped back and hesitated before he glanced at AJ. "I'll let you two say your goodbyes. I'll meet you at the top of the stairs."

Lando kissed AJ on her cheek, shook Finn's hand for the last time and retreated down the stairs. AJ watched him go as she blinked back tears.

"You're not going to shed any of those for me, are you?" Beckworth's mocking retort held a note of tenderness.

She wiped her eyes before glaring at him. "Don't be silly."

They stared at each other until Beckworth spread his arms wide. "If I may be so bold."

AJ threw her arms around his neck, inwardly pleased to see his shocked expression. In just a few months, they had turned from bitter enemies to fast friends. An understanding that had developed into a friendship as strong as the ones she had with

Ethan and Lando. And she was happy when his arms tightened around her.

When she pulled back, and he released her, she tilted her head and studied him. "It feels odd not to stab you."

"I'm willing to offer you my shoulder."

She laughed. "I'm not sure what I'm going to do without wondering where you are and what you're up to." She hoped Beckworth would find someone who would love him for who he was under all his bravado and misplaced charm.

His smile was rakish in that manipulative way he had. "I'm only a stone's throw away."

She could only shake her head. A wise-ass to the end. "I will miss you, Beckworth."

He tugged at his sleeves, and his smile turned solemn. "Take care, AJ. You'll always be welcome at Waverly." He took a step then turned back. That mischievous smile returned. "And if our paths should ever cross again, I'd be pleased if you called me Teddy."

M aire stood in the cozy sitting room that overlooked the bay. Her lips thinned as she watched the *Daphne Marie* sail toward the Channel. Her quick trip to check on Jamie's healing wound might well be the last time she saw him, Lando, Fitz, or any of the other crew members.

Ethan had rushed her back up to speak with Sebastian, depositing her in this room to wait for them. Now, as dawn approached, their way back to England sailed without them. She ignored the sound of boots entering the room and the whoosh of Sebastian's robes.

She remained rigid when Ethan's hands rested on her shoulders, but he didn't remove them.

"I know you're mad, but come over and let's talk about it." Ethan's tone was one used for a small child to prevent a tantrum. As much as she'd like to throw one, she'd only say things she'd regret later. She allowed him to turn her away from the window and guide her to a sofa. He sat next to her. She trained her focus on the fire warming the hearth.

Pages turning in a book made her gaze shift to Sebastian. He sat in a chair that was turned to face both the hearth and the sofa. He held the *Mórdha Stone Grimoire*, otherwise known as the druid's book, on his lap, slowly flipping the pages. She'd given him the book earlier, but he wouldn't have had time to look at it until now, busy as he'd been with the cleanup.

Maybe she could talk Ethan into staying at the monastery until the war was over. That would give her a few years to study the grimoire and *The Book of Stones* with Sebastian. She should have some say in her life.

More footsteps approached from the hall, and she didn't have to turn to know it was her brother and AJ. No doubt, the architects of her future.

"Now that we're all here, let's get started. We don't have much time. I've already sent for the army." Sebastian closed the book and glanced at Maire.

Finn and AJ took seats across from Sebastian, also facing the hearth and sofa. "Sister, I can see how upset you are. And you have every right to be angry, but you need to listen to Sebastian."

Maire stared at her brother, wanting to scream at him, but she held her tone with tight control. "You're going to blame this on Sebastian?"

"This is no one's fault but Reginald's. And we have no choice but to consider Dugan's last words." Sebastian leaned forward, trying to get her attention. "Look at me, child."

Maire couldn't resist his chiding tone, and she glared at everyone before resting her gaze on Sebastian. He looked tired.

God knows the last time he'd slept or eaten. And now he'd have to deal with the army before he got any rest. "I understand the danger of his words. But he could have just as easily been lying. We have no proof that anyone else knows about the Heart Stone or its powers."

"Which is why this will only be for a short time." Ethan reached for her hand, and when she didn't pull away, he held it in both of his. It was so cold against his warmth. "We'll wait until the war is over. Between Sebastian, Hensley, and the earl, they'll know if anyone is whispering about some magical stone that can travel through time. When we return, they'll be able to tell us if it's safe to stay."

AJ moved to sit next to her. "We'll get you in touch with Professor Emory and his friend Gallagher. They would love to spend time with you and your notes." She smiled at Maire, but her eyes were full of concern. "We didn't mean to make the call for you, but you can be a bit stubborn."

Maire held back a grin, still upset. "I hoped to have more time to discuss the books with Sebastian." The monk frowned and nodded his agreement.

"I'll do one favor for you. If you promise to keep it a secret." Sebastian rubbed his hands together. "I'll tell you where I'll leave the second portion of *The Book of Stones* and the grimoire." He shook his finger at the group. "They won't be kept in the same place, and they won't be with the first section of the book or my personal journal. We already know this Gallagher person will find those. We don't want everything found, or the trouble with the stones will truly follow you into the future."

The idea pleased Maire. If she couldn't study them in this time period, she felt relief in knowing they'd be available in AJ's time. Her eyes glistened. "I'll miss you."

"I still have a few years left. And who knows what the future truly holds."

"Will you keep the stones separate?" Ethan asked.

"For those I have, yes. They will be spread around the monastery."

"You should have them all but the one Ethan will take with him." Finn glanced around, and everyone nodded.

"And the one Beckworth has," Sebastian added.

"Beckworth has a stone?" Maire was startled by the news, but when AJ's expression relaxed, hers did as well. Beckworth hated his time in the future. Allowing him to keep the stone added an extra layer of safety. The man was notorious for hiding his valuables. And without the Heart Stone and all the smaller stones, the torc would never have full power. Whatever that actually meant.

"Then I guess we're safe. Beckworth will never use it." Finn appeared confident in his statement.

Ethan laughed. "I don't think I'll ever forget the terror in his eyes when we had him tied to that chair at the inn and we told him we were going to leave him stuck in the future."

Maire couldn't hold back a laugh at that image. She caught Sebastian's gaze on her. His expression was cheerful and full of promise. He seemed to honestly believe he'd see her again, and the thought comforted her. "All right. As if I have a choice. Let's get this over with before we have the army to contend with."

The group walked through the tunnels. AJ made note of the stone and earthen walls for the last time. She let Sebastian lead the way, then Ethan and Maire. She held Finn's hand, his grip tight as if he finally decided to worry whether he might not materialize on the other side. Their shared fear of that fate would continue until they landed on the dock in Baywood. Then they would know the Keepers' legacy had survived.

They said their final goodbye to Sebastian on the landing. He waved with that happy grin that told them all would be well. He'd never been wrong.

The walk down to the beach was long, and no one rushed. If Sebastian's last words hadn't been enough to convince her all would be well, the gulls gave their final blessing. As the sunrise brought a new day, the gulls filled the air with the frenzy of their morning feeding, and she laughed with them.

A calmness had settled within her by the time they reached the beach and dropped their duffels.

Though AJ had said her goodbyes to the others, their sudden loss hit her in the chest with the power of a hurricane. This would be her last time in this century. She didn't know how she knew it to be true; it was just one of those insights that carried no explanation. In a few short minutes, everyone she knew from this time period, those she'd fought with, those they'd lost, would be nothing but distant memories. Their voices long dead. She could only hope that those that still lived would live a good life.

"Are you ready to go home?"

She glanced up at Finn, and his lopsided grin was all she needed to see. She reached for the necklace that now lay around her neck, her fingers caressing the Heart Stone as she recited the incantation she now recalled from memory.

The four of them slung their duffels onto their shoulders and held hands as they watched the fog roll in.

51

———

Baywood, Oregon - Current Day

S tella poured the wine, and after taking a sip from her glass, returned to tossing the salad. The smell of ribs made her stomach growl, and she stared out the inn's kitchen window. Adam was at the grill, his wife Madelyn leaning against the railing. Stella had been surprised by the woman's warmth toward her. She expected Madelyn to be irritated by how much time Stella spent with Adam. But it seemed the two of them were at peace with their marriage.

Helen bumped her hip into Stella's as she placed a bowl of mashed potatoes on the counter. "I think you've tossed the salad enough. The tomatoes are starting to puree."

Stella glanced down. "Sorry. I don't know where my mind is."

AJ's mom gratefully changed the topic. "I think you should take those origami birds to the library. They could hand them out during the children's story times."

Stella gave the long line of paper birds that ran along the edge of the windowsill a rueful sigh. She really needed to find something else to help focus her mind. The birds were multiplying as quickly as tribbles.

"I honestly believe these are the best ribs I've grilled." Adam set the platter of ribs on the table, the enticing aroma spreading through the kitchen. "We should eat now while they're hot."

Madelyn's laugh followed him in through the French doors. "I think you say that every time, dear."

Stella handed her a filled wineglass. "I suppose that's better than knowing he's still practicing."

"At least you don't look at my cooking like you did when I made you that first bagel." Adam teased as he sat in front of the platter.

"Actually, I do. I just don't let you see it." Stella's quip made everyone laugh.

Helen settled in next to Stella. "My garden club is coming out to the inn next week. I want to finish the beds in the front."

"Are you still planning an end-of-summer party?" Madelyn glanced around the table, absently passing the green beans with blanched almonds to Adam.

"Absolutely," Stella answered. "We're just waiting on a date." Her voice tapered off.

No one spoke about when AJ and Finn might return. No one wanted to put a time frame around it. When did they stop waiting? When did they pull out that piece of paper AJ had given Helen and her? The page that listed all the places AJ might leave a message from the past, telling them they were fine though they'd never return. Stella's heart cramped at the thought.

Madelyn stood, breaking the silence. "We forgot the dressing."

"I think I left it on the counter by the sink." Helen sipped her wine before placing salad on her plate.

"Well, isn't that the strangest thing." Madelyn walked toward the bay window as if in a trance. "I don't think I've ever seen fog move in so fast."

Three sets of chair legs scraped against the wood floor as Stella, Adam, and Helen jumped from their chairs and raced for the front door.

"Where are you going?" Madelyn's question blew around them as they raced toward the path to the dock. "Oh, my God." Her next words were more of a shrill. "Is this the fog you were talking about? Are they coming back?" Her voice continued to rise in pitch. "Oh, my God. You weren't joking about where AJ went?"

Stella stopped at the end of the path where it met the edge of the wooden dock. Adam stopped behind her and held up his arms to block Helen or Madelyn from venturing farther.

The mist thickened, and the ethereal streams, thin as twigs, moved as if reaching for something just out of reach. Stella took a step back, forcing Adam and the others to do the same.

A bright light blinded her before a figure dropped onto the dock, followed one-by-one by three other forms, and apparently, their luggage. Stella waited.

Adam grabbed his mother before she could run to the prone figures. "Wait until the fog begins to dissipate and sound returns."

Stella had forgotten about the loss of sound. He was right. Other than the heavy breathing from the four of them, there was no other sound. No waves, no creaking pier, no gulls. Then the sun began to break through, and the screech of a gull could be heard. As if it was welcoming AJ home.

52

Baywood, Oregon - Three months later

The new sailboat rocked gently against the pier. AJ perched on the hatch and watched as their guests arrived, finding a place to store their personal items before grabbing something cold to drink. Ethan and Finn were preparing for the sail. Before they'd gone back in time to find Maire, Finn had refused to go sailing. The sixteen-foot sailboat he'd first purchased to give her sailing lessons all those months ago had been moored at the marina. Yet, he'd always watched the sea from the back deck of the inn.

Many people watched the sea, staring at its endless boundaries, but only a few actually dreamed of being on the water and sailing to unknown places. Finn had yearned to be out there, but something always held him back.

After their last jump, something had changed. Maybe it was Finn's last time at the helm of the *Daphne Marie*. But at some point, he came to terms with the man he'd become after their fantastical journey.

During their first month back, they rarely left the inn. When they did leave, it was for the family's weekly dinners, which had grown with the addition of Ethan and Maire. Sometimes they visited Ethan and Maire at the McDowell house or went horseback riding, a pastime AJ had grown to love. The rest of the time was spent at home, on their own, taking the time to properly mourn those they'd left behind.

AJ smiled as she watched Olivia, Jackson's wife, coerce her husband up the gangway. Jackson didn't like sailing, but as it turned out, Olivia loved it. This was their second time onboard, and though he would never admit it, he didn't appear to be grumbling quite as much. Though he swatted furiously at Isaiah, his grandson, who pushed him up the ramp, eager to get going. Isaiah's previous summer jobs on crab boats and salmon trawlers gave him an instant spot as one of Finn's crew.

Helen sat next to Madelyn with her granddaughter, Charlotte, tucked between them. Adam was helping Finn and Ethan at the sails, his own childhood dreams come true. His sons, Patrick and Robbie, sat close enough to watch, but in a place they couldn't get into trouble while they were still in port. Patrick wasn't as interested, but if AJ had to guess, Robbie would soon be challenging Isaiah for the first mate position.

"You're not leaving without us, are you?" Stella's voice rang out over the bay. She wasn't a fan of sailing either, but refused to be left behind. Steven, her Realtor friend, strained under the baskets of food Stella had piled in his arms. AJ wasn't sure how long the romance would last. Stella seemed fond of him, but AJ suspected Stella's true love was still out there. AJ hadn't become a psychic, but she had a better grasp of time and the miracles that come with it.

When Stella stepped aboard, Charlotte raced to her and wrapped her tiny arms around Stella's legs. Stella wasn't comfortable around children, but her relationship with Charlotte was different. Adam's youngest was fascinated by the origami shapes Stella made and had begun trying to create her own. When Stella saw her attempting to fold one at the end-of-summer party, otherwise known as Finn and AJ's impromptu official wedding ceremony, she took pity on the child. After Stella taught the young girl how to make her first swan, the two were inseparable at family dinners.

"AJ, come down here. You have to see what Adam brought." Stella was pouring her famous sangria into plastic cups and passing them around.

AJ jumped down and ducked under a boom as she made her way to the stern where everyone had found their favorite spot.

She patted Jackson's shoulder. "I loved your latest sketches for the third-floor remodel."

Jackson grunted. "And I could be working on that as we speak rather than going out to the middle of the ocean, risking life and limb from a freak fall storm."

AJ glanced up at the cloudless sapphire sky, then gave him an impish grin. "I'm going on a hunch that we'll survive the afternoon. Would you feel better in the cabin?"

He vigorously shook his head. "I want to look death in the eye when it comes for me."

The others laughed, assuming he was joking. AJ wasn't so sure, but Jackson laughed along with them. She picked up a cup of sangria and found a place against the railing next to Maire and Ethan.

Maire glanced up, her eyes shining with excitement. "Aren't they beautiful, AJ?"

"He got them already?" AJ asked as she leaned over Maire's shoulder.

Ethan nodded and handed the passports to her. Ethan's hooded expression in his photo would probably earn him a luggage check at customs. Maire's ethereal beauty came through as if the photo was like the ones in the Hogwart's Daily Prophet, where the characters moved around as if real.

"Should I ask when you're leaving?" AJ's heart sank. She was getting used to having them around.

Maire's tinkling laugh was one of the first AJ had heard since they returned home. Her friend was adjusting well, learning the computer, reading books on history and travel. She spent hours in the library and an equal amount watching television, immersing herself in the new century. But AJ had seen the brochures for Ireland and Trinity College. Maire also dragged Ethan to Eugene on a regular basis to have lunch with Professor Emory so they could discuss *The Book of Stones.*

"We'll probably wait for spring. We want to try out the passports locally first, so we were thinking of a trip to Vancouver Island." Ethan handed the passports back to Maire then jumped up to thank Adam.

AJ studied Maire. She continued to run her fingers over the passports. It was like Maire was being released from another imprisonment. She was free to go anywhere she wanted, as long as it was within the US borders and this timeline. With the passports, Maire was free to return to France and visit the monastery or head to Dublin and bury herself in the library at Trinity College. Would that be enough? AJ had no delusions that Maire and Ethan might leave them one day. And with everything else she'd learned from her adventure, patience was now something she took to heart.

"When do you think Finn will have the second end table finished?" Madelyn asked. "The women at my book club can't wait until he starts taking orders."

"I think he just needs to stain it." AJ took one of the deviled eggs Madelyn offered.

"I knew that boy had a way with wood the first day we began the remodeling." Jackson gripped his plastic cup of iced tea, a squashed sandwich gripped in his other hand. "I just don't know where he got the passion for making furniture."

Then everyone glanced at AJ.

"What? Just because I run an antique brokerage doesn't mean I have that type of influence." AJ sipped from her cup of sangria. "I think I'd have to blame Isaiah."

Olivia nodded. "It was the four of them. Jackson, Isaiah, Adam, and Ethan. When they got it in their heads at your wedding party to build a wooden model of the first *Daphne Marie.*"

AJ nodded in agreement, just to settle the discussion. The truth was, not even Finn could explain where his new obsession came from. It didn't really matter. He'd found a purpose in this new century. Something that connected him with the old. His future began with the purchase of the fifty-six-foot sailboat, officially christened the *Daphne Marie II.* With the horses, the new plans for the inn, and his fledging cabinetry business, he'd be kept busy for years.

AJ pitched her empty cup in the trash and made her way back to her perch. She split her time between watching the men work the sails as they left the bay and her new family gathered at the stern, watching the shoreline grow smaller. She considered the trip Maire and Ethan would eventually make to Europe. Maybe she and Finn could join them for a week or two.

She glanced at her husband. His forearms strained as he wheeled in a sail while Isaiah worked the second one. Ethan steered the boat while Adam tied a line. When the sailboat left the bay, Finn replaced Ethan at the wheel. Ethan moved to the stern and dropped next to Maire, folding her into his arms. She laid her head on his shoulder and listened to the conversation around her.

AJ left her perch and ducked under the boom again, this time heading for her husband. She ran her hands over his shoulders before sitting next to him. His arm slipped around her waist, and his cedar scent enveloped her as he leaned over and placed a kiss on her lips.

"Is everyone settled, wife?" He pulled out a silver compass, the one she'd seen on the first *Daphne Marie*, the one with the filigreed *M* on the cover.

"Stella was pouring the sangria before we left the dock."

Finn grinned. "And Jackson?"

AJ laughed. "I imagine he'll be glued to his seat until we make land."

She reached out and touched the small piece of wood that had been mounted behind the wheel. Before the *Daphne Marie* had sailed out of the bay the last morning at the monastery, Jamie had one of the crewmen dangle from the bow of the ship and chip a piece of wood from the masthead. The piece had come from the mermaid's wooden lock of golden hair, and it was one of the first things Finn had permanently added to this century's *Daphne*. A remembrance of the family they'd left behind but would never forget.

She stared at his long fingers as they gripped the wheel, his silver wedding band glistening in the sun. She fingered her own band, happy to have it on her finger where it belonged.

"Have you decided what to do with the Heart Stone?" Finn never questioned AJ's ownership of the stone. As far as he was concerned, she was the current Keeper.

"I think it's fine where it is for now." She had placed it back in the safe in the third-floor closet. The picture of Lily covering its resting place. That particular room would be modified to a holding room for antiques. While AJ was satisfied at being just a broker for now, she thought she might want to open her own store one day, someplace Finn could sell the occasional piece of handmade furniture. Her store would be one of rare collectibles.

Until then, she would need someplace to keep the treasures she found. Keeping the Heart Stone in that room just made sense.

The matching earrings that had been chipped from the Heart Stone were still in their velvet bag, stuffed in the rock grotto, five feet from the edge of the dock, where Stella had placed them months ago. AJ checked them occasionally, and Finn promised to make a strong box for them so they'd stay safe from the elements.

"Any particular place you want to go?" Finn signaled Adam and Isaiah, and they moved into position to prepare for the course change.

AJ glanced up at the sky then back at the point where the inn perched proudly on the cliff. Home. She had everything she could possibly want.

She set her sights on the horizon before reaching over to pull Finn's head toward hers. She kissed him long and hard, their tongues touching before she released him and snuggled into his arms. His right hand firm on her belly.

"Captain's choice." She slid her hand over his and squeezed. "I trust you."

THANK YOU FOR READING!

I hope you enjoyed AJ & Finn's story. There may be more in store for their family & friends. Time, as they say, will tell. As a thank you for joining their journey, I'd like to offer a free book, assuming you don't already have a copy.

Your free book is waiting!

A LEGACY OF STONE

Nine months after the attack at Pearl Harbor, for Lily Travers, the war seems far away. She's forced to flee her home in the Pacific Northwest to avoid a green-eyed stranger who seeks a rare heirloom in Lily's possession. She heads for the safety of Boston, a city large enough to hide in. When she runs into Louis Mayfield before ever leaving the train station, the troubles she left behind soon fade.

Louis is a young naval officer with a two-day pass before he jumps on a convoy to London. Suddenly the war is as real as it gets when Lily realizes she may never see him again. And when the green-eyed stranger finds her in Boston, she must decide if she's willing to step into her ancestral role as keeper of the stone.

Get your free copy by clicking this link!

Stay connected with Kim to keep up with next releases, book signings, and other treats by following her on Facebook, her website, or joining her newsletter.

OTHER BOOKS BY KIM ALLRED

ABOUT THE AUTHOR

Kim Allred lives in an old timber town in the Pacific Northwest where she raises alpacas, llamas and an undetermined number of free-range chickens. Just like AJ and Stella, she loves sharing stories while sipping a glass of fine wine or slurping a strong cup of brew.

Her spirit of adventure has taken her on many journeys including a ten-day dogsledding trip in northern Alaska and sleeping under the stars on the savannas of eastern Africa.

Kim is currently working on the final books for the Mórdha Stone Chronicles series and the next books in her sizzling romance series—Masquerade Club.

To stay in contact with Kim, join her **newsletter**, visit her website, or visit her at any of the social media links below.

9 781953 832016